Lunch with
Elizabeth David

Lunch with Elizabeth David

A Novel

ROGER WILLIAMS

CARROLL & GRAF PUBLISHERS, INC.
NEW YORK

First Carroll & Graf edition 2000

Carroll & Graf Publishers, Inc.
19 West 21st Street
New York, NY 10010-6805

Library of Congress Cataloging-in-Publication data is available.
ISBN: 0-7867-0707-0

Manufactured in the United States of America

For Joby

Contents

'If, as a memorial, I leave behind me nothing
but Eric, it will suffice to prove to posterity
that I have not lived in vain.'

Norman Douglas

Part One

UNCLE NORMAN

CHAPTER 1

The Invitation

Villa Tuoro, Capri
3 April 1951

My dear Eric,
    You are coming in July? How fashionable you are, to arrive when there is least interest on the island, between spring flowers and autumn fruits. Never mind. Oleander, hibiscus and jasmine will be in full cry and you can see how well the Hottentot fig has caught hold: it will remind you of Africa. I can find no indigent of this island who has had the wit to put a local name to the 'Carpobrotus edulis'. If you pick its flower and ask a Caprese what it is, he will look at you as if you have asked him why he gets up in the morning: he has not the slightest idea or interest. It's the same with fish.
    July should at least seem a suitable distance from winter, which I spent being guinea pig to the Dottoressa's cures. She makes them up like the lunch-time 'piatti del giorno', which ensures they are far more efficacious than anything a real doctor might prescribe. There is some warmth back in the sky now, but I am still confoundedly shrivelled and chilly, as you have no doubt deduced from this arachnid scrawl. Come and see me, before I give it all up. And don't forget to bring everything on the list that I sent you. Will you be in uniform? Or do Tanganyika police superintendents disguise themselves in mufti?
    You won't like it here, I warn you. It may look the same but it's

full of shits. Expatriate gossip gets quite out of hand. I have been obliged to circulate a memorandum inviting various guilty parties to stuff their incorrect information up their arses.

One or two friends rise above it. You will meet them. Ettore and Macpherson you know, and we might get a visit from Harold Achtung bearing all the gossip from Florence. (Achtung the Panama hat! If it is ever removed, it is after lunch when slicing a peach suddenly reminds him of a moment from his youth: he gets going then, and starts recalling how I set him on his career by telling him to go East. I don't remember it myself, but I am not wrong when it comes to putting young men on the right path, as you well know!)

Mrs Elizabeth David promises to turn up. She is the woman I got to help me reach Lisbon in '41, after I had shown her how to make an omelette and not settle for a drop less than a bottle of wine for lunch. She is a handsome woman, a little shy but sharp as a lemon. Her first book came out last year, not too bad, on Mediterranean food. If it does anything to stop one single Englishman from eating the frightful stuff the septentrional nations pass off as cooking, she will have done Western civilisation favours beyond the dreams of Epicurus.

I have finally finished with 'Venus in the Kitchen', which is going through Heinemann at the moment. They are assembling the scraps of wine-marinated pages I have been sending them over the months in the hope of some fucking cash. Graham Greene is going to write the introduction, and I suppose I should be pleased but he conjures up to me neither a love goddess nor an aromatic stove. They are even proposing to use that picture David Lawrence gave me of a naked couple romping round a kitchen: Lorenzo had no more idea of good draughtsmanship than he did of the erotic. Nowt to do about it now.

I look forward to lunch together in an umbrageous restaurant near the marina: you and me and Mrs David. Books still keep me afloat, but a good lunch is a greater levitator and far more enduring.

Yours ever,

Uncle Norman

*

Eric Wolton read the letter twice, then put it down on the table before him. The small squares of paper flushed under the last rays of the engorged African sun that was sinking in a crimson furnace across the long horizon, making the giant acacia trees in silhouette look no more than burnt stubble. To the right, to the north, Mount Kilimanjaro answered the high and mighty dusk with an immutable radiance from its headdress of snow. The evening jabbering had begun, though few animals were visible around the whitewashed bungalows: nattering monkeys occasionally swung into view, birds squawked, unseen dogs and cats of various sizes and degrees of danger barked and roared and yelped. An ageing Great Dane spread out at Eric's feet kept one eye open, the pupil swivelling back and forth, which was as much as it felt like doing to chase the savage choristers of the familiar evensong.

In this rosy glow, Eric's smooth, freshly shaved, round face looked flushed. Out of uniform, fattening in a clean, short-sleeved white shirt, his dark curly hair wet from the shower, he sat by a low carved rosewood table on the porch with a pipe clenched between his healthy white teeth and a whisky-and-soda sundowner half drunk. His left arm hung down the side of the wicker chair and idly scratched the hound's ear, which made it close its eye with a shuddering sigh. Eric drew heavily on the briar: the tobacco smoke helped to keep away tsetse flies, though soon it would be time to move indoors, behind the screens, when the lights would come on and everything that was small and winged and nasty would begin to bite. The ceiling fan was already whirring in the sitting room; pots banged mutely in the kitchen, which spread aromas of well-spiced curry, a sure defence against unwanted insects. Curry was the only thing he missed about East Africa when he was in Europe.

For untold nights Eric had gazed at Kilimanjaro. There was nothing so dramatic, so awe-inspiring, in all Europe. But it was no compensation. For all its grandeur, it could not compete with the intimate landscapes and rocky coasts of Sorrento and Capri; for all its wildness, it could not compare with the mysteries of the Calabrian jungle; for all its brightness, it never possessed the raw warmth of the Mediterranean's radiant light. He was alone here now, except for the servants. Helen was away for a few days up-country, doing good. He felt washed up in Arusha, condemned to the enormity of Africa.

He picked up the letter and read it through once more. Uncle Norman had been badgering him to come for more than a year, but it was not easy to take time off, and he had had to persuade Helen. She had not wanted to go, of course, but he suggested that she might include a visit to her family in Germany, and besides she had never been to Capri, an island that enchanted everyone. Perhaps it would not be so bad this time; the presence of another woman might help. Mrs David might be the person to show Helen what a great man Uncle Norman really was. He had touched so many people. Hah! He heard the old man's explosive laugh. He was, what, eighty-three? It was unlikely that he would see out another winter: this really could be the last time they would see him. God knows how he kept going after the life he had led. He had looked half starved that time they had met up in Paris thirty-five years ago, living off chestnuts and sorrel. He got by on neat *joie de vivre*. Didn't everyone want to live on that? Eric suddenly shuddered as he thought of Paris and his visit to the hospital at Amiens, and once again he wondered if he really did want to go back to Capri.

The second half of his drink disappeared in one swift movement, but his throat closed and he swilled the effervescent malt whisky around his mouth and pressed it to the back of his lips as if he had second thoughts about allowing the drink to come to an end. No, there was no pulling out. He had agreed to go, and Helen would come, too. It was good of her. Really, she had been very understanding. But it all seemed so unresolved. Every time he thought he had put it all out of his mind, it would return with another memory, another card from Uncle Norman, another day when he realised he had not heard from Violet, another year wondering if he would ever see Annetta again. Sitting here, at the start of another solitary evening in this boundless country in this eternity of a continent, everything seemed unfinished, without purpose, without end. Perhaps this trip would provide a resolution.

He would try to go to London, he thought. Perhaps he would go back to Camden and show Helen the house where he was born; knock on the door and ask if they would let him look around. And he suddenly recalled its odour of boiling nappies, Macassar and rose-water, beeswax and Cherry polish, smoothing irons and bubbling soups, and fresh bread of such warm and doughy deliciousness that he used to dream his pillows could be made of it. He had no relatives left in the city where he was born, but he might look up some of the blokes he had met on a training course at Hendon a few years ago. There may be work there. He was fifty-three and he had solid experience in the colonial police force which should not count for nothing. He had given up asking Uncle Norman to pull strings for him years ago. There was a time when he thought Uncle Norman was deliberately not trying – that, having got him out here, out of the way, his responsibilities had ended. Well, perhaps they had.

He tickled the dog's ear again, and he grinned. As always, the nightmare chill of the memories was accompanied by a recollection of the good times. There was the Odyssean voyage in Ciro's boat, the driver in Lucera, the escapade with the Americans in Manfredonia, the rowboats at Richmond, crazy Count Jack . . . He started to chuckle, which made him cough. The dog opened both eyes, raised its brows and looked up.

The sun had hit the horizon and rapidly shrunk, and as it

faded, first Venus then the larger stars were turned on in the lowering sky. The netted door to the sitting room opened and Salem, the houseboy, came out to say that the cook was about to serve dinner and the wireless was warming up for the World Service news. Eric raised his empty glass in a toast to the mountain and to the sun for another great show. He found a last lick of whisky and downed it with a shiver. He knew he really couldn't wait to go to Capri. It had been such fun with Uncle Norman from the start.

CHAPTER 2

Bonfire Night, 1910

'Where have you been?' Violet scolded. 'I've been waiting ages.'
Moments earlier, catching sight of her brother coming up the
road, she had silenced her spinning top, opened the coal-hole
door, thrown it in, raced up the basement stairs and stood by
the iron gate, her hands in her muff, ready to dish out her
complaint. Her long fair hair was tucked under a felt hat tied
under her chin with a scarf. A thick box-cloth coat hung midway
down her heavy serge skirt and hidden woollen stockings were
snug inside scuffed and scarred high-laced boots.

'Working,' said Eric, a sturdy, dark-eyed boy, hands in heavy
coat pockets, his face half hidden beneath a cap. He took no
notice of her reproachful gaze. 'What d'you think?'

'Come on, let's go.'

'What about Mum? I'll just poke my head in.'

'She's putting Percy to bed.'

'How is he?'

'He'll live.'

It was cold and getting dark. Lamplighters were doing their
rounds. Breath was forming clouds around the people who
hurried home to their Saturday tea. Already there was a smell of
bonfires in the air.

'I should go and see,' Eric said.

'Oh, come on, we'll be late. I told Mum I'd meet you and
we'd go on. She'll only nag at you to wrap up and keep out of

trouble. I can do that for her.'

'Go on, then.'

She put on a grown-up voice: 'Wrap up, Eric dear, and mind you just stay out of trouble.'

'Bog off, Mum.'

Violet laughed. 'Come on, duck. Squid and Chalkie might not wait for us.'

She put an arm in his and propelled him up the street. Violet was eleven years old, Eric was twelve, and they got on well, even though she always liked to tell him what to do. They approached the underground station, which stood on the sight of the 'Cow's Cathedral', the local dairy where they had bought their milk and cheese until only a year or two ago. Down-and-outs and heather sellers gathered round the new electric building, seeking warmth. Violet dug her hands deeper into her cony muff. It was a gift from cousins who kept rabbits in Essex, and she was very proud of it. In some degree of agitation, two shadowy figures in boots and caps and mufflers watched them approach.

'Race you down,' said the stouter of the two, stepping forward as they drew up.

Chalkie's drab serge coat, an overlarge hand-me-down, hung heavily on his shoulders. Unlike either his companion or Eric, his voice had broken and he shaved. The boys had been at school together, and had left a few months ago. Chalkie had a job with an uncle in a furniture store in the High Street and Squid took what work he could around the locks and barges, often legging narrow boats through tunnels, lying on a board on his back and walking his feet along the dank brick roof. Eric's father worked as a clerk in the office of Gilbey's in Camden Goods Yard and there he had found work for his son in the General Forwarding floor. Eric spent nine hours a day, six on Saturdays, moving around crates of wine and spirits, imported and exported through London Docks via barge and train. Most of his meagre wages went towards his keep, and what was left seldom survived the weekend.

'Ride Number One,' said Eric as they boarded a waiting train. It was a game of theirs to see how many forms of conveyance they could take in a day: though an errand boy, he seldom got out of the distillers' warehouse.

'First today for me, too,' said Violet. There were only two vacant seats and Violet took one of them. The boys stood over her, hanging on to leather straps.

'I was on a tram this morning,' said Chalkie, 'and on the delivery bike at lunch-time, so this is Number Three.'

'What about you, Squid?' asked Violet.

Squid did not answer but began instead to cough and did not stop until he pulled out a cigarette and cadged a light from a pipe smoker opposite, sticking it into the proffered, glowing bowl. He was thin and wiry, though no taller than Chalkie. His coat fitted him, but a gap between his corduroy work trousers and his boots showed that, as usual, he had no socks. He wore woollen gloves without fingers.

'Only the second,' he said finally. He was an Irish cockney and his voice was high and thin. 'Unless you count the barges individually, in which case it's the twenty-second.'

'You made that up,' said Violet.

'What?'

'Twenty-second. You just said it without counting,'

'No I didn't. I counted them all as they went through and the last thing I said to the gaffer was, "That's the twenty-first bleeding barge I've legged through the tunnel today that hasn't given me a bleeding tip."'

'You never,' said Violet, laughing.

'I'll give you a tip,' said Chalkie: 'don't swear in front of young ladies.'

'I never do,' said Squid, making Violet laugh again.

Eric grinned. At Euston they got out of the smoky underground and took an omnibus through the West End to Charing Cross. It was cold, but they liked being on the wooden seats upstairs in the open, Violet and Eric in front, constantly tossing back their heads and shouting at Chalkie and Squid in the seat behind. Shining motor cars drove past with honking horns, toffs at the wheels and women beside them so covered in fur and feathers it was impossible to see their faces. In Tottenham Court Road they overtook a horse-drawn bus decorated with posters and manned by suffragettes. In Oxford Street there was a carriage drawn by a zebra advertising tea. At Shaftesbury Avenue a black face played a squeeze-box and boys tossed diabolos. Posters advertised glittering productions and Violet said that she had heard Sarah Bernhardt was being paid £1,000 in gold every week.

'Let's go and see that,' said Chalkie, pointing at the dancing figure on a poster from Covent Garden, which proclaimed: 'At last, the veil is lifted!'

'Salami?' said Squid.

'Salome! Get your eyes tested.'

'What's it about?' asked Eric.

'The dance of the seven veils,' said Chalkie. 'That's all Salome's wearing, and as she dances she takes them off one at a time. It's been banned, 'cos it was written by that nancy Oscar Wilde. Now he's dead, they're doing it.'

'What's a nancy?' asked Squid.

Chalky said incredulously, 'You don't know?'

'I'm adopted,' said Squid. 'I don't know much.'

'It's men that like doing it to men.'

'Doing what?' asked Squid.

'It,' said Charlie.

'The dance of the seven veils?' said Squid.

'Oh Squid, duck, you are a disaster,' said Violet.

'Don't you like me?' said Squid, rubbing his eyes theatrically with his knuckles.

''Course we do,' said Violet. 'We think you're a pet.'

'That's all I'll ever be to you,' he said. ''Cos I only like boys.'

'Get away,' she said and gave a high-pitched laugh. 'You've been having us on.'

At Charing Cross the four climbed on transport number three, a special steam train going to Crystal Palace High Level station at Sydenham. Forty minutes later they emerged from the station's grand cream-and-gold-tiled underpass to reach the massive bulk of the hilltop exhibition halls. The night-time glow of London and the twinkling town lights of six counties – all the world, it seemed – were at their feet. Thousands had gathered for the annual Brocks fireworks display, and they trooped past the great glass structure: twenty-five acres of crystal halls enclosing exhibits of natural history, archaeology, science, engineering, arts and Empire. Through the glass they could see stern statues of Egyptian gods and the thunderous organ that pulled out all the stops for the Handel festivals, but the building was rusting now, in need of repairs, and closed for the day. Eric could not hide his disappointment, for however familiar he was with the palace, he enjoyed wandering among its exotic treasures. He had been coming here every year for as long as he could remember, and he loved looking at the exhibits from the different places in the world so full of mysteries and possibilities: African tribes and Egyptian gods, wild animals, exotic plants. They brought a hint of the fame and fortune that were waiting to be won.

Dwarfed by the structure that rose like a ghostly skeleton behind them, the four walked through the park, past sphinxes and dinosaurs, towards the fountains, lagoons and watershoots that had been introduced in attempts to entice the public.

Finally they reached a point on the garden terraces with a view of the unlit bonfire near the boating lake where people had paid to be pushed out on the water in pleasure craft.

'It's blooming cold,' said Squid. 'Can't we get nearer the bonfire?'

'I won't see from down there,' said Violet. 'I'm only little.'

'I could give you a lift,' Chalkie volunteered.

'They'll light it in a minute,' said Eric. 'We'll get a good butcher's from here.'

'I want a snossidge,' said Squid.

'Try a drop of this,' said Violet, taking a small lavender water bottle from her muff and unscrewing its silver top.

Squid frowned as he put it to his lips and took a tentative taste.

'What is it?' Eric asked with a frown.

'Mother's ruin,' said Squid, holding the bottle up for inspection.

'Vi!' Eric appeared to be rather shocked, but he was not entirely surprised. His sister got up to all sorts, which was what made her more interesting than most girls. 'Where'd you get that?'

'Don't you want some?' she asked. 'It's good when it's cold.'

'Just a drop.' But he swigged back half of it, so as not to leave her too much. Once, back in the summer, they had both got drunk by the tow-path on a bottle of half-hinched Gilbey's gin, and he had had to carry her home and explain to his father how she had suddenly been taken ill. Fortunately there was little she could do wrong in her father's eyes, and their unlikely tales about food poisoning went unquestioned.

'I'd still like a snossidge,' said Squid, handing back the bottle. 'They usually do them.'

'I'll get a bag of chestnuts,' said Violet, screwing the cap back on. 'Give me some money, duck.'

Eric took a thrupenny bit from his pocket and gave it to her. 'I haven't got any change. Get a couple of bags, not too burned.

Where did you see them?'

'There.' She pointed to a small queue gathering around a glowing brazier at the back of the crowd about twenty yards away.

'Don't get lost,' he said.

''Course not,' she said, walking confidently away.

Chalkie shook his head as he watched her go. 'Why couldn't you have a sister who was easily impressed and slightly shy, like other girls.'

Eric grinned.

Chalkie hunched his shoulders. 'Hell's bells, it's cold.'

'Freeze a monkey's,' said Squid, blowing into his half-gloved hands.

'I bet it's hot in Egypt,' said Eric, thinking of the colossal, upright, seated deity in the warmth of the palace. He pulled his muffler tight under his chin. The sky overhead was now sparkling with stars and crystal clear; a frost would not be far behind. His toes curled in his woollen socks as he thought about the chilblains of winter yet to come. Chalkie pointed out the plough, Orion's belt and a bright star he said was the planet 'Venice'. Images of Egypt and the classic world remained with Eric as he noted the aquiline nose of a tall man standing in the queue next to his sister. Outlined against the glow of the brazier, he wore no hat, in spite of the cold, though the collar on his heavy wool coat was about his ears. He was talking to Violet who was laughing. They both turned and looked in Eric's direction. The man smiled and nodded towards him. He looked rich. Eric smiled back.

'Africa's always hot,' said Chalkie.

'I want to be hot,' said Squid.

'How long do you think it would take to get there?' Eric asked, turning his attention back to his friends.

'Egypt?' said Chalkie. 'Oh, a couple of weeks.'

'If that,' said Squid. He took a loose cigarette from a pocket and asked a man next to him in the crowd for a light. A match flared in his gaunt face.

'Depends how you go,' said Chalkie.

'I'd go by canal barge,' said Squid, nodding his thanks to his benefactor after taking a puff. 'I'd get a horse to walk me round the coast of Spain to Cape Trafalgar and into the Mediterranean. I wouldn't have to do nothing.'

'You'd miss Switzerland,' said Chalkie. 'All the mountains and snow.'

'If you wanted snow,' Eric pointed out, 'you wouldn't want to go to Egypt.'

'You might want the contrast,' said Squid, 'a bit of skating on the way, when the canals froze over.'

'There's no canals in Switzerland,' said Eric. 'It's too steep. The locks would be like steps.'

'Egypt's a land of contrasts,' said Chalkie. 'Ancient and modern. Do you know why there aren't any Egyptians here tonight?'

Eric looked back towards the man with his sister: he was quite tanned and might have been Egyptian for all he knew, but he said, 'No.'

'Because they don't like leaving their mummies.'

Eric laughed. He laughed easily and he smiled a lot, which made him popular, especially among friends who told jokes. He was still smiling when Violet returned just as all the lights in the Crystal Palace went off. The sudden pitch darkness left the crowd in such a silence it was hard to believe there was more than a handful of people there. In a few minutes the quiet was broken by a rustle, then a crackle as torches were laid at the foot of the house-high bonfire, and cheers went up. Flames began licking hungrily at the dead branches, boxes, crates and broken furniture, flashing towards the figure of the treacherous Guy Fawkes, an elegant scarecrow in a top hat and frock-coat, with a painted, grinning mask, pink as a port-drinker, above the flames that illuminated the faces of the cheering crowd. People called out, urging the figure to die painfully and to rot in hell. 'Down with the Pope,' they shouted and, 'Death to all traitors.' Some of their language was not fit to be heard. Then rockets shot into the night and the air shook with almighty explosions that blasted cascade after cascade overhead, mirrored in the inky lake.

The brilliant eruptions of rockets, Catherine wheels, Roman candles and Mount Vesuvius cones went on for more than an hour, filling the air with the aroma of burnt gunpowder, of Guy Fawkes Night and leaf-dead, chilly autumn, and the four were held by its spell. Just before the end, however, Squid said his tummy was rumbling, and he wandered away to find a sausage, returning ten minutes later. Residue pork fat on his thin lips sparkled beneath the finale of rockets. Their overhead bursts were followed by a slow fall of sticks which glowed ever dimmer as they headed silently earthwards, their short lives sublimely spent.

When he could no longer make out the smallest spark of life, Chalkie sighed and said, 'Well, that's it, I suppose. Not bad, was it?'

'Topper,' said Eric with the grin that had barely left him since the pyrotechnics had begun.

They turned and began to follow the mob back down the hill. Squid took out three small cigars and handed them out, lighting them with a gold petrol lighter, which he cupped in his hands to provide a little warmth. They barely had time to savour the first puff when there came a shout.

'That's him. That's the little mizzler.'

Squid might have coughed a lot and he might have looked small and not too well sometimes but when he wanted to he could move like the wind. One moment he was there, the next he was gone. Eric and Chalkie dropped their cigars and kept their heads down, trying to continue at a normal walking pace, aware that many eyes were on them. A police whistle blew.

'And them,' the same nearby voice shouted. 'Them's his pals.'

The crowd seemed to be closing in. Violet was wide-eyed in disbelief. Chalkie looked indignant. As nonchalantly as he could, Eric put his hands in his pockets, only to encounter the unexpected shape of a well-stuffed leather wallet. A restraining fist tightened sharply on the back of his collar. He laughed, as if this were some sort of joke.

'Who's your friend, sonny,' the copper asked. He was solid as the nearby monumental *Tyrannosaurus rex*.

'You leave my brother alone,' said Violet. 'He hasn't done nothing.'

The policeman's face was close, and from the corner of his eye Eric could see Chalkie being treated in the same way. 'What's your name?'

'Eric, Eric Smith. I don't think it's me you want, sir.'

'And who's your friend?'

'Him? Chalkie White.'

'Not him, the one that just ran off.'

'Oh, I don't know him. He was just standing here. I think he was an Egyptian.'

Violet let out a frightened, high-pitched scream. 'My purse!' She had pulled her hands from her muff and was looking vainly around her. 'The scallywag has taken my purse. Officer, I want to report a robbery by an Egyptian.'

'I thought he was Scottish,' Chalkie said. 'He sounded to me as if he came from Glasgow. 'Strewth, where's my watch gone? It's been pinched! Eric, have you got your watch?'

Eric reached inside his jacket, tight though the fit was with his collar still being stretched. 'Heavens, Chalkie, no I haven't . . .' But there was still just a possibility Squid might get caught, and he didn't want him facing more charges than he deserved. 'But I'm not sure I brought it with me. I'd have to check at home.'

'That Egyptian will be halfway to Glasgow by now,' said Chalkie.

'I hope you're not saying anything rude about the Scots,' an educated voice broke in. 'You know your Uncle Norman is sensitive about his ancestry.'

With a ramrod back that suggested either the military or a stern grandmother, the stranger surveyed the scene with avuncular blue eyes that twinkled beneath flying brows, his fair hair shorn short at the back and sides and sweeping out of a centre parting. He looked as if he did not really care too much what happened to this trio.

'Do you know these children, sir?' Chalkie's policeman asked.

'Know them? Officer, even if I were a total stranger and not their Uncle Norman, I should be able to perceive these children to be as innocent as the day is long. Anyone can tell at a glance that they don't have the physiognomy of the criminal classes. Mind you, they probably do deserve a lesson for allowing themselves to be taken in.'

Eric smiled. Violet glowered: 'I want to report someone's stolen my purse . . . Uncle Norman.'

'How much was in it?' Uncle Norman asked.

'Half a crown,' she said.

'Two and sixpence! My dear girl, I am not rich, as you know, but even I could find a few bob to save you from police reports that will take half the night and like as not make you miss the last train back to Camden, where your poor parents will be worried sick. Besides, I'm sure the police have better things with which to occupy themselves.'

'I want to report it,' she said firmly.

While she had been talking to the stranger at the chestnut

brazier, Eric realised, she must have told him they had come down from Camden, though why he should stick his neck out for them now was hard to know. He could also see that Violet had not much choice: once a story had begun you had to stand by it, or you might get copped worse.

'Half a crown's a lot of money,' Eric agreed. 'And there's the matter of Chalkie's watch.'

Uncle Norman seemed amused by their doggedness. 'Have it your way. Do you have transport, Officer, or do we have to find a cab?'

A police wagon took the four of them, plus the man who had been robbed and his girlfriend. He was aged around thirty, clean shaven, and wore a Derby, and he had no wish to speak to anyone not in uniform. At the police station in Dartmouth Road a collection of complainants were sitting on benches awaiting their turn to report their losses at the duty sergeant's desk, and it seemed hours before the victim could make a statement about his loss of a wallet, gold cigarette lighter and hunter watch which, he said, amounted in all to more than £20. Meanwhile the boys were taken to separate rooms and made to give statements. They also had to turn out their pockets. There was no sign of Squid, and Violet, who sat on a bench with the stranger, waiting to file her complaint, looked up anxiously each time someone came in through the door.

'Expecting someone?' one of the arresting officers asked, catching her look of concern.

'Horrible criminals,' she said. 'Isn't this where they come?'

Finally, with a grave look and a nose barely above the desk, she gave her details to the sergeant, who took them down in a large ledger in a laborious longhand. She gave her name and age and address in St Paul's Street, Camden Town. She gave an elaborate description of the purse, remembered that the half crown was dated 1907, and described the Egyptian who, she said, had seemed very polite and had introduced himself to her as Mohammed, though she had declined the cigar he offered. Uncle Norman aided in the spelling of Mohammed. His presence seemed to be sufficient to stop the officer wasting energy questioning her unlikely tale, especially after he had promised to see them safely home.

It was not until ten-thirty that they left the station, just managing to catch the last train to Charing Cross. On the way they did not mention the incident, but talked instead about the fireworks, and the stranger recalled his own attempts as a child at producing a Roman candle out of household substances, resulting in the conflagration of a country barn.

'It was a terrific fire,' he said with enthusiasm. 'My sister and I hid behind some rocks and watched it until we were very nearly caught. It was so blazingly hot we thought we'd bake like potatoes, but we couldn't resist staying to watch the old farmer, who was beside himself with rage. He was such an idiot.'

At Charing Cross, they alighted from the special train and Chalkie, explaining that he had to meet a pal in Piccadilly, disappeared into the feckless night. Uncle Norman hailed a motor cab and told the driver to take them to St Paul's Street in Camden Town. Sixth today, Eric thought as he sat with his back to the driver, facing Violet and their new acquaintance who was lighting up a Gold Flake. It was the first time in his life he had been in a taxi and he thought he could get to like it.

Uncle Norman said, 'I'd better give you this back now.' From a pocket he produced the leather wallet Eric had secreted there, in the back of the police car on the way to Dartmouth Road. Eric accepted it guardedly, but he couldn't help a quick smile.

'The important thing is to have fun without bringing yourself to anyone's attention,' said Uncle Norman. 'Especially the authorities. They're out to find trouble. That's what they're paid for, so it's best to avoid them. There are plenty of ways of amusing yourself without alerting them.'

'What sort of things?' Violet asked suspiciously.

'Don't you play games? Have you a hoop or a top?'

'She's got three tops,' Eric volunteered.

She stuck her tongue out at him.

'Hah!' Uncle Norman exclaimed. 'What have you got? A whipping top? Klondyke? Boxer?'

'Whipping top, humming top and a dumb bargee.'

'Dumb bargee! There's a new one. What does it do?'

'It's like a bargee, but you can't get a rise out of it. So it's dumb, see, stup . . . ?' She bit her tongue.

He did not take offence. 'I should love to see it. I collect children's street games and one day I'm going to put them into a book.'

The animated, brightly lit streets of London suddenly went dark and quiet. They had passed out of the West End and entered north London where shadowy drunks and whores grouped on street corners and gas lamps flickered and died over the cobbles. Even the interior of the cab felt colder and it seemed to intensify the smell of tobacco on the man's breath.

'Do you write books?' Eric asked.

'Now and then, when I feel like it.'

'Do you live in London?'

'Not if I can help it, especially at this time of year. I'm usually loafing around the Mediterranean, in Naples or Capri.'

'I've heard of Naples,' Eric said, pronouncing it 'Ny-paws'. 'But I never heard of Capri.'

'It's an island surrounded by a warm sea swimming with mermaids who live in grottoes. The sun shines with unfailing regularity. You can drink and eat all day if you wish, and talk about whatever you like and do whatever you care. Everybody has nothing whatever to do, and they do it rather well.'

Violet made it clear she found the story inane and patronising and she stared out of the window into the dark. When Eric said, 'Gosh, I'd like to go there,' she wriggled her shoulders to show she was even less impressed with her brother.

'Why not?' said Uncle Norman. 'Anyone can.'

When the cab driver came to a stop and Eric and Violet got out, they were surprised to find Uncle Norman following them. He handed the driver some coins, and the vehicle – the only one in the street – drew away in a cloud of exhaust fumes. The night was cold and thick and smoky. There was no sign of the stars that had hung over the Crystal Palace. The three of them stood on the pavement without moving. Icy drops of rain started to fall.

'Well, which one is your house?' asked Uncle Norman, flicking his cigarette stub on to the cobbles. 'I'm looking forward to meeting your parents. Only the most sympathetic and enlightened couple could have produced such delightful children as you two.'

Violet sighed and looked away with obvious contempt for his flattery. Neither she nor Eric moved. The street lamps had gone out and there were lights in no more than three curtainless windows in the entire street. A man was shouting obscenities in one of the houses. Rolling stock rattled and clanked in the distance. Glass broke.

Suddenly Uncle Norman laughed. 'Pah! I've been duped! You gave the desk sergeant a false address. Why didn't I think of that? You're too clever for me. Come on, do an old chap a favour. I've come all this way, I think the least you could do is give me peace of mind by letting me deliver you to your mother and father. Is it in walking distance?'

Violet sighed. She was tired. 'Yes, Uncle Norman.' She put an arm through his, and started to lead him up the road, Eric falling in step on her other side.

'And I suppose you aren't Eric and Violet Smith either?'

'Wolton,' said Eric, 'but it's best to keep your first name in case your mates forget and shout out to you.'

Uncle Norman suddenly roared with laughter. 'An Egyptian! Called Mohammed! I have never heard such an outrageous story in all my life.'

They all started to laugh. 'Any Egyptian called Mohammed living in Glasgow should be worried tonight,' Eric said.

'Would you really have given me half a crown for not reporting the robbery?' Violet asked.

'You aren't one of the shrinking Violets, are you, my dear?' Uncle Norman said with another gust of laughter.

So it was that Mrs Wolton opened the door to three happy revellers. The look of relief on her face showed she had been worried about where they had got to; that and the smell of gin on her breath as she kissed them. She was a cheerful, full-figured woman, with Eric's dark eyes and hair that had started to grey.

'I brought them home safely for you,' Uncle Norman said. 'My, what is that smell? I haven't smelt fresh baking like that since I was a boy in Austria.'

She could tell at once he was a real gentleman and she happily invited him in.

CHAPTER 3

Naples, April 1911

Signor Douglas was giving a private lesson in Villa Sarno when Eric returned with some Felino salami and Castellammare olives, bought on the way back from the nearby summer residence of the British Ambassador in Naples. The boy stepped down from a carriage behind Raffaele Amoroso, an elderly man with a thin moustache who wore a light linen suit and straw hat and moved in a haze of lavender cologne. Wagging a gold-tipped cane, he ushered the boy down the drive towards the side of the villa.

'The garden is this way.' There was hardly a trace of an Italian accent in his English.

Dressed in a collar and tie and navy serge suit with full knicker-bocker trousers, Eric grinned and fell into step across the tiled path. Behind them, unbidden, the coachman gee'd up the pair of boot-black horses and trotted out of the wrought-iron gates on to the road that led down to the port and the city. They headed around the side of the villa, the old man's head set forward, the boy, with a fixed grin, looking this way and that, and catching sight of the twinkling metal of an automobile through an unbolted stable door.

'What kind of motor car is that?' Eric's voice was starting to break, and his rough London accent seemed out of place.

'A Lancia Delta,' said Amoroso.

'Is it fast?'

'Fast? It has cost me two hats and I have had to borrow this one from my gardener's donkey.'

Eric's even, white teeth glinted. 'Didn't the donkey mind?'

'No. I gave him ten lire for it.'

They rounded the solid whitewashed villa that smelled of a stone cave and stepped into the garden bathed in the April morning sunshine. At its edges pine trees, cypresses and eucalyptus rose above banks of myrtle, erica and broom. There were sweet scents in the air, and the clean and unfamiliar aroma of pine. Deep greens of the shrubs were brightened by the colours of flowers Eric had never seen: hibiscus, oleander, pelargoniums, cistus, as well as exotic succulents. Pervading it all was the excited whirring of the cicadas. A hundred yards from the back of the house the garden sloped sharply away towards the sparkling blue sea. Eric stopped for a moment to look at it. This was the Mediterranean Douglas talked so much about. There really did seem to be diamonds scattered across its surface, stretching out to the nearby islands, and it was suddenly easy to imagine Greek traders, Roman emperors, sirens, sea gods and the whole cast of exotic characters Uncle Norman had introduced him to in the months since they had met.

Uncle Norman had promised Eric that he would wake up in Naples on his thirteenth birthday, and this morning that was exactly what he had done. They had arrived at the villa in the dark, around midnight, and they would stay here for a few days before heading south. He had awoken to the sound of Amoroso's carriage, and from his bedroom window had seen him step down with a girl who had come to have tuition from Douglas. By the time he reached the breakfast table the lesson had apparently begun. Amoroso introduced himself and told Eric that his Uncle Norman had suggested he accompany him on an errand to the embassy. The errand done, he was now exploring the villa for the first time.

'Ey, Don Amoroso!' came a crusty greeting.

Their host, Salvatore Lo Bianco, was sitting at a large table in the shade on a tiled patio by wide-open sitting-room doors. He was a huge man, a blackamoor who spoke as if hollering up from some subterranean cavern. His lips were thick, his brown eyes bulged and his dark face was unshaven. He wore a white singlet and shorts, had no shoes on his flat-toed feet, and he was brandishing a broad dagger which he tapped on the corner of the table as an invitation for Eric to put his two parcels down. A jug of water and an unlabelled bottle of wine were surrounded by flora and fauna from the deep: lumps and twigs of coloured coral; rocks and seaweed; bones and other scraps of fish. It was pungent with iodine, ozone and the salty sea. Also on the table was a copy of Douglas's latest book, just published, *Siren Land.*

Lo Bianco's complete lack of English did not stop him talking to Eric; he did so in thunderous Italian, using his large, loquacious hands to help explain everything. '*Che cosa hai fatto, amico mio inglese, eh?*' He patted the bench next to him as an invitation for Eric to sit down, squeezing the boy's thigh as it spread across the seat. Eric grinned.

'Where's Uncle Norman?' Eric pronounced the word 'uncaw'. Then he tried the word '*Dove?*' And when Lo Bianco replied, '*Ah, dove? Benissimo mio caro*', he knew that three days of Italian lessons from Douglas on the train had not been in vain.

'I expect he will be out in a minute,' said Amoroso.

Lo Bianco said nothing without using his hands, continuing this manual communication as he reached out and picked up a purple spiky ball, which he prised open with his knife. He dug out the five quivering fingers of rose-coloured eggs and pointed the loaded blade towards Eric, gesturing for him to eat. The boy squirmed and laughed. '*Bene, bene, molto bene,*' Lo Bianco entreated, until it was clear that the boy really could not be persuaded, and he shrugged and put the dagger's tip into his own mouth where his large mauve tongue engulfed the entrails.

Amoroso took a thin knife from his waistcoat pocket, flicked it open, and prised the life out of another of the prickly balls. Eric watched closely. By contrast, his was a serpentine tongue and it chased over the dry old lips and along the bottom edge of the grey moustache. He dabbed his mouth with a large silk handkerchief, which he then shook in the general direction of the sea.

'See that roof down there,' he said.

Eric followed the direction of the handkerchief to a stand of umbrella pines on a promontory at the edge of the sea. Beside them was a solid, square building with a vaulted structure on its flat roof.

'The red one?' he asked.

Amoroso nodded. 'That was the Douglases' home until a few years ago, a very beautiful place, one of the finest in all Posilipo. Villa Maya. Maya-Illusion Signor Douglas called it.'

'Ah, Villa Maya.' Lo Bianco nodded vigorously. '*Bella, bella, molta bella.*' The nodding changed to a shaking.

'Parts of it were from a Roman villa,' Amoroso went on, removing his hat and wiping his brow with the handkerchief. 'In one amphora Signor Douglas even found some olive oil, untouched after two thousand years. The oldest virgin in the world, he called it. He had floor tiles designed like Roman ones, and he asked Queen Margherita of Denmark to be the first to walk on them, for luck.'

'Was that when he was married?' asked Eric.

Amoroso nodded.

Eric asked, 'Do you like olive oil?'

'Of course I do. I am Italian.'

'I think it's horrible.'

'Of course you do. You are English. Down there, also, was one of the biggest villas in Italy. It belonged to a Roman called Vedius Pollio who was a famous devotee of Epicurus, the Greek philosopher who loved only pleasure and avoided all pain. For his own pleasure he fed his lampreys on the flesh of his slaves.'

Eric looked horrified at the idea, but not quite as horrified as he might have looked had Douglas not told him the same story on the train the day before. He also now knew that lampreys were not a breed of dog. Lo Bianco dug him in the ribs, chucked his head back and made a gesture with his open hand, the thumb jabbing at his open mouth.

'*Vuoi un po' di vino, ragazzo?*'

Both gesture and words were lost on Eric until Lo Bianco picked up the wine bottle and swigged from it, then, grinning and nodding vigorously, passed it to the boy. Eric screwed up his nose at the tart, vinegary smell, before tentatively putting it to his lips.

'Temperance, Eric. The nurse of youth!' The voice from the house behind them was clipped, imperious, captivating, and courted no response. Eric immediately put the bottle down and turned round with a broad smile to see his friend, who went on: 'For boys your age to drink wine is like heaping fire on fire. Only when you reach our age will you find it beneficial, as an ally against the moroseness of advancing years.'

Six feet tall and carapaced in a three-piece wool suit, in spite of the warmth of the day, Norman Douglas had stepped out from the sitting room with all sense of purpose, his back mop-pole straight, his fair hair shorn around the neck and ears and parted in the middle with twin hanks that flopped down above flying eyebrows. The sharp features of his face, the aquiline nose, jutting jaw, thin lips, were all softened by the twinkling, deep-set blue-grey eyes. Eric grinned back. This was the man who had led him from the dull toil of Camden into this warm and sensuous world of adventures and light. Douglas greeted his friends in Italian, just as at home here among foreigners in Naples as he was among his fellow countrymen in Camden or Crystal Palace.

'And how is the birthday boy? All the better, it would seem, for your ambrosian slumbers. What did you have for breakfast? Don't tell me, let me guess.'

He leaned down and pointed his long nose towards Eric who exhaled a cloud of breath as if testing the air temperature on a frosty morning. It was a game they had played on the train. As he moved his head round to do this, however, Eric was distracted by the sight of a figure beside a large earth-coloured urn sprouting pelargoniums by the back door. It was the girl he had seen arrive in the carriage with Amoroso.

'Hard-boiled, speckled brown egg,' Douglas pronounced. 'Bread from an oven fired with umbrella pine, a Sevilliana orange without pips and some second-rate salami which this kitchen should be ashamed of.'

'What was that snossidge I had?' Eric asked, still with half an eye on the girl.

'That was the salami: the "snossidge", as you call it, of the south. What do you think of it?'

He pulled a face. 'I don't like it much.'

'Get used to it. Some days it may be all we have to eat. Have one of these to take the taste away. A birthday present.' From his jacket pocket he took out a cigar and handed it to Eric, lighting it with a silver lighter. The boy coughed on the first intake of breath, and his eyes watered, making Lo Bianco laugh. Eric tried to laugh too, at the thought of what an ass he was making of himself. This wasn't a little pencil-thin cheroot that he was used to, like the ones Squid nicked at Crystal Palace. This one was like inhaling a whole bonfire.

'It is your birthday today?' Amoroso asked.

Eric beamed and nodded.

'How old are you?'

'Thirteen.'

'Congratulations. An Aries, eh?' And he gave the news to Lo

Bianco, who slapped him heartily on the back.

'*Tredici, tredici,*' he said, holding up first two open hands, then three fingers.

'*Tredici,*' Eric repeated.

'Bravo!'

Douglas caught sight of the parcels on the table beside the copy of *Siren Land* which he had brought for Lo Bianco. 'Ah, the first taste of the south. Best olives in Italy.' He pushed his fingers into the paper and helped himself to a shiny fruit. 'Did you tell the ambassador we would be delighted to see him tonight?' Amoroso began to explain, in Italian, that the ambassador could not see them as arranged. 'Ha!' Douglas said. Amoroso continued his soft-spoken explanations, and Eric was again distracted by the figure near the back door. Her sharp eyes were watching them, but nobody seemed to notice or care. Douglas gave a loud laugh. 'Christ, the diplomatic service hasn't changed. To hell with them. We'll leave for Sant' Agata tonight.'

This about turn was a surprise Eric did not welcome. He had heard so much about Naples that he felt let down by the idea that they would not stay a few days, as they had planned. Noticing the boy's disappointment, Douglas tried to make amends.

'But we'll make your birthday a day to remember, Eric. How about a ride in that car of yours, Salvatore, for a start? *Andiamo áell'automobile, Salvatore?*' he said. 'We'll go down to the old town first and take my new pupil home to her aunt. This afternoon Salvatore can show you around the Zoological Station.' He repeated the sentence in Italian, for the benefit of Lo Bianco, who nodded amiably, winked at Eric, got up and ambled into the house.

'*Annetta, ti presento Enrico.*' Acknowledging at last the figure by the urn, Douglas wagged his hand as if he were paddling a canoe, bidding the girl forward. After a moment of what seemed like indecision, of wondering whether she did or did not want to do his bidding, she swaggered out of the shadows. 'This is Annetta, Eric. *Enrico, ti presento Annetta.*'

She wore a white blouse and a plain cornflower-coloured cotton skirt which fell loosely to her mid-calf, where her brown, down-covered legs appeared, stockingless, in rope-soled canvas shoes. Her long, straight hair was the colour of jet, her skin pale, her lips vermilion and her eyes like anthracite. There were gold studs in her ears. Eric grinned for ever. She replied with a perfunctory twitch of the lips and swaggered over to where Amoroso was sitting.

'No lessons for you on your birthday,' Douglas said to Eric. 'But tomorrow in Sant' Agata we will start again with forty minutes of Italian followed by an hour of general studies, which will include, on alternate days, Latin, History, Geography, Geology, Mineralogy, Botany, Topography, Mathematics.' He took out one of the small notebooks in which his life was regimented. 'Tomorrow: a history of the Emperor Tiberius will also be appropriate.'

'Will we come back here again? To Naples?' He still called it 'Ny-paws'.

'Of course, at the end of the summer, when we have discovered all the secrets of old Calabria and have had enough adventures to last for a winter.'

'Annetta is very pretty,' Eric said, quite unable to keep this observation to himself. She was now sitting astride the bench beside Amoroso, and he longed to speak fluent Italian.

'So she is,' said Douglas. 'But don't put your trust in women, Eric. Not even in the kitchen. They are all vampires.' He said these things cheerfully, talking and smiling in Annetta's direction. 'All, without exception, if you give them a chance. What you must do is vampire them first, slowly and systematically' – a devilish grin towards the girl was met with a fleeting smile in reply – 'it takes time and study, but the results are worth it.'

Annetta's thin fingers picked away at the contents of one of the spiky sea urchins. She ate the eggs matter-of-factly, slipping them unhesitatingly between her quick lips. Eric was suddenly overtaken by the idea that he really was looking at a vampire – a vampire enjoying a bite. And he wished he had been tempted to try a sea urchin himself.

Fifteen minutes later the thrilling blue motor was roaring down from the heights of Posilipo, bumping over the tramlines and darting in and out of tunnels. From its high, black leather back seat, Eric had his first sight of the city. He grinned so infectiously that even Annetta, sitting on the far side of Amoroso and glimpsing him through a tussle of windblown black hair, could not help but smile back. Eric's stomach somersaulted. And when the old man suddenly snatched at thin air and roared in frustration as his gardener's donkey's hat flew from his balding head into the wild blue day, they laughed out loud.

Lo Bianco, at the wheel, did not give the incident so much as a backward glance, and his foot depressed the accelerator with greater resolve. Properly dressed now, in a linen jacket and open-necked shirt, though still unshaven, he steered a creative course. Beside him sat Douglas, gesticulating and telling him how best to drive.

Naples Bay, the talk of all Europe, was opening up fully before them. Even Eric's mother, who had travelled no further south than Sydenham, knew Naples sufficiently by reputation to appreciate how lucky her son was to be there. Thinking of her now, the boy put his hand on his chest, feeling beneath the serge jacket the outlines of the Pelican pen his parents had given him for his birthday before he had left home. They had chosen it especially, she explained, reading from the leaflet that came with it, because it had a shut-off valve, so that it could be carried in any position without leakage, and its feed was made of 14-carat gold instead of vulcanite, so that it was 'unaffected by Hot Climate'.

'Write and tell me about Naples,' she had said. 'Describe the Bay and make me wish I was there.'

Douglas had made him write to her every other day, and Eric had promised Violet that he would write to her every week, too. Throughout the winter Uncle Norman had sent them post-cards from Italy every week. Now it was Eric's turn to be the source of news from abroad.

At the bottom of the hill they reached the pleasure ground of La Villa Nazionale, where fashionable villas included the Villa Pignatelli.

'Belongs to the Acton barons,' Douglas called out. 'Going back to Sir John, Ferdinand IV's first minister, 1780s.'

'I've been to Acton,' Eric said.

On the sea side of the park was the Via Caracciolo, the popular promenade where Neapolitans went for their evening stroll and where bands played on summer nights. From here there was a view across the sparkling bay, dotted with lateen-sailed fishing boats as it had been for two thousand years.

'Capri!' Douglas shouted, pointing to the great boulder out in the bay. 'And the Sorrento peninsula. Siren Land!'

Eric stared.

'The white buildings there,' Amoroso indicated with a wave of his hand towards the park, displaying a thick gold band on his second finger. 'That is the Zoological Station where Signor Lo Bianco works. He will show it to you this afternoon.'

'What do they keep in them?'

'The Aquarium, the middle building, has everything that lives in the sea.'

'Even mermaids?'

'If there are mermaids in the sea, then there are mermaids in the Aquarium.'

Douglas's turn: 'Virgil's temple. Mark it, Eric. We'll read him tomorrow.'

The boy furrowed his eyes, trying to look impressed. At the end of the park they turned down around Pizzafalcone, a spur from which a small bridge led to the islet of Megaris and the great angular prison of Castello dell'Ovo, the castle on the wizard Virgil's egg. Just beyond it, in the district of Santa Lucia where a recently unveiled bronze statue of King Humbert I shone like the sun, the road swung north, and the naval port came into view. Men-of-war lay out in the bay, threatening steel-hulled bulks as well as romantic barques with ribbons of bunting and laced with ropework.

'Your Admiral Nelson sailed in here,' Raffaele Amoroso said to Eric. 'He rescued our royal family and stole the heart of Emma Hamilton, the most beautiful woman in the city. We are still always very busy when your sailors are in port. Your admirals have always been particular.'

'She was a harlot,' Douglas cried from the front of the car. 'She made Nelson weak.'

Eric looked proudly at the ships anchored in the bay, scanning the masts and yardarms for signs of flapping white ensigns, imagining himself as a particular English admiral, willingly weakened by Annetta as Lady Hamilton. But the port quickly disappeared as they drove up past the coal magazines of the Arsenal and the Palazzo Reale, slowing behind the traffic of carriages. Douglas pointed to the statues on the palace façade.

'Tell him who they are,' he shouted at Amoroso.

'Eight centuries of Neapolitan dynasties,' Amoroso recited obediently. 'The Sardinian Victor Emmanuel, Napoleon's brother-in-law Joachim Murat, the Bourbon Charles III, who built the Teatro San Carlo opera house behind here, the Austrian Charles V, Alfonso I of Aragón, Charles I of Anjou, Frederick II of Hohenstaufen and Roger of Normandy.'

'Gosh,' said Eric.

Via Toledo, or what was fashionably being called Via Roma, the city's main thoroughfare, opened up before them. Saturday night in London's West End had always seemed to Eric to be the most exciting and animated place in the world: now he knew better. Here was complete chaos. Pedlars, news-vendors and shopkeepers cried out and shouted. Carriages rocked and drivers hooted, gesticulated and yelled while the Guardia Municipale, in dark coats with yellow buttons and numbered caps, conducted the cacophony as if they were conducting at the opera house. The Lancia's 115-kilometre-an-hour speed capabilities were completely useless in this mêlée and children began to form an escort around it. None had shoes, all had bright eyes, and there was a quickness about them. They shouted and laughed and pulled faces, and shamelessly went through a lexicon of gestures. Eric grinned.

Amid the cacophony there was music, too, provided by an old man playing a mandolin and building workers singing popular songs. The workers were signs of the *sventramento*, the disembowelling of the city that had been going on since the catastrophic cholera outbreak of 1884. For a quarter of a century, the authorities had been pulling down the worst slums and rebuilding, but work had recently slowed while money was diverted into the earthquake that, more than two years earlier had flattened Reggio, on Italy's toes, and Messina, the Sicilian port that faced it across the straits. A tax remained on train tickets as a means of raising funds.

Halfway up the street Lo Bianco drew to a stop, ignoring the shouts of the carriage driver behind. His passengers got out, and with Douglas leading the way they headed into the maze of alleys, followed by a group of urchins.

'Watch out for your valuables,' Amoroso advised. Eric grinned and dug his hands deep in his jacket pockets. He thought about

Squid, who had turned up to work on the Monday after the incident at Crystal Palace, cheerfully accepting the wallet Eric gave him: they had split its £10 contents in half. Now his right hand slid down beside a notebook and gripped the Waterbury nickel watch his father had given him, while his left hand sunk into a treasure trove: marbles, string, a cork from the dining car on the train, a used ticket, and the chatelaine knife with a tortoiseshell handle that was a present from Violet.

In Via Toledo they passed elegant shops selling leather and cameos, pastries and parasols, before turning off into a street where stalls were hung about with salamis and sausages, set out with buckets of olives and baskets of vegetables and bolstered by sacks of dried peas and beans. Eels and dragonfish lay on fishmongers' slabs. Portable stoves cooked sardines, anchovies, mullet, mussels and macaroni, and the air, spiked with garlic, was warmed in patches by draughts from pizza and bread ovens. There was also the passing stink of spilled wine from *osterie*, which displayed the price of half-litres, and the fusty smell of tobacco from tobacconists where flames were kept alight for the free use of passers-by. Second-hand cigar butts were a popular pedlar's line, as were rags.

The street led to a maze of lanes, myriad canyons festooned with washing and running with cats, dogs and children. Here society seemed turned inside out: kitchens, dining rooms, sitting rooms and workshops were all in the streets. Above them, like landings, were the washing-hung balconies, chirping with caged birds and clucking with chicken. From their railings people shouted to each other, to wayward children, to market sellers who bartered a price for their wares before putting them into the baskets lowered on the end of ropes. Goats, led through the streets to provide milk every morning, were still doing the rounds, and there were signs a cow had been making deliveries, too.

Of the half million people who lived in this city, a full fifth lived *sotterraneo*, in underground rooms that were little more than caves, without windows and with only the entrance doors through which Eric could see little. Sometimes there was a bed with a sick or elderly person in it, sometimes a candle burned, perhaps before an image of a saint. Sometimes there was a small portable stove, though most of these were out of doors.

The complete nakedness of some of the children added to Eric's feeling that he was intruding on so many private lives, and made him particularly aware of his tailored suit and leather shoes. A small gang followed them, continually calling out ('Monsieur', 'Signor', 'Cigars') and availing them with a whole vocabulary of gestures. One small boy followed Annetta, his hands in the air, wiggling his bottom until Eric dispatched him with a flick on the ear. Amoroso rebuffed calls for money with *'Niente, niente'*, chucking back his head and raising his eyebrows, while Douglas simply ignored their call for coins, an attitude Eric thought impolite.

As they turned into a wider lane, Annetta suddenly quickened her pace and skipped ahead of them, disappearing inside the door of a laundry. They followed her, stepping into the steaming sweatshop's gloom. A large and friendly middle-aged woman appeared from the Stygian dampness and greeted Douglas with a flurry of hand-waving and excited chatter. Her hair was black as Annetta's, her flesh white as flour, and she was introduced to Eric as Annetta's aunt, Maria Spasiono. Thick, doughy fingers smelling of overcooked pasta patted his cheeks. He grinned.

'Ah, che bel ragazzo,' she said with a throaty laugh and she produced from her pocket a bon-bon, wrapped in paper, and gave it to Eric who politely said, *'Grazie'*, which greatly delighted her. The confection tasted of aniseed.

With exaggerated politeness, Douglas declined an offer of a drink – though cakes suddenly appeared on a plate. When it was clear they really would not stay, the aunt turned and shouted Annetta's name into the shadows. In a moment the girl appeared, a pallid, almost theatrical face in the surrounding darkness. She stepped forward and kissed Douglas quickly on both cheeks. Then she turned to Eric, who awkwardly held out his right hand. With a movement so quick he did not notice, she took it in both of hers and brushed both his cheeks with kisses so light they seemed like a warm breath. Before his flushed skin had time to cool, she had gone.

They turned and left, stopping at the end of the street because Amoroso was going in a different direction. He spoke in Italian, and Douglas pressed a small bundle of lire into his hand. Amoroso made no attempt to conceal the money, which he placed deliberately inside a pigskin wallet. Then he shook hands with Eric in a formal, English way.

'Goodbye, young man,' he said. 'You will have a good time with Signor Douglas. He is the best of cicerones.'

'I'm sorry about your hat,' Eric said.

'I will buy a cupboard full,' said Amoroso, tapping the pocket which held his wallet, 'for the season. I hope we will meet again. Have a good journey.' He gave a nod, and turned on his heels, thrust his walking cane forward and went deeper into the warren of lanes.

'Come on, Eric,' Douglas said, making off at a good clip back towards Via Toledo. 'If we are to leave tonight there is plenty to do. After lunch I will deliver you to Lo Bianco for a couple of hours, while I sort out our arrangements.'

'He doesn't speak English,' Eric pointed out.

'All the better to teach you Italian. Listen to everything he says. He has a pure Neapolitan accent, though I suspect his ancestors came here from Africa. He is also the best marine scientist in Naples. He goes fishing and diving himself, a great innovator. I will pick you up in good time to return to his house before we get the train to Sant' Agata. There is one at six o'clock this evening.' He turned down a small, sunless alley.

'Can we go by boat?'

'It only runs in summer when . . .'

A tremendous crash made Eric spin round. Suddenly Douglas was no longer beside him. Instead, standing over the sprawled, inert figure of his friend was a young man not much older than himself. He was dressed in a loose shirt, short trousers and canvas shoes, and in his hand was a length of wood tinged with a red patch which matched the red liquid glistening in Douglas's hair. Eric did not think twice before hurling himself at the assailant. The sheer force of his rush pushed the other boy back against the wall, where Eric punched and kicked and wrestled until the two of them tumbled on to the cobbles in a panting, grunting, silent fury. If either felt pain they did not show it, and neither was going to give in.

Their furious silence was broken by an unexpected and familiar 'Hah!' Douglas had shaken himself into full consciousness, and he emitted such a roar of laughter that the two could not help but stop their fight. With a twinkle in his eyes that defied his undoubted pain, Douglas proceeded to quiz his assailant, who had rolled away from Eric and was squatting, panting, against the wall. He was sullen and monosyllabic, his broken voice scratchy and deep. His knees were grazed, there was a trickle of blood from his nose and his ruined shirt was stuck by sweat to his back. Eric was in a similar state: his tie was ripped to ribbons and his shirt had lost two buttons. He found one but could not see the other and as he searched for it he kept an eye on his adversary in case he should decide to strike again. Douglas continued to be thoroughly amused as he extracted information, grunt by grunt, from his assailant.

'Eric,' he said finally, getting up. 'Meet Michele, Annetta's brother.'

Eric was surprised and confused, but Douglas put a hand on his shoulder and said, 'Come on, I think you have taught him a lesson he won't forget. Get up and shake hands. *Pax.*' He took an arm from each of them and raised them into the air in the manner of a boxing referee. 'Joint winners,' he proclaimed. '*Bravi!* The prize is as much ice-cream as you can eat. *Gelati, Michele, per i magnifici pugili.*'

Eric was angry: he had been winning a fair fight, and he couldn't see why Michele had to be appeased. As they walked to the Gran Caffè d'Italia on the teeming Via Toledo, he kept eyeing the other boy. Douglas, deliberately between them, explained to Eric that there had been some sort of mistake, that Michele had thought he was a German who owed his aunt money.

Inside the grand café, a small ensemble was playing 'Torna a Sorrento', and though the clientele was generally animated, the blooded and scraped boys did not escape scrutiny. Led to a table at the back of the premises, they sat down and an ancient waiter, efficient and indifferent, awaited the order. Without consulting either the menu or his young friends, Douglas asked for three kinds of ice-cream, *gelati alla vaniglia, alla fragola* and *al lampone*, two full portions of each ('so you don't fight over them'), to which he added two glasses of *spremuta di amarena*, lemonade flavoured with the perfumed cherry, mahaleb. For himself, a vermouth with seltzer. He lit a cigar. Eric sat back cautiously, stroking his sore fists. The only good thing about it was that his mother wouldn't see him in this state. The thought of her made him check his pocket for the pen she had given him. It was gone.

'Are you going to Capri?' An American voice broke in overhead. Two women had materialised at their table. The one who spoke wore a suit nipped tight at the waist, erupting into a bustle. Her felt hat was adorned with a spray of false flowers, her lips were painted red, there was powder on her face and she lacked the natural sunshine of someone from the south. Eric supposed her to be in her mid-thirties, a little older than her companion, who was pale and did not attempt conversation, nor was she invited to do so.

'No, Gertrude.' Douglas sat back in his chair and looked up at them but he did not get to his feet. 'I have other plans.'

'There have been tales of phenomenal indecency,' she said, inhaling very slowly from her cigarette holder. The whole room was already in a cigar haze that the sun was finding hard to penetrate.

'I should hope so,' said Douglas. 'It's all in the ancient tradition.'

'Oh God, you're not going to go on about the Emperor Tiberius again, are you?' she asked.

'You know my views on that subject,' said Douglas.

'I would if I knew what "the gerocomic method" meant,' she replied.

Douglas chucked back his head and roared just as the waiter arrived with a silver tray full of ice-cream and lemonade.

'Wouldn't you be better off buying your little *scugnizzo* soap instead of ice-cream?' she asked, raising a querulous eyebrow in Eric's direction.

Eric stared back at her. 'My name is Eric Wolton,' he said, 'and I am a friend of Mr Douglas.'

She returned his stare with a quizzical gaze. 'An English *scugnizzo*? Be sure to write to your mother, Master Eric. She should be concerned for your welfare.'

CHAPTER 4

Siren Land, May 1911

It was a sky-blue day. The Sorrento peninsula, a ragged finger of limestone pointing at the island of Capri, rose in deep green stripes from the flat, violet sea. A heat haze blurred the horizon, and Mount Vesuvius, which four years earlier had blown off its cone and poured forth such a weight of ash that the roof of a Naples market had caved in, puffed an innocent pillar of smoke. Its unshaken column rising straight up into the sky was a sign, said farmers, fishermen and women in black, that the weather was about to change. But change seemed an outlandish notion on such a tranquil day animated only by lazy bees and hummingbird moths, by swallowtail butterflies and by the few birds which had escaped farmers' garrottes and snares and hunters' guns. Finches were flitting through the vineyards, orchards and olive groves, blue rock thrushes hopped in and out of limestone niches above the shore, wall creepers and kingfishers added darting colour; gulls and peregrine falcons swooped around the islands.

Beneath the crumpled folds of the south side of the Sorrento cliffs a fishing boat made slow headway, propelled by a single, silent oar. From its gunwales a sweet falsetto swam out in waves across the Gulf of Salerno, drifting up towards the giddy cliffs of the Amalfi coast in search of echoes. The notes had about them the bewailing sadness of a *canzone di personale*, a primeval peasant's song, but on closer hearing, the words were not in

Italian and the sweetness of the music was both suspect and a little flawed ... '*Hoio hoiotoho-swar, eia-weia opopoil; Ai! Ai! Papaiax attatai papai pai; io, moi, moi, omoi ototototoi; wallawahupla, ja, ja, atcha!*' In this mixture of Neolithic, Teutonic and Hindustani tongues which he thought to be the appropriate language of the Sirens, Norman Douglas, lips pursed, head back, eyes closed, was wooing young Eric Wolton who, dressed in just his blue woollen swimsuit, was blindfolded and lashed to the mast.

'Odysseus, my hero,' cooed Douglas when the song was complete, 'won't you put your hand through my golden hair? Will you not feel my breasts and my slippery, scaly tail?'

Eric giggled. 'No no, Parthenope, I know your tricks. I will never set eyes on you. Be gone. Go away, go away.'

'You are the one with the tricks, you cruel captain. How can I ever tempt a blind man tied fast to a mast? My fishy heart is broken, what am I to do?'

'Go and do something useful and leave me and my brave crew alone.'

'O, despair! I shall dash myself against the rocks in the next bay, on the island of Megaris, thus founding the settlement which shall be named Parthenope, after me, and which in 474 BC the Greeks, having defeated the resident Etruscans, shall call Palea polis, the old town, and build beside it their new town, their Nea polis, their Naples. Thus I shall be founder of the great city yonder.'

'Go on then.'

The morning history lesson, which had begun in the garden of the Hotel-Pension Villa Petagna in Sant' Agata on the heights of the Sorrento Peninsula (Virgil, Tiberius and Homer had all been touched upon), had been transferred to this fragile barque for the sake of a picnic lunch. The vessel belonged to Ciro, a broad young man, taciturn, serious minded, not yet old

enough for the military but already burdened with the responsibility of keeping his family in fish. He stood in the stern of the
boat, one thick hand gripping a single oar that was tied to the
stem. A constant, slow swishing back and forth kept the boat
moving steadily forward. He had said nothing since they left
the shore, but now he spoke.

'Eh!' He pointed over the starboard bow.

Douglas looked towards the small group of islands they were
approaching. 'Aha, a real siren.' He stood up enthusiastically
and reached forward to take off the boy's blindfold and undo
the loose rope around his wrists, so that he, too, could enjoy the
spectacle.

'Where is it?' Eric asked, blinking into the sunlight.

Douglas pointed. 'Over there, near that cave.'

The boy rubbed his eyes and peered out across the sparkl-
ingly clear blue-green water, over the silver flash of fishes and
the dark patches of rock and seaweed on the sea bed. Li Galli,
the Siren Islands, fortified in the Middle Ages but now abandoned, were strewn across the sea before them, and there, by the
water on the largest of them, a character peered out. It was
tanned brown, dog-faced and quizzical, and it seemed to be
wearing some kind of a hood or wimple.

'*Bove marino*,' said Douglas.

Ciro nodded knowingly, adding further information about
the beast. Eric had seen similar monk seals and manatees only
two days earlier, at the Neapolitan Aquarium. The afternoon
with Lo Bianco had introduced him to life in the Mediterranean, to octopus and cuttlefish, crabs and crayfish, and to
electric rays he was allowed to touch to feel their tingling
charge.

'Does it live here?' he asked.

'It's hard to say, it's so infernally sly,' said Douglas. 'Ciro says
that on moonlit nights it comes to these rocks to eat the

celebrated *frutti di mare*. And sometimes it goes to see its relations in Capri. Two years ago one was washed up on the beach near Ciro's house and they fed it bread and beans. But it died all the same. Sometimes, Ciro says, they climb into the vineyards at night to steal the grapes. And when they have had enough, they fold themselves into a sort of ball, like an orange, and roll back into the water.'

'Don't you think someone else might be stealing the grapes?' Eric asked.

'Marine scapegoats, you think?' Douglas said.

They were a hundred yards from the island when the monk seal wavered, then tipped into the sea, its tail flipping up as it dived.

'My last gift to the South Kensington Museum,' said Douglas, 'was a seal from the fresh-water lake of Saima in Finland.'

'How did you catch it?' asked Eric.

'I sat beside it and sung a few verses of the Finnish epic poem *Kalevala*. Like a Siren's victim, it was entirely mesmerised.'

'Can you mesmerise this one?'

'Of course. If I get the chance to sit beside it .'

The boat tipped to one side as all three of them leaned on its edge to get as close a look as possible should it reappear, hoping it might pass by the boat where it would hear Douglas's songs. Eric gave a shudder of excitement at the thought of the great dark body bumping against the fragile craft. It might tip them all into the water, and though he was hoping the next few months would be the time he learned to swim, he had several times imagined himself clinging to the hull of this vessel in a dramatic rescue scene. They could have seen the seal approach from some way off. The water, clear as an aquarium, was now less then ten metres deep. A tremulous flicker of silver showed up a shoal of fish the size of sticklebacks, and it was possible to make out the molluscs and flora, the black urchins and mussels, the red starfish, anemones and coloured coral. Douglas pointed to an octopus, its legs waving breezily over the sand. But there was no sign of the seal.

The boat pulled in beside a deeply shelved rock a hundred yards from where the seal had sunk. This landing point had clearly been used for centuries as the island's jetty and, from the ruins of a small building, an ancient wall crumbled down into the sea. Eric put on his collarless shirt, khaki shorts, socks and shoes, took hold of a towel they had borrowed from the hotel and scrambled on to the rock from where he held fast to the side of the boat to keep it from floating away. Douglas, in his shirt sleeves, and hatless, threw a jacket over his arm, handed him the picnic basket and stepped deftly ashore. As Ciro pushed the boat out again and rowed off around the island to attend to his pots and lines, Douglas led the way up a path overgrown with scrubby vegetation which scratched Eric's legs. Around them the island's treeless slopes sparkled with spring flowers, with thistles, rose garlic, irises, rock roses, orchids, fritillaries and such myriad small bright flowers as stork's-bill, campion, scarlet pimpernel and the white star of Bethlehem, their thick fragrance mingling with lavender, thyme, rosemary and rue. Dark lizards flicked their tails and disappeared into the undergrowth, crickets jumped in a whir of blue and red wings, and a brace of quail squawked out of the undergrowth, prompting Douglas to boast of his prowess with a gun.

By the time they had reached the summit of the island, Douglas had explained the island's flora (he had once tried counting the flowers here but had been forced to give up), fauna (the swifts were Alpine), geology (part of the Apennine limestone ridge and not, as some would have it, a volcanic eruption, as the circular nature of the island group all too easily suggested) and history (Eric liked best the story of the Amalfi pope who had had his eyes put out and was exiled alone and sightless on this island of exceptional vistas).

The view from the top of the island was unsurpassed, taking in the Amalfi coast, dusted yellow with broom, the silhouettes of islands, the peaks of the hinterland and the great sweep of the Gulf of Salerno from Capri to Sapri. Eric stared around and around, but Douglas barely took in the scene before he began searching the ground, occasionally pushing stones over with his foot, or picking them up to examine them more closely. Now and then he stamped a foot. Eric, curious, stared at the ground around him, too, wondering what there was to see.

'Ah, look here: white penthellic. And here' – Douglas dived on a patch of ground, rubbing its surface – '*giallo antico*, which the Romans used as paving slabs. Each time I find something new.'

'Did somebody live here?' asked Eric.

'I'm sure there must have been a large Roman villa. See how the summit has been flattened for about fifty yards, enough to have put up a temple if they wanted to.'

Eric looked hard but did not know how to tell the difference between something that had been flattened and something that was flat.

'And over there are the substructures of two first-century walls. A systematic hunt might yield brick stamps which would decide the actual age of the building.' Douglas tapped his foot on the ground, then jumped on the spot. 'Come and try this,' he yelled excitedly.

Putting down the picnic basket and towel, Eric went over to Douglas and started stamping and jumping, too.

'Now try it over there. See if it sounds different.'

For half an hour they jumped up and down all over the summit of the rocky island, deciding – after much discussion and repeated jumping – that there were several distinct areas where the resonance of their falls seemed different, confirming to Douglas the existence of underground chambers. Sometimes they jumped together in one place, sometimes they leaped separately, sometimes they hopped, sometimes they stomped one foot at a time, marching on the spot. They considered the height of their jumps and the weights of their bodies and they endeavoured to jump higher and higher. In the heat of the spring afternoon it was a perspirational activity, but they did not stop until they had become quite out of breath from both their jumping and the laughter it evoked. Finally, pretending dizziness, Douglas zigzagged towards what looked like a ruined farm building, and Eric followed after him.

They fell together on to the ground beneath a knotty carob. 'Think of the number of gales it has taken to bend its boughs into such an ideal shady spot for the benefit of the happily unemployed.' He opened the hamper Eric put before him. 'Do you like strawberries?'

'Oh yes.'

'These aren't too bad.' He pulled out a punnet, examined it, and carefully placed a fruit in his mouth. 'They come from the market stall of Maria A'Paponnessa in the Strada Tasso in Sorrento. She has a patch of land on the south slopes of the Torre de Sorrento and uses manure from the neighbour's cow mixed in with straw bulk, which is never less than one year old.'

Eric, about to put a fruit in his mouth, hesitated. 'Cow pats? Can't you taste them?'

'Only if you have exceptional imagination. Go on, eat up. Don't be a baby.'

Eric shut his eyes and pressed the fruit between his tongue and the roof of his mouth. The flavour squirted out into his cheeks, down his throat and up the back of his nose. It was delicious and he grinned. Douglas took another for himself.

'The important thing is to know where to find what you

like – and don't tell a soul where you found it. It's good to keep people jealous. Who wouldn't be jealous who could see us now? Two friends lunching alone on a Siren Island.' He searched in the hamper. 'I also asked the kitchen to pack bread and olives and that wretched salami you cannot abide, and some cheese made from buffalo milk, which you also forbear, and four tomatoes.'

'I like the tomatoes,' said Eric. 'They're like cricket balls. Do tomatoes come from Italy?'

'The navigator Christopher Columbus who was from Genoa in northern Italy – the man you remember sailed the ocean blue in 1492 – brought them back from the Americas, but the English deemed them poisonous and thus, as usual, denied themselves the pleasure, a sacrifice that lasted nearly two hundred years. Here, on the other hand, as soon as they saw them they invented the pizza. Oh, I forgot, there is a slice of Margherita for you. There, wrapped up in the greaseproof.'

Eric put down the tomato he was contemplating and unwrapped the pizza.

'I've never known a boy who didn't like it,' said Douglas. 'If we were dull and interested only in money we would open a restaurant in London selling nothing else.' He took two bottles from the hamper, handing the lemonade to Eric and opening a dark green bottle of wine with the corkscrew on a complex knife. 'Eat whatever you like. That's the first rule. As for this' – he took a mouthful of wine – 'it's the closest approximation to that gold of Sant' Agata: *oro stravecchio, oro del padrone*. How is the lemonade? It was freshly made this morning.'

'I like it.'

'Not bad for a Monday afternoon, eh?' Douglas settled back. 'But we have not been idle. I think we have hit upon an import-ant discovery here today. Jumping. The trouble with most people is that they don't jump enough. It's not inability, it's wilful. At every opportunity they fail to leap.'

'I don't often see people doing it,' Eric admitted.

'The problem is that they don't allow themselves enough leisure.' He cut a lump of cheese with the pocket knife. 'Like all animals we are the products of leisure moments, but unlike beasts, we walk upright because leisure has made us curious. A real gentleman is someone who knows how to use any amount of leisure. But leisure is so often wasted or used unwisely. In this country it has produced the vendetta. It is in the blood. Odysseus and the whole *Iliad* is nothing but a vendetta. If you suggested expeditious English methods of settling accounts – like you, Eric, undertook on my behalf with my mad assailant Michele – the southern Italian would laugh at you. He does not want his accounts settled; the brooding is what he likes.'

'They should do more jumping,' said Eric.

'Hah! Yes they should.'

For an hour beneath the gnarled carob they discussed at their leisure the subject of leisure and the subject of being at their leisure to discuss what they liked. They talked of the nature of *vendettas* and recalled their best fights, which were the fights in which they had come off best. And as the lemonade and the wine went down and the hamper gave up its load, the talk turned again to their favourite food and the best fruit they had ever had.

'Who lived here?' Eric asked at one point. 'Apart from the pope who was blinded.'

'There were two villas. I like to think they were built by some solitary Siren-worshipper, who spent the summer months among his fruit and vines and books and flute-girls, reflecting perhaps on how men's boyhood friendships give way to their distrustful later years as shaggy solitaires.'

'Are you a shaggy solitaire?'

'Undoubtedly.'

'But I thought I was your friend.'

'You are, Eric. My very best friend.' He put his hand round the back of the boy's neck and looked so intensely sincere that Eric did not for one moment doubt it. 'Come on, now. Let's do some exploring.'

Eric jumped up and pulled at Douglas's outstretched hand to yank him on to his feet. They put the picnic away and set off round the island, looking at flowers and stones, and insects and views.

'Do you know what everything you can see is called?' Eric asked when they reached a rock at the edge of the island and sat down again.

Far below, near a neighbouring island, Ciro's boat drifted. He was paying out a line of earthenware pots, strung together, to trap octopuses, the way they had been trapped since the times of the ancient Greeks. In a moment, he would take hold of the oar and push the boat round to the south side of the island, unknowingly watched by his passengers.

Douglas looked around him at the hillsides, then out across the sea to the shore. 'Yes,' he said. 'I think I have a name for everything I can see.'

'What's Ciro's boat's name?' Eric asked.

'Hah! I have no idea.'

Eric grinned. 'Does anybody come to this island?'

'Hunters, sometimes, and fishermen if they get caught in a storm. Ciro won't come ashore, though. He says it is a *male sito*, a bad place, and he claims things go flying about here and strange lights appear at night.'

'Do they?' asked Eric.

'I have never seen them,' said Douglas.

'Does Ciro really think the seals steal the grapes and turn themselves into orange balls?'

Douglas gave a shrug. 'Yes, of course he does. Or not,

depending on the moment. He sometimes talks about a beast called the *gatta marina*, the sea cat, which puts its head out of the water to see where the nets are, then dives down to eat the fish. It has four feet with prodigiously long claws, and only comes in certain seasons – and then not always. Its colour is black – or sometimes white; and it weighs less than a hundred-weight – but often more. It is covered with a sort of fur – like a dolphin. Nobody eats the sea cat – except some people, who do . . .'

Eric laughed at the faces Douglas pulled at each change of heart. The water near Ciro's boat, now hidden from the sight of the mainland by the island, suddenly erupted and a small white spume rose and fell back on to the water. A few seconds later an explosion thundered across the bay, bouncing off the hills and echoing back and back towards distant heights. The small boat rocked violently. Eric stood up, alarmed. 'What was that?'

'Dynamite. Ciro's making a fish soup for his supper.'

'Why does he want to blow them up?'

'Because he is lazy and cannot be bothered to fish properly. Sometimes he uses cyclamen roots or the juice of euphorbia, which he squeezes on the water to poison the fish, and no doubt half his family in due course as well. It is nothing short of a miracle that any kind of swimming, crawling creature continues to frequent these coasts. There is hardly a fish in the Mediter-ranean worth eating. Here they make soups with the *guarracino*, a pitch-black monstrosity, one or two inches long, a mere blot with insufferable manners. Or the *scorfano*, which got its name because that's just what it sounds like – the spitting out of bones. The only difference between the *scorfano* and a toad is that a toad has more meat on it. Or the *aguglia*, all tail and proboscis, the very nightmare of a fish, as thin as a lead pencil, which the peoples of Siren Land have fought for centuries over. Or the noble-looking *palamide*, whose flesh tastes like shoe leather soaked in paraffin, which is exported in thousands to the epicures of Naples. Or the *totero* or squid, an animate ink bag whose india-rubber flesh might be useful for deluding hunger on desert islands since, like American gum, you can chew on it for months but never get it down.

'The French can make fish soup, but not the Italians. The French could produce an excellent and nutritional substitute out of cigar stumps and empty matchboxes. But even as a Turk is furious with a tender chicken, because it cheats him out of the pleasure of masticating, so a Neapolitan would throw a boneless *zuppa di pesce* out of the window: the spitting and spluttering are half the fun. He eats with his eyes, like a child who prefers tawdry sweets to good ones. Neapolitans pay untold sums of money for showy sea spawn, for green and golden scales and rococo dorsal fins. Their flesh is either flabby or slimy and full of bones in unauthorised places . . .'

And so, for a while, Douglas, with the help of another glass or two from the picnic hamper, continued to describe, in as graphic a detail as could delight Eric, the unpalatability of Neapolitan soup, adding descriptions of rancid oil and garlic, weeks-old breadcrumbs, decaying sea shells, and onion peel swept from the kitchen floor. As he did so, they kept an eye on Ciro, but there were no more bangs. Eventually the boat got underway, heading back towards the jetty, and as the fisherman passed below, he caught sight of them and waved as a signal for them to come down to be picked up.

By the late afternoon the land, heated by a full day's sun, had become warmer than the sea, and the air rose above it, sucking in cooler air from over the water. Taking advantage of this on-shore breeze, Ciro unfurled the triangular canvas sail and, still steered by the single oar, they drifted back towards the coast. By Ciro's feet were several buckets full of unrecognisable carnage from the dynamite blast. At the bottom of the boat was a collection of small, coloured fish and three octopuses which Ciro had tenderised by biting out their hearts with his teeth. Eric took off his socks and shoes and dangled his feet over the bow, kicking the sea, and imagining his toes being attacked by any number of creatures. As they blew homeward, Douglas taught him a song about the wretched local *guarracino* fish that local boys had elevated to a dish of great rarity and delight.

They came ashore in the Cove of Crapolla, a steep-sided inlet with a stream tumbling down its back. Half a dozen other fishing boats were drawn up on the shore. Three more were on the edge of the water, preparing to leave with acetylene lights, which had recently taken the place of pine torches in attracting fish at night. There was no sign of any foreigners: the season for bathing had not yet begun.

The sun had gone off the cove some time before their arrival and Eric, drying his feet and pulling on his socks and shoes, shivered in the chill of the early evening. They did not wait for Ciro to sort out his catch and his nets, but started at once on the hour-long walk up the steep, paved path to Sant' Agata. Douglas, swinging the picnic basket, recited lines from the *Iliad* in Latin as they went. Dusk was not a drawn-out affair, and by the time they were halfway along the path, moonlight was guiding their steps and cicadas had started to whir. Eric remembered he had left the towel in the boat.

'Go and fetch it, then,' said Douglas, without stopping, 'or they'll charge us for it. But you better hurry or there might not be any supper.' When Eric hesitated, he added: 'Not afraid of the dark, are you?'

'No,' said Eric.

'Good boy. We're not halfway yet, you might catch me up.' And he disappeared, declaiming further verses from the *Iliad*, even though there was no one to hear them.

Eric turned and tried to run back down the path, but he had

to be careful where he put his feet. The full moon, set in the centre of the pitch-black, star-pricked sky, made a brighter night than he had seen in all his life, but parts of the path lay in deep shadow. It was true he was not afraid and, though he was tired from the sea air and the climbing and the jumping, he sped down the path to the beach. He expected to pass Ciro on the way, but there was no sign of him and when, fifteen minutes later, he climbed down to the shore, he found it deserted. Nothing stirred under the moon, among the shadows of the cliffs and the fishing boats, in the secret crevices of the rocks and in the black ink of the sea. Trying to slow his panting breath to a whisper, he looked around, listening to the tide lapping half-heartedly on the pebbles. A small olive-green crab scuttled sideways down the stones in front of him, then another further on. Out at sea lights glowed by the uninhabited islands, and Eric thought of the *male sito* Ciro described, of the strange lights and things that went flying about . . . and he thought of the *bove marino* visiting relatives, and the black *gatta marina*, weighing more than a hundredweight and showing its long claws. Behind him there was a thud. Looking round he saw what he thought was a red ball, like an orange, which had fallen from the vineyards above, rolling down the beach towards the sea.

Without further hesitation he found Ciro's boat and he clambered up the side and tipped himself in, landing on something so slippery that he immediately slid to his knees. His palms pushed down on more slimy things he could not see, one of which moved, he was sure, when he touched it. Frantically he felt around for the towel, working his way through he knew not what wet substances until, through ropes, lines, buoys, pots and rags, he connected with the familiar roughness of the hotel linen. He grabbed it, jumped from the boat and without a backward glance headed up the beach for the path, not slowing down as he pounded up the almost vertical slope.

Away from the cove, Eric thought he was surrounded by unseen men smoking cigars, as he could not put a name to the fireflies that glowed by the path. He tried to run from this new *male sito*, whirling the towel around his head to keep it at bay. So he was glad when at last he arrived at the unlit hamlet of Tosca and the towel seemed to fly more like a triumphant banner: he had not let his friend down. He was even more pleased when he reached the outskirts of Sant' Agata, but he was suddenly brought to a halt by an unaccountable howl that chilled his blood. On a dusty street corner at the edge of town, in the light of the moon, he saw what looked like a wild beast. A lunatic on all fours, shaggy headed and ragged clothed, put his face up to the moon and bayed like a wolf.

He was more grateful than he could articulate when he finally reached the Hotel-Pension Villa Petagna. On the doorstep before the lobby, he folded the towel carefully into a manageable size, wiped his hands on it, regained his breath, tucked in his shirt and then stepped into the hotel. The dining room, overlooking the moon-carpeted garden, was heavy with chestnut furniture and decorated with Christs and calendars and views of Paris, the Alps and Rome. Fewer than half of the dozen tables had customers and the emptiness gave the place a subdued air. It also meant there was no problem finding Douglas who, looking relaxed as any man faced with good food and company, was deep in conversation, this time with a bearded foreigner who was wearing dark glasses.

'Ah, here comes my best friend,' Douglas called when he saw the boy advancing towards them. Eric grinned, though he felt tired and rather sick. 'Come and meet an old acquaintance. This is Doctor Axel Munthe. Axel, this is my protégé, Eric Wolton.'

'I am so pleased to meet you,' the guest said in an accent too good to be English. 'Any good friend of Mr Douglas is a good friend of mine.'

'Axel, that is one of the most implausible platitudes I have heard you pronounce,' Douglas said amiably. 'It simply will not wash. You are sliding into the Italian habit of exaggeration and hyperbole: you have been coming here too long.'

Munthe took little notice of the admonishment. 'Are you a friend of Archie and Robin's?' he asked.

'No,' Douglas said, 'he is not.'

Eric held the towel behind his back. It was smelly and crumpled and seemed out of place. 'I'm rather hungry,' he said.

'I expect you are,' Douglas said. 'Unfortunately, the dish of the day is fish soup.'

The sick-making images of tough and bony fish Douglas had evoked earlier arose in Eric's mind, and his fingers felt again the slippery textures of the bottom of the boat. 'Oh well, perhaps I am not that hungry,' he said.

On the table before Douglas, beside the litre carafe of wine, was a plate on which bread, a boiled egg and some raw vegetables were lying half eaten.

'This is all I could get out of the kitchen,' said Douglas, 'and that not without a fight. When it comes to fish soup they just won't take "No" for an answer. I told them we had joined a new sect called The Piscine Preservation Fraternity, but they were quite undeterred. In the end I had to go into the kitchen and fetch these myself.'

Munthe said something in German, which Eric did not understand, and the two men laughed, falling into conversation.

Fifteen minutes later, looking back on the evening from the quiet of his hotel room, where a hunk of bread, a tomato and two radishes kept him company, Eric could not decide if they had been talking English or Italian or German or the language of the Sirens. *Hoio hoiotoho-swar, eia-weia opopoil; Ai! Ai! Papaiax attatai papai pai; io, moi, moi, omoi ototototoi; wallawa-hupla, ja, ja, atcha!* He slept as he lay on his bed, in his clothes, the bread half eaten and the radishes untouched. None of the recent distresses of the evening disturbed his dreamless slumber. But by the time the moon had spread a silver river across his counterpane he was woken by the simple click of a light switch. He opened his eyes to the moonlight, aware of a figure at the end of the bed. At first he had no reason not to think he was at home in north London.

'Who's there?' he asked sleepily.

'Ah, you're awake,' said Douglas. 'Your light was on. I just came to switch it off and say goodnight.' He drew the curtain. 'Moonlight must never touch your bed. It's unlucky. Did you have enough to eat?'

'I fell asleep.'

'You should get those clothes off and put your pyjama suit on.'

'I'm too tired. I'll do it in the morning.'

Douglas chuckled and bent down to kiss the boy on the forehead. His heavy breath was thickened with cigars and wine. Eric's dad never smelled so sociable, and he wondered what Uncle Norman's children made of their father.

'When will you see Robin and Archie again?' he asked.

'Oh, in the summer holidays, if they're good.'

'Wouldn't they rather be here with us?'

'Perhaps, but they have to go to school.'

'Do they ever see their mother?'

Douglas let out a loud squawk like a chicken. 'That old hen won't ever see them again.'

Eric thought about this for a moment, then he said: 'I'd like to meet them one day.'

'So you will. Goodnight, my brave captain.'

Eric heard Douglas shut the door behind him, and he lay

awake for just a few minutes wondering what a terrible woman Uncle Norman's wife must have been.

When he woke again it was light. He rolled off the bed and walked over to the window and pulled back the curtains. A smell of fish and the sea came from the towel strewn across the base of the bed like an exorcised ghost. From the pocket of the jacket on the chair Eric took out the Westerbury watch. It was 5.13 a.m. Sant' Agata, 1,280 feet above sea level, looked out on both sides of the Sorrento peninsula: to the south were the Gulf of Salerno and the Siren Islands; to the north, the direction in which Eric's room faced, was a full view of the Bay of Naples. It was different today. There was a low, grey blanket of cloud. A spray came off the sea in small white tufts. The sweep of the land around the bay and the continuing islands of Procida and Ischia were dark as pitch and seemed menacingly close, as did the steamboat heading for the Marina Grande on Capri, bobbing and dipping through the sea horses. A south wind was blowing. Siren Land was losing its magic. Their adventure from Campania into Apulia, Basilicata and Calabria was about to begin.

CHAPTER 5

Moving Along, June 1911

By mid-May Eric and Douglas were in 'thirsty' Apulia, the wide, dry limestone plain east of Naples which extends south from the promontory of Gargano, the 'spur' on the familiar Italian boot. The journey had been carefully planned, the route mapped, *postes restantes* anticipated, and their bags packed with no space for any object or garment that was not absolutely necessary. At the start, in London, Douglas had insisted they needed no more than one piece of luggage each because, apart from anything else, any bag that could not be carried on to an Italian train would be charged at the rate of 4.65 centesimi a kilometre. Eric found it hard to squash everything into his canvas portmanteau. He had been given a list of what to bring: the suit he stood up in, a pair of 'tropical' khaki shorts, four shirts with detachable, sponge-clean celluloid collars, pyjama suit, gauze vests, cotton pants and half-hose, swimming costume, towel, washing bag with coal tar soap, Cherry toothpaste and brush, nail scissors, pen (since replaced), pencil box, blotting book, stationery box, four lined notebooks and a pocket Italian dictionary, in which he had looked up every rude word he knew and discovered a number of interesting other ones besides, including *baffona*, meaning a woman with a not unpleasing moustache. Douglas suggested he tried to learn a column of new words each day.

'No one washes south of Naples,' Douglas declared on their

first day in Sant' Agata, and Eric was glad not to be pressed for an inspection of his hands before each meal, as happened at home. That did not mean he was not encouraged to keep reasonably clean, and if they stopped anywhere for more than one night, Douglas would find a washerwoman to deal with the contents of their shared blue cotton laundry bag, though a box of washing soda was kept for emergencies. A set of Indian cotton sheets added to the weight of Douglas's small compressed-cane trunk, but in some bug-ridden places without fresh linen or iron beds, they would help in the diurnal fight against the enemies of repose.

Neither Douglas nor his charge pried upon the other – they would not think of entering each other's hotel room without first knocking – but as they moved from town to town, packing and unpacking, their lives grew mutually familiar. A source of great interest to Eric was the shirt tray in Douglas's trunk, which was not used for shirts but was full of the traveller's needs. 'Everything useful,' said Douglas, 'and nothing indispensable.' There were seven books, including the *Odes* of the Latin poet Horace, who had been born in Apulia; Roget's *Thesaurus*; a small volume in Italian, dated 1759, on an obscure monastic order; a book on local architecture, and one on local customs, of which some pages were still to be cut; a well-thumbed zoology in German, and a copy of his own recently published *Siren Land*. There were also half a dozen notebooks, diary, invaluable address book, collection of calling cards, stamps, maps, pen and ink, carbons, pencils, wax and seal, pack of playing cards, bootlaces, stud box, razor and leather strop, tin-opener, clasp knife, toothpicks, magnifying glass, Zeiss prism binoculars and steel-rimmed reading glasses. There were pipes and cigars and a few packets of Gold Flake cigarettes, which he kept to himself, smoking just one each day, before breakfast. For general dispensation he had brought a quantity of snuff and sweets for the old and the young, who were the only people, he declared, who were worth talking to.

Among other items in his trunk was a small medicine box containing bandages, gauze and aspirin, chlorophyll, lanoline, iodine, quinine, camphor and Bengu ointment for insect bites. There was also a waterproof tweed knapsack, to be used, he said, on small excursions. Finally there was a small, firm cushion he called Albert, without which he was quite unable to sleep.

As far as Eric knew, Uncle Norman had not lived in a house since he was divorced and had given up the family villa that Signor Amoroso had pointed out in Posillpo. In fact, it never occurred to Eric that Uncle Norman should have a home at all. None had been evident, none mentioned. Instead this trunk seemed to be his well-furnished residence. It implied a complete and sturdy domestic interior with a fussy kitchen, an airy living room, a book-lined study that smelt of wood polish and tobacco, and a bathroom and bedroom with a slightly antiseptic, chemical odour, where Uncle Norman entertained in his Paisley dressing gown. Who needed the encumbrance of a roof, when there were inns in every town, friends in every city, and carob trees in every field?

A routine had set in early. Douglas was up at dawn each day and had usually read half a book, drafted several pages of another and written a handful of letters by the time Eric appeared, dressed and tidy. Breakfasts were a disappointment, consisting generally of a small cup of coffee, black, and sometimes stale bread, perhaps some fruit, such as a fig, and little else. "Strewth, I couldernarf do with a kipper and treacle puddin'," Douglas said at breakfast on the first day of their travels, mimicking the accent of his charge. After this slender repast there would be two hours of formal lessons. Eric was no academic but he applied his mind to his studies with a steady patience, as he did to everything else. Although his Italian was coming on, he was still to be convinced that anything he said in the language might actually be understood.

To encourage him in his endeavours, Douglas told him: 'I was three years younger than you when I first went to school in England, and my English was abominable. German was my first language.'

'Didn't you speak English at home?' Eric asked.

'Not after my father died when I was five. Not much before either: he was hardly ever at home, always up in the mountains, hunting chamois for days on end, till it finally killed him. Hah! Good way for him to go.'

'What happened?'

'He lost his footing in the snow, though nobody knew the mountains better.' Then, as often when recalling family matters, he changed the subject. 'But we'll soon have you speaking like a Calabrian. Listen out. They speak differently down here, and it pays to remember your Latin. When they swear they don't say "Corpo di Cristo", they say "Corpo di Bacco", Body of Bacchus. You have to delve.'

Douglas encouraged delving up to a point. Eric would have liked to have known more about Douglas's past, more about Archie and Robin, but it was an area into which he did not feel encouraged to delve. For all his own curiosity, Douglas considered social curiosity vulgar. During the interview with Eric's parents in Camden, however, when they had been trying to ascertain where exactly he came from, Douglas had explained that he had been born in Vorarlberg near Lake Constance in Austria, and he had even pointed out the rough direction of the place on a pocket map. His mother was Austrian, he said, but his father was a Scot, Laird of Tilquhillie on Deeside, who had inherited the cotton mill that Douglas's grandfather had set up in this alpine region. It was a respectable and promising background.

Eric was not good at descriptive writing, and in his letters home he sometimes borrowed phrases of Douglas's, or asked him for help. 'I couldn't half do with a kipper and treacle pudding,' he wrote the same evening Douglas had suggested it. If he often mentioned the terrible food, it was his way of complimenting his mother on hers, of flattering her, and implying that he missed her, which he occasionally did. But he was careful not to include any details to alarm her, for if there were any hint that he might not be in safe hands, his parents might order him home. He also wrote to Violet every week as he had promised.

Douglas liked him to write down the meals they had eaten in a daily diary he persuaded him to keep. On those evenings that Douglas was lost in conversation with some old crone, or had gone out for a stroll, Eric would write up his diary in his room, often surrounded by pictures of saints lit up by devotional candles or bare bulbs. And he would skim through his dictionary, looking for words he could use to surprise and impress Uncle Norman, who was never mean in his praise.

Their first long stay was a week in Foggia, a railway junction and the market town of the Apulin plain. It was a community of small, creamy white, comfortable houses and the centre for wool and corn. Brick kilns blew smoke into the clear skies and the *fosse granarie* – huge corn vaults capped at street level with tombstone slabs – showed this had long been a bread basket of the south. There was electric light in the streets, but it was extinguished by 8 p.m. when just a few beams spilled out of the doors of the *osterias*, which were marked by limp red flags. More mysteriously, some houses' doors bore crude blue plaques with red crosses and the inscription: VIGILANZA NOTTURNA. However much Douglas denied their existence, brigands never seemed far away.

On their first day in Foggia, Eric and Douglas despatched by swift examination the grain stores, the palace of Frederick II and the Norman cathedral where, Douglas explained, the great stone slab on columns which served as the altar had been Frederick's dining table, ample proof, if it were needed, of the civility of the Swabian Hohenstaufen king. Then he played a few notes on the organ and told how, as a child prodigy, he had broken five keys on a piano playing a Liszt polonaise. His teacher, himself a pupil of Liszt, had told him not to apologise, and said that a polonaise like young Norman's was worth a piano.

Eric believed their journey was taking them clear to the heart of world history, where Greeks, Romans, Normans, Saracens and all the empires of Europe had played their part. Uncle Norman, who was so at home here, took on the mantle of resident guide, pronouncing the name of the Emperor Frederick II Hohenstaufen with such Germanic rectitude that he sounded like a respected distant relative. And just as Frederick was descended from the Normans – the Norsemen from northern France who gave England its nobility and Sicily its first kings – so Uncle Norman was part of the same pan-European family. He was just another Norman in the south.

In the next few days they made sorties from their base. On excursions into the country Eric often found it hard to keep up, even though Douglas, swinging a walking cane, made allowances, shortening his stride, stopping now and then with some questions, taking notes, pacing sites, examining, measuring, leaping.

Devoid of trees and hedgerows, and depleted of the half a million sheep that had left for the higher summer pastures, the countryside was stilled. It was already losing its lush greenness to the parching sun, and after Naples and the coast it felt empty and lifeless. A few peasants wandered into the landscape, some in ox-hide leggings, some in conical hats, scraping at the land with timeless hoes, riding high-wheeled carts and driving milk-white, long-horned buffalo that would be yoked to elm ploughshares and used to drag hurdles as harrows. In the towns and villages Eric became accustomed to the sight of the black-dressed women, the indolent, often blue-eyed girls and the stubble-chinned men, and he listened patiently to the tales Douglas drew from them with the aid of his snuff and chocolates and cigarettes. They would tell him about their horticulture and husbandry, their saints and superstitions, and about the problems of the young, who were going to live in America where they pursued a purely material life. Their absence was already marked by untilled fields and untended vines.

In Venosa they explored catacombs, stared at Casa d'Orazio where in AD 64 Horace had been born, and visited the Norman church of La Trinità, where old women foregathered on their knees, licking the cold stone floor, before kissing a fissure between two stones on the wall. Douglas asked a priest the significance of this yoni worship.

The bald man shrugged and said, '*Sono femmine.*'

They made an overnight sortie to Lucera, staying at the Albergo Sirena in the Corso, where Douglas, as usual, questioned the tariff. 'They expect it,' he told Eric. 'They don't respect you unless you make a fuss and complain.' The landlord deducted two lire from the bill. In the afternoon, after further bargaining, a young man took them in a mule-driven carriage to the great castle of Frederick II a few miles west. He knew nothing about the 'Sultan of Lucera' and was more interested in telling them about a current trial of a triple-murderer in the town, which he thought they would find amusing, though murderers were no longer hanged in Italy as they were, he had been told, in England. Did they come from London? Was London much bigger than Naples? Bigger and richer, no doubt, though there were many millionaires in Naples, and at least three in Lucera. The two *signori* must be rich. How much had they paid for their hats, their boots, their binoculars?

Bored with the young man, Douglas said: 'The binoculars were ten thousand lire.'

'Ten thousand! That's an enormous sum of money.'

'It is.'

'And what did your watch cost?'

'I can't say. It was given to me by the Sultan of Turkey.'

'I wish he'd give me one. And your walking stick?'

'My stick cost one thousand five hundred lire. It is made of wood that grows in the island of Zamorgla and nowhere else.'

'You must be millionaires.'

'We are.'

The young man's eyes were bright with astonishment and Douglas said to Eric in English: 'Never call yourself poor when you talk to these people. Say you are a millionaire, and that you mean to keep every penny of your money and to pay them rather less than what everyone else pays. That will make them respect you. And if you want to make them hate you, never call them robbers or cut-throats – they like that. Call them rich. Say you know they are rich, and that everybody else knows it, too. It makes them furious.'

From the imposing, turreted fortifications of Lucera there were views down across the whole emerald plain, spattered with blood-red poppies and yellow fennel flowers, towards Foggia and the distant cone of Monte Vulture near Melfi in the south. Overhead, falcons were gliding, looking for mice and rabbits among the ruins. Of all things that were new to Eric, birds attracted him most: he could sit and watch them for hours.

Striding around the walls, Douglas, the proud pagan, was pleased to explain how Frederick worshipped both God and Allah and kept his crack army of 20,000 Saracens in this fort, where he built a mosque from the old cathedral and minarets from which the muezzins' call echoed across the plain. As the lights of distant Foggia began to twinkle through the lambent dusk, Eric imagined, with Douglas's help, the king's caravan coming towards them over the plain, sparkling with swords and scimitars, with silks and gold thread, and enchanted by elephants and by hunting jaguars riding on horseback, by falcons gripped to the wrists of handsome boys, and by cushioned carts plump with girls from the harem, girls with long dark hair, yashmaks and nothing beneath their diaphanous pantaloons.

If Frederick was a heroic figure, his bastard son Manfred was even more brilliant, not least because he was, according to Douglas, very beautiful. Two days later they left Foggia and headed for the eponymous Manfredonia on the east coast twenty miles away. The stopping train, which was crowded with people returning from market, took an hour and a quarter to get there.

Manfredonia greeted them in the mid-afternoon with overcast skies and no sign of the 5,000-foot summits of Gargano behind. A strange metallic light infused the remaining, inner world with a startling silvery clarity, giving a brilliance to the lime-washed houses. But fifteen minutes before the train arrived, Douglas had been afflicted with a sudden fit of wheezing and sneezing of such ferocity that he hurled a perfectly good ten-centesimo Cavour cigar from the window. When the train finally stopped, a porter was summoned to help bundle him into a carriage which conveyed them straight to their hotel at the end of a street leading down to the beach. Their rooms overlooked the small harbour and the Adriatic Sea.

The landlady, a stout, blunt-faced *baffona*, dismissed Douglas's theories that his virus had been borne by a sprite from a stagnant river, and said he had merely caught a dose of the sirocco, which had by now drawn a veil over the view from the window across the Gulf of Manfredonia to the Hohenstaufen Castel del Monte at Barletta forty miles south. Douglas took to his bed with a large dose of quinine and told Eric: 'Leave me to sleep and let us hope this is not the last we have seen of each other. If it is, take the train back to Naples and go and find Lo Bianco. He will look after you very well, and he knows I wish to be buried on Capri.'

For the first time in more than a month, Eric was suddenly quite alone. Of course he hoped Uncle Norman would not die, but to pass the time in his room, he looked up words that might be useful, such as 'burial' and 'coffin', and he pieced together a scenario in which he would use the words: 'My uncle is dead and wishes to be buried on the island of Capri. I am from London, and you must be sure I get home.' He also considered the idea of calling on Annetta to deliver the news and imagined being received by a comforting embrace. In the late afternoon he watched the returning fishing boats, spotlit in this brilliant electric light beneath the steely hood of low clouds, their unfurled lateen sails displaying golden moons and silver stars, leaping blue dolphins and spangly butterflies. They could not be resisted for long, and he soon slipped out for a closer look.

There was a small fortress on the north side of the port, and near by was the ancient gate that led to the *corso*, the avenue at the heart of Manfredonia's old town, but he did not venture in, nor did he speak to any of the few pale-faced people he passed, but he sat on a wall for a while, sifting through beach stones watching the boats and following the flights of the feasting terns and gulls. He wished Violet could have been there; Chalkie and Squid, too. They could have played football on the beach. Violet might have brought her spinning tops.

When the silver light began to fade, Eric returned to his hotel room where he closed the shutters before turning on the lights, to keep out the mosquitoes. He knocked on Douglas's door, but there was no reply, so he went downstairs for his supper, taking his diary to record the day while he ate. Hams hung from the ceiling of the small dining room, where half a dozen other diners sat in silence. The landlady's daughter, an unattractive, self-possessed young woman in her late teens or early twenties who had not yet begun to shave, brought bread and wine to his table, and from an old pot she served a stew of puréed beans and rice on to a terracotta plate, adding from a pan on the fire veal cutlets that had been soaked in eggs, dusted in Parmesan cheese, fired in butter, then simmered in a tomato sauce. It looked as if she had given him Douglas's portion too, but he managed it all and when he had finished she put a bowl of fruit on his table and asked if he was American. She showed him a ring costing hundreds of lire which her boyfriend had bought her. He was in America making his fortune, and when he had saved up enough, he would send for her. Eric was pleased he could understand so much.

After the meal, he went back upstairs and knocked lightly on Douglas's door. There was no reply. He hesitated, then thought he had better go in, in case Douglas was dead, and he opened the door slowly. Moonlight was spread over Douglas's counterpane, and his silvery hair flopped across Alfred. His breathing was heavy. As quietly as he could, Eric walked across the room to draw the curtains and stop the moon spreading its malevolent beams.

Back in his own room he took out a piece of paper to write to Violet. His sister had not been impressed by Uncle Norman the way Eric or her parents had been, though she had come to know him well enough on those occasions when he asked her to guide him around the streets of Camden looking for boys and girls at play so that he could record their games. When Eric had told her he was going on this trip to Italy with Uncle Norman, she had run to her room and slammed the door and didn't talk to him until the next day. He did not know if she was jealous, or if she just didn't want him to leave home; she would not say. It was more likely, he thought, that she was incapable of understanding friendships between men. Yet he still hoped he could make her see what an entertaining man Uncle Norman could be, and he never gave up telling her about the sport they had and the funny and rude things he said. With the gold-nib pen that Douglas had bought him in Sorrento to replace the one lost in Naples, he began to write in a firm but uneven hand.

Dear Sister,

We are at the seaside, a different one, called the Adriatic where Greece and the Balkans are, and I have just had supper on my own because Uncle Norman has a cold. I met the landlady's daughter. She is called Maria and she has a ring worth hundreds of lire which her fiancé in America gave her. People talk about America a lot and some people ask if we are Americans or if we have been there. Uncle Norman tells them he doesn't like to go to places that have already been discovered. The food isn't so awful in this hotel but I haven't had breakfast yet. I would like it if you were here, and Percy too. You would like to see the sea though the sun isn't shining but the boats have very gay sails. Everyone looks pale and the girls aren't very pretty, not like in Naples. You would stand out a mile. We are supposed to go to a cave in the mountains where the archangel St Michael lived though Uncle Norman says it's all mumbo jumbo. Last week we went to a shrine where old women kissed cracks in the wall, and Uncle Norman said they were doing something very rude, if you can guess. He told me another limerick on the train:

> *There was a young lady of Louth*
> *Who returned from a trip to the South.*
> *Her father said, 'Nelly,*
> *There is more in your belly*
> *Than ever went in by your mouth.'*

I hope he is better soon so I can tell you some more. I will try to post this letter myself tomorrow. I don't know how I will get on buying stamps in Italian (a stamp is 'francobollo'). If it doesn't reach you, write and let me know!

Your loving brother, Eric

PS: If you don't understand the limerick, I'll tell you in my next letter.

The following morning Eric breakfasted alone on black bread and an orange. He didn't want coffee and he asked for milk, which was sour and he could not drink it. At midday he finally found Douglas awake, sitting propped up in his iron bedstead in his Paisley dressing gown, his reading spectacles on his nose, a handkerchief alert in one hand and a pen in the other, resting on Alfred. He was better but not well, he said, and promptly sneezed. He had a list of errands for Eric to run which he handed him along with a dozen letters to post, including the regular letters addressed to Robert and Archie Douglas at Uppingham School in Leicestershire. From a pile of change beside his bed he counted out some coins.

'This is all we've got till we get to Taranto. These five-centesimo pieces are called soldi and people in the market count in soldi. So if they say *"dieci soldi"*, they mean fifty centesemi.'

'How much are soldi in English?' Eric asked.

'There are five to a bob,' said Douglas, 'so a soldi is about . . .'

'Tuppence farthing?' said Eric.

'Between tuppence farthing and tuppence ha'penny,' said Douglas. 'There are about ten centesimi to a penny. Only accept Italian coins, or coins from the Latin Monetary Union.'

Eric kept the money deep in his trouser pocket as he headed into the town, ignoring a group of boys who shouted at him, and keeping a resolute pace. He queued up at the shops and stalls, where people talked and gesticulated, their voices sometimes loud and excited, their gestures sometimes elaborate, sometimes minimal. He said *per favore* and *grazie* more times than anyone else, and his smiles were often greeted with blank stares. When he was not understood, he pointed to things, smiling, and, smiling further, used his fingers to show how much or how many items he required.

He was careful with the money, though on two occasions he was unsure if the transaction was correct. At one market stall he knew he had been short-changed and he resolutely stood his ground until the stallholder, a mean-faced, middle-aged man, waved his hands in the air and produced the right coins which he thrust at the boy as if he were a beggar to be rid of. On this occasion Eric did not smile, though he said *tante grazie* by mistake. Finally, happy that his mission had been a success, he returned to the hotel, where he took the stairs two at a time, knocked on the door and rushed in. He spread the spoils triumphantly on Douglas's bed and the invalid scooped up the remaining coins, sifting through them. He picked out half a dozen.

'These, my dear Eric, are worth rather less than a swallow's fart. Not only have you been short-changed, but you have been hardly changed at all.'

Eric was dumbfounded. 'I was very careful. Let me see again.' He took the coins Douglas had selected. 'Aren't these Italian?'

'They are from the Papal states and the Duchy of Lucca and both have been declared illegal – and banished to Apulia by the look of it.' Douglas was quick to reassure him. 'Never mind, it's all sport. We'll try to get rid of them. I like to end up my trips thinking I have outwitted them more times than they have outwitted me. There is nothing easier than to swindle a southerner, all you have to do is change your moral gear.'

Douglas pulled a face to try to cheer Eric up, and he opened a bag of fresh *fichi di Pasqua*, second-crop figs. 'This is the female sexual organ,' he pronounced, turning a fruit over in his fingers and, nose raised, peering at it through the demi-moons of his reading glasses, as he might have done a geological find, 'the yoni, the quim. And most of the time – as the shepherd will tell you of the succulent shoots of the *ficus indica*, and the fisherman of the plump gills of the ray fish – far more enjoyable and certainly less contrary or temperamental than the real thing. Black, white, green, brown, red or purple – no two are alike. And unlike all other fruits, which are called by the feminine form of the name of the plant that bears them – *melo* for apple, *mela* for apple – when *fico* becomes *fica* it does not become a fruit of the fig tree, it becomes the *pudendum muliebre*. Both are best, by the way, after they have been warmed a little in the sun, which we cannot appreciate on such an overcast day, and most men and women will never appreciate in all of their lives. Here, eat one like this. Put it whole between your lips and hold it gently with your teeth as you push your tongue forward. Then see if you can't suck all the flesh from it without disturbing the skin.'

Douglas closed his eyes and made a soft, slurping sound. Juice trickled from the corner of his mouth. Then it was Eric's turn, and for a while they had a great deal of amusement and face-pulling, practising this new game. He was glad that Uncle Norman was better, but something still pressed on his mind.

That evening after supper Eric went back into the town where he sat in the square for nearly two hours until he saw what he wanted to see: the man who had short-changed him and who had eventually given him a pocketful of dud coins. It was not difficult to follow him from the café to his home in a slum on the outskirts of the town.

Back in the hotel he lay awake until he heard the landlord climb upstairs to bed. It was one o'clock when he slipped from his room, shoeless, in order to decrease the noise. It took a full five minutes to negotiate his way out of the hotel, moving quietly to avoid bumping into furniture he could not see. The front door was heavily bolted, so he slipped out through a kitchen window into the courtyard, then through a high carriage doorway into the road. The night was warm and silent and a quarter moon gave enough light to move freely through the streets. Still barefoot, he made his way through the town to where the man lived.

His door was not locked, though the latch made a loud 'clack' as Eric lifted it. In a moment he was standing inside a single room with the remains of a fire in the centre, and a sink with no tap in the corner. Steady snores came from behind a door leading from the room. There was little furniture, no ornaments, and a picture of the Virgin above a table. Methodically, Eric searched around, looking for valuables or any money he thought rightfully Uncle Norman's, hunting through the drawers of a cupboard, on shelves around the sink, until he was convinced that there was absolutely nothing here of any worth. He was deeply frustrated. Perhaps he would try the bedroom. He went over to the sink and picked up a large kitchen knife, just in case he should be attacked. Silently, he crossed the floor and eased the door open.

It took him a minute to adjust to the sight he saw: the moonlight, that unwelcome visitor in Douglas's room, wandered over many shapes, and only gradually the scene came into focus. The man snoring lay on the bed with a woman, loosely draped with a single sheet. There were three others in the bed, all huddled up, children ranging in years, but all younger than Eric. On a ledge beside them an old couple slept head to toe. Above the main bed two slings hung from the ceiling, with a small child in each. There was no money here. No money and no way of making good. Eric closed the door and walked over to the picture of the Virgin Mary. He gripped the kitchen knife tightly and, as quietly as he could, he sliced the picture into fragments, leaving them scattered about the floor.

On the third day the rain was beating down, but Douglas could no longer wait for either the weather or his health to improve. He had secured a carriage and a big moustachioed driver to take them to Mont Sant' Angelo and they set off on the three-hour journey straight after breakfast. There was no view and the aspect became gloomier and colder as the road wound up to the 2,500-foot summit. On the way they passed bedraggled pilgrims, most walking barefoot, though the festival of St Michael had been held three days before. When they reached the chapel, Douglas temporarily dismissed the carriage driver with a few lire, and they entered through a huge bronze door, made in Constantinople in the eleventh century. Eric had begun to connect centuries to his age, starting with the birth of himself and Jesus Christ. He had arrived in the Roman world, some time after the Etruscans, Phoenecians and Greeks, all of whom were of his parents' generation. In the fifth century the Roman Empire fell to the Barbarians: at five he had started school. At eleven he was free of formal education and between the eleventh and thirteenth centuries most things seemed to have happened in this part of the world, and between the ages of eleven and thirteen most things seemed to have happened to him.

Inside, at the end of a long passage, was the grimy, rock-dripping grotto where there was a shrine to St Michael. Eric did not like it; it was dank and echoing, and an old organ wheezed to the collection of pilgrims whose collective stench could have been harnessed to power electric light.

'Now you know why incense was invented,' Douglas whispered.

Afterwards, walking down the village street, he said: 'Poor brutes are just bored.' He had an arm around the boy's shoulder, pulling him close to try to keep warm. It had begun to rain again and neither had coats: they had not been prepared for this weather. 'For four months a year they are cooped up in dens an Englishman wouldn't keep a dog in. The rest of the year they struggle to wrest a few blades of corn from the ungrateful limestone. They have no games or sports, no peg-tops or klondykes or tomtits or dumb bargees, no buttons for Bang-Out or balls for French cricket. There are no cattle shows or fox-hunting or rat-catching. They don't even have the mild excitement of debates between church and chapel or the scandal of the vicar's daughter's love affairs. These visits to the archangel are their sole amusements.'

'Sons of bitches!' The expletive blew on to the pavement followed by a gale of laughter.

Douglas stopped and raised his tufty eyebrows. 'Come on, Eric,' he said, 'I think we may have found somewhere for lunch.'

They followed the sound of English and Italian voices down a long flight of stairs into a cavern Eric thought quite as dark and dank as the archangel's. But this was a candle-lit *osteria*, unsullied by daylight, infused with cigar smoke and heady with the smell of wine spilled from three enormous barrels. Cheerful, gravel-voiced men in suits and shiny shoes were raising voices over games of cards, over heated discussions, over jugs of wine. The new arrivals were welcomed to join them.

'Drink this, Mister,' said one with a large moustache, thrusting a glass of darkest red wine into Douglas's hand; another was put down in front of Eric. Chairs were found for them. Plates of ham and salami, olives and black bread soon arrived. Questions poured out, stories were exchanged. All these men came from around here but now lived in America, in Pittsburgh mostly.

Each year they returned for the festival, of course, but some were no longer sure why they had come. Though Douglas clearly spoke Italian, they all insisted on speaking English.

'This saint business is dead,' said the one with a large moustache who had pulled a chair up beside them. 'I don't know why I'm here.'

'For the *vino di montagna*?' Douglas suggested appreciatively.

'Hah, damn right. Pretty fine stuff. Maybe the only thing you can't buy in America.'

Another spat his mouthful of wine across the floor. 'You can keep the wine for everything else you can buy in America: shoes, clothes, good linen, food. There is money there. Who wants to live where there is no money?'

'What is there to keep people here?' another one said. He had his feet up on a chair, one hand on the chain of a fob watch across his belly. 'The villages in the south, around here, they have half the populations they had twenty years ago. Everybody goes to America. Why not? Eh? Just these angel-worshipping ass-holes stay behind.'

Eric looked at Douglas, expecting him to protest, but his blue eyes twinkled as he took another draught of wine. One of the Italian Americans ruffled Eric's hair, grasping a hank of it for a moment and shaking his head in a rough gesture of friendship. 'What's a nice boy like you doing with this man here, eh?' He winked at Douglas, who said: 'He is being *mediterraneanised*, an indispensable part of the educational curriculum for every young northern European.'

'You won't learn how to make a buck here,' the first man said, 'and that's what's important. I mean, what are the prospects? We could bring in some merchandise, set up shops selling saints' images. The archangel could look nice with his toy sword and helmet, a *bel ragazzo*, a pretty boy you might want to have some romp with. You could sell that. Put a price on it. Or holy water, which is nothin', or angel wings or incense or somethin' that lights up. People love things that light up. Some crap like that. But who's gonna buy it?' He banged the table again. '*Corpo di Bacco*, there's no fuckin' money here.'

Douglas smiled. 'How right you are. There is no fucking money here. And that is why I like it.'

The man looked at Douglas's twinkling eyes for a moment, wondering if they were patronising him. Then he laughed and clapped Douglas on the back. 'More wine for this Mister,' he shouted, and he put his face close. 'Of course you like it,' he said, 'because in the land without lire the man with a soldo is king.'

'They don't know how to work here,' another was saying. 'Never stop working, that's the secret of success.'

'I cannot drink to that,' Douglas said. 'It is an awful doctrine.'

The philosophies of Douglas and the new Americans could not have been further apart, yet they all got on well, all pioneers in their own way, none beholden to tradition or stuffy mores. Eric liked the company, too, and they taught him how to play poker, using gnocchi pasta as chips. As they talked and played, the wine kept pouring, and Eric forgot to worry about what he was eating, dipping into the bowls and dishes that were offered to him as they arrived on the table. The men from Pittsburgh were paying and they were insistent, jabbing at their own mouths with bunched fingertips, and he could not insult them too often by refusals: he picked at the bones of finches and fieldfares, and dipped bread into terracotta bowls full of nameless offal.

Two hours after they had entered the cellar they staggered up the stairs into the daylight, which, in spite of the continued low level of cloud, seemed shockingly bright. Unsteady but grinningly happy, Eric felt the air rush into his lungs like iced water.

The driver had deduced where they were and was waiting for them, leaning heavily against the wall, grinning and pulling knowingly on one end of his drooping moustache.

'And how much have you drunk?' Douglas asked.

'Just a glass of wine,' he said, a little too loudly. 'Because of the bad weather.'

'Just one glass?' Douglas asked.

'Maybe two. But the horse is perfectly sober.'

On the way down the mountain, Douglas sang songs from Garibaldi's popular revolution, accompanied enthusiastically by the driver, and declaimed limericks which had no Italian translation.

> 'There was an old man from Peru
> Who was looking for something to do,
> So he picked up a carrot
> And buggered his parrot
> And sent the results to the zoo.'

Eric laughed, but he did not feel as happy now. The lurching coach did nothing to steady his stomach, which was beginning to regret, in particular, one small dish of offal he had dunked some bread in. The aroma of its dark, rancid juices clung to the back of his nose, making his stomach heave in volcanic spasms which blew out his cheeks. As they reached the plain, the sun burst forth like a sign. Eric jumped up wildly and shouted for the carriage to stop, leaping from it just in time for his vomit to hit a myrtle bush. Douglas cheered. Eric remained doubled up, retching, sweating, one hand on his forehead, the other clutching a handkerchief.

'Take your time,' Douglas called from the carriage. 'It was probably the spleen. I try to avoid it.' He then asked the driver if he would take them to the ruins of the Greek city of Sopanthum. 'I have been ill for two days and have a lot of sightseeing to catch up on.'

'Anywhere,' the driver called back. 'To London, if you like.'

Eric groaned and got back into the carriage. He was ill now and it was his turn to take to his bed. He put his head in his Uncle Norman's lap and felt a caress on the nape of his neck. He closed his eyes and gave himself up to the rhythm of the carriage, his nose pressed close to the rain-dampened tweed that was suffused with cigar smoke and vapours of wine. It was a familiar, comforting lap.

'Can we go back to the hotel?' Eric asked weakly.

'What, now?' Douglas said. 'Just as the sun has come out? Life must be lived, Eric, not just endured.'

CHAPTER 6

Magna Graecia, July 1911

Eric and Annetta swam naked among the islands in a wide, wet sea. Caressed by the currents and tickled by trails of bubbles, they moved beneath the water as round-eyed as fish, without effort or need to draw breath. Eric flapped his arms like a bird on the wing, looking down on Annetta's black hair waving behind her, getting to know her breasts, her kicking legs, her twisting hips, the soft black tufts under her arms and between her legs. A shoal of anchovies sparkled by, followed by mullet and wrasse. He was Odysseus, the brave captain, come to rescue her from the deep, and she would surrender to her saviour. He stretched out his hands to pull her to the shore where they might lie on the rocks so her *fica* could be warmed by the sun. But as he was about to take hold of her slim wrists, an old woman, a wrinkled crone, came swimming up between them in a billow of black skirts. Tears like oyster pearls hung from her eyes as she reached out and pressed her thin, lifeless lips against Annetta's sweet vulva, whispering, '*Santissima, santissima.*' The girl's divine face broke the surface and her sparkling dark lashes closed under the glare of the sun. Her head tipped back to show her vulnerable, cod-white neck, while her arms drifted wide. The smile of an ecstatic martyr washed over her face and Eric felt his first moment of religious conviction. Then, overwhelmed with humility, the crone turned away, muttering, '*Tutti santi, tutti santi.*' Her mane of white hair drifted off and her bovine face grew whiskers. Wriggling out of the black skirts a monk seal, licking its lips, swam leisurely into the blue.

The wet of the yoni, the wet of the sea: all pleasure was liquid and flowing. But the sea rapidly faded leaving Eric in darkness, in a chasm of confusion, for the damp pleasures of the sea had been replaced by the certain knowledge that, lying in the dark on a mattress, fully dressed and with no immediate knowledge of his own whereabouts, he had urinated in his khaki shorts. He lay still for a moment, disturbed by the unexpectedly thrilling spasms that the passing of water seemed to have caused. Little by little, he recalled the unseen hut around him and smelled the stale tobacco of his travelling companion. He had not urinated at all. As quietly as he could he searched in vain for a handkerchief to push down the front of his trousers to try to stem the flood of embarrassment.

'Horace recounted a wet dream in Apulia.'

Douglas's voice was quiet, and only a foot or two away, and it took Eric a moment to realise he had begun quoting in Latin. They were lying side by side on mattresses in a building beyond a marsh by the station at Spinazzola, having missed their connection, the last train to Taranto, and there had been nowhere else for them to stay.

'If you put a cotton reel down your back it can stop it.' said Eric, trying to be helpful. There was no one else for half a mile, but they kept their voices low.

'Have your tried it?'

'No, but my dad said it worked.'

'The only way to stop it is to do it yourself, and as often as you want. You do know how to, don't you?'

''Course I do.' Not only did he know how to do it, but it was as often a topic of conversation with Chalkie and Squid as was talk about girls.

'"Sexual malpractice" is not only common practice, it's also very handy to get yourself thrown out of places you don't like. When I was at Uppingham, I told my mother I would deliberately get caught doing it, so I would be thrown out and she would have to send me to the gymnasium in Karlsruhe.'

Never in all the world could Eric imagine such a conversation with his own mother. 'What did she say?'

'Oh, she always did what I asked in the end.'

'What was so horrible about Uppingham?' He moved the 'h' from 'orrible' to 'Huppingham'.

'The food was too vile to eat, the masters were humbug, and they only wanted to make you part of the herd. When my older brother left, I made sure my mother had no choice but to take me away, too.'

'Why do Archie and Robert go there?'

'It's changed.'

Eric imagined Uppingham like a huge workhouse on the hill, where herded boys in dull-coloured uniforms performed rituals, and masters in mortarboards spoke in Latin and Greek. The idea of such a place gave him a fright, and the idea of going there until he was sixteen or even eighteen beggared belief. What was there to learn all that time? It was much better to travel the world like this to find out all about it.

'Who was your best friend at Uppingham?' Eric asked.

'We all called him The Bug,' Douglas said.

'What was he like?' Eric imagined a scrofulous being who lived in Douglas's bed or his socks, at which point an insect struck. 'Ow, I think that was a real bug!'

'Watch out, I've already been well bitten. The Bug was always dirty and always in trouble, but he was a lot of fun, and he played the violin like the devil and had a passion for music. We got up to all sorts of things together.'

'Did you two, you know, masturbate together?'

'Oh, all the time. He could come more quickly than I could,

and he usually ejaculated further than me.

'I've done it in twelve seconds,' said Eric, scratching himself as another bug bit.

'Bravo,' said Douglas. 'Sometimes, though, it's fun to see how long you can take. Women like you to take a long time.'

'How long?'

'Oh, days, some of them. Days and days.'

Eric laughed, and he thought of Annetta. 'Perhaps I should practise.'

'There are all sorts of tricks to it,' said Douglas. 'So many things they like you to do.'

'What sort of things?' Eric asked.

Douglas did not have to be asked twice. The tutor, the sage, the mentor, liked nothing more than giving young people advice. For the rest of the night, without prefect, monitor or teacher to spy on them, the two talked and experimented, trying to find what gave pleasure, what games were fun. Eric learnt new words, *titillare*, to tickle, and uranism, meaning a spiritual love between men. With no one to hear them, they laughed like hyenas and giggled like girls. Palm Over, Corkscrews, Swolo, Wallie, Gulley Hole, Rabbit-in-the-Hutch, One-Two-Three-and-a-Lairy: Uncle Norman knew all the children's street games.

Early next morning the two tired, sated, bitten and newly bonded travellers arrived at the station in the industrial suburbs on the north side of Taranto. A motor cab took them over the bridge to the old town where Douglas knew somewhere they might stay. The house belonged to a plump, grey-haired woman in black who expressed her pleasure in seeing Don Douglas by cupping his face in her hands and kissing him damply on both cheeks. 'What a surprise, what a pleasure, what a delight to see the signor again. I knew something was going to happen when I woke up this morning and there were two cats on my window-ledge and a swallow in the kitchen.' She was also delighted to meet his latest pupil, of course, what a beautiful boy, and he did not escape a similar welcome.

'*Molto lieto*,' said Eric with a brief smile. The secret pleasure he had shared with Uncle Norman had given him a confidence and an introspection that set him a little apart from everyone he now saw. He no longer felt like a small boy, smiling to try to please doting women his mother's age. This one continued to prattle, saying she had not expected them until the following week.

'I couldn't stand another day of those Apulian breakfasts,' Douglas said. 'Nutrition is the secret of a nation's character, and those thimbles of black coffee in the morning are so mean, they are enough to make anyone envious and vengeful. They must take responsibility for all the revenge murders in this country. Your breakfasts will revive our natural blitheness.'

Oh, she knew how Signor Douglas liked his fresh eggs in the morning: exactly three and a half minutes in boiling water, how could she forget? Of course the rooms were available: her daughter and son-in-law were away at the moment. She would make up the beds straight away.

After she had gone, Douglas said to Eric, 'You'll get used to her. At five lire a night she needs to be cultivated: we're down to our last few. We could stay with some dons or signors of my acquaintance, but if you have a letter of introduction they never leave you alone from morning till night. Much better to try to pay your own way. Now, let's go and see if there is any money waiting for us in the post office.'

It was nearly midday and the sun was furiously hot, and for the first time Eric began to realise just how intense its heat could be. Uncle Norman tucked a handkerchief under the back of his hat to protect his neck and he urged Eric to do the same.

Nobody else in the town walked around looking like this, and Eric continued to find something admirable in the man's insistence on being different, however preposterous: in his refusal to follow the herd.

The whitewashed walls radiated heat, and shoeless children and timid, scraggy cats and dogs all avoided walking over the baking, dusty ground. Several dons, dressed in smart suits and hats, sat in barbers' shops and in the shade of coffee houses, with gold rings on their fingers and silver tips to their canes. Nobody seemed to be going anywhere: America was much too far away.

The old town was on an island dividing the inner and outer harbours. In the inner Mare Piccolo oysters and mussels grew by the ton on ropes looped over poles, and discarded shells of murex, which had produced purple dye since ancient times, were piled on its banks. There was also an arsenal and dockyard for the Italian navy, and warships slipped in and out through the iron Ponte Girevole swing bridge on the south end of the island, which led to the mainland new town.

At the post office Douglas despatched twenty letters and as many postcards and, producing a calling card, enquired after their mail. There were a dozen letters for him, which he quickly glanced at before pushing them into his jacket pocket. There was one for Eric, in his mother's familiar round handwriting, with a St Pancras watermark over the stamp of the late king. They went to find a café, taking the Via Garibaldi beside the fishermen's quarters along the Mare Piccolo. Oyster sellers called to them – 'Only ten soldi a dozen' – and fishermen wanted to give them tours of the oyster beds – 'Very cheap for an hour, signor. Bring bread and wine and have a picnic feast. Best oysters you ever tasted, signor.' They spoke with thick accents, and a dialect muddled with ancient Greek.

Douglas walked faster than anybody in sight and he did not stop to talk beyond remarking that this was not the right season for oysters. They crossed the swing bridge to the Corso Due Mari, and sat in the shade of a café awning facing the flaking circular bastions of Taranto's Angevin castle. Douglas opened his letters at great speed, scanning their contents and feeling inside the envelopes for bank drafts or further missives. Using his chatelaine knife, Eric approached his single envelope carefully, savouring the moment as he took out a letter from his mother, written closely on two sides, and an envelope with his name on, in Violet's loopy hand. Attached to his mother's letter was a bank draft for ten shillings.

'Well,' said Douglas, looking at the correspondence in front of him, 'seeing as how the letter I expected to contain remuneration contains only the news that ninety per cent of the copies of my latest book are due to be pulped because of poor sales, and the letter from Conrad is all praise and no pennies, we are down to our last few lire. So it will be a light lunch.'

'I've got ten bob,' Eric volunteered, holding up the note.

Douglas brightened. 'Good for you. But it can't be your birthday again.'

Eric scowled in the sunlight and read his mother's letter to discover why he had been sent the money. 'It's from my Aunt Beat in Essex,' he said. 'She expected to see me before we left to give me my birthday money. She says there's extra so I can bring her back a cameo from Naples that she's always wanted.'

'Shall we consider it a loan?' said Douglas.

'All right.' Eric handed it across, glad to be able to contribute, especially after losing the money in Manfredonia.

'This town has nearly a hundred kinds of fish and shellfish in its waters,' said Douglas. 'Until the Romans reached Colchester they thought Taranto oysters were the best in the world.'

'I'd like a vanilla ice-cream,' said Eric, suspecting something terrible might fetch up on his plate. 'Or a lemon *granita*. I'm very thirsty.'

Douglas ordered both the ice-cream and the *granita*, as well as a plate of *cozze*, *coccioli* and other shellfish, and mineral water to drink. They returned to their mail. Apart from news of his aunt and cousins in Essex, Eric's mother had written to say that it had been unbearably hot and thousands had died of the heat. There was great excitement because the Festival of Empire was finally going to take place at Crystal Palace, just after the coronation, and it was a shame Eric was going to miss it. Some fifteen thousand Londoners were going to enact thirty-two scenes from the history of London, and the contribution from themselves and their neighbours in the borough of St Pancras was to be a scene set in the time of King Arthur. There had been a fund for King George V's coronation: everyone in the country named George had been invited to contribute between a penny and five pounds. A good job it wasn't King Percy or King Eric, his mother said. Had he read about the coronation in the papers in Italy? They had all gone up to Westminster: it was a wonderful day. She hoped Eric was doing his lessons properly and being a credit to the family. She hoped he wasn't too close to the Balkans because they sounded dangerous.

Eric folded the letter and put it back in the envelope, then slit open the smaller one.

'Il mio piccolo brothero,' Violet began her pencil note, which was littered with random Italian words, each one underlined. She had been to Hampstead Roller-Skating Palace the previous settimana, and she had seen Chalkie and Calamari. They asked after Eric and told her they'd pulled an uomo out of the canal. 'Have you seen any gondolas?' she wanted to know. She had found the Italian words in a dictionary at a friend's house. 'Have you made any Italian amici?' she asked. 'Or do you just go around all the time with nosy Uncle Norman?' Eric pulled up the edge of the page in case Uncle Norman could read upside down. 'Do they have spinning tops in Italy? Or marbles? What are they called in Italian? <u>Toppi</u> and <u>marbelli</u>? Do they play Queenie? Write me a joke in Italian and I'll see if I can translate it using the dictionary. You better come back soon, or I'm moving into your room, which is much too big for just Percy who would be fine in my cupboard. <u>Addio</u>, brothero, ducks.'

'How is everyone at home?' Douglas asked as Eric folded the letters and replaced them in the envelope.

'All right,' Eric said. 'Mum says it's hot in London.'

'Has Violet found any new games for me?'

'No, she wants to know if there are any spinning-top games here.'

'A chapter on Italian games? Not a bad idea. I will talk to her about it when we get back.'

Eric carried the letters about in his pocket over the next few days while they set about exploring the town, seeking out its historical, geological, botanical, zoological and anthropological secrets, roaming from its imposing museum and ecclesiastical buildings to the pageant of its indolent street life. He found excuses not to write home: he thought he had nothing much to say to his mother and he no longer felt like sending Violet Uncle Norman's rude jokes. Smoky, damp Camden Town was such a long way away.

After they had been in their lodgings five days the landlady's daughter and family returned to redeem their rooms, so Eric and Douglas moved to a small *locanda* in the old town, the Risorgimento in Piazza Fontana, where Douglas complained at the lack of vegetables served with his supper. 'If the *signor* can afford meat, why does he want vegetables?' was the patron's response. Money was still a problem and Douglas had wired several friends.

A highlight for Eric was a visit to a barber's in the Corso, where a gleaming cut-throat razor, honed on a long leather strop, scraped away the down that had been darkening his upper lip and his chin. This was his first shave. He also had his head closely cropped, which was not the intention, though he sat and watched without complaint and in some fascination as his dark curls, bleached a little at the ends, fell to the floor. When Douglas returned to meet him he was upset at the sight of the scalping. For a full thirty minutes Eric sat and listened to Douglas berating the barber who, with no signs of remorse, reflected on the different way people interpreted the word 'short'.

Some days they went to the beach and looked across the Ionian Sea to the instep of Italy's boot, a flat, swampy shoreline to the west and south where the hills of Calabria hung in a haze. Douglas would sift through the pebbles on the shore, deciphering the kind of marble or porphyry that had been imported for use in Taranto's villas and temples. The town had been the capital of Magna Graecia, founded by Parthinians, illegitimate sons of Sparta who had been born when the men were away fighting the Athenians. Plato, Socrates and anyone else who was anyone in the Greek world had been here. It was a centre of Pythagorean philosophy and its famous sons included Arsitoxenes, author of the earliest known treatise on music, around 400 BC – 'Four years BE, Before Eric,' said Douglas, who had delighted in Eric's egocentric way of determining the epochs of the world. It was a new city on a new land and historians had called it the classical New York. But today, unlike the situation in Apulia, no Tarentines harboured ideas of seeking their fortunes elsewhere. All they thought about was walking up and down the Corso for their evening *passeggiata*, looking their best. Joining in the ambulation, Eric – scalped as he was – had no trouble catching girls' eyes, for they were bored as butterflies, and sometimes they looked at him so frankly he looked away, convinced his antics with Douglas must be starting to show in his face.

Douglas, an expert on courtship ritual and avid reader of the lovers' missives in the local papers' personal columns, held out no hope. 'What you need to do when you find a girl,' he said, 'is to visit the pharmacist and explain your love sickness, and you will be prescribed some poison in such an amount that is guaranteed not to kill you, but leave you writhing and foaming at the feet of your lover, who will be so impressed by your sacrifices she will weep for your life. It's supposed to be flattering. Every day the papers here have stories of young men attempting suicide because of some girl and not once have I ever heard of a woman who was properly flattered by a decent, decomposing corpse.'

During the day, people stayed indoors. It was too hot for work, too hot for school, but in the late afternoon gangs of young boys dived into the harbour and roamed the beach, shouting and laughing, splashing and pushing each other into the sea. Eric was jealous of their easy company and he recalled what Violet had said about playing with people his own age. One afternoon a crowd of boys on the beach drifted over towards the unlikely couple sitting on the beach fully dressed, in straw hats and handkerchiefs, sifting through the stones. One of them called out, and asked if they were German.

'*Scozzesi*,' said Douglas, and he pumped his elbows into his sides and blew raspberries through his lips, mimicking the bagpipes playing 'Scotland the Brave'. It meant nothing to the boys except confirmation of the eccentricity of foreigners, but Douglas got them all at it and in a while they were dancing and blowing raspberries in a line that wandered over the beach. Eric broke away, wanting to show some independence of spirit, and he went down to the water's edge and began skimming stones. Some other boys followed, and they competed to see how many skips they could make, calling out loud in unison at each attempt: '*Uno, due, tre, quattro . . .*'

Large mauve urchin shells edged the tideless waters, along with razor shells, flotsam from the port and bleached canes from the marshes on the opposite shore. Green crabs as big as pennies scuttled among it, and a small boy suddenly picked one up, tore it open and ate its flesh. The others laughed and did the same thing, pulling off legs and chewing them and throwing the empty carcasses around. They offered one to Eric to eat, but he declined, so they put it down the back of his shirt, and then they tried to put them in his pockets and down his trousers. They lifted up his hat and put them in his hair, and they threw his hat into the sea, after which they filled it with water and used it as a water bomb to lob at each other. Some of the boys were older than Eric, and though he remained good-natured, he did not smile much. It was like playing with Percy's friends.

Finally Uncle Norman distracted the boys by making a great game of eating the crabs himself. They all liked him, of course, and he showed them how to suck out the meat from the claws, and how to tell a cock crab from a hen. But it wasn't as much fun as trying to put them down someone's trousers, and after a while they wandered off, back to their own families, their domestic routines, leaving the strangers to return alone to the town.

Across the sea, the afternoon sun was drifting down on the distant hills of Calabria but there was still a lot of heat in the day. Douglas sat on the beach beside Eric who was sifting through small stones.

'The money should be here tomorrow,' he said, 'then we'll be on our way.' He arched his hand over his brow and gazed at their destination out across the bay.

'Is it very different in Calabria?' Eric asked.

'Yes,' said Douglas. 'It is quite different. The train will take us around the coast, then we will head into the mountains, where there are wolves and marmosets and boars and bears, and a lynx I have read about, called a luzzard, which has a spotted posterior.'

'Can we shoot them?'

'If someone will give us a gun.'

'What else is there?'

'Liquorice grows wild, and in the marshes is a plant called *agnus castus*, which the ancients employed for its anti-venereal properties. I take it you know all about venereal disease.'

''Course I do.'

'The best cure against infection is always to go with a virgin,' said Douglas. 'And if you don't want any trouble it has to be carefully planned through the family. I learned that when I was in the embassy in St Petersburg. An old Russian general taught me how to get in with a girl's family. He was governor of one of those central Asian regions of Russia and he always had more girls than he could usefully deal with at one time. It wouldn't surprise me if he threatened to send their families to Siberia, too, if they complained. Hah! Other soldiers there often picked up girls, but when they did they usually picked up something else as well. I asked him to find someone for me, to help me learn Russian, as well as for pleasure, and so he did. Anyuta Ponomoreva was about your age and she lived with her mother and younger brother, though to my regret I never met the boy. She had a wonderful spontaneity and capacity for abandonment which the Russians possess.'

Eric stared out across the dead calm, opaque sea. The warmth of the sun had left him. A chill fist gripped his stomach. 'Did you . . . did you pay for Annetta in Naples?' he asked.

'Of course,' said Douglas. He sounded surprised to be asked such an obvious question but, like a good teacher, he was happy to explain the secrets behind a particular success. 'Didn't you realise? Amoroso is a wonder at looking after visitors to his city, from admirals to ambassadors, as well as all the idle local counts and dons.'

'Blimey,' Eric said, trying to sound impressed as he took in the information.

After supper, for which the main course was a *fritto misto* of fried liver, brains and artichoke, Douglas went off for a stroll with his pockets fully supplied with snuff and chocolate. Eric retreated to his room to write his diary, but he could not settle. Soon he found himself wandering out into the night, his feet taking him back towards the moonlit beach where they had met the boys. For more than an hour he sat and rhythmically threw stones into the water. They plopped like tears in a well, disturbing the moonbeams and spreading their ripples out towards Calabria, towards the next stage of their journey. Uncle Norman was right about women: before they vampired you, you had to vampire them.

CHAPTER 7

Calabria, August 1911

Eric Wolton was ravished by Norman Douglas the length and breadth of Calabria. In every way this remote, mountainous, extreme southern tip of Italy was a climax of their adventure. During these exhilarating, hazardous days, Eric felt further and further from the urban bustle and smoking trains he had left behind in Camden Town. Most of the small villages they visited, without electricity or mains water, had never encountered a foreigner before. Roads were poor, and even the main highways were in a state of disrepair: the price of labour had increased dramatically since the emigrations to America had begun. Reducing their load to one small bag each, they often walked from village to village, and sometimes, to avoid the intense heat of the day, they travelled through the night, on mules or bumping around in the backs of wagons. They rested where they could during the swooning quiet of midday to late afternoon, when neither humans nor creatures stirred and even the whirring cicadas grew weary.

To Eric, the most intoxicating features of the landscape were simply the air and the light. It was as clear and clean and brilliant as the fancy-free waters in which he had swum with Annetta, who had not yet left his dreams. The aromas in this vivid landscape rose from the damp floors of the chestnut woods and the chill caverns of the oak forests, but most of all they exuded from the embalming scrubland of myrtle, juniper, rock roses, rosemary, lavender, fennel and thyme. This was at its sweetest in the evenings when the sun exploded on to a fiery canvas of Biblical dimensions, shaping mountains and slipping away, leaving the westering sky to pass through all the colours of the rainbow.

It was cooler on the high ground. The rugged country rose to more than 4,000 feet, and even in July there was snow left on peaks. Paths negotiated steep ravines, dry now, but torrential whenever rain fell. Yet there were still trickles of icy water, and every village had grown up around a cool, mossy fountain. The riverbeds, hot and lifeless and hard underfoot, were sometimes the only highways. There was shelter when the paths led through beech stands and woods of holm oak and ilex, sweet chestnut and manna ash, and groves of mulberries and olives. Butterflies and bees hummed about their labours, flies were a nuisance, mosquitoes a pest. Most of all, Eric loved the birds, which, though not plentiful, were astonishing for their size and colours. He borrowed Douglas's Zeiss binoculars and was constantly alert for the liquid mewing of the golden oriole, yellow as the sun, the 'pu-put' of the hoopoe which would swoop from the pines like a count in a cockaded hat, the scream of an eagle, the shocking azure flash of the roller bird, or the twitter of bee-eaters, king-sized kingfishers which perched on high twigs. He longed for a gun to take trophies home.

There were trophies in some of the places where they stopped: stuffed eagles, foxes, marmots, polecats, weasels and red squirrels, wolfskin rugs, deer antlers and wild goat horns. Taxidermy turned out to be another of Douglas's skills. As a boy he had ridden badgers, he said, and a squirrel slept under his mother's pillow. *Locande* were fewer and farther between and when they did find a place to stay or to eat, there was sometimes little more than hard bread, onions and curd or goat's cheese. Douglas had abandoned his bedsheets because of their weight, and on many nights it was far too warm for any covering anyway, but the rooms had more than mere entomological horrors to guard against. One morning Eric awoke with a rat on his chest, but the hotel keeper took no blame. It was the signor's fault, he said, for keeping his bedroom door closed during the night and preventing the circulation of the cat.

Calabrians were, on the whole, taciturn, solid mountain people. The men were unshaven and moustachioed and protected from the sun by conical hats, and many did not reach Eric's height: Douglas stood out wherever they went. The women, barefoot and barelegged, tucked up their skirts as they walked, showing their muscular calves, carrying pitchers of water, baskets of washing and babies about on their heads. The most vividly dressed were the Albanians who occupied whole villages, worshipped at Greek Orthodox churches and wore brightly coloured clothes. They had been here since the sixteenth-century diaspora from the lands of the Turks, and their poor houses and lack of domestic pride contributed to the notion that they were still only temporary residents, waiting for a country called Albania to be born again.

For several days they stayed at a remote Albanian mountain college, where Douglas told the priests how they should inspire the three hundred pale, thin boys. In his tireless quest for knowledge, he found out all he could about the Albanians' culture, which he clearly admired, especially their readiness to set fire to their own homes and move on if the government started demanding taxes or giving them any other trouble. It was boat-burning on an epic scale. And as he struggled to master a few words of the Albanian language and its thirty disputed alphabets, he was further gratified to discover that there was a word for house, but no word for 'home'.

The Albanians' costumes were shown off to their best effect at a Catholic festival to the Virgin near Monte Pollino on the first weekend in July when thousands of pilgrims arrived by foot and mule at a chapel 1,500 feet above a ravine. Stalls were set up selling food, wine and souvenirs, as well as wax *ex-votos* to take to be blessed. Douglas pointed out the lumpen shapes representing spleens enlarged by malaria, and Eric wondered if the food he had eaten with the Americans in Sant' Angelo had looked so foul.

On the eve of the feast, there was a bonfire and fireworks, and dancing and music from bagpipes and flutes and double flageolets called *fiscasols*. More than half a dozen Albanian towns were represented, each with distinctive pleated and brocaded silk gowns the colours of sapphire, amethyst and wine trimmed with lace and gold. Hair was entowered in architectural arrangements, which twisted down in ringlets at the temples. Eric's eye was caught by a girl with a radiant face, who wore a simpler scarlet-dyed dress that whirled round and round, flashing white calves and glistening cleavage. This was the night, Douglas said, when young couples would run off to the woods together, and Eric longed to abscond with the girl in scarlet, but he did not know how to begin. Instead, he ended the night in a bed sandwiched between two priests in the same room as Douglas who shared a bed with two more. The offer of accommodation by the church was a kindness that could not be ignored, though they were kept awake long into the night by the bagpipes and fireworks exploding overhead.

The next day there was a grand procession of the saint to the chapel, and the younger of the priests who had slept beside Eric invited him on a stroll through the woods. His teeth were misshapen, his mouth was loose and his breath smelt of sleep, but it was the only invitation Eric had had. '*Amici*,' the priest said, jabbing himself in the chest. Eric nodded and said: 'Friends.' They walked for a while on the dry, dead vegetation that crunched underfoot, pointing at fungus and ferns and trying to make conversation. Eric explained how clever and famous his travelling companion was but he could not explain that he was not a millionaire.

The festival ended in the early afternoon, when Eric said goodbye to the priest and sought out Uncle Norman and their muleteer. The pilgrims were gathering their belongings and loading up their braying mules and high-wheeled carts ready for the exodus down the mountain.

'A two-priest night in Calabria,' Douglas mused as they set off. 'That must be something to write home about.'

It had been a week since Eric had sent a letter to his parents and he had not written to Violet since Manfredonia. He vowed now he would make up for it: in the next town he would buy a card of an Albanian woman in her traditional dress and write to say how exciting the evening had been. He would not relate anything rude that Uncle Norman had told him. He would not mention Uncle Norman at all.

At the bottom of the hill the pilgrim party was held up by the authorities: everyone was to be fumigated because of the cholera. The muleteer and many of the village people complained, but the foreigners thought it a sensible precaution. Cholera, typhoid and malaria were never far away.

As they continued their journey, heading south through the deep green woody mountain range of the Sila, on the ball of the Italian foot, they passed through villages where open drains discharged water and sewage into the streets and houses were tarnished by fires that burned not in hearths or stoves but on the floor in the centre of living rooms. Malaria was known to thrive on the marshy lowlands of the coast, but during the summer months seasonal workers had to spend time labouring among the malarial fields and swamps of both the Ionian and Tyrrenhean seas. Douglas had many theories on the disease, which he believed may have brought an early end to the local

Greek civilisations and reduced the number of people with fair complexions, whom it favoured most.

They did not reach the coast until Reggio, the largest town in Calabria, on the top of the toe of the Italian foot, which kicked the ball of Sicily into the middle of the Mediterranean Sea. Around the town the fever threatened in the clusters of mosquitoes that hovered over the wells in the lemon and orange groves, and in the town it showed in some of the weary faces of the people. But these faces were also wracked by strain and bereavement. Nothing but shacks had been built to replace the buildings lost in the earthquake of three years ago. Even the early morning sunshine, which began its daily work on the travellers' tans as they stepped from a train into the Piazza Garibaldi, failed to cheer them or their miserable huts. Some 5,000 had died in the earthquake and the whole town was reduced to rubble.

Douglas and Eric did not linger. They headed for the ferry to take them across the straits to Messina fifty minutes away. Messina was also flattened by the thirty-two-second quake and ten-foot tidal wave that had left both towns some twenty inches closer to the level of the sea. Here 70,000 of the 167,000 population had died. It was a ghostly town that for the most part was still locked in those few seconds of chaos. Some façades remained, some had been ripped away leaving first- and second-floor rooms exposed like dolls'-house interiors. Stairs went nowhere, doors swung open on to nothing, and a few remaining roofs were so twisted it was a surprise they had not long since fallen in. This was not a promising place to find a good lunch.

Douglas, however, knew the very spot. By one o'clock they had booked into an inexpensive hotel near the ferry terminal on the south side of the port, which had escaped the worst of the devastation. Eric whooped with pleasure in his first bath in more than a week, singing 'Torna a Sorrento' over and over again, rolling his 'r's like a *scugnizzo*. After they were both washed and scrubbed, they went off in search of their reward for their long journey: a menu that offered more than one dish. In straw hat, crumpled linen jacket and bow tie, Douglas strode through the streets to the restaurant he knew, a plain and respectable dining room, with white tablecloths and waiters in waistcoats and black ties, making Eric conscious of his frayed collar, of the tears in his jacket pocket and sleeve, and the dry mud stains on his knickerbocker trouser knees. At least his short hair did not need combing.

Douglas ordered olives and a plate of hams and salami for himself, some macaroni soup for Eric, then braised swordfish steaks with a bean salad, followed by quail stuffed with cream cheese and raisins in vine leaves, and finally *cassata alla siciliana*. To drink, Calabrian wine would spin out the effects of inebriation rather longer than the sledgehammer of a Sicilian. The whole idea of the meal, even before it arrived, put Douglas in a state of unusual excitement.

'The *cassata* alone,' he promised, 'will be worth the trip. They have the balance between the fruit and the cream exactly right here. The ice is solid on the plate and evaporates in a puff as your tongue squeezes it up against the roof of your mouth and the flavour courses through every extremity.'

Over the mellowing meal, between reflections on each course's deliciousness, they discussed the earthquake, and compared it with the last great southern Italian earthquake of 1783, the effect of which Douglas had often pointed out. The only known catastrophe larger than this, he said, occurred in Syria in AD 526 when 120,000 died. He talked about the visit he himself had made to Messina shortly after the event, when he had brought the money collected from the expatriates on Capri.

'There were corpses in the street then,' he recalled, 'pecked at by seagulls and pulled apart by dogs, and during the night, people said, vampires came down from the hills of Calabria and plundered the ruins and stripped gold and jewels off the dead. The living had nothing: to stay alive they ate grass.'

As he went on to describe what he saw, elaborating the most horrendous details, Douglas made it sound exciting, and Eric rather wished he had been with him. He wondered if Douglas would have been any different then; if he had come alone, or brought a friend. Sometimes he found it hard to imagine him at any other time in his eventful life.

A second bottle of wine had already been ordered: Douglas's early injunction not to put fire on fire by giving alcohol to young people had long since evaporated, though since Mont Sant' Angelo Eric had learnt how to moderate his intake. When the *cassata* came, it was as delicious as predicted, and they began to reflect on their journey.

'You promised me you'd teach me how to swim,' Eric said. 'Is there anywhere good we can go?'

'There certainly is. When we have surmounted our last hurdle, the Aspromonte, we will go back to Cotrone on the Ionian. It has a fine sandy beach and is the best place in the world to learn how to swim.'

'What's the Aspromonte?'

'It's the last lump at the very end of Italy, high and empty, with a few remote, Greek-speaking villages, and the home of southern Italy's great bandit, Musolino.'

'Is he alive?'

'Yes, imprisoned on Elba, and there are people who remember him well.'

Through the *cassata*, coffee and cigars, Douglas talked about this local Robin Hood figure, and it was not until around 6 p.m. that they finally left the restaurant, feeling mellow and replete. The air outside was still heavy with heat and they headed slowly back to the hotel for a few quiet hours, Douglas stopping now and then to talk to people about the shacks that had been built, and about the clearing work that still needed to be done. The hotel lobby was cool and shady, and at first they did not see the dapper businessman sitting in an armchair. He arose immediately he saw them approach.

'Mr Douglas?' he said. He was English, though he looked as if he had lived in the south for some time.

Douglas said: 'That is me. Who are you?'

'My name is Heynes. I am the British vice-consul in Messina.' He studiously avoided looking at Eric. 'Harold Trower, the British Consular Agent in Capri, asked me to look out for you here.'

'Good God, is there no escaping that pompous little ass?'

'There is a telegram for you from Austria.' He took an envelope out of his pocket and handed it to Douglas who raised an eyebrow as he opened it.

His reaction was clearly not what the vice-consul expected. Hooting a high 'hoo-hoo-hoo', he flapped his arms at his side and clucked like a hen, then he fell into something approaching hysteria, tottering back against the wall at the bottom of the stairs and laughing like a drain. The colour left the vice-consul's face, and Eric noticed his hands opening and closing in tight fists. When the man spoke, it was in a broken whisper.

'I take it, sir, that there is no reply.'

That set Douglas off into hoots again as he shook his head and tried to say 'No'. The vice-consul hurried out of the building.

'What is it?' asked Eric after the man had gone. He was grinning at Douglas's antics, wanting to share the fun.

'I've won! She's dead! She's finally dead!' He leaned back against a wall, his arms hanging limply. His convulsions had caused a small rivulet of saliva to fall from the corner of his mouth, which drooped in a crooked smile.

Eric stopped grinning. 'Who?'

'My wife! Archie and Robin's mother.' There was triumph in his dark voice.

Eric was appalled. 'How did she die?'

'Conflagration!' Douglas chuckled. 'Burnt to a crisp after smoking in bed. So there is justice, for the wicked. Never, my dear Eric, never underestimate the power of the evil eye.'

Eric did not evade Douglas's triumphant and pitiless stare, and for a moment those deep-set blue pools seemed to look out not from under flying eyebrows but from under horns. This was not his Uncle Norman. This was not just somebody Eric did not know well; it was somebody he did not know at all.

The last leg to the south was a terrible slog. It took two days to find anyone willing to guide them over Aspromonte, which reached a peak at Monalto 6,400 feet above the sea and was reputedly still a haunt of bandits. The views from its heights should have been perfect: over the sea to the east and south towards Malta, and to the west, over Sicily where Etna stood proud. But they were only halfway up the summit when the bad weather closed in, the mist wrapping a cold blanket around them. They had begun the climb at 6 a.m. and by 10 a.m. Eric was cold and shivering.

Now and then his mind returned to the other Uncle Norman, the strange figure he had seen in the Messina hotel. The moment had not frightened him; he was seldom afraid. In retrospect Eric felt privileged to have seen this heroic figure at such an important moment in his life. He was glad he had been there and in some way he hoped that his own presence had helped Uncle Norman at that emotional time. The vice-consul clearly had been shocked, but he didn't know Uncle Norman the way Eric knew him, as a man of great integrity and devotion, who wrote to his sons twice a week and would do anything for the people he cared for. There was no doubt that Uncle Norman was a great man: no one else in southern Italy, for example, was brave enough to have attempted the mountain crossing they were making, over such rough, unmarked high land, even if it did turn out that they were ill-equipped for the cold.

'Come on, dear Eric, not far now,' Douglas kept saying to keep their spirits up.

It was a tedious journey, with nothing to look at, no views, no wildlife, and even Douglas fell into long silences. The soles on Eric's boots were worn thin by sharp stones, the damp cold made him cough, and he had painful stomach cramps. The crossing took fourteen hours, and to Eric it seemed like fourteen days. When they finally arrived at a Greek-speaking village on the other side of the mountain range, nobody believed they had walked all that way. Eric was ill now. On a mattress in a small windowless room he vomited until dawn. Douglas sat beside him in the candlelight, taking potions from his medicine bag and damping a cloth for his heated forehead.

Just before dawn, Eric fell into a deep sleep, and when he awoke around 10 a.m., his legs and feet ached from the walk, but otherwise he felt quite better again. As soon as he had breakfasted they were on their way, heading down to the coast at Bova Marina, the very bottom of the Italian boot. But they did not tarry. From there a train whisked them 120 miles up the eastern coast, and in less than a day they were in Crotone. It was the last week of July: lessons stopped and Douglas abandoned all but the most cursory research in this town which had been founded by the Greeks in who-cared-how-many-centuries Before Eric.

Crotone was a popular resort with two new hotels and a fine beach, as Douglas had promised. Eric barely stayed out of the water and Douglas showed him how to swim, an exercise that involved a great many splashing games.

'Believe me,' said Douglas, 'it's an act of faith. Our natural state is to float.'

'The water gets in my eyes,' Eric complained.

'Just put your head under,' said Douglas, 'and keep your eyes open.'

Without thinking twice, Eric did as he was told, and after a couple of attempts, he was surprised and delighted to find that he could actually see under water: he could make out little fish with spots on their backs, and translucent prawns. It was as if they were flying like birds in a pure azure space. And he could see crabs and urchins, so he knew where not to tread.

Each evening the two of them would sit at a restaurant table on the hotel terrace overlooking the port and the beach, watching the lights of the boats flickering across the water and stars pricking the sky. After the meal they would smoke cigars and by turn eat ice-cream and drink lemon *granita* and coffee until midnight when Eric would go to bed, and Douglas would order a final bottle of wine for himself, for the day's end. On the third evening, sitting at the restaurant table, Eric wrote a letter home, saying he could swim three strokes. And he told his family he would see them soon after they received this letter. He also dropped a card to the priest at St Domenico, saying he hoped he might visit London, knowing there was no chance of it happening.

When he had finished he looked up and asked, 'When's your birthday, Uncle Norman?'

'Birthday? December the eighth, the Day of the Immaculate Conception of the Blessed Virgin Mary. Why do you suddenly want to know?'

'I was just thinking. We've been together every day for more than three months, and I still don't really seem to know you.'

Douglas was amused. 'I'm sure you know all there is to know, and what you don't know can't be worth knowing. I must say it has been a wonderful three months. I cannot imagine a better companion. You have been steadfast and uncomplaining all the way. But I have noticed some changes: you have become more serious, and now that your balls have finally dropped, your voice is an octave lower, and I swear you have grown at least two inches. You will be taller than your mother when you get home. What about you? Tell me what you have enjoyed best?'

Eric thought back. 'That day on the Siren Islands,' he said, 'and the festival with the Albanians.' But really he thought the best part of all was his first sight of the Bay of Naples and the ride in the Lancia with Annetta. He asked: 'Will you see Annetta again when we get back to Naples?'

'I might do,' Douglas said, and his tongue slipped over his lips. 'Perhaps I could arrange with Amoroso for you to meet a girl, too, and we'll see if all this practising has worked.'

'It may be inconvenient,' said Eric. 'I could go on for *days*.'

That was the last time Eric and Douglas laughed during their whole adventure. That night Eric began vomiting again, and for two days he was so sick and delirious he did not know where he was. On the second day Douglas began vomiting, too. There was no point in delaying the journey home any longer. Naples, the most vibrant city Eric had seen, would remain in his memory and he could only be thankful he had seen it before he died.

All he could recall of the city on the way home was sitting in a café at the station where they changed trains, shivering, trying to keep even a glass of water down. He was so glad Uncle Norman was with him, administering the quinine and helping him when he wanted to wash or change his clothes: there was no one else in the world he wished to look after him, not even his mother. Lo Bianco had been alerted and was waiting for them at the central station, but even his solid, kindly, reassuring figure could not take away the miserableness and pain. He offered to put them up until they recovered, but Douglas said they should get on the night train for Paris and London: they were both consumed by malaria and he knew that the best place for Eric was home.

CHAPTER 8

Return to Sorrento,
1911–13

Eric imagined he would die like a bird or a fish: a brilliant life
one moment, the next moment a pile of indigestible bones. At
home, in the winding tangle of summer sheets, with fleeting
recognition of his father, sister, a visiting doctor, but mostly
his mother, he lay in the shivering heat of delirium with pains
so savage that his barely conscious moments convinced him it
would be better were his life to end. For days the whole flat in
Camden Town tiptoed in near mourning. His mother's
concerned voice sometimes penetrated the nightmare, as she
pushed spoonfuls of medicine down him, helped him to the
lavatory, gave him blanket baths and told him he would be
better soon.

On the afternoon of the fourth day Eric awoke alone,
rational and free of all fever. He was in the small bedroom
which until he left home had been Violet's domain. The smell
of London, of soot and roses, breathed in through the small,
barely open sash window that gave on to part of the yard.
Sitting up, he realised how hungry he was. He climbed from the
bed and, in his pyjamas, walked barefoot out into the hall, down
the scarlet runner that led to the front room where he found the
familiar smells of beeswax and Macassar, pipe tobacco and coal
dust which even in summer never quite left the house. The clock
on the mantelpiece struck four quarters and chimed five: outside,
the sounds of London's traffic and bustle were as familiar as old

nursery rhymes. Not everything around him was immediately recognisable, however. It took a moment to recall that the boy in the photograph on the mantel by the clock, dumpy and grinning, with a small girl at his side, was in fact himself, taken with Violet at the fair on Hampstead Heath two years earlier.

He left the front room and retraced his steps past the bedrooms to the kitchen. The back door was bolted, the stove was not lit, but there was a fresh loaf on the table and he pulled off a chunk which he chewed with caution. Then he went out of the back door to the lavatory, and to find some kindling which he used to build a fire under the stove. He filled the kettle with water, rinsed out the teapot, found two eggs in the larder cupboard, and put a pan on to boil.

It was surprising how weary these small tasks had made him. His joints ached and, while he was sitting down to rest, trying to avert his eyes from the kettle so that it might boil, his mother emerged from her bedroom with Percy in tow. Her grey hair hung in hanks; her face was alabaster and her brown eyes were rheumy, but she lit up at the sight of her son who stood up with a broad grin and accepted her tight embrace laced with rosewater and the dry sweat of sleep. For the first time he felt pleased to be home.

'You're bigger than me,' she said, standing back to look at him. 'I hadn't realised till now.' She apologised for her state, pushing her hair back coyly, like a schoolgirl. 'I must have let the fire go out.'

'I was just going to boil a couple of eggs. Do you want some tea?'

'Have you learnt how to cook? Let me do it.'

'Three and a half minutes. And I wanted some fresh bread and dripping.'

'Oh, it's grand when a man has an appetite,' she said, and she took an egg-timer out of a drawer. It was a souvenir from

Southend-on-Sea and it reminded her of her sister-in-law. 'Did you get Aunt Beat the cameo?'

'I was going to, but I got ill.'

'You'd better give her money back, then.'

'I will.' Eric did not mean the note of petulance in his voice, but he thought it insensitive to start asking an invalid for money. Uncle Norman would have called that bad manners. Percy appeared and pulled at Eric's pyjamas, pressing a wooden train into his hands.

'Have you heard from Uncle Norman?' Eric asked,

'No,' his mother said. 'He just dropped you and ran off. We have no address for him.'

'He was ill, too.' Eric felt defensive.

'How did you get in such a pickle?'

'It's only malaria. Everyone gets it in South Italy.'

'Well, if Mr Douglas had told us that in the first place, I'm not so sure we'd have let you go. The doctor said your spleen should go on show at the Empire exposition. Your father's been praying for you every day.'

'Where's Violet?'

'At the shop . She'll be home soon.'

'I forgot she worked now.'

'We'll soon have you on your feet and earning a wage, with all your new knowledge, that must be worth something . . .'

Eric excused himself and went to the lavatory. He returned as his father was coming in through the front door.

'On his feet, is he?' he called out. 'That's more like it.'

William Wolton was the same height as his wife but thinner, dressed neatly enough for Gilbey's office, his hair oiled, his moustache trimmed, his fingers uncalloused by labour, his stomach a stranger to excess. His two great interests were the church and his own health, for which he bought patent tonics, electronic belts and devices, and copious reading material. There was no malice in him, and he had only ever thrashed the children after consultation with, or on the advice of, his wife. He had, however, a well-developed sense of disappointment, which he expressed when he recalled Douglas dumping his son at their door.

'I thought he'd just come by with some laundry,' he said, 'till you groaned.'

'It's only malaria,' Eric said again in stout defence.

'So Mr Douglas said. And he told us how to treat it, as if he was a proper doctor. Not a word to say he was sorry. A gentleman would have apologised for bringing home a dog in such a state.'

Violet came in shortly after, kissing her father on the cheek before turning to Eric and remarking: 'Tea in your pyjamas? Some people are always spoilt.'

Soon after his tea, Eric returned to bed where he slept for a couple of hours. When he woke, his sister was sitting on the end of his bed. She was twelve now and a working girl, a full inch taller, breasts starting to swell, her total confidence replaced by a shade of shyness, a wariness.

'I'm earning fourteen-and-six a week,' she said, 'and I've been skating in Hampstead Palace on Fridays. Squid's sometimes there. He's very good at not falling over.'

Eric said, 'I'll come with you next time.'

She said, 'You sound different.'

He said, 'My voice has broken.'

'You mean your balls have dropped. Or did nosy Uncle Norman pull them out for you?'

Eric said, 'I thought you'd grow into a lady while I was away.'

'Away becoming a man with your beloved Uncle Norman.' She dragged his name out theatrically, clasping her hands at her throat as if about to swoon.

'You're jealous because it couldn't happen to a girl.'

'Of course I am. But that doesn't mean I want nosy Uncle Norman sniffing round me like an old tom-cat. Imagine if I told Daddy I was just off for a few months with an old man I met in the park.'

Eric was tired and he did not want to continue this conversation. 'And anyhow,' he said, 'I met a girl.'

Violet frowned. 'What's her name?'

Even though he had only been back in the land of the living for a short while, Eric had already thought of Annetta several times, just as he had done every day in Italy. He described her to Violet, and related the tale of the drive in the Lancia. It was like an act of contrition: by admitting one lust, he could deny another.

'When we left, she kissed me on the cheek,' Eric said as he finished a description of the day in Naples.

'Oh, they all do that,' Violet said. 'The girl I borrowed the dictionary off, she's Italian, and they go around with their lips out all the time waiting to bump into anyone they know.' She puckered her lips, half closed her eyes and waved her head around until Eric laughed.

'Anyway,' he said, 'don't tell anyone about it. It's a secret.'

'You didn't say. I'll want a quid.'

'You're joking. I haven't got a brass farthing.'

'You'll have to get working, then. Are you going back to Gilbey's?'

'Not if I can help it. Uncle Norman said he'd get me a better job.'

'Not good enough for you now, are we?'

'He could find you a better job, too.'

She put a hand to her throat. 'What would people say, duck? Both of us, you and me, getting rich on an old man's favours.'

*

But Eric did not have to work for more than a year. In that time Douglas, recovered and rehabilitated as a family benefactor, continued, with parental blessing and gratitude, to keep Eric beneath his wing: first for a four-month period of convalescence spent mostly at a boarding-house in Leigh-on-Sea, then, in the New Year, in Richmond, where he could be nearer to the contacts in London he needed for work. It was an appalling situation, Douglas told anyone who would listen, but until such time as his literary talents were appreciated, he would have to stay close to the city to make a crust. At the Richmond flat books piled in for review and Eric was given chunks of works by Edward Thomas and other poets to learn by rote along with the daily dictionary lists.

When he was better, Eric was trailed around galleries, museums and sites, occasionally sitting in on restaurant gatherings and music evenings, where he would imagine himself back in his first weeks in Italy listening patiently to incomprehensible conversations. Though their names meant little to him, Eric knew that the people they met were of no small importance, and he was always polite and usually rather quiet. They several times visited Joseph Conrad and his family in Ashford, where Douglas had convalesced, and they saw Hugh Walpole and Henry James in Polpero. In West End restaurants Eric met Compton Mackenzie and his actress wife Faith who behaved like a charming surrogate mother. The young Rupert Brooke and the ancient W. H. Hudson came and went. In Earl's Court they met Chaliapin, Gertrude Stein and Nijinsky at *soirées* where the hosts' four-year-old son was whisked away immediately Douglas appeared with his blasphemies, blue jokes and general reputation. They went to the Wigmore Hall at the invitation of Violet Gordon Woodhouse who was giving a harpsichord recital. Dressed in a fashionable turban, she was an exotic, dark-featured woman of Indonesian blood. They had first met at an Earl's Court *soirée*, and Douglas was delighted to discover the rumours of her *ménage à cinq*.

Douglas made sure Eric saw his family at least once a week, just as he had insisted on regular letters home from Italy. Eric returned home for school holidays, when Douglas sometimes went abroad. These were the boarding-school holidays of Douglas's boys, whom Eric had still not met. After he had gained custody of them half a dozen years earlier, Douglas had put them in the care of friends: Archie in London, Robin in Yorkshire. Eric asked after them several times.

'It is quite surprising,' Douglas replied on one of these occasions, 'how many children survive in spite of their mothers. Nobody can misunderstand a boy like his own mother. Mothers can bring children into the world but this performance marks the end of their capacities. They can't even attend to the elementary animal requirements of their offspring.'

At the end of the year they moved into Albany Mansions, a large-roomed, inexpensive Victorian block overlooking Battersea Park which Douglas could fill with the trophies of his travels. Just before Christmas he announced that Robin was arriving at St Pancras from school. Eric was due in Camden for the weekend and asked if, before he went home, they could go together to the station to meet this boy who by now seemed like his own relative. Douglas agreed in an offhand sort of way. He had some proofs to deliver and a dinner was planned. When they arrived at the station they discovered that Robin's train had been delayed. They waited half an hour, then Douglas found a policeman and asked him to pass on a note to any lost-looking twelve-year-old arriving on the delayed train, saying that his father had gone on to the *English Review* offices whence he should proceed. They then took a cab to the magazine's premises, where Douglas delivered his proofs and picked up a bundle more. After waiting a further thirty minutes with no sign of Robin, he pinned a note to the door: 'Gone to Gennaro's for dinner. Follow.' Over spaghetti and ice-cream, Douglas was irritable, and he argued so heatedly with the other guests that Eric was glad, around 10.30, to be offered his train fare home. At the same time Douglas paid the bill, leaving another note for his younger son: 'Gone home, what's the matter with you?'

Eric was appreciative of the escape he had made from the drudgery of Camden, and though he missed his friends, he sensed their distance. Several times he went skating with them at Hampstead Palace, but it was increasingly difficult to find common ground.

One time at the rink, Squid said, 'Vi says you've got a secret girl.'

'That was supposed to be a secret,' Eric said.

'Yes, I know, that's what she said.'

So Eric found himself again telling the story of the encounter with Annetta: this time the young lovers had kissed goodbye fully on the lips; she was the best kisser he had ever met, he said. Squid whistled and said if he were Eric he wouldn't be standing there, he'd get his skates on and be back in Italy like a shot.

Eric, more worldly, explained, 'You've got to be careful with women. You have to vampire them before they vampire you.'

Squid said: 'What are you talking about? Are you bats? You have to tell them how lovely they are and give them presents and make them feel like queens.' He grinned, revealing the absence of a couple of teeth. 'Then they're nice to you and they let you do what you want.'

A few days later, over breakfast in Albany Mansions, Eric told Uncle Norman he would like an Italian penfriend, someone he could practise his written language on; perhaps somebody he had already met, someone about his own age, someone like Annetta, for example.

'Why don't you write to Michele?' Douglas said.

'Michele?' Eric was shocked.

'He writes to me regularly,' Douglas said. 'He is contrite and I know he respects you for coming to my rescue.'

Though he knew only a small percentage of the senders and recipients of the daily deluge of correspondence that flowed into and out of the flat, Eric had no idea Douglas had kept contact with his would-be assassin.

'In the meantime,' said Douglas, 'I have found you a job in the Ministry of Pensions. There will be an interview next week but it's not much more than a formality. There is a vacancy for Violet, too, if she wants it.'

'Will I have to work all day in an office?'

'You don't want to be a manual worker, do you?'

'I just thought I might do something where I don't have to stay in all the time, like I had to at Gilbey's.'

'My dear, to compare the Ministry of Pensions with Gilbey's is to compare the British Empire to a gin house. In a few years you might get a posting. And anyway the salary is decent enough for you to live at home or even to rent a modest room, for however much affection I have for you, I do have my own life to get on with and you are, as you realise, an expense – one I cannot much longer endure.'

'Of course. I'm sorry. Thank you, Uncle Norman.'

'But I have also told them that you can't take up a position until the beginning of May. I promised we would go back to Italy, and I am planning a trip for just after Easter.'

Eric gave a whoop of joy. But he was not the only one excited by the idea of going to Italy. As the time grew nearer Douglas's bad London began slipping away.

*

The train pulled into Naples station just before lunch on 21 April 1913, six days after Eric's fifteenth birthday and almost exactly two years after their first visit. 'The sixteenth century in Eric years,' Douglas said. 'The Renaissance, the rebirth, the Cinquecento.' The dream was recurring. Lo Bianco was on the platform to greet them. The big man had put his arm around Eric and kissed him on both cheeks. Eric grinned hugely and immediately began asking about the aquarium and his latest catches as well as his latest car. Lo Bianco was histrionic in praising the boy's Italian, its deep resonance now more fitting for the south. As they walked through the station concourse Eric continually looked around for Annetta though he knew she would not be there. He had written to Michele but had no reply.

For the first week they stayed at Sant' Agata on the Sorrento peninsula and Uncle Norman immediately came into his stride: up mountains at four in the morning, down into coves and out to remote hamlets to seek out old friends. Dinner tables were once more animated with his opinions and conversation; children had tricks played on them and were given sweets; old people imparted their wisdom and their foolishness. Eric was sometimes left alone while Douglas went his own way, especially in the evenings. The old routine quickly set in.

At the start of the second week they went over to Capri where Douglas was welcomed and fêted like visiting royalty. Every resident expatriate, every bar owner, market vendor and restaurateur came out to greet them. Babies were brought out for him to pat on the head, as if in benediction; boys and girls came to kiss him, some carrying flowers. Offers of hospitality could have stretched out through the summer, and blandishments to stay, even offers of free villas, tempted Douglas sorely, while many of the invitations were received with his usual air of amusement. He even enjoyed meeting the weaselly consular agent Harold Trower.

'Dear God,' Trower said on seeing him with Eric, 'I hope the floodgates haven't opened again.'

Douglas chuckled. 'My dear Trower,' he said, 'you must realise that men of substance cannot be dammed.'

Compton and Faith Mackenzie, enchanted by Douglas's descriptions of the island, had just arrived for a rest after a mauling of his latest play on Broadway. Faith grabbed and kissed Eric as if he were a favourite nephew. But the high point of the first week was a tea party given by the American party doyennes, the Wolcott-Perrys, cousins who had hyphenated their lives and names for social ease. Douglas expressed indifference to the event but they went anyway. Eric had never seen such a high-society circus. Local children, dressed as sailors, waited on the guests, handing them éclairs, praline ice sponge cake, and tall glasses of *crème de menthe frappée*. The guests were of every nationality in every kind of dress, and the mix of languages made cockney just one more linguistic variant; nor was anybody wrongly dressed, for any kind of dress was acceptable among the pergolas and loggias, the follies and terraces of the Villa Torricella which looked out over the twinkling olive groves across the indigo bay.

'Girls or boys?' a bearded old man said quietly to Eric as he sipped a cup of tea by an isolated Doric column.

'Pardon?'

'Which do you prefer?' His English was too impeccable for him to be an Englishman: he was German or East European.

'Boys for friends, girls for fun,' Eric replied cautiously, adding the Normanism, 'turkeys for Thanksgiving.'

'Good chap. Not biased, of course. Anything goes here. It's in the air: dogs, chicken. All immoral. Can't help it, poor dears. Know Douglas, do you?'

'He's been helping with my education,' Eric said.

'Ah, one of his little protégés. He's responsible for bringing today's guest into our midst.'

'Who's that?'

'Le Comte d'Adelswård-Fersen. Over there.'

A good-looking, fair-haired man in his mid-twenties, slim, over-dressed, effete, was standing on the patio haloed by the magenta stars of a mesembryanthemum. No doubt he was one that Trower imagined should be the other side of the floodgates.

'We call him Count Jack. Pederast. Various jail terms in France found out by the mayor here, no doubt through old Trower, got chucked off the island, now reinstated, thanks mainly to these two old biddies who think the sun shines out between his pleasure domes, hence the knees-up. Anyone you fancy yet?'

Eric looked around. Everyone was posing, pouting, batting *bons mots* back and forth. Some were already clearly drunk. He expected at any moment to see the American woman who had been so disparaging in the Gran Caffè d'Italia on his first day in Naples two years ago. This time he would be ready for her. They were all something of her type. There was no one quick and fresh as Annetta. He shook his head. 'Not yet.'

'Well, let me know if there is, old chap. See if I can fix you up, though if they're over thirty you might as well just plunge ahead on your own, they're all so bored, poor dears.'

An hour later, having spoken to, and decided against, several thirty-year-olds, Eric found Douglas on the shady terrace in a wicker chair drawn up beside the French count. Two glasses and a bottle of brandy were on the table before them and the count was offering cocaine from a small enamel box.

'Have a pinch?' His voice was rasping, his French accent strong.

'Thanks, I will.'

Douglas took it as casually as he took snuff, placing it on the back of his left hand, spreading it out for scrutiny before raising it to his large nose for a loud, honking snort. A passing Wolcott-Perry did not raise an eyebrow.

'I didn't know you took snow,' the count said, after taking a pinch himself.

'I don't make a rule of it.'

'Pouf! I do. My life has been messed up.'

'It is you who are messing it up.'

'Messed up by other people.'

'I know. Send them to hell. Don't go there yourself.'

'Ah, *mon vieux*, if I had met you when I was a boy . . .'

The count looked up at Eric who, caught eavesdropping, smiled innocently. Douglas introduced the count to Eric: 'My favourite nephew.'

'Snow?' the thin Frenchman asked.

'Thank you,' Eric said, with automatic politeness. He took a pinch of this social condiment, thinking it a kind of snuff, until a large inhalation told him otherwise. His eyes bulged and he grinned.

'Just so you know what it is like,' Douglas said to him. 'For your education. You are not to have more.'

'Quite right,' the count said. 'Now tell me, Uncle Norman's current little favourite, what are you going to do with your life, now that you have had such invaluable instruction?'

'I am about to start a career in the Ministry of Pensions.'

'My God!' the count exclaimed in a roar, banging the table before him with the flat of his hand. He took a handkerchief from his top pocket and dabbed his moistening eyes. 'How can one so young have such courage? Such fucking courage!' And his melancholy gradually dissolved into helpless, soundless laughter.

Eric smiled happily. Everyone seemed to enjoy themselves on Capri.

*

Over the following week, Eric followed Douglas on jaunts and errands, and though he liked the island he had heard so much about, he felt tied to Douglas and increasingly he looked across the bay to Naples. The desire to escape became so strong that one morning he left a note on the kitchen table of their villa: 'Gone to Naples, back tonight.' It was time to take Uncle Norman at his word, to do as he damn well pleased and to take the consequences. With ten lire half-inched from Douglas's wallet and a small twist of paper that was a gift from Count Jack, he caught the midday ferry which arrived at Naples at noon.

He had not forgotten the city's layout, which in his imagination he had run through many times, and he headed up the Via Toledo, hanging on to his wallet and savouring every step. Even though Maria Spasiono's laundry was in the middle of a warren of unnamed streets he soon found it, just as he remembered it, though now the front door was firmly shut. He banged long and hard until Signora Spasiono appeared at an upstairs window, her dark hair falling about her like a witch.

When he set out, he had not known what reception to expect: he had no idea if Annetta would either remember or care for him. But he was desperate: desperate to find a girl who had touched him; desperate to prove he could live a life without Douglas; desperate to capture a real kiss to take home to Camden; desperate to prove he was not a nancy. And he knew that he might never visit Naples again.

Signora Spasiono remembered Eric, but she did not seem pleased to see him. He asked if Annetta was at home. '*Aspetta!*' she said impatiently and disappeared back behind the window. A minute later Annetta's unmistakable, slightly husky voice came from overhead. Eric stepped back to look up at a second-floor window.

'What are you doing here?' she demanded.

'I wanted to know if you were as beautiful as I remembered,' Eric shouted up.

'Where's Uncle Norman?'

'In Capri, with the goats.'

'Ay-ay.'

'Let me come up.'

'No.'

'Throw down the grocery basket and pull me up.'

'Sshh! People are trying to have a *siesta*.'

'*Siestas* are for old people. There is no time for sleeping. I'm only here today. Come for a swim. Come for a boat ride. Come to England. Marry me.'

'You are stupid,' she said.

He took out the small twist of white powder, unwrapping it dramatically. 'I have a poison from the chemist in Capri. He assured me it would be the best way to take my life. If I don't receive a kiss from you . . .' He licked his finger and picked up a few grams to taste on his cautious tongue. 'He said it works very quickly.'

'*Mamma mia!*'

People had begun to take notice: a young man who had been pitching coins asked Annetta who her lover was. An old man on a balcony shouted to Annetta to warn her against having the blood of a foreigner on her hands. A young girl in a doorway called out to say she would take him if Annetta didn't want him.

'All right, all right,' Annetta finally agreed, if only to keep the neighbours quiet. 'At five o'clock. By the bandstand outside the Villa Nazionale.'

Eric's grin could be seen on the planet Venice and in his whoop of delight he threw the twist of paper in the air, scattering its dust into the street to be sniffed at by curious cats. In the next few hours he discovered the deep, glowing satisfaction of anticipation, a feeling that surpassed every real event that had so far occurred in his life. He kicked his heels around the old town, and made his way gradually down towards the bay just as the evening stroll was starting.

Annetta was on time. She wore a white embroidered blouse, cornflower-blue plain skirt and canvas shoes, as he had remembered her, with dark hair and lustrous eyes full of the history of the whole Mediterranean, the complete magic spell of the south. She sauntered up and kissed him perfunctorily on both cheeks, and he beamed. They had both grown in confidence, as in everything else. Without asking, she picked a pistachio from a bag he was carrying and then slipped a hand inside his arm to lead him among the perambulating crowd.

They walked past hurdy-gurdies, storytellers and performing monkeys, and sellers of water, bananas, nuts and ice-creams. They dismissed beggars and invitations to card games. They walked through the Villa Nazionale pleasure ground, rode a merry-go-round and bought lottery tickets. They looked in on the Zoological Station, which was so popular it stayed open late. Lo Bianco was not there, and they strolled among the fish, mimicking their expressions, and trying to find the specimens each thought the other looked like. By the bandstand Annetta swung her hips and tried to teach him the Tarantello. They drank lemonade made with a great iron lemon squeezer and brought to life with teaspoons of bicarbonate of soda. They had their photograph taken, arm in arm.

He told her about his trip to Calabria, and how he had become too ill to come back to Naples where he had hoped to see her again. He asked after Amoroso and wanted to know if she had had a ride in Lo Bianco's new car. He told her of the social highjinks on Capri. They agreed their favourite food was a Margherita pizza, and pistachio their favourite ice-cream flavour. She taught him some new words, and he bought her a carton of contraband cigarettes. After dark they went down to the shore and took off their shoes and paddled in the water, looking out across the bay, to the distant lights of Sorrento, Ischia and Capri.

'I must be back at ten o'clock,' she said.

'Or what happens?' Eric asked.

'I will be disgraced and thrown out of my home.'

Eric did not doubt it. 'I'll look after you.'

'They would kill you.'

'Who?'

'Michele and his friends.'

'You could marry me.'

'Hah! Then they would kill us both. Besides, you're much too young.'

'I'm only a year younger than you. How old do you expect your husband to be? As old as Uncle Norman?'

'Perhaps.'

'Are you going to see him again?'

'He'll be back on Monday, he said.'

'Back? You have seen him already?'

'Twice. Last week.'

Of course, that's just where Uncle Norman would have been on his evenings away from Sant' Agata. He always went back: he was always faithful. Annetta walked up the beach and sat down on the sand. Fireworks began to explode over the bay.

'Now you are grumpy,' she said as he sat down beside her.

'I didn't know he was still seeing you,' he said.

'And you,' she said. 'You have sex with him.'

He evaded an answer. 'Do you think he is homosexual?'

She shrugged as if she did not really care. 'Michele goes with him.'

'Michele! My God, how does he fit us all in!' His Italian for 'fit us all in' was not exact and she laughed.

'Would you like to marry him?' Eric asked.

She said: 'Stop talking about marriage. It's so English.'

'I won't say another word.' He cupped her face in his right hand and kissed her, lightly at first, then as long and as hard as he had in his boastful stories, as softly and fully as he had in his dreams; letting her tongue run over his lips as it had run over the urchin eggs on that first day in Lo Bianco's garden, running his own lips around her small gold-studded ears, supping at her white neck and letting her blow gently on his eyelids. It was an enormous relief to know he could find such pure joy in kissing a girl, and he was bursting with the pleasure of it. Fireworks again exploded over the bay.

'Does that always happen when you kiss?' Eric asked.

'Always,' she said.

And he kissed her again, touching a breast beneath her blouse, thrilling to the firm nipple for a few moments until she pushed his hand firmly away. However impossible the dream remained, he longed to find a way for them to be together, so that all he had practised with Uncle Norman could be put into effect. He had imagined this moment: he had anticipated the kiss, the touch, but he had not anticipated the shock of the ecstasy. Nor had he planned for premature ejaculation. The unthinkable event made him shudder with despair, and although he tried to pretend it had not occurred, when he instinctively touched himself, she said softly, 'I am pleased you like my kisses so much.'

He looked away. He was ashamed. Her fingers touched the back of his neck, but he continued to stare at the lights across the inky water, the sea that seemed now to flow through his veins, towards the jutting island and the man who had brought them together.

'What time is the last ferry?' she asked. 'You mustn't miss it.'

'It won't matter.' He kissed her lightly on the cheek. There was no denying the happiness he had felt, no denying he would always think of her. 'I could walk across the water.'

But after walking Annetta home, he did catch the ferry, with minutes to spare. Uncle Norman was not in his room when he reached Capri, and Eric went straight to bed.

Throughout the rest of their stay Douglas never mentioned Eric's day of escape, or the money that had gone missing from his wallet.

CHAPTER 9

France, 1917

The second pair of messengers that Sergeant Wolton had sent to the front line had not returned. For more than an hour he had been at the top of the trench ladder, half sunk in mud, looking out across the scarred landscape. The moon smudged the clouds but failed to break through the grey blanket that offered protection from the night's prying eyes. He had not turned away from the darkness, not lit a cigarette, but kept his gaze steadily in the direction the two soldiers had gone. Another burst of fire flickered across the horizon, outlining the charred trees. Nature had long since breathed her last here: the battle was over her dead body. The front-line trench was only yards away from the Germans', which meant that from any distance it was impossible to tell who was shooting at whom. The mission should have taken the two young recruits less than forty minutes. One was a Londoner, like Eric, who had joined up the previous week.

'See anything?' the Captain's voice called up. He was a Yorkshireman, not a toff like many of the officers: there weren't many toffs left.

'No.'

'Find two more men, then, and I'll get the message copied out again.'

'I'll take it myself,' Eric said, climbing down from the ladder and pulling a packet of Gold Flake from his battle jacket.

The Captain looked at him steadily under the lamplight. Eric was the cheerful cockney, the ready volunteer, who since joining in June, seven months earlier, had soon risen to sergeant; a rise caused through the rapid wastage of officers and men. Eric had been here for nearly four months continuously: he had missed Christmas and would probably miss his nineteenth birthday, too. By next Christmas he would be a general or in his grave.

'If you want a job done properly,' Eric said, 'you have to do it yourself.'

The Captain, who was only a few years older than Eric, went into his cupboard-sized office in the trenches to write out the order once more. Eric smoked the cigarette evenly, one hand in his heavy khaki trouser pocket, gripping the penknife Violet and Percy had given him, and as the Captain emerged with the envelope he took the Westerbury watch from his shirt pocket: it was three o'clock in the morning. Everyone in Camden would be asleep, except perhaps for Violet, who would probably be down at Charing Cross, in uniform, looking after the 'poor lovely boys' who arrived by the trainload to fill the hospitals and graveyards.

Eric pocketed the rewritten message with a brief salute and then, with a bayonet fixed in his rifle, nipped up the ladder and headed off into the dark. Although he had watched the other messengers go, he had no better idea than they had about which way to advance. With no God to put his trust in, no mantra to chant, he just kept his head down and ran at as steady a pace as the shell-shocked landscape would allow. At least there were no mines between here and the front line. Machine-gun fire opened up on his left, then a flare shot up from the right. He dived into the mud and lay there as it passed overhead. He rose again, and headed onwards. Rifles exchanged fire. The direction only had to be roughly right: if he kept running he was bound to fall somewhere into the front-line trench.

He had volunteered not just for this mission but for the war. He had been restless since he returned from Italy, and anything seemed better than working another day in the Ministry of Pensions. Uncle Norman had promised to try to find him a better job, but nothing had transpired. Besides, he wanted to try to put an end to this fight that had gone on more than two years. Everyone knew someone who had been killed in it. Both his cousins in Essex had died. Squid had been reported missing just before Eric joined up, and this time he was not so optimistic of his friend's chance of survival. It was immediately after receiving news about Squid that Violet began to devote all her spare time to ministering to the wounded. Their father said she was too young, but she shouted and made a scene until, as usual, he gave in. Chalkie had joined up at the same time as Squid, and there had been no news of him for a while.

Eric could have done with a little more moonlight, but he could not worry too much about where his feet fell or his pace would slacken, and he wanted this job to be over soon: he was carrying orders for the morning, and he knew how vital such information could be. Without warning, he fell headlong into a trench, landing on a soft mix of sandbags and mud. A frightened voice shrieked at him: 'Who goes there?' and before he could reply, a .22 bullet tore through his jacket. The oaths that Eric found were loud and long, and it was all he could do to stop shooting back. He had caught the sentry off-guard, or asleep, and now all hell had broken loose, with guns going off on all sides and another flare going up.

Fortunately, the bullet had passed through Eric's epaulette and not even drawn blood. When the sentry had finally seen the error of his ways, Eric asked him to take him to the commanding officer, and they walked through the squalor of the trenches. He stepped into the small office, saluted the captain and gave him the envelope. The officer, grey, gaunt, and in his early thirties with a thin moustache defiantly clipped, read it with no apparent interest.

'Getting here's the easy part,' he said. 'This is the third time this message has been delivered tonight.'

Eric left as quickly as he could, up and over the top and back through the mud and craters. As he ran he was reminded of another time running at night, in Siren Land, chased by the demons of the *male sito*, by the ominous fireflies, and by the howling wolf man. Just as the sound of that idiot began to return to mind, when his eyes were beginning to be able to make out the shapes and shadows in the dark, he heard a moan, as if someone were answering the wolf man. Heading towards the sound, Eric soon came upon the pair from the second party: one dead, and the cockney recruit half shot to hell.

'Soon have you back,' said Eric.

He picked the lad up and hoisted him over his shoulders. The moaning increased, but it did not last long. It was a corpse that Eric eventually delivered back to the trench. He mustered a burial detail and went off to bed.

Two days later the mail arrived, the first there had been for a couple of weeks. For Eric there were three letters from his mother and two postcards from Uncle Norman, both from Paris. The letters from his mother had been opened and were stamped by the censor. They kept up her cheerful tone, describing daily life in the Wolton household in Camden Town in a similar vein each time she wrote. Percy couldn't wait to join up, Violet was working round the clock at her nursing, and his father was worn out at the factory which kept him till late every night. She herself was working for the Red Cross, and though she seemed to write about her sewing, Eric was never quite clear what her duties were.

He had to look at the dates on the postcards to make sure he read them in order. In the six years they had known each other, Douglas had sent cards regularly whenever they were apart, so although he had not seen him for a couple of years, Eric always knew where this nomadic uncle was. Some months ago Violet had sent a newspaper cutting, which he kept, along with several others, inside his copy of *Old Calabria*, the book of their travels, which had been published in 1915. Beneath the headline 'REMANDED IN CUSTODY', *The Times* reported the arrest and remand in prison of Norman Douglas, forty-eight, 'a well-dressed, middle-aged man, described as an author, of Albany Mansions, Albert Bridge Road, Battersea'. He was charged as a suspected person, of assault on a sixteen-year-old boy he had importuned at the Natural History Museum. Eric did not know how Douglas had escaped or been let off prosecution, and had not mentioned it in letters to him. As Douglas himself might say, it was none of anyone's damned business. Violet, however, had clearly been delighted by the news, which confirmed all her suspicions about him.

Soon after the cutting arrived, postcards from Douglas came from Italy, where they continued to be sent through the summer until the last one, which had come from Paris, saying he had taken a room at 45 Rue Pigalle, Montmartre. It was comforting to know Uncle Norman was in the nearest city. The first card had a picture of a windmill and read: 'Saw Archie last week: gassed and in hospital. Awful business, but he's very cheery. Hate to think of you in the thick of it, only sixty miles away. Can't you get leave and come to Paris? Things pretty tight and not much fun, but we could share a few chestnuts and recall sunnier times. Bring money for a decent meal.' The second one was printed in neat capitals: 'To whom it may concern: I wish to ask permission for Sgt E. F. E. Wolton to be granted leave to see me, his Uncle Norman, on a family matter of some delicacy, concerning his cousin, a young lady from Louth . . .'

Eric grinned. There was nothing he would rather do after months in this miserable muddy hell-hole than spend twenty-four hours in the company of Uncle Norman, and he certainly would show this plaintive note to the Captain, in whose good books he had been put after the escapade of the other night. Anyway, leave was long overdue.

Eric was given a thirty-six-hour pass and the following Saturday the train from Amiens on which he was travelling arrived at the Gard du Nord two hours late. Douglas was waiting in the station café writing in a large exercise book, which he closed on seeing the smoking engine shunt into the iron-and-glass cavern of the terminus. Eric was in uniform, with peaked cap, tunic blouse, webbing belt and gaiters, and shining hobnailed boots. He carried a small leather case containing his overnight require-ments and his copy of *Old Calabria* which went everywhere with him, like a talisman. As the steam cleared from the hissing train, Douglas came into view, a gaunt but still imposing figure, the hair greyer but thicker, the eyes greyer, too. Beneath a thread-bare coat, he remained broad-shouldered and upright, if a little underweight. He was half a head taller than Eric, who had no hope now of catching him up.

'Can't expect to win this war when the trains don't run on time,' Douglas said, stepping forward and shaking Eric warmly by the hand.

Eric grinned. Paris in wartime, bleak, bombarded, rationed, and run by women and the un-able-bodied, would be another adventure with Uncle Norman.

'I'm starving, did you bring any cash?'

'As much as I have,' said Eric who had known what the first question would be.

They strode off through the press of soldiers to the con-course and the outside world.

'I've booked you into a *pension* in Montmartre not far from me. You can't stay in my room, because there's no heating, and it's flea-bitten. I can't stay there myself during the day, it's so damned cold. But I've had some luck. Last week I took this coat to be mended and it turned out that both the tailor and I had boys at the front, so he only charged me thirty francs. When I went to pick it up this morning he mistook my fifty-franc note for a hundred-franc note. In other times, of course, I would have mentioned the overabundance of change. Despicable conduct, I know, but when one's stomach is so completely empty one does not hesitate. Besides, it's all part of the great give and take. The other day Marcel, my young *voyou*, a rather unstable urchin who looks like an angel in disgrace, ran off with a hundred-franc note of mine, which I had given him to buy medicine, which was particularly mean of him since the medicine was designed to relieve an ailment he had freely given me. I shan't leave Paris before I have found him and told him what I think of him.'

They walked through the side streets towards Montmartre, Douglas talking of other city characters, and declaiming against the war, the waste, and the lack of food and creature comforts. A shell burst somewhere in the city, which was in range of the German big guns. There were soldiers everywhere: French, English, American. It was from them that Douglas had cadged cigarettes and other rations, and he pointed out the corner of Rue de l'Agent Bailly, which was a favourite spot for 'passionate farewells'.

At Place Pigalle they entered a brasserie, Au Rat Qui n'est pas Mort, and settled themselves at a window table. Douglas ordered wine and porterhouse steaks, insisting on seeing them before they were cooked. He had not had meat, he said, since he left England. They had much to catch up on and there was no gap in their conversation. Archie was all right, he said, but this gassing was appalling. Eric asked where he was in hospital and said he would try to go to see him. He had still not met either of Douglas's sons, though they often talked about them, and he looked forward to introducing himself to Archie whom he instinctively felt would be like a brother.

When the steaks arrived, Douglas sniffed the rare-cooked meat deeply. He seemed to waver a little, then he quaffed half a glass of wine and cut into the meat. He had swallowed only a couple of pieces when he had to rush to the lavatory. Eric watched him go, and wondered how long it was since he had eaten a proper hot meal. Life in the trenches was a particular horror, but at least they were fed.

On his return, Douglas apologised, and had to have the plate of meat taken away, for even its odour, it seemed, caused convulsions among the gnawing pangs of his stomach. Lunch lately, he said, was usually a few chestnuts, and perhaps some boiled sorrel, sometimes just boiled sorrel. Eric ordered him an omelette, and recalled happier times. *Old Calabria*, he said, patting his case, went everywhere with him and he had been re-reading it on the train, though it wasn't all how he remembered the experience. He did not mention his disappointment that he himself had not been included in the narrative. He talked about publishing the diary he had kept, but Douglas pointed out that nobody was publishing anything at the moment.

Old Calabria had had some critical acclaim, and although it failed to sell in any numbers, at least it had not been pulped, like *Siren Land*. The previous year *London Street Games* had come out, and again its sales were few. Douglas's lack of success seemed to be summed up in the newspaper cutting Violet had sent, which showed that, as an author, Douglas was quite unknown to the general public. Eric asked what he was writing now.

'Conrad suggested I did a novel, said there might be more money in it. The first one, *South Wind*, should be coming out in a month or so, if Secker have done everything I asked. It's about a mythical island called Nepenthe full of immoderate people doing just as they please, and a bishop who loses all sense of right and wrong and comes to condone a murder. Great fun.'

'Is it based on Capri?' Eric asked.

'Sort of. It's certainly designed to be an antidote to this silly war, and I hope it will cheer everyone up.'

'And what's next?'

'I have put aside Theophilus, which is too demanding at the moment. Hunger is no bad thing sometimes: it's like an emetic, cleans you through, but it has been going on too long, and I'm starting to feel listless. I've begun putting together my war memoirs instead.'

'What war memoirs?'

'Hah! Exactly. What did you do in the war, Papa? I loafed, my boy, I loafed around Italy. I will call it "Sunshine". But I'm having a damnable hard time writing it here on this empty belly. You know me.' He grinned. 'I need all the juices to be flowing.'

Eric thought this a good time to ask if he was allowed back to England. 'Violet sent me a cutting from *The Times* about what happened at the Natural History Museum. Were you really jailed on remand?'

'Only for a week,' said Douglas. 'Not bad, at least I was fed. No, I can't go back. Burnt my boats again. Everyone buggered off, no one stood by me, not even Conrad. It's ridiculous when some trifle becomes a crime just because it used to be a sin, and it only became a sin because some impotent old antediluvian once got jealous of someone else's pleasures.'

Eric smiled ruefully. 'You should watch out you don't cop it.'

After lunch they wandered the city, Douglas warning that they might have to dive down into a metro station if the bombardment started again, which it did most afternoons. It was cosy down there, he said, among the Parisians and their children. As they strolled across the Pont Neuf, the bells of Notre Dame chimed and he looked at his watch, which had stopped. He took it off and hurled it into the water.

'Burn your boats,' he said. 'That's the way to do it. Paris is so dreary, I've had enough of it. I'll go to St Malo to finish the memoirs, though not before I have settled with that young cherub, Marcel. Come on, let's hunt him out.'

They trawled the seediest bars in the city, where Douglas seemed entirely at home, and where Eric, in his uniform, felt out of place, though his money was in demand wherever they went. There was no sign of the boy. Towards the middle of the evening, between bars, they were propositioned by a well-painted, middle-aged *madame*, who invited them to meet her girls, refusing to take their pleas of poverty as an excuse for turning down her offer. Her girls, she said, were so depressed with the war, they just needed to meet new people, to have some diversion, to cheer up.

'Ladies in distress,' Douglas said to Eric, 'are, in my experience, easy to refuse, but in this case we might make an exception.'

Eric was apprehensive but he did not have much appetite for continuing the quest for Marcel. They entered an apartment block, walking passed a dozing concierge. In a room on the second floor, half a dozen women were sitting around on chairs and sofas, all of them around twice Eric's age, their countenances shadowed by the red scarves draped over the lamps, their cheeks rouged, their breasts half covered, their legs in holed stockings. The *madame* produced some rum and handed it out in opaque, chipped glasses. Douglas made complimentary remarks and was soon speaking fluent French, amusing the *madame* and charming the women. Eric felt as he had often done in the early days in Italy, made mute by the lack of language, patient and passive at the side of his master, though he caught the drift. Douglas was asking details about the acts of coition as performed by different nationalities, as he might have asked some Calabrian peasant about the nature of particular plants.

As they were talking, a woman close to Eric leaned over, unfastened his trousers and began to arouse him. The others took no notice, and in a short while he removed her hand and she led him behind a curtain. In this small space, on a lumpy bed, the woman's looks and loose-skinned body became immaterial. Eric lost his virginity listening to Douglas, his tutor, whose lessons had been so instructive that the act in which his pupil was now engaged threatened to go on for eternity. Only by conjuring thoughts of monk seals, warm figs, bustling Naples and the sweet kiss of Annetta could Eric bring the matter to a suitable close.

Eric spent his next short leave visiting the 41st stationary hospital in Amiens. This turned out to be in the former home of the writer Jules Verne. It was not a particularly warm day, but patients were encouraged to breathe the fresh air, and had taken up places in the overgrown parkland that surrounded the mansion. They were in their dressing gowns, blankets and slippers, patched, plastered and sewn up, some hobbling, some in wheelchairs, some on benches. Among the Red Cross nurses there were several English girls and Eric would not have been surprised if he had seen Violet there.

Eric had never met Archie Douglas, or even seen a photograph of him, and a French nurse had to point him out, sitting in a chair out on the lawn. A few months younger than Eric, he was plump as a pudding and round-headed, and Eric thought he looked like a Kraut. His eyes were bandaged from the effects of the mustard gas.

'Hello, Archie. I'm Eric, Eric Wolton, a friend of your father's.' He reached out to shake hands, but Archie's remained folded in front of him, the fingernails, Eric noticed, bitten to the quick. Eric immediately sensed himself to be at a disadvantage, for, without sight, Archie could not appreciate the sincerity of his warm smile.

'What are you doing here?' Archie asked, unimpressed. His Uppingham education had given him the same clipped public school accent as his father. His breath was short.

'I met Uncle Norman a couple of weeks ago and he told me you were here. I said I'd try to look you up. Smoke?'

'Oh thanks, just what burnt-up lungs need.'

'Sorry . . .'

' I take it you're not an officer?'

'Sergeant.'

'I won't get up then.'

Eric laughed because Archie could not see him smile. 'No, don't get up. There's some fruit here – Egremont apples and Seville oranges. I'll give them to the nurses to wash and put in a bowl. How are your eyes?'

Archie sniffed, and seemed uncertain whether or not to answer. Then he said, 'Better. I just keep them covered up in daylight. They don't think the blindness will be permanent.'

Eric asked how it had happened, and Archie told of a mustard gas attack one night near Cambrai. He had been injured, too: the shrapnel from the exploding canister had torn through his left leg. Two people had been instantly killed and several had been permanently blinded. It was disgusting stuff, he said, explaining the effects of the gas in detail. Eric said it must have been terrible, and how lucky he himself was to have escaped uninjured so far.

Archie shifted uncomfortably and said, 'Most of the poor bastards here haven't seen their families in months, because they aren't allowed to cross the Channel. My father is less than a hundred miles away, and he has been to see me once.'

'He doesn't have much money,' Eric said defensively

'And when he did come here, do you know what he did? He buggered a drunk Madagascan soldier by the road. He thought the Madagascan would be too far gone to remember, but he wasn't, and the story got out, so I'm left here with the usual humiliation and derision. It's just another insult to add to my bloody injuries.'

Eric was deeply shocked and acutely embarrassed. He had no idea that Douglas's sexual activities were so public, nor had he imagined Douglas's children would know about them. He himself had not the faintest notion if his own parents had any sexual life at all.

Lamely, he said, 'He likes to take his pleasure where he finds it.'

'I don't know what the hell I'm doing here.' Archie began to bite his nails. 'My mother was German, but I don't remember her: I was seven years old when he took me away. Robin was four. We just got dumped in England, like he dumps everyone, for his own convenience. Mother died broken-hearted. We were forbidden to get in touch. You can't talk to him about her: he goes into complete paroxysms if you mention her name. When she died she had absolutely no idea where we were, and hadn't had for years; his vengeance was absolute. Her sister, my aunt, was at the hospital and she told me my mother's last words were *"Meine Kinder in England"*.'

Eric recalled the strange figure of Uncle Norman in the Reggio hotel, holding the telegram and hooting hysterically. 'I'm sorry,' he said.

Archie said angrily, 'Oh, do piss off, you fucking little cockney cunt.'

CHAPTER 10

East Africa, 1925

Assistant Inspector Eric Wolton was in the Hotel Africa in Moshi drinking a beer. His sun helmet was on the counter, his pistol in a leather holster at his side. Local colonials, all acquainted and all but a handful of them English, were wandering in for lunch, and talk at the bar was of two Englishmen killed by a rhino the previous day. Did the Assistant Inspector of Police have any news of the animal? As far as he knew, Eric said, it was still on the loose. The previous morning Norman Douglas had arrived in Mombasa, and taken a train up to Voi where he had stopped overnight. Unable to get away, Eric had this morning sent a driver to bring him over the border from Kenya, a bumpy four-hour ride, which should by now be nearing its end. The last time Eric had seen him was more than four years ago in Marseilles just before setting sail for East Africa and the post Douglas had secured for him in the Tanganyika police force. Uncle Norman had been promising to come and see him ever since, and Eric wondered now if he might have changed: if he would get on with Eric's wife, Helen. She was a German widow of a customs official who had been crushed to death beneath a badly stowed assignment of sisal some years earlier, and they had met in Dar-es-Salaam where she lived, and where Eric had been seconded for a couple of months. Among the expatriate community there was no great matter of choice, and everyone knew everyone. In the three years before they met, Eric had encountered no one else with whom he felt he could form a relationship. Their affair had blossomed fast, and within two months of its start they were married. For the first time since he had left home a couple of days before his thirteenth birthday, Eric felt settled. It was a pity they had not had children, but they kept trying.

Dust suddenly billowed in the road outside the hotel beside his police lorry, and a Ford drew to a halt. Eric picked up his hat, and stepped outside into the midday heat of the street. Douglas, overdressed as usual in a thick wool suit the colour he called 'pressed cockroach', strode towards him.

'My dear Eric, I hope you've ordered. I'm famished.'

Eric grinned with immediate pleasure. Any trepidation he had had at the thought of their meeting immediately vanished: it was as if he had seen Douglas only the other day. He wasn't quite as tall or as broad as Eric remembered, but he was as fit and agile as when they had first met.

Eric said: 'You're looking better than I've seen you in a long while.'

They ordered German beer and sat down to steak, potatoes and beans, with guavas and strawberries to follow. Douglas asked after Helen, said he was looking forward to meeting her, and wanted to know the local gossip. Eric told him about the two Englishmen who had been killed by a rhino, and Douglas was immediately reminded of the story of a young subaltern who had got himself killed by a tiger in India. His parents in England had wired the regimental colonel, asking that the coffin be sent home for burial. Some time later a large coffin arrived and they were horrified on opening it to find the body not of their son but of a tiger. They wired the colonel: 'Some mistake here tiger in coffin not James.' To which the colonel had replied: 'No mistake tiger in coffin James in tiger.'

Others in the restaurant overheard the story and laughed.

Eric beamed, and offered brief introductions. The tom-toms had begun: Douglas was famous now. *South Wind*, his pagan novel of manners set on an island based on Capri, had been a post-war hit, bringing him the acclaim and financial freedom he needed. News of his arrival would soon spread. This was not the first time Douglas had been to Africa, but he had, he said, already found things of new interest: the great baobab trees around Mombasa, marabout storks, snake-devouring secretary birds, boundless herds of gazelle, and giraffe that sauntered 'like ships in a breeze'.

After lunch they climbed into Eric's vehicle and headed the last fifty miles west to the boma where Eric lived, in Arusha. They were on a high plateau, around 4,000 feet, and the land was flat and expansive, with clumps of forest occasionally interrupting grassy plains. There was nothing like this, Douglas said, in all Europe. It was May and the rainy season, such as it was, was ending, though there was not much to choose between the seasons, being so close to the equator.

They passed enormous herds of game – of impala, buffalo, topi, sable, wildebeest, zebra, ostrich – and Douglas marvelled at the beauty of the Masai shepherd boys: dark, proud, leaning on their spears. Eric was glad to be the cicerone for a change, and he explained that since the end of the last century, when smallpox felled the native population and rinderpest killed off the cattle, the animals had reconquered the land, turning it into the world's greatest meat larder. There were no restrictions on killing any animal. Douglas asked Eric to give him his gun. Obediently, Eric took his pistol from his holster and handed it over. As the car bounced along, Douglas took aim at a flock of guinea fowl and let off a shot. The birds flew off, leaving one headless animal which they stopped to pick up.

'I hope you've got a decent cook,' Douglas said.

In the late afternoon they approached the coffee plantations and lines of sisal fibre, drying in the sun around Arusha like an open-air blond wig factory. They swept up a dusty track to the house, to be greeted by a houseboy who wanted to take the cases in from the back of the vehicle, though not before Douglas had insisted on being introduced to the lad. Helen came out on to the porch of their white wood bungalow to greet them. Stocky, with a plain but open face, grey eyes and light brown hair, she was, at thirty-one, four years older than Eric. There was a calm about her and she did not rush to greet their guest, though Eric knew she was nervous at meeting the man she had heard so much about.

'I have a present for you,' Douglas said, holding up the guinea fowl as he approached the porch steps.

'Thank you,' she said, a little flustered at the unexpected gift. She held out her free hand to shake his, and Douglas reciprocated the Germanic rectitude. 'Do I call you Uncle Norman?'

'Naturally,' he said. 'It goes with the privilege of marrying my favourite nephew.'

The fact that the cook had prepared an evening meal did not deter Douglas from insisting that they should have the guinea fowl instead, since it was fresh. Helen had gone to some trouble organising the marinated haunch of impala, but Uncle Norman was a guest. He was immediately at home, going into the kitchen to talk to the cook and make sure the bird was properly plucked, drawn and trussed. Luckily, prepared for all eventualities, he had some garlic in his jacket pocket.

After leaving full instructions with the cook, he took a shower and rested until it was time for Scotch and beer on the patio, prior to the sun's rapid departure, just after seven. The houseboy brought out a tray and, as the drinks were poured, Eric told Douglas that Helen was from Munich, hoping it would inspire a rapport.

'A Bavarian,' said Douglas. 'Things seem to be hotting up

there these days. I hope intolerance isn't going to come back into fashion.'

'And where are you from?' she asked politely.

'Originally, from Vorarlberg,'

'Ah, Austria, yes, of course I know it. It's not so far, on the Bodensee. But you are English?'

'Scottish. My grandfather, the fourteenth Laird of Tilquhillie, built a cotton mill at Bregenz. But I am one quarter German, through my mother's side: her mother was Scots, too, a daughter of the seventeenth Lord Forbes and Scotland's premier baron, but her father, Baron Ernst von Poelnitz, came from Schloss Frankenstein in Franconia.'

There was always an element of fiction about Douglas, Eric thought. There were so many aspects of his life, so many stories he told, that seemed too far-fetched. When he met somebody new, Eric often wondered if they were going to believe he was real, that he was telling the truth about himself and his adventures. But what else could he be, except the product of brave-hearted Scottish lairds and Frankenstein's castle? Helen ingested the information, and made no mention of her own humble origins as the daughter of a Munich merchant, nor was she encouraged to do so.

Summoned to supper, they went indoors, where the oppressive heat of the evening was dispersed by an electric ceiling fan. The guinea fowl was pronounced far too tough, but Douglas refused to take any blame, heaping it instead upon the cook for setting the oven temperature too high. Eric tried to soothe the situation with copious French wine he had managed to import, and after supper they took cognac and coffee out on to the porch, puffing their African tobacco in pipes to keep the midges away. Douglas proclaimed the coffee appalling.

'East Africa produces the best coffee in the world, but makes the worst. How do you put up with it?' he asked Helen.

She shrugged. 'You get used to it,' she said.

'Well, you shouldn't. It grows perfectly well. The best coffee I ever had was in Bludenz, d'you know it?'

'I haven't been there.'

'In the south of Vorarlberg. I once asked my hostess there how she roasted the beans. She said she puts them in the oven until they begin to sweat, when they are no lighter or darker than a Capuchin's frock, then she takes them out, piping hot, and puts them in a glass jar and immediately covers them in a thick layer of powdered sugar. As they slowly cool, they hold in all their flavour. "Isn't that how the English do it?" she said. Hah!'

'Well, I must try that,' said Helen.

In a short while she declared the mosquitoes were getting too much for her and she retired to bed, leaving the two men to listen to the wild sounds of the African night. They sat in contemplative silence for a while, Eric occasionally identifying the sounds. The brandy slipped away.

'I don't suppose you had any luck with jobs for me in Australia or South Africa,' Eric said.

'I have asked,' said Douglas, 'but I don't think it's on. What's wrong with Tanganyika anyway? It's wonderful here, much more dramatic than Europe.'

Eric said, 'It's the people. They're so narrow-minded, it's worse than Leigh-on-Sea. They're always gossiping and you can't get away. Everyone knows what everyone else is doing. I'm happy with Helen, but it was like a shotgun wedding: everyone knew all about us from the first night. The expatriate community is so small and you can't make friends with the natives: they are not encouraged to learn English. I would resign if there was anything else here I could do.'

'Oh, you're all right,' said Douglas dismissively. 'You're just restless, like everyone who went through the war.'

When hostilities ceased, Eric had tried to return to the Ministry of Pensions but he hated every minute of it. Violet, meanwhile, had followed a soldier to India. Percy and his mother had died in the flu epidemic at the end of the war. His father remained in Camden, working at Gilbey's.

It was true, though, that the war had left its scars. Eric had walked away from it with a Military Medal, but he had also brought home wounds that were nothing to do with the battle: he was still haunted by the image of himself as an educated pederast's working-class receptacle, a highly disturbing image he had not considered until the hospital visit in Amiens. Archie's damning rebuke continued to chill him all these years afterwards, even though whenever he met Douglas, he felt reassured that their friendship was above reproach. He had not mentioned his conversation with Archie, whom he had not met again, though he always asked after both of Douglas's sons.

'Robin's in America,' Douglas said. 'Archie keeps wandering off. I think he's in Germany.'

They sat up a long while, talking, and though Eric introduced Helen's name on several occasions, Douglas had nothing to say about her.

Over the following weeks Douglas set up a routine. He would rise early, around six o'clock, and be off for long walks, seeking out insects and reptiles, birds and butterflies that he had never seen before, sometimes returning at lunch-time, sometimes not coming back until the evening. He explored the volcanic slopes of Mount Mura, found flints in nearby caves, and spent hours among the natives in the market at Arusha, admiring the fruit and trying to converse with the stallholders in gesture and sound. There were 120 tribes in Tanganyika, according to Eric, and though most spoke Swahili, Douglas was not going to be there long enough to learn the words he wanted to use.

'Poor Uncle Norman hates not speaking the language,' Eric said one evening among a party of expatriates.

'I suppose,' said a local official, 'that it makes it more difficult for him to pick up native boys.'

Helen looked shocked.

'He's just joking,' Eric said.

That night in bed Helen asked Eric if Douglas really picked up boys. Eric had never lied to her before. He said: 'Of course not. I wouldn't have someone like that in our house.'

Every other night they went to a different household of expatriates and it was not long before Douglas had got to know most of the Europeans in the area. By and large they did not amuse him, except when he could shock them. He clearly was not one of them.

'Why do you walk everywhere?' one wanted to know.

'I thought most people in this country did,' Douglas replied.

Eating out meant driving to another white person's bungalow, where native cooks prepared a variety of dishes. Douglas was particularly fond of the curries, and he could not understand why the servants were not taught how to cook other things properly, but were left to 'serve up the same old things, and get up to their old tricks'. Eric could tell that Douglas was restless among the same people night after night. Sometimes he wondered if he wouldn't be happier, whatever the dangers, being out in the bush, just prowling around.

At weekends, or when Eric could take time off, they went on longer jaunts. They visited a friend on a distant coffee plantation who lived in roaring range of a well-known man-eating lion; they sat up through the night at another friend's house awaiting the return of a leopard that had clawed the houseboy; they went south to Dodoma, where tribes had gathered, and climbed aboard a railway inspection trolley, propelled by a pump-action lever, and were driven off into the countryside where, *en passant*, they slaughtered quantities of game with an armoury of weapons.

Douglas was intrigued by everything about the natives, and never ceased asking questions. He thought that the Masai were bored because the English had put a stop to their principal amusements of fighting and cattle stealing, and he was cheered to discover that the girls made their bangles from cut-down telegraph wires. At Dodoma a boy in post-circumcision costume and armed with a bow caught his eye and for a while, with Eric's help, he tried to engage him in conversation.

'Ask him,' he said to Eric, 'if he has a god.'

Eric hesitated. His Swahili was not fluent and he could not recall the word for 'god', so he described a supreme being. To Douglas's delight, the boy found the concept of an all-powerful divinity highly comical and he laughed, baring his perfect white teeth. In the end, though, the language defeated them, and Douglas said to Eric: 'I shouldn't have stayed with you and Helen. I should have hired a native guide from the start.'

On the way home they pulled off the road to sleep in the Jeep. Eric handed Douglas a nightcap from a flask and finally asked: 'What do you think of Helen?'

'Another vampire,' said Douglas. 'Don't leave any books lying about if you don't want them burned.'

Eric smiled grimly. There was no point in pursuing the subject. But he was disappointed they had not become better friends.

The day after their return, Douglas, as usual, went out for his morning walk, coming back at lunch-time to find Eric sitting in an armchair in the spacious lounge, reading the court reports in the local paper. An electric fan whirred overhead.

Eric looked up and smiled as he walked in. 'Did you know,' he said, 'that in Kikuyu law the penalty for biting off someone's ear is thirty goats?'

'Nanny or billy?'

'It doesn't say.'

Douglas stood before him with his hands in his jacket pockets. 'I've decided to go back to Europe this week,' he said.

'Really?' Eric was disappointed, but not too surprised.

'The truth is, I have taken a shine to your houseboy, and for the first time in my life, for your sake, dear Eric, I think I must exercise restraint: not something I wish to do for long, as you will appreciate. It has, after all, been nearly six weeks.'

Eric suddenly held up his hand and looked across at the bedroom. Helen had been resting since lunch. The door was ajar.

'Let's sit on the porch,' he said.

But the damage was done. That night in bed, Helen would not believe that this time anyone was joking. 'You did it, too, I know it. In Italy. When you were just a boy. I don't want him in this house. He is probably full of diseases.'

'No he isn't,' said Eric wearily.

'How do you know?'

Eric sighed. 'Because he is always very careful.'

He walked from the room, leaving her to her inconsolable tears. Half the night he sat on the porch, sinking Scotch, listening to the sounds of the jungle and thinking back to Italy when the sun shone and, because no one had said what they were doing was wrong, everything they did seemed perfectly right. Did the others feel like this? The hundreds of nieces and nephews whom Douglas had tutored and sent off into the world? What had happened to Annetta? Where were they all now?

He would drive Douglas to Moshi tomorrow morning. Helen's headache would be too bad: she would send her apologies for not seeing him off. Then he would come back and see if he had a marriage left.

CHAPTER 11

Antibes, 1939

The novelist watched the old man coming towards the café, tugged along by a small boy who gripped his right hand and led him through the morning market shoppers, just as a peasant child might drag an unwilling doctor or a reluctant priest from his home to comfort his sick mother six leagues away. The child wore a large straw hat against the sun and beneath it his brows were scowling and his dark eyes were concentrated in mulish determination. The reluctance of the old man, however, seemed part of a game and, besides, he was far too full of life to be a part of any fiction.

The novelist had originally planned a diversion to the Côte d'Azur to attend a small film festival that was to be inaugurated in Cannes. When the political climate forced the cancellation of the event, he decided to come anyway and make the most of a few weeks alone to finish a book that had been filling him with the usual doubts and causing some depression. Coming towards him now was the only certain tonic to dispel any misgivings and divert unnecessary introspection. Who was it who had described this towering figure as 'half Roman emperor, half Roman taxi driver'? They had it just right. The imperial profile, jutting and aquiline, rose from a suit most would consider too hot in July; others might notice the wayward threads around the collar and cuffs. Letters and papers sprouted from his pockets and he swung a stick purposefully, every few steps putting it down firmly on the cobblestones. The tie was in need of an iron and the shoes were down at heel, yet he walked with an aristocratic lightness, his white hair and eyebrows, yellowed by nicotine, were all animated as he chatted to the boy who continued to pull him along.

The pair approached the blue-striped umbrellas on the pavement outside the busy Chez Glacier, and they looked around to see who was there. The winter season this year had extended through the summer, and few shops were boarded up or hotels closed down. These out-of-season visitors included exiles and refugees, Jews and gypsies, communists and general dissenters escaping the fascist regimes to the east. Sometimes it was hard to get a table for so much as a coffee, and as the old man looked around to see if one were free, he found himself caught by the watchful emerald eyes of the Englishman, a tall, boyish figure in short-sleeved blue shirt and flannels.

'Good morning, Grr Grr,' the old man growled cheerfully.

'Good morning, Norman. *Bonjour*, Antoine.'

'*Bonjour, Monsieur Vert.*'

The novelist was halfway through a dry Martini and had been picking at a bowl of small black Provençal olives. A corner of the overseas news pages of *Le Matin* flapped in the light breeze like the fin of a beached mackerel. With a satisfied sigh, Douglas sat down beside him, placing his stick against the table. Without consulting the boy, he ordered coffee and two lemon ice-creams. The novelist picked up a brown paper parcel he had been guarding by his feet and put it down on the newspaper in front of him. 'I brought some books, including Huxley's latest. I thought you might be interested.'

'Oh, very good.' Douglas opened the book on the top of the pile and read through the preliminary pages. 'Not too much preaching this time, I hope. He always ruins it by bringing on a character to deliver a sermon.'

'I'm afraid I won't be able to catch your final appraisal, but if you have the time, do write and tell me what you think. I'm clearing out this afternoon on the Blue Train.'

Used to comings and goings, Douglas expressed no surprise, but of course it would be a loss. 'I'll miss our chats about books, about who's up and who's down.' He glanced at his companion. 'Antoine does not fulfil every need.'

The boy was sucking a cold metal ice-cream spoon and he looked up at the sound of his name, but said nothing. He was the landlady's son, and Douglas liked to have the boy with him in case he had one of his giddy spells.

'I'll miss them, too,' the novelist said.

'Will you fight?'

'Of course, if it comes to it.'

'It's long past time those two gangsters were exterminated. I was up at the border, at Castellar, yesterday. Scores of refugees are coming in. Half of them have nothing more than the clothes they stand up in. Do you realise how many are being done to death in prison camps in Italy and Germany? Building prisons has become a new industry. To hell with this Peace with Honour. Hitler and Mussolini need to be put on the spot, so we can all take our leisure undisturbed. Nothing ever comes at the right time, have you noticed that? Just when authors are broke and can least afford a paper shortage. Just when people think they're settled, it's all up with them. You have to burn your boats before He burns them for you.' He pointed skywards. 'He doesn't approve of people having a good time or getting ahead. He steals their money so they pray to him for help, and He makes them kill each other off now and then, so He can add to his collection of martyrs. That's why He makes these gangsters.'

'I have some hope for you, Norman, with all your superstitions. You complain about God too much to be a complete pagan.'

Douglas laughed and said, 'Believe what you like.' And he

took some snuff from a small box, put a pinch up each nostril, sneezed heartily into a large, freshly laundered handkerchief and changed the subject. 'Faith wrote from England a few days ago and told me they are selling *Brighton Rock* nightdresses in John Lewis's. Hah! Imagine the thousands of housewives from Surbiton climbing into bed thinking about your damned Pinkie every night!'

There was a genuine modesty in the novelist's grin. It was his turn to change the subject. 'What about you? What are you going to do? You can't go back to Italy.'

'Not to Florence. Ridiculous business. But I've had an offer of a villa on Capri from Bryher . . .' He raised a large, quizzical eyebrow. 'Sir John Ellerman's daughter?'

'Yes, yes, I know her poetry, but I have never met her. Isn't she married to the film writer, Macpherson?'

'He's a good man. They're both wonderful people, devout homosexuals. Never had a couple more in common, which of course is the undoing of the marriage. Anyway, they've had enough shambollocking about, and she's settling various of her father's millions on Macpherson, buying him the Villa Truoro in Capri on condition that I live out my life for free and for nothing in its annexe, which is very charming and sensible of her. If we ever see the light at the end of this tunnel and it turns out not to be the Blue Train approaching, you must come and visit: you'll find friends galore.'

'I can think of nothing more pleasant.' The novelist smiled and paused to reflect on the prospect. He had dreamed of Douglas the previous night. The old man had been in Florence where, like the Pied Piper, he was followed by a crowd of children, whom he was instructing by pointing his stick at the fine Renaissance monuments they passed. Each time he called out, '*Cinquecento!*' With increasing giggles the children all chorused back, '*Cinquecento!*' until he had merely to point to a façade for the boys and girls to shout out, '*Cinquecento*! *Cinquecento*!' Then the police arrived noisily, their flapping capes and black hats bursting out of small Fiats. 'Move away from him!' they shouted through megaphones. 'You're quite safe as long as the son-of-a-whore doesn't try to dandle you on his knee!'

The novelist had no wish to relay this dream to Douglas and he said, 'I'm sorry I didn't get any further with the film script of *South Wind*.'

'Oh, you did what you could: much better than I would have done. The film world seems even more precarious than publishing, and you know I don't expect miracles.'

'Everything useful and nothing indispensable; everything wonderful and nothing miraculous.'

'Hah! That's it.'

'What about you? What if there's war and Germany or Italy invades?'

'Oh, I'm not going anywhere. I've run out of countries. I'll sit here and get so fat I'll need six coffin bearers.'

'Are you writing any more?'

'Very little. I was seventy-one at the last Immaculate Conception. Hah! Now there's an event that might be miraculous if it happened every year – and it could explain why I'm just a recycled old cunt: it's in my stars. No, everything's slowed down. And I've always needed, you know . . .' He laid his right hand on his left biceps and made a fist of his left hand. 'A bit of that . . . a bit of passion to write. It's always been part of the process.'

An image of Dorothy Glover came into the novelist's mind, as it had done every time he had sat down to write his present book, of that first startling tingle when their forks clashed over a dish of onions at Rules in Covent Garden. He said, 'You dedicated *Looking Back* to "Eric". Was he your companion in *Old Calabria*?'

Douglas's thin lips stretched like elastic and he cast a steady gaze at the novelist. 'Eric was a wonderful boy. I couldn't keep him a complete secret. Besides, why should I? Sometimes I think I should have written him into the narrative, we had such fun. He deserves to be more famous than me. But Conrad was always telling me to excise characters from my books, and in those days I listened to him.'

'Whatever became of Eric?'

'I found him a job in the colonial service, and he married a Bavarian *Frau*. They've been living happily ever since in Bampopo land.'

'Do you still keep in touch?'

Douglas patted his pocket full of letters. 'Old habits . . .'

'It's a great responsibility,' Graham Greene said, 'being a writer.'

After Graham Greene left for London, Douglas watched others come and go. Among the new arrivals was his oldest son, Archie, who had given up on Munich and rented a flat in Vence, a hilltop town twelve miles inland from Antibes, 1,000 feet up, with views across undulating fertile tracts to the sea. He had been there more than a week before he contacted his father. When they did meet, Douglas was affable, and he began the civilities by asking after his daughter-in-law.

'I've left her,' Archie said with a note of defiance in the upper-crust Uppingham voice. He was forty now, nearly as tall as his father but slightly stooped, with thick-lensed glasses, a legacy of the mustard gas. It was in the middle of the afternoon and he was half full of brandy, half full of self-pity. 'I thought you did not approve of her.'

'Why should it matter if I approved of her or not? If I had worried about what my father would have approved of, I would probably now be an Austrian mill owner making dull grey uniforms for the German army. '

Archie looked down into his tumbler of brandy. 'I lie awake every night,' he said, 'wondering which bits I most regret inheriting.'

The conversation was heading for its usual collision point, and when, inevitably, Archie asked for money, Douglas simply emptied his pockets and handed over all that he had except for his bus fare back to Antibes.

The uneasy peace was a strange time. Not knowing what was going to happen next gave the present a carelessness and an urgency: parties had not stopped; people danced until dawn. It also presented moments of reflection, a chance to look around the past, like looking round empty rooms in a newly vacated house, checking that nothing had been missed. Among those forced to give serious consideration to their position were the Duke and Duchess of Windsor. When, on 3 September, news that Britain and France had declared war on Germany was brought to them by the pool of Le Croë, the château they had just rented in Cap d'Antibes, there was not much left to say and the duke dived into the pool. There was little he or anyone else on the Côte d'Azur could do about it, though many thought it their duty to have even more fun. France was the only civilised country in the world left to live in, and the best place to be was in the south. Carnations, roses and gladioli still brightened the markets; balconies in Antibes' old town were strewn with geraniums and washing waved airily in the bleaching sun. All along the Riviera, the familiar landscapes of purple Alp and sapphire sea, of olive and vine, lemon and fig, provided the bedrock of civilisation; here generous kitchens were infused with herbs and cooled by terracotta tiles, making cuisine the crucial element in the culture; and though barbarians were rattling the gates, the Riviera kept its spirits high. Sleek black Citroëns rumbled over the cobblestones, champagne had not run out and the funnels of snow-white yachts puffed idly in Port Vauban. It was also possible to live frugally, as most locals did, and as did Douglas and a contingent of artists who had come here specifically to do so, eating simply, unconcerned with fuel and lighting bills, freedoms that could never be claimed in colder climates.

But the war was on, and soon waiters hung up their aprons and went off to man the Maginot Line, while the hotels filled up with arrivals from Paris, as well as escapees who continued to make their way from Italy and Germany. Lectures were given on what to do in an air raid, blackouts began, and the British consul in Marseilles commandeered red-ensigned ships to evacuate the affluent who took as much luggage as they were able. Their staff were left to fend for themselves, and a number of them picked up the aprons discarded by the conscripted *garçons*. The Royal Navy called by to pick up the Windsors and take them to the Bahamas. Military units began to appear, and there were some English and American soldiers as well as lorry-loads of French. Newspapers were sold quickly, new arrivals scrutinised, rumours of spies proliferated and anti-Semitic graffiti appeared on walls. Douglas grew used to saying goodbye to friends, sure he would never see them again, and he settled into a last routine in the room that he rented from Antoine's mother, a friendly dressmaker in Place Macé, in the centre of the old town. From his second-floor window he could watch the world go by. 'Life more mundane than *mondaine*,' he wrote to Nancy Cunard in Paris.

At first there were no great shortages or hardships, though bureaucracy was tightened and travel became restricted; even visits to Menton or Nice required a *permis de circulation*, mail began to slow down, both inland and from abroad – there had been no news from Eric in East Africa since the outset – and money became an important topic. Fed up with all the talk of what might happen, Douglas decided he had better volunteer to do his bit, but he did not receive a reply from the British Consul in Cannes, with the suggested date of an appointment, until the New Year.

He needed a travel permit to make the short journey, and he took Antoine out of school for the jaunt on the motor-bus. His mother was pleased: the boy seemed to learn so much more on his outings with his Uncle Norman than he ever did sitting behind a desk at school. It was raining and miserably grey when they set off on the ride. To the right, inland, hilltop villages had given themselves up to the gloom; to the left, the Iles de Lérins were lost at sea. They wiped the condensation from the window to see what games they could play, and they counted sea horses, and established the difference between terns and seagulls. After twenty minutes, the bus slowed along Cannes' puddle-soaked Boulevard de Croisette where the palms shivered and rocked. It stopped beside the dripping memorial to Edward VIII just before the bleak and unlit municipal winter casino. As they stepped down on to the street Douglas, in a dark blue beret and turned-up jacket collar, extended a large black umbrella beneath which they made off up through the old town, across the Rue d'Antibes where shop lights shone gamely, and up the small Rue Maréchal Foch where the elegant town house of the consulate was guarded by a British soldier in a peaked cap that shaded a fine suntan. Douglas produced his passport and letter of appointment.

'What about the boy?' the soldier asked. 'Who's he?'

'He is my nephew,' Douglas said. 'He takes care of me.'

As they were about to enter the building, a woman emerged, a Frenchwoman, perhaps, wanting asylum or maybe married to an Englishman. She looked first at the douching skies, then at Douglas, with a glance that went straight through him, nailed firmly to a distant thought. She had the hauteur of a boutique owner, the indifference of a museum attendant and the posture of a catwalk *vendeuse*.

'*Vous aurez besoin d'un parapluie,*' Douglas said conversationally, making no effort to offer the protection of his umbrella.

She was hatless, but the collar of her white blouse was turned up, her dark hair was pulled tightly back over her wide cranium and her brown eyes gleamed. In response to Douglas's remark, her head flicked away, as if she would not talk to anybody to whom she had not been properly introduced.

'*Anglaise,*' Douglas said to Antoine, who was following the strides of her white tennis shoes that disappeared into the crowds of Rue d'Antibes.

Inside the consulate, they were led into a picture-lined hall to wait, and were left to find further diverting games to occupy a full thirty minutes. Other British citizens came and went, and there was a change of sentries. Finally, Douglas was summoned into a large drawing room, leaving Antoine sitting stoically outside, writing in a small notebook and ignoring anyone who looked at him. The consulate occupied a handsome villa, and the drawing room, which had become the main office, was grandly proportioned, stucco-ceilinged, chandeliered, and furnished not just with money and taste but with a whimsy that included some modern sculptures, Biot glassware, a lionskin rug and Indian tea caddies, as well as the obligatory vivid painting of the king and a map of Europe stuck with pins. The room was occupied by two civilians at mahogany desks, one more ornate than the other, and a major who had captured the high ground, standing with his back to the large French windows that gave out on to a verandah leading to unseen, drenched gardens below. Rain battered on the glass. The major, not a tall man, aged about thirty, looked the interviewee up and down as if he were on a parade ground inspection.

'Sorry to have kept you, Mr Douglas,' the civilian at the

larger of the two desks said, continuing to run his eyes over papers, sorting them, shuffling them, signing them, putting them into piles. 'Busy times.' He waved Douglas towards a chair in front of him. 'White – John White.' He indicated his colleagues: 'Mr Ian Woodford, Major Anthony David. I'm standing in for the consul, who is in Marseilles today, organising embarkations. We've told Somerset Maugham he can only take half a dozen servants, but he won't listen. There have been complaints about the lack of games decks. And of course they all want to take their motor cars. One chap pushed his Rolls-Royce into the harbour last week, said if he couldn't take it he was damned if he was going to leave it for the Bosch. What can we do for you?' He now looked up, an ordinary chap in his late thirties, wearing a suit; a civil servant, a perfectly decent human being, in charge, in control, incontestable.

'Absolutely nothing,' said Douglas, picking at his nails as if he were not quite sure himself why he was here. 'I came to find out if there was anything I could do for you.'

'Such as?'

'I may be old, but I am not yet gaga, which I assume is rather more helpful than being gaga and not yet old. I speak English, French, Italian, Russian, some Greek, and German, which was my first language. In the late nineties I was undersecretary at the British Embassy at St Petersburg, where I fraternised and made many contacts to some effect . . .'

A light tapping came from over by the window. The major was flicking his swagger stick against his left thigh.

White said, 'We know about you, Mr Douglas, and of course your books, which we have all enjoyed, but to be honest, I am not sure what help you could be. We are not certain ourselves what is going to happen here. For the moment we have been instructed to try to persuade all British people to go home.'

'I have just had to leave my home, in Florence.'

'To England.'

'In December?' He frowned. 'What could I do in England anyway? What I have to offer is a Mediterranean perspective, a slightly different point of view.'

'You mean, not a British point of view,' the major intervened. He was dark, with a clean, pinched face, and the creases in his uniform undoubtedly extended well below the skin. There was a menace in the way he played with his swagger stick, but perhaps, like so many in uniform, he was frustrated at not being able to get on with the job.

'Intelligence fails,' Douglas said, 'if it is not drawn from a broad kirk.'

'You are well known, Mr Douglas,' the major said. 'But you are not usually talked about in the context of churches.'

Douglas stared at the major and said, 'Ask the parishioners of Sorrento about my restoration work on the church of Sant' Agata.'

'Hard to do now,' said the major. 'Besides, the fabric is not the faith.'

'Did I mention my shooting skills?' Douglas said laconically. 'And my particular aptitude for taxidermy?'

White held up a hand and said in what were clearly meant to be conciliatory tones: 'I don't think you need worry about any previous difficulties, Mr Douglas, if you want to go back to England. Really, they're the least of our worries.'

Douglas suddenly had no idea what had possessed him to write to the consul in the first place, and he got up to leave.

'Can you tell us,' the major said as he rose, 'the name of your nephew who is sitting outside?'

Douglas straightened up to make himself several inches taller than the major. 'Antoine Laubreaux is my landlady's son. His address is 1 Place Macé, Antibes, the same as mine.'

CHAPTER 12

Antibes, 1940

It seemed as if this war was going to be the same as the last one for Douglas: once again he would be left to loaf through the hostilities, surviving on little more than what wits he had left. Friends and acquaintances, however, had other plans. As the Côte d'Azur drifted through the blackouts of winter into early spring, cheered with the annual golden crop of mimosa and lemons, they advised him to get away. The chances of sailing from Marseilles were diminishing daily, and berths were hard to find. Archie would have left earlier had cupid not placed in his path an American woman, whom his father treated with a politeness that only thinly disguised his disapproval. Robin, his younger son, whom he had not heard from since a row many years earlier, wrote from America suggesting his father should go to stay with him; Faith Mackenzie urged him to return to London, saying she was willing to provide an alibi should the warrant still be out for his arrest over that matter in the Natural History Museum; Nancy Cunard, with whom he had journeyed through Tunisia two years earlier, wrote from Paris, saying she thought that she might be able to get him out through Spain, where she had tirelessly given the Republican cause her support.

Their words fell on stony ground. Douglas still had energy, though his movements were restricted by the petty rules, and his scientific enquiries were limited by lack of access both to historic sites and to a decent library. When he could, he made sorties into the hills, to watch their flowers, inspect their minerals, look for fauna and find restaurants and cafés with authentic food. Most mornings he visited the market in the Cours Messina, and it was here on a halcyon day in the New Year that he recognised the young woman from the consulate in Cannes. In a cream cotton skirt and crisp blouse, a loose shantung jacket and white espadrilles, she might well have been French: she was certainly *mondaine*. Her dark hair fell to her neck and bounced around her striking face, and if she looked a little out of place among the women of Antibes who favoured black, so did he. A couple of shining lemons, a handful of loose potatoes and a clutch of eggs lay in her wicker basket and she was picking over a mound of dew-fresh sorrel.

'If you want some good, true French tarragon to go with that,' Douglas said in English, 'try Louise Barre's stall, the second to last on the right.'

She looked at him with quizzical, raw umber eyes. 'Tarragon?' Her county voice was low and breathy, but her enunciation would have been at home at Buckingham Palace.

If you're making a sorrel omelette, mix the tarragon and mustard in with the raw eggs first. Gives it a bite.'

'You are an expert on sorrel, are you?'

'I have lived on it.'

She smiled and nodded at this immense lunatic and went on her way. The following weekend Douglas saw her again when he and Antoine went for a mid-morning walk down to the port. She was strolling on the quayside with the major from the consulate in Cannes. There was an awkward familiarity between them, as if he were a friend of the family sent to keep an eye on her, and she had no desire to be chaperoned.

'How was the tarragon?' Douglas asked as they drew close.

The woman said, 'Sorrel is quite sufficient flavour for

omelettes.' She looked away, across the serried masts in the old port towards the Fort Carée.

'You have met?' the major asked in some surprise.

'We bumped into each other,' Douglas said. 'The Riviera is such a small place.'

'*C'est mon oncle*,' Antoine suddenly said to the major, tugging at Douglas's jacket. '*Il est grand comme j'ai dit.*'

The major smiled thinly. '*Bien sûr, Antoine, il est grand.*'

'You have met?' Douglas raised his eyebrows.

'*Il s'appelle Antoine comme moi,*' Antoine said.

'*Je ne connais personne,*' said the woman, who looked as if, had she been a jot less well bred, she might have yawned.

'This is Miss Gwynne,' The major, driven by courtesy, felt introductions were necessary. 'Miss Gwynne, Mr Norman Douglas and his companion, Antoine.'

Antoine looked up at the woman and smiled.

The woman said, '*Bonjour, Antoine.*' Then, frowning: 'Norman Douglas? Should I have read something you wrote?'

Douglas said, 'Most certainly not, my dear, you look far too young and impressionable. But if you will have lunch with me tomorrow, I will see if I can find a copy of something that may improve your mind.'

'That's rather insulting,' the major said.

'Only minds gripped by rule books or *rigor mortis* cannot be improved,' Douglas said breezily and, turning to the young woman, instructed: 'Bring me a book in return. My library is about to be requisitioned by the *Firenze fascisti*, who will use it as kindling; reading material is hard to come by these days.'

'Do you read French?' she asked.

'Provençal, if you like.'

'And where will we eat?' She looked suddenly defiant, rising to the challenge, lifting her head and lengthening her fine neck between the starched collars of her blouse.

The major said, 'I'm not sure that you should . . .'

'Do you know Giorgio's, up the first street there on the right?' He jabbed his stick into the air.

'I can find it.'

'One o'clock tomorrow.'

'One o'clock,' she said.

With a light nod, her neck still ennobled, she walked off, turning down to the quay where she stepped on to a gangplank laid on to the teak deck of a black ketch. On board, a thick-set, sunburnt man in dungarees was at work among rags and paraffin bottles and engine parts. He looked up as the boat swayed to Miss Gwynne's steps. She passed him without a word and disappeared into the aft deckhouse. The sailor glanced at the trio left on shore.

'Morning, Major!' His voice came from the rougher end of Bermondsey market. 'Lovely day for a cavalry charge, wot, wot!'

The major smiled tightly, turned on his heels and marched off.

'*Au revoir, oncle Antoine,*' Antoine called after him.

Douglas was amused to discover later that Major David had met Antoine twice: once when he had come around to the house shortly after their visit to Cannes, and another time in the street when he had bought the boy an ice-cream. His landlady confirmed it. The major had been charming, like so many Englishmen, and had asked about her lodger and his friends as she talked with him in the kitchen and served him an infusion of tisane.

The next day, Monday, was slow getting started. Douglas strolled alone through the market, where not all the stalls had opened and few flowers were being sold, arriving at Giorgio's promptly at one. There was still a choice of tables and there was no sign of Miss Gwynne. The day's menu was discussed with

Georgio, an unhurried, large man, who put up a stout defence when Douglas told him he should be ashamed of himself for putting fish on the menu on Monday. Then the old man settled down in the umbrella shade of the small, square luncheon table, unburdened his pockets of cigarettes, matches, snuffbox, pencil and book, put on his gold-rimmed spectacles and began to re-read with a critical eye a publication that he had written a dozen years earlier. Two cigarettes and half a jug of wine later Miss Gwynne arrived. She did not apologise and he did not complain.

'If you know what is good for you, you won't have the fish,' Douglas said as she sat down.

'I am well aware what is good for me, thank you, Mr Douglas.'

'No one under the age of thirty calls me Mr Douglas; they call me Norman.'

'I am Elizabeth to everyone older than my mother,' she said.

'Hah! And do you always know what is good for you, Lizzy?'

'Yes,' she said. Lizzy was not what most people called her, but he was clearly not the type to take much notice of what anyone said.

She had pushed her sunglasses up to look at the menu. She was twenty-six years old, and had a good figure. Her dark eyes were decisive, her dark hair shone. She had a strong face, the high cheekbones and deep forehead adding to a wilful air. She shook her head in reply to his first suggestions as to what she might eat.

Then he said, 'If you can bear to wait, we could try the macaroni. Georgio makes them with the right kind of flour and they are close to the authentic version, of lily-like candour, to be found in the best village *locande* in Italy.'

She smiled and looked up at him. 'I think I might enjoy reading your books.'

Douglas shut the small volume in front of him and pushed it across the white tablecloth. 'Here's one to start.'

'*Birds and Beasts of the Greek Anthology*,' she read, turning to the title page. 'It sounds rather grand. Will I understand it without a classical education?'

'Oh, it's very lightweight. Hi-deal for the hoi-polloi. You can dip in and out.'

Giorgio appeared and they ordered the macaroni, followed by *aïoli garni* for her, and for Douglas veal with *prosciutto*, fresh sage and tomato sauce. Giorgio brought him the raw meat to inspect. Douglas thought it barely worth cooking, and Giorgio said that, with the shortages, he was lucky to get any meat at all.

'And the sauce is fresh and the sage newly picked?' Douglas asked.

'Of course, and the *aïoli*. We are preparing it all now, Monsieur Douglas.'

'Break the leaves, don't cut them. And grate some of this on the top.'

Giorgio accepted the small lump of Parmesan Douglas took from his pocket as gratefully as he might accept a tip. Elizabeth smiled, then she dipped her hand in her basket and pulled out a rather tattered brown cloth volume of *The Gourmet's Guide to Europe* by Lieutenant-Colonel Newnham-Davis and Algernon Bastard, an original edition from 1903. She handed it across the table.

'Hah!' Douglas said. 'I haven't seen this for a while. Is it yours?'

'I borrowed it from the library at the consulate. You have three weeks.'

'Quite long enough. That's where we met, if you remember. You were coming out of the front door. I had an interview with that tight-arsed little major of yours. Is he a relation, or do you work for him?'

She smiled quickly and looked away. 'He wants to marry me,' she said.

Douglas was delighted by his *faux pas*. 'My dear, it's clearly not just the fish I have to warn you against.'

'Well, I'm not very good at taking advice,' she said, and sipped a good mouthful of white wine which she pushed around her mouth before swallowing. 'Everybody warned me against Charles and I don't know a soul who likes him.'

'Who is Charles?'

'The man I live with on the boat.'

'My dear, how can you possibly live on a boat? The world's unsteady enough without inviting further motion. Man was designed to have both feet on dry land, and the dryer the better, none of that boggy northern stuff that poses as countryside. Though I must say the last time I nearly drowned was in a motor car in the Chott Djerid in Tunisia. Have you tried Africa . . . ?'

Norman Douglas was not prying or censorious and Elizabeth Gwynne found that she liked his company very much. She had been to Cairo, she said, with her cousin a few years ago, and for the rest of the meal they talked about the food and the markets of the Middle East.

In the coming weeks, avoiding the confines of the boat and a relationship that was clearly not working out, she was frequently in his company. And though he voiced no opinion, when Douglas did meet Charles Cowan, it was evident that, like the rest of her friends, he was less than impressed. There was often little reason to pry among the expatriate community, for gossip made everyone's lives common property. Elizabeth and Charles had met at the Open Air Theatre in London's Regent's Park, towards the end of her brief attempt at an acting career. He was a chancer, and he didn't have a bean: it was obvious that Elizabeth, with family income, had paid for the boat. *Evelyn*

Hope had journeyed down from the River Hamble to the Riviera through the canals of France, arriving in Antibes for the winter in November. That the captain continued to live off his crew was no great matter for comment among the Riviera crowd, but the fact that he was a committed pacifist and frequently declared that if it came to a war he would certainly not fight, did not add to his popularity.

Douglas provided relief from the expatriate community whom, with her family connections, Elizabeth could count as her peers. She wanted to escape their petty preoccupations and their constant conversation about the unfolding events of the war. Instead of reading newspapers, she read books, and now she began reading *South Wind*, which she borrowed from the consulate's library. For his part, Douglas found in her a flattering audience, but though he knew most of the well-connected families of the day he did not place Elizabeth's until one morning over coffee in the Place Macé when they were talking about vegetable gardens and she mentioned the manor house in Sussex where she had grown up.

'It's that high forehead and slightly olive skin colour,' he said. 'Indonesian. Violet Gordon Woodhouse, she of the *ménage à cinq* – wasn't she a Gwynne?'

'I always thought *cinq* rather greedy,' said Elizabeth. 'Aunt Violet was my father's sister. I used to hate having to stay with her and all her old men.'

'She was very good on the harpsichord.'

'I don't like music much.'

'Never mind,' Douglas said. 'It's our imperfections that make us interesting.'

She talked of her aunt and her aunt's unusual and publicly acknowledged arrangement of a husband and four lovers. And she talked of the boarding-school she loathed in Tunbridge Wells, the fluent French that came from doing a course at the

Sorbonne and staying eighteen months in Paris with the Barettes where she encountered the Continental enthusiasm for food, and from whose home expeditions to the market stalls of Les Halles were undertaken up to three times a day.

'The Robertots were the greediest family I have ever met,' she said as they sat in the sun on a bench above one of the many small bays of the Cap d'Antibes. 'Madame once went on a diet that didn't last the first meal. When she saw what the rest of us were eating, she wept like a baby, so we felt we had to offer her some of our beef casserole, which she gobbled down.'

They had walked to this spot after lunching in Juan les Pins. The Cap provided perhaps the best vantage point on all the Riviera, with a view of the snowcapped Alpes Maritimes from Mont Mounier to the Baisse de St Véran, as sharp and warm as the blue of the bays. Elizabeth had not been there before and, full of a good lunch, she talked happily about the family in France, about her sisters, nursery food, her stage performances and her stint as a *vendeuse*, her passion for the town of Munich and her visits to Cairo and Malta, until the sun went down. Never had she talked for so long about herself.

Archie knew her. He was still in Vence and it was there that they met in a café by the fountain in the Place de Peyra just inside the gate to the concentric streets of the old Roman town. Archie had not actually been introduced to Elizabeth Gwynne before, but he had seen her among the Aryans and Amazons in the glittering cafés of Munich. His bottle-glass spectacles hid any glimmer of recognition, and she gave no sign that they might have run across each other before. Marion, his American paramour, was with him. She wore a straw cloche hat and floral frock, and her nervous and insistent talk suggested some desperation.

'I'm going to join up,' Archie said. The Norwegian army had

capitulated to Germany the previous week.

'They wouldn't have me,' Douglas said.

'We've talked it over,' said Marion, 'and I understand. Men seem to have to prove themselves sometimes.'

Douglas arched an eyebrow. 'To whom?'

'Well, not to me, obviously,' said Marion, laughing with a nervous trill in response to the threatening whiskers of her potential father-in-law and the withering silence of his young lady friend. 'He's already done that.'

'We've got a place on a ship leaving Marseilles next week,' Archie said. 'Why don't you come with us?'

'You're too old to need a chaperon.'

'Robin told me he wrote to you,' Archie said. 'Will you go to America?'

'That rambling lunatic asylum? You know I only go east or south.'

'You're determined to be the *Gauleiter* for the Côte d'Azur, aren't you?' Archie looked at Miss Gwynne as he pronounced the word in heavily Bavarian-accented German, but she was staring absently at a passing group of young French soldiers and seemed not to have heard.

Later, on the way home, Douglas said: 'I think he deliberately picks them to annoy me. If only he could see properly, they might at least be halfway attractive.'

Elizabeth said, 'Did you spend much time with your children when they were growing up?'

'It was difficult,' Douglas admitted. 'If there hadn't been so many money worries, so many writing pressures . . . But then, if my grandmother had had wheels, she would have been an omnibus.'

'Having children must be rather frightening,' she said. 'Like living your own ghastly childhood all over again.'

*

The day before Douglas went to see Archie and Marion off on a ship to England, Nancy Cunard arrived. Only there for a day, she joined Douglas for lunch, and was pleased to meet his new English friend. Nancy had come, she said, to make sure Norman was all right and to try to persuade him to leave. Taking little notice of his rebuttals, she gave him detailed instructions of how he might make his escape through her contacts in Barcelona, and she left a list of addresses and phone numbers. She herself had abandoned the Hours Press and her Normandy home and was heading for Latin America and the hospitality of one of her poets. Thin, white and weary, she conveyed an image of the faded flapper: a silk scarf was thrown about her throat, heavy African jewellery enslaved her wrists and her hair was flattened beneath a bandeau. Her thin mobile lips were dashed with bright red lipstick and her eyes, large, curious, hungry and usually dramatically framed in kohl, lurked behind dark glasses that failed to conceal a black eye.

'Picked up another bad one, eh?' Douglas said, chuckling. 'Don't ever learn, do you, Chawlie? That's what you get for do-gooding with the natives.' Douglas had begun to call her Charlie in various accents on their jaunt a couple of years earlier, to keep up their spirits when their car had come off the track and half sunk in a Tunisian lagoon.

She said, 'I notice, Norman darling, that however many new Arabic or Albanian words you consign to memory every day, however many improving books you read and however many scientific discoveries you make, your own life is not without repetition.'

'Hah! Perhaps it is, but I'll surprise you yet.'

'Of course you will. You do it again and again.'

'Where is your house in France?' Elizabeth asked. She felt an affinity towards this old friend of Douglas's, who could confront him head on, who could get knocked about by disastrous affairs and still have more social confidence than she would ever know.

'La Chapelle-Réanville in Normandy,' Nancy said, 'in the Seine Valley.'

'I lived in Paris with a family for a while,' said Elizabeth. 'They had a farmhouse in Normandy, in a village called Bieville in the Cotentin. There was always fresh butter sent up from there.'

'I hope nothing happens to it,' Nancy said. 'I don't have a lot of faith in the Maginot Line.'

The German army did not break through the Maginot Line: they went around it. On 10 May they walked into the Lowlands, and from there poured in through the top of France, heading for Paris. The road to the south coast was jammed with refugees escaping the advance, and all the accommodation along the Côte d'Azur was soon accounted for. The homeless began knocking on doors, food became short, and there was a new kind of cosmopolitan raggedness to the resorts. Endeavouring to ignore the commotion, and to stay out of any excitable debate, Douglas roamed around with sheaves of papers and books in his pockets as well as chunks of Parmesan, occasional pickings from the market and handfuls of herbs, which he would thrust at waiters to add to the increasingly tasteless dishes.

One day at the end of May, Douglas met Elizabeth Gwynne in the market and she said that the time had come for her to make an escape. Major David had already left to join his regiment in India, and she and Charles were getting ready to set sail for Italy and, she hoped, the Greek islands. Douglas immediately suggested a farewell lunch, for it was unlikely they would see each other again. He knew just the place, and the following Sunday they took a midday bus towards Nice,

Elizabeth in a wide straw hat, Douglas in a beret and carrying an old wool rug in case he felt like sitting down. Halfway to Nice they disembarked and began walking up the road to Grasse. In twenty minutes, a couple of laden donkeys had passed but only one black Citroën: petrol was getting expensive.

'How far is this place?' Elizabeth wanted to know, stopping to take a breath and inhaling the heady, cicada-whirring heat of the day.

'Only a couple of kilometres,' Douglas said, striding on.

'Espadrilles aren't made for hiking.' She stooped to pick a couple of deep violet tassel hyacinths to add to a clutch of campion and anemones already in her hand. 'We could have taken a taxi.'

'We wouldn't have had any money left for lunch. And we wouldn't have seen the flowers.' He put on his spectacles and examined her latest picking, brushing the fan of flowers at the top. 'These are infertile. The flowers underneath, dark blue with white teeth, they're the fertile ones. *Mascari comosum* is of the lily family, related to the Tyrolean fritillary which grew wild in our garden in Thüringen.'

Over the next kilometre he talked about the lily family, the garlics, dog's-tooth violet, alpine squill, and the poisonous meadow saffron, not to be confused with the saffron crocus of the iris family whose stamens produced the most expensive herb in the world. He was explaining the Arabs' love and use of saffron as they turned up a steep road through a wood of pungent umbrella pines. Here Douglas found a cone of nuts which he offered to Elizabeth for encouragement. In ten minutes the hilltop village of Villeneuve-Loubet appeared, its ancient streets deep shadows around a medieval castle. It was after one o'clock and the place was empty except for a couple of panting dogs.

'Up there,' Douglas said, pointing his stick, 'is where Auguste Escoffier was born.'

This piece of information revived Elizabeth. The culinary wizard of Monte Carlo and Mr Ritz's Savoy, who had died five years earlier, was probably the only chef English people knew by name. She suggested they knocked on the door of the house to see if it was inhabited by relatives or friends. Perhaps they could look at his kitchen, perhaps they would be offered lunch. They knocked but there was no reply. Cupping his hand against the reflection of the sun, Douglas looked in a couple of the windows, then urged her to do the same.

'The kitchen,' he said, 'must have looked like that when he was a baby.'

He helped her up on to a stone to peer in. The home was clearly lived in and it could not have changed much since Escoffier was born there at the end of the last century. Shelves were stacked with heavy pans and terracotta pots, herbs hung in hanks from the ceiling, tomatoes and onions were hooked up and a rusting wire basket was bright with fat eggs.

'It's a work of art,' she said, 'like a painter's studio. It has all the earth colours of a master's brush. It could have been painted by Vermeer or Zurbarán.' She climbed down, clapped her hands together to remove the dust and laughed dryly. 'If I said that to somebody in England, they would think I was mad. Half the time food is a taboo subject even at the dinner table. At home, when I was a child, we were never allowed into the kitchen except at Christmas, when we were permitted, under cook's watchful eye, to stir the Christmas pudding. Talking of which, I am famished. Where's this restaurant of yours?'

'Half a kilometre, the other side of town,' he replied.

'Oh, Norman, you are impossible. I'm dying for a drink.'

The restaurant they finally reached was shaded among pines on the edge of the village, a shabby establishment with just one table outside in the shade of a Judas tree, and half a dozen within. There was no view, four male diners ate in silence, and the only sound was from the cicadas. The smell from the pines was intense. Elizabeth slumped in one of the chairs outside and began to unlace her espadrilles so she could massage her sore feet.

'This had better be worthwhile,' she said.

'We won't know till we've tried it,' Douglas said, and he went into the darkness of the restaurant. She did not have the energy to go with him. When he returned, he was followed by the owner, a middle-aged, rotund woman who carried cool earthenware jugs of water and wine. Douglas had been entrusted with a plate of small black olives marinated in garlic and herbs.

'We're in luck,' he said to Elizabeth. 'She has a glass of wine by the stove, a sure sign of a sensitive and enthusiastic cook. She has stuffed cabbage today and I have made the presumption that we can also deal with a kilo. They make the wine themselves.'

She smiled and said, 'I could certainly deal with one.'

'Long life,' she said, raising her glass. The first sip of the cold red wine coursed through her veins and thrilled her with well-being.

'To Italy,' he said, 'and the Greek islands, but I warn you, you won't think too much of the food.'

She smiled. 'I hope to try out that recipe in your Greek anthology, the one for a saddle of boar.'

'Not a dish for every day,' he said, 'but then no dish should be.'

He went on to describe the best way to prepare the dish, to talk about the food of Greece and the food of France, and they pooled their knowledge of Auguste Escoffier, inventor of the Peach Melba and, Douglas liked to imagine, the verb to scoff. Meanwhile the meal arrived: the stuffed cabbage was authentic, as was the subsequent goat's cheese, and the fresh-made *crème brûlée* which the owner brought out with an unlabelled bottle of sweet muscatel. Elizabeth excused herself and went into the restaurant to the lavatory. While she was gone, Douglas remembered the book he had brought her: he took a green clothbound volume from his pocket, unscrewed the cap from his fountain pen, turned to the title page and wrote: '21 May 1940. N'. The ink had dried by the time she returned, and he closed the book and gave it to her.

'Something to remember me by,' he said.

'*Old Calabria*,' she read. 'Is it like *South Wind*?'

'No, it's a book about a journey, a travel book, if you like. Old-fashioned stuff. Heavy-going. I don't know whether you'll be able to get through it. But it has a great importance for me. It was a special journey, one in which I became particularly . . . involved.'

She read the inscription and said, 'I will read every word.'

'You should write a book, my dear.'

'Me?' she said, turning her head sharply away. 'Oh no, I have nothing to say.'

'Of course you have. Only people with strong points of view should write books. People who can bring rigorous enquiry to bear on any subject they choose, and not be afraid to say what they think, should help everyone else to a better understanding. But you must keep reading and learning. Everything needs to be put into an historical perspective. You have enchanted me with your enthusiasms: you could enchant and entertain the whole world. You should not be parsimonious with your gifts: they are to be shared.'

'What should I write about?'

He picked a fresh greengage from a small plate of fruit and cut a slice, which he handed to her on a fork. 'Things you are passionate about,' he said.

They talked on beyond the end of the lunch, finishing every scrap of food and wine they could find. Then they left the restaurant, congratulating the woman on her fine stuffed cabbage, and headed back down the hill. Douglas began to declaim: 'There was a young girl from Antibes . . .'

Elizabeth took it up: 'Who one night encountered a grebe . . .'

Douglas: 'He said, "If you're after a duck, you're quite out of luck . . ."'

Elizabeth: '"On the other hand, if you would like sexual intercourse, I'm your bird."'

Gusting with laughter, they turned into a field where, amid lavender and rosemary, among scrubby myrtle and dusty clumps of thyme and with a view of the sparkling Mediterranean more than a thousand feet below, they set out the rug and settled down beneath an olive tree, floating in the late afternoon heat. *Old Calabria* slipped from her bag on to the rocky ground, but neither could be bothered to pick it up. She rested an arm on his knee. They seemed the only two foreigners left on the coast.

Douglas said drowsily: 'Warm-blooded people know instinctively that peace and happiness begin, geographically, where garlic is used in cooking.'

'Anthony hates garlic. Can you imagine?'

'He isn't your type. He's a cold-blooded northerner, not warm-blooded like you and me.'

'He doesn't understand about going to the market every day. He thinks people should stock up with tins. But that's the army for you, I suppose: drinking and horses, Kipling and Wodehouse.' She sighed. 'Anyway, he has gone now, but perhaps I should have said yes. I never seem to fall for men with an income, which I sometimes think is what I need more than anything.'

'So you'll carry on with Charles.'

'We're going to give it one more go.'

'There's no point in it; it won't work.' Douglas put an arm around her shoulder and she slipped hers around his waist. 'Stay with me and see me out, my dear. When the time comes I would like to think of myself putrefying gracefully in your arms.'

'Dear Norman, you know I would love to stay. But I am committed.'

'Do as you please and send everybody to hell and take the consequences. Damned good rule in life.'

She smiled and not without effort leaned down and picked up *Old Calabria* and handed it to him. 'Write that in there,' she said, 'so I don't forget it.'

Laboriously, he took out his spectacles, produced the stub of a pencil and scribbled the missive in the back of the book.

'You must leave, too,' she said, looking at him with great seriousness.

'Where would I go?'

'I have a cousin in the embassy in Lisbon. You'll get a ship to England from there.'

'I haven't been to England for twenty-five years.'

'It's the best way out for you. I'll write to him before I leave.'

'We won't meet again. I had hoped to be buried on Capri, but now I'll probably end up next to that little shit David Lawrence at the cemetery in Vence. Hah! Life's ironies.'

'You're going to live to be a hundred.' She kissed him on the cheek, let her sleepy head rest on his breast, and put a hand on his knee.

He enclosed her hand with his, shifted himself awkwardly and inhaled the sweet herbs of the hills, the aroma of the south. 'I do believe,' he said with a sigh, 'that I could write another book.'

Elizabeth Gwynne and Charles Cowan sailed away three weeks before the Italians, encouraged by the fall of Paris, declared war on Britain and France. Alarmingly, if half-heartedly, troops crossed the border and for four days occupied Menton and Sospel. An armistice halted the German advance around Lyons, after which Marshal Philippe Pétain, a Provençal farmer, governed unoccupied southern France from Vichy, giving Champagne, Burgundy and the Loire to the Germans, and leaving Bordeaux and the Côte du Rhône to Vichy France. New laws were brought in by this regime: two-piece bathing costumes were banned, and women were forbidden to smoke in the streets.

News on the French radio was suspected of being censored, and the residents on the Côte d'Azur preferred to rely on the BBC, but the postal system, bringing what Douglas called 'real news' from abroad, was disrupted, and letters were reduced to a trickle. There was no word from Eric in Tanganyika. By September, when the Blitz was starting in London, a brief note from Archie arrived to say he had failed his army medical because of poor eyesight and he was now living in Scotland with Marion who was pregnant. Food became scarcer and scarcer. In October, new laws in Britain allowed no more than £10 a month to be sent to British citizens abroad. One package did get through, though not without being opened and scrutinised by the Customs, and it arrived bodged up with string and tape. There was a brief note inside the cover of a new novel, *The Power and the Glory*: 'Nothing miraculous . . . See you in Capri – Grr Grr.'

In December, with extreme reluctance, Douglas had to admit that his time in Antibes was up, and boats once more would have to be burned. He procured a visa for Spain and Portugal and applied for an exit visa from France. Just before he left, in January 1941, a long, breathless and barely punctuated letter arrived from Elizabeth Gwynne in Athens. *Evelyn Hope* had been confiscated in Sicily the day Italy declared war, and they had been deported on an absolutely frightful journey via Venice and Yugoslavia, which involved many days of incarceration and hunger. What she hoped to do now was find a small island to hide away on until the whole boring shooting match was over.

In a last letter, Douglas replied that the food really had become too appalling, and that he was looking forward to meeting Elizabeth's cousin. The morning he left Antibes, the BBC broadcast the news that the Germans had occupied Capri. He said goodbye to his landlady and to Antoine, climbed into a black Citroën taxi and headed for the station, where he would start his train journey to Lisbon, via Barcelona and Madrid.

It was dreadful to think that he might have to live in London again.

Part Two

MRS DAVID

CHAPTER 13

Eastbourne, 1985

'You'd better light it, Max, we can't wait for John. Molly, I'm going to cook now! Isabel, tell your mother, I don't think she heard.'

'Mum, Dad says he's going to start cooking.'

'Can I light it, Uncle Max?'

''Course you can, Jack. Here, I help you up.'

'What are you doing, Uncle Max? You know he's a pyromaniac.'

'Oh, Mum, you're not going on about that again, are you?'

'The boy's just curious. And if nobody had been curious fire would never have been discovered and we wouldn't be here today enjoying a barbecue. . .'

'And looking at the empty space where the shed used to be.'

'We needed a new one. Anyway, the insurance paid up.'

'Aaah! Christopher, you beast. I'm drenched.'

'I was aiming at Jack.'

'Hey, Christopher, have we got enough chairs out.'

'Yeah, I reckon we're twelve. Isabel, is Lucy still watching television?'

'I suppose so.'

'Ask her to let me know when Tina Turner comes on.'

'Count me in on that.'

'She's too old for you, Dad.'

'You think so? Maybe you're right. Anyway I've told Pauline

to pledge twenty-five pounds for me. I know what it's like to be hungry.'

'Pauline, we're three forks short.'

'What are you cooking, Grandad?'

'Tuna steaks. Didn't I tell you? Your Uncle John got them for us yesterday. Here, Max, look at these. *E un bellissimo tonno*, isn't it?

'*Sì, molto bello, Angelo*. Where is little John?'

'Probably sleeping off his Saturday night out, as usual.'

'You can't blame him. Sunday's the only day he gets off.'

'He's lucky to get a day off. People don't know these days.'

'Mum, do you want a hand in the kitchen?'

'Someone bring a tray out. Lucy, ask your father if he's got the bread knife.'

'Dad, have you got the bread knife?'

'Who wants to know?'

'Mum.'

'Here, Peter, take your grandmother the bread knife.'

'Dad, don't give him a bread knife like that. Peter, don't run with a knife!'

'We got some potato salad to go with this. And some nice lettuce salad, too. I made the mayonnaise myself.'

'Emily, look where you're going, sweetheart.'

'I don't like fish, Mum.'

'This isn't real fish, it's tuna, the hamburger of the sea.'

'Don't forget the dill, Max.'

'I got it here. I need to wait a minute till the flames die down before I put it on.'

Family lunch at the Barnet home of Angelo and Molly Dorelli was the same most Sundays. Sometimes neighbours were involved and friends might drop by, too, and they would all cram into the back room of the three-storey Victorian house around a long table on an assortment of chairs, with an assortment of cutlery, crockery and glasses. In summer, whenever they could, they carried the table outside and turned their narrow semi-detached garden into an alfresco event, where a barbecue would smoke away, children could bike about or play with balls, and the fresh air helped down unstinting quantities of home-made white wine, which was ritually pressed in an old bath in the garage each October. Making wine like this, said Angelo, was a typical southern Italian thing to do, though his contemporaries in Italy had long since given up such a chore and had been buying their wine from supermarkets for years.

Even at the age of sixty-three Angelo remained a tall and upright figure, and his grey eyes were bright: he refused to accept that he needed glasses. After living in London for more than thirty years, his accent was still strong. His wife Molly was a Londoner, born to Irish parents less than half a dozen miles away. She was plump as a pudding, most of her long, grey-flecked brown hair was caught up in a large tortoiseshell comb and, except when shopping and on Sundays, she wore a floral house-coat and slippers. She smoked with a passion, laughed easily and had the even temper of someone with a healthy, slow-pumping heart. Most of the world passed her by and she had been content to bear and bring up the five children who had become her life. There were three boys and two girls, and they in turn had progeny, so that anyone walking in on a Sunday lunch would not be expected to remember who they all were, even after Angelo had proudly introduced them. The oldest was Lucy, married to Brian, mother of Peter, Jack and little Zoë. Two boys came next: Tony lived in Swindon with his wife Sandy and two daughters, and he phoned on Sundays if he couldn't get home; Christopher was married to Pauline and they had a son called James and a daughter, Emily, and now Pauline was six months pregnant. Angelo hoped, were it to be a girl, his grand-daughter would be called Diana, after the enchanting young Princess of Wales. If a boy, he suggested that he might be called David or Daniel or Donald. Names were a constant subject of mealtime conversation.

Isabel, aged twenty-five, was not married and was the only one of the children still to live in the four-bedroom home where they had all grown up wanting nothing except a little breathing space. John, the youngest, was twenty-three, and rented a flat with two friends in Camden, north London, not far from the family's wet fish shop where he worked. His father and his father's oldest friend, Massimo – Uncle Max – wiry, with a grey moustache and exuberant nasal hair, also owned Dorelli's restaurant nearby. That was the full extent of the Dorelli family.

It was not until the meal was nearly over and several places at the table had been vacated by those wishing to go indoors to watch the Live Aid concert that John, the youngest son, finally arrived. He was six feet tall and big-featured, with a full head of brown hair, strong hands, full lips and a nose large enough to feel comfortable inside a brandy balloon. On his left cheek he had a distinctive birthmark the size of a kidney bean, and he had long since been nicknamed John Dory, after the fish that had a similar blemish on its cheeks, and also because of his occupation and his own surname. He arrived with an old friend, Nick Dimitriou, a food importer who had come to know the family through the business. As the two older Dorelli sons had each married in turn, he had moved his friendship down the ladder until he had reached John, the only bachelor left, and half a dozen years separated them.

John's mother, who had begun clearing away the plates, greeted them both with kisses on the cheeks. Nick commented on how pretty her housecoat was, and she said there was still sufficient lunch for them both. The tuna could go under the grill, she said: it wouldn't take five minutes. Before sitting at a vacated chair next to his father, John kissed other cheeks, touched arms and backs, gave his brother Christopher a playful slap and roughed his nephews' hair.

'How was the tuna, anyway?' he asked his father, picking up a scrap of bread and throwing it at Jack.

'Not as good as the *tonno* from Sicily.'

'Dad, when you were a boy I bet even barnacles tasted good.'

'That's what people were eating in the war,' said Uncle Max. 'Before that, all the fish was good. The fish soups had so many kinds, so many colours . . .'

'And so many bones,' John said.

'That was half the fun,' said Angelo. 'Here, have some wine.' John held up a hand. 'Not for me.'

He poured it anyway, and some for Nick, too. 'You can't eat tuna without wine.'

'Dad, lots of people eat tuna without wine. It doesn't kill them.'

'I didn't have any wine,' Pauline pointed out.

'Of course not, you're pregnant; you have to look after the baby. Every house needs a baby and we don't have one at the moment. You must be careful.'

Molly produced plates of salad, said, 'The fish won't be a minute', and returned at once to the kitchen.

'You had a good time last night?' Angelo asked his son, raising a bushy eyebrow.

'Great,' John said, conscious that his London accent was deep and rough from his nocturnal excesses.

'Why don't you ever bring your girls here for us to meet?'

'There aren't any girls,' Christopher said. 'They're all blokes. That's why we never see them.'

'I'm not a poof, you fucker,' said John, flicking a lettuce leaf at him.

'Don't use that language in this house,' his father said sharply.

'Well, I don't like to be called a poof.'

'Christopher, it's true,' said Angelo, 'you mustn't call your brother that. It's a terrible accusation. But also, I won't have bad language of any sort, especially on a Sunday.'

When Molly came out with the tuna, she said, 'Tony called. They're coming next weekend.'

John said, 'I won't be here.'

'Where are you going?' his father asked suspiciously.

John explained that he and Nick were going to Eastbourne where Nick had taken up a short cookery course, and had found a girl he liked. Angelo said he wanted to meet her and told Nick to bring her to the house for dinner soon.

'Oh no, you get me into too much trouble,' said Nick. 'You muddle up their names.'

'Hah! You make enough trouble on your own. Besides, you are growing bald: it's time you settled down.'

'I'll settle down when John settles down, when there will be no more Dorellis to go out and play with.'

'So you won't be here next weekend then? That's a pity, I was thinking of making a pavlova.'

An enormous crash came from the house.

'Christ,' said Christopher, 'I hope that's not one of ours.'

Angelo said, 'Don't worry. It's just the noise children make.'

It was the last Sunday in July when John and Nick drove down to Eastbourne. The schools were out; the grass was fresh; corn was ripening; and the blue sky billowed with bright scudding clouds. Small excitable waves played on the green sea; flags and empty deckchairs flapped in the breeze; and the ice-cream business flourished, though not along the sea front, since William Cavendish, seventh Duke of Devonshire and founder of the south coast resort, had decreed that no commercial premises should sully the view of the town from the sea and, more than a hundred years later, the wish was still respected.

Traffic on the journey down from town had been heavy and they were late. With Nick, in wraparound sunglasses, confidently at the wheel, and John in charge of the music, the BMW swooped down from Beachy Head, drove along the sea front past the pier, then turned in towards the old town. A few minutes later they stopped in the middle of a side street and Nick hooted. His girlfriend, John knew by now, was called Joely, and when the front door opened and two young women stepped out, he immediately identified which one was Nick's. They were always skinny blondes with a penchant for shiny shoes, aspirational jewellery and bright lipstick. They were also cheerful, often to the point of boisterousness. This blonde had her hair cut short, and though she wore lipstick, her face was pale. She was wearing a white T-shirt, short black skirt and dark tights that were rooted in a pair of black Doc Martens. Her companion was a complete contrast. Celtic-looking, dark-haired, with dark eyes, fine cheekbones and a high forehead, she was dressed conservatively in a plain white blouse, long plain cotton skirt and sneakers. She carried an old-fashioned picnic hamper.

Nick got out of the car to open the boot, kissing the blonde lightly on her extravagantly outstretched lips. As well as the picnic hamper, they had brought a coolbag and a couple of bulging plastic bags through one of which poked a sharp knife. A rug and a couple of books were also tossed into the boot, where a coolbox of wine had travelled down from London. Nick opened a rear door and Joely was the first to climb in.

'I'm Joely,' she said to John, 'and this is my flatmate, Cherry.'

'I'm John,' John said in his gravelly Sunday voice and he half turned towards them, out of politeness and to see if he fancied Cherry. She looked confident, elegant, a bit remote, a little severe. His dad would have thought her classy.

'We know,' Joely said. 'Nick told me on the phone. He said you were Italian and unattached.'

'Do I sound Italian? Do I look unattached?'

'Definitely. John, meet Cherry, who's English and un-attached.'

'Joely!' Cherry reprimanded crisply. She looked delightfully embarrassed and John turned away, smiling.

'The others have gone on ahead,' Joely said.

'How many are there?' Nick asked.

'Oh, about five thousand.'

'You should have brought some fish,' Nick said to John.

'Do you believe in miracles?' Joely asked John.

'Absolutely,' John said.

Joely gave Nick directions and they headed around Beachy Head, through the Cuckmere Valley to the small village of Wilmington tucked beneath the South Downs. Kites and hang-gliders brightened the sky. Even before they reached it, they saw the giant graffito of the Long Man of Wilmington. They parked next to the old Priory, gathered the constituent parts of the lunch and began walking up the hill towards the Long Man, a vast, priapic chalk figure cut into the hillside. From way above, a group of about twenty people began to wave and shout, and before long they had joined them, spreading their rug on the clover-flowered grass, and laying out the meal. Although Cherry and Joely knew most of the group well, they kept to their patch, beside Nick and John. Bees buzzed, Meadow Brown butterflies chased high and low, and Cherry took off her shoes and pulled her skirt above her knees so that her slender legs could catch the sun. Two girls had stripped down to their bras, several boys had taken off their T-shirts, but Nick and John, overdressed townies in proper shirts, kept buttoned up. John started to make a daisy chain as Joely handed around the goose gizzard and spinach-leaf salad, and the sliced duck breasts with mango. Nick uncorked the first bottle of Pinot Grigio.

One of the shirtless students produced a flute and began to

play. The folk songs were sporadic but tuneful, the words picked up here and there around the party. They were a mixed bunch and covered a wide age range, and though most were in their late teens and early twenties, Nick was not the oldest. 'What's he up to?' he said as he drained his glass for the first time. He nodded towards a figure who had appeared in the corner of the field; a young man who was standing quite still with a hooded falcon perched on his leather gauntlet. They all turned to look and wondered if the bird was about to fly. For a while they stared at the figures, which remained motionless, and in the end they looked away and continued to pick at the imaginative dishes that were scooped from plastic boxes, bags and jars.

Ten minutes later, John heard a distant tweeting and he looked up to see four or five skylarks, hardly larger than flies, careening in their unsteady flight. He glanced across to the hawker. Cherry was already watching him. In his hands was the leather hood. The bird was gone. In the sky, high above, the falcon was reaching the apex of its flight, its beating wings audible now that they had all stopped talking and had begun to watch. If the skylarks heard their predator, they did not show it, continuing on their erratic course like school-children too busy talking to walk in straight lines. The falcon hung for a moment in mid-air, then it fell like a stone with all speed and accuracy, snatching one of the small songbirds on the wing and taking it out of sight behind the brow of the Downs. There was a silence. The other skylarks carried on with no more noise, their unsteady course looking now more like panic than abstract wandering. The picnickers, too, had fallen silent. They watched the hawker turn and climb unhurriedly over a fence to follow after the falcon. The flautist took up his instrument and played a few melancholy bars of 'A Lark Ascending'.

'Perfect,' Cherry said. 'A perfect kill.'

'Nature in the raw,' Nick said.

Joely said, 'Poor little birdie.'

John said, 'It was so quick, I don't suppose it felt anything.'

John wrapped the small daisy chain about Cherry's left ankle, linking the last stem, and finding unexpected pleasure when his fingers brushed her smooth skin. After the meat and salad, the cottage cheese and cucumber, the lemon sorbet from a vacuum flask, the goat's cheese, grapes, wine and coffee, there was a suggestion of a walk, which was greeted by groans. The flautist was playing 'Greensleeves'. The sun encouraged sleep.

Joely said to Nick, 'Let's go and see the butterflies.'

'What butterflies?' John asked.

'We'll show you,' Cherry said.

They walked back down the hill, Cherry barefoot and daisy-chained, carrying the picnic gear, which they packed away in the car. Beyond the car park, behind the Priory, was the Priory church where a vast and ancient yew was held up by chains and poles. Joely pushed back the creaking porch door and they inhaled the musty interior. It was a simple, unprepossessing space out of time. In a small alcove on the north wall was the font, and above it a stained-glass window richly decorated with exquisite butterflies of the deepest lapis, vermilion, emerald and sun yellow. John was enchanted by them, and he studied them carefully, trying to remember their names. Cherry gave several of them the different local names that they were called in her home county of Hereford.

Outside, Joely said, 'To the woods, to the woods', and she and Nick set the pace, following a sign that said 'Folkington 1 mile', and a path that led through dappled beechwoods. Collared doves cooed and flapped away. John asked Cherry if she was a country girl and she said that she came from Ross-on-Wye, near the Welsh border. And they talked about themselves. Cherry told him how, after some false career starts in London, she had thought she might try her hand at catering, which was why she had gone on this course in Eastbourne, where she had met Joely. John told her of the family fish business, and she took a serious professional interest. She liked dancing, she said, and she had a collection of fifties dresses. He replied that his father liked dancing, which had put him off: his father was Italian, but he himself did not speak the language. Italy was the country she most wanted to visit.

There was something heady in the summer air, pungent with ripened nature and a good lunch, and when the backs of their hands accidentally touched, John felt butterflies fluttering in his stomach. He thought she felt it, too, and when he looked at her, she gave a quick smile.

They lost sight of Joely and Nick long before they reached Folkington, but as they neared the end of the path, the couple emerged from the woods, red-faced and dishevelled, with a loud 'Boo!'. John and Cherry were not at all surprised. The path emerged by the church at Folkington, a small community tucked at the foot of the Downs at the end of a lane, and without any commercial premises: just the church, a few houses and an unending flint wall enclosing an unseen estate.

'Someone told me Elizabeth David's family owned the manor house here,' Joely said.

'The cookery writer?' Nick said, impressed. 'Is she still alive?'

Nobody knew. John said he had her book on bread and yeast. Joely said her mother had several cookbooks by her. Nick said he had her *Mediterranean Food*.

'My mother's got an old copy of *Mediterranean Food*,' Cherry said. 'It's signed.'

'You never told me.' It was Joely's turn to be impressed. 'How did she get that?'

'Oh, it was when she worked in a hotel. Elizabeth David was just a guest.'

'What was she like? Did you meet her?'

'It was before I was born. Mum says she was nice and polite, as you'd expect. But I wouldn't know her if I saw her.'

An old woman was coming towards them, walking a black labrador.

'Do you think that's her?' John whispered.

'Ask her,' said Cherry.

'Excuse me,' said John as the woman drew near. 'Are you Elizabeth David?'

'Of course I'm not,' the woman said, passing briskly by.

The four of them scuttled off, chuckling, into the church. There were no more butterflies; its windows were unadorned. They looked for a plaque or a tombstone that might belong to Elizabeth or any other David and Nick said that as far as he could see, the only evidence that the cookery writer had ever existed at all was that Cherry's mother had seen her. Joely dragged him out to the graveyard for further research, leaving John and Cherry reading the tablets on the wall, pronouncing the names of Scots who had come down from Fifeshire, and noting a memorial to Violet Gordon Woodhouse, a harpsichord and clavichord player whose 'genius for music' had revealed hidden beauty. John read the inscription out loud, as Cherry had not brought her glasses, and they guessed that she must have been a pillar of the church. Sunlight shone through clear windows and warmed her dark hair, and when she turned to speak, it glinted on her eyes and chased across her lips. She smelt of fresh air and cucumber.

John said, 'Have you ever been kissed in a church before?'

She shook her head. So they kissed and the butterflies took wing.

*

From that first, effortless kiss, Cherry became part of John's life, and he often whistled as he worked. His parents would have been delighted to meet his new girlfriend, but for several months he did not take her home, not wanting to raise their hopes falsely, not wanting to put her off, not wanting to share her too soon. At the end of the summer, she went on holiday with Joely and he missed her. In her absence he did not console himself, as Nick did, with someone else, and when he pushed the food around his plate at Sunday lunch at home, there was speculation that this might be true love.

It was not until late autumn, when Cherry had finished her course and her holiday and moved into a shared flat with friends in south London that they finally went together to a Dorelli Sunday lunch. Cherry had never seen such a gathering. Members of the family, of all sizes and ages, were milling around the kitchen and back room; conversations were layered on conversations; questions were asked without waiting for replies; children darted in and out.

John introduced her to his mother, who shook her hand warmly and said, 'So pleased to meet you.' His brothers grinned at her, his sisters kissed her on the cheek and the children said, 'Are you Uncle John's girlfriend?' She said, 'Yes.' Unused to the easy familiarity of large families, Cherry felt touched. Molly refused her offers to help with the lunch and Angelo, the proud father, invited her to sit next to him at the head of the table where he filled her glass with his potent, greenish brew and demanded to know what they taught on her cookery course.

Molly did not sit down. Throughout the entire lunch she was on her feet, making sure everyone had what they wanted to eat and drink. Cherry knew no other Italians, but imagined that Molly had learned to behave like an Italian wife, which she found both endearing and deplorable. What was without doubt completely acceptable, however, was the food that Molly produced: *lasagne al forno*, salad with a mix of red and green salad leaves in oil and wine vinegar, followed by treacle pudding.

'Your mother cooks?' Angelo asked when Cherry expressed enthusiasm for the meal.

'Yes, she's a good cook.'

'You have a big family like this?'

'Nobody has a big family like this,' Christopher said with a grimace.

Christopher had John's features, though not his height, and Cherry felt that had he lived closer, they would have seen much more of him. Her only sibling, she explained to Angelo, was a step-brother in South Africa, whom she hardly remembered. Her father, a saddlemaker, had died the previous year, but her mother was one of six children, so she was not deprived of relations.

'It doesn't take much to make a big family,' Angelo said, grinning and showing gold fillings in his back teeth.

Over coffee and a little brandy Cherry said, 'John says you are from Naples, Mr Dorelli.' The table was emptying. The children were off out in the garden, though it was grey and overcast. There were cries and shouts and muddied knees and a little blood.

'Yes, from Naples,' said Angelo, offering cigars, which John declined but Cherry, to his delight, accepted. 'That was a long time ago.'

'What brought you to England?'

'My father was English, but he died just after I was born.' He waved a hand towards a picture of a young couple high on the bookshelf, in an ornate silver frame among a clutter of souvenirs.

'They look very young,' said Cherry who could not quite focus on them without her glasses.

Angelo nodded seriously. 'And very much in love. But I don't remember my father. He died of tuberculosis. He met my mother when he was visiting the San Carlo opera house. He was a violinist.'

Molly put a plate of sliced fruit in front of them. John had turned away and was looking out of the window at the children. Angelo sighed. If he were slightly tipsy from the meal, Cherry would not have guessed.

'The rest of my family died in the war,' he went on. 'I didn't want to stay in Naples after that. I had to go somewhere. My father had an uncle in London, and I found his address, Albany Mansions, in Battersea. That was where he lived.' He pronounced Albany Mansions as if it were a palace to be respected. 'But of course, I didn't speak a word of English, and I still had my mother's family name, Dorelli, because they did not have time to be properly married before my father died.'

John had been tugged off his chair and out into the garden to play with the children in the garden. Molly had begun washing up. Max went out to help her.

'Did you find him?' Cherry asked. 'Your father's uncle?'

'No. We went there, but there was nobody in Albany Mansions of that name. It was a big, exclusive-looking place.'

'You didn't try to look for him after that?'

'We didn't know where to look. But I read about him later, when he died. It turned out he was a famous writer. Well, not very famous. Nobody ever heard of him now.'

'What was his name?'

'Douglas. Norman Douglas.'

'No, I have never heard of him,' she said. 'I'm surprised John doesn't speak Italian.'

'Tony, our eldest boy, he speaks it a little. But our home is here now.'

Cherry looked out of the window. It had started to rain, but no one outside was taking any notice. The cigar smoke was thick and the windows were misting up as steam drifted in from the washing-up water in the kitchen along with occasional flutters of Molly's laughter. Among the figures racing around the garden, Cherry could barely make out which was John's: the world was closing in. It seemed so comfortable here. The room, the house, were not elegant or tasteful: there was no obvious attention towards comfort or style and it was all the friendlier for that. She thought she could get used to coming here.

She said to Angelo, 'You must miss sunny Italy.'

'Not for one moment,' he said. 'I want to be where my family is, and my family is here.'

He picked up the brandy bottle and topped up her tumbler.

'Here's to rainy days,' she said, raising the glass.

'Hah! Oh yes, I love grey, wet England.' He filled his own glass and shook his head emotionally. 'John is a good boy.'

'Yes,' she said, 'he is a good boy.'

He clinked his glass against hers and smiled. 'Here's to rainy days. And here's to sunny days, too.'

CHAPTER 14

Moving In,
Autumn 1987

John Dorelli and Cherry Ingram were married in church in
Barnet on the first Saturday in September two years after they
met. He turned out in a herring-bone suit, a loud kipper tie and
thick-soled brogues. She was in a white fifties frock with
voluminous petticoats, white satin high heels and a daisy-chain
anklet which did not survive the reception during which she
danced with every Dorelli from old Angelo to little Zoë. Her
mother and a handful of relations came up from Herefordshire
and, though made to feel very welcome, they were hopelessly
outnumbered by John's family who were clearly running the
show.

It was Cherry's idea that they honeymooned in Italy, and
John said he did not want to go to Naples or anywhere in the
south, which he said was dirty and noisy. Cherry called him a
snob, but she was more than happy to have a fortnight in
Tuscany and they had a wonderful time. Over long lunches in
the square in Siena and among the historic streets of Florence,
they talked about the Italian evening classes they had signed up
for, about their new flat in Camden and how they would wait to
get properly established before starting a family. Strolling
Tuscan city and village streets, they had been alert to architectural detail, choosing the tiles they would like to live with and
wondering if pots were too heavy to carry home. Though they
were disappointed by the bony *cacciucco*, fish soup, they

discovered hare stew made with citrus fruit and cocoa, ate *pecorino* cheese with Chianti, and tried all the sweetmeats they could find. At the end of two weeks, looking healthy and well fed, they returned to a new routine, arriving home just after ten o'clock in the evening for their first night in a two-bedroom garden flat near Camden Underground station.

'This place has probably doubled in value since we've been away,' John said as he carried Cherry over the threshold.

'So let's sell it,' said Cherry, landing on the bare hall floor, 'and buy two more.'

They went into all the rooms, switching on the unshaded lights, and throwing their holiday luggage on the new, sprung double bed. Black sacks and boxes of possessions were tossed about the rooms, among them the wedding gifts which they had only glimpsed before they left.

'The lounge is wider than I remember it,' Cherry said, 'and the kitchen is definitely smaller, by about one hundred per cent.'

On the pine kitchen table was a welcoming note from Joely, who had a key to look after the place while they were away. Beside it was a vase of golden chrysanthemums and a bottle of Bardolino. Fresh bread was in the bin – 'not made by me, I'm afraid' – and in the fridge was semi-skimmed milk and some lettuce and cheese, plus a bottle of San Gimignano.

'That girl is a brick,' Cherry said, distributing the contents of the fridge across the kitchen table.

'We need some bricks, to chuck at those cats,' said John, who had opened the back door at the sound of whining toms and was peering into the darkness at a whole new responsibility. 'This garden is going to take some clearing. You could get a chest freezer in this outside loo easily, though I think I was wrong about a larder fridge. Maybe we should dig down and make an ice house.'

'Talking of which,' Cherry said, 'do you know how the heating works?'

'Probably.' John closed the back door and went to find the thermostat in the hall cupboard beneath the stairs that belonged to the flat above.

'*Eccolo*,' he said as the boiler hummed into life and the pipes began to gurgle.

She said, 'We 'avva *ben caldo*.'

He said, 'You 'avva Ben Caldo, dollink. I 'avva eez seester.'

She said, 'Open a bottle and I'll get the bread and cheese. We could use some of that Lucca olive oil we bought, to put on the lettuce.'

They were not really hungry, they had eaten a few hours ago on the plane, but it seemed essential to break bread at the kitchen table on their first night home.

John said, 'I've got to be up at four.'

She said, 'You poor lamb, back in the old routine.' She kissed him on the lips and caressed him under his ear. 'If you like, we could go to bed now.'

He said, 'What kind of cheese is it?'

She said, 'Dolcelatte.'

He said, 'Let's have supper in bed.'

Up at four each morning and in bed by nine-thirty, John's life as a fishmonger was not geared to be a greatly sociable one, and Cherry had to start getting used to it. John had now taken charge of the family fish shop, some fifteen minutes' walk away. He had renamed it John Dory, Purveyor of Sea and Freshwater Fish, and he was gradually gaining a reputation for supplying unusual species, for which the newly enriched, in particular, were glad to pay. Parrot fish, lizard fish, shark sucker, black-spotted rubberlip and even sea cucumber, which few had heard of and even fewer knew how to cook, had all decorated his slab, and his own enthusiasm for them overcame any concern about modest sales.

Over the coming weeks, Cherry filled her time by going to the shop to help John and Bernard, his assistant, sometimes running errands in the van, which was their only means of transport. Her own work, as a freelance for catering companies, mostly for corporate clients, was sporadic and unsatisfactory, often relying on caterers' desperate last-minute calls. On Saturdays, when John had the afternoon off, there were often wedding receptions, but one Saturday she suddenly found herself free, so she invited Joely over, ostensibly to help paint the kitchen, but it was really a poor excuse for a big picnic lunch.

The affair with Nick had lasted six months, and now Joely was going out with Oliver, a contrastingly large, bookish man who worked in information technology, and after lunch John set him to work helping to clear the garden. It was going to be an edible garden, he said, which sprouted nothing but herbs and plants with leaves or flowers you could eat. Cherry and Joely went up to Camden Lock and the markets, leaving John and Oliver to the weeds.

'It's great you're in Camden,' said Joely, who was working in a hotel and living in Kennington on the opposite end of the Northern Line. 'It's an excuse for me to come to the market.'

'So who's Oliver?' said Cherry. 'Is he serious?'

'Unfortunately, yes,' Joely said, 'but at least he's reliable. Oh, look, there's the perfect shop for you. You didn't tell me about this.'

Cherry followed Joely's pointing, scarlet fingernail down a road off Camden High Street and saw the sign for a shop called The New Look. She had not noticed it before. From the outside it was unassuming, another clothes store, but inside it was full of possibilities. Watched over by a man in a Terylene suit, Haworth shirt, club tie and short-back-and-sides, they wandered through three rooms stacked with racks of fifties clothes: billowing dresses, pneumatic tops and fake-fur coats and jackets, with shelves of plastic belts and bright jewellery, stockings and long-sleeved gloves, scarves and Alice bands, boxes of high-heel shoes and dozens of hats, some shaped like coolies'. Petticoats that could hardly have got through the door were hung high on the wall and a Dansette was surrounded by LP sleeves picturing squeaky-clean high school gangs. 'Let's Go to the Hop' was playing, and a host of songs by harmony singers, bobby-sox backing groups and brilliantined sax players were piled up on a spindle waiting to come on.

Cherry ran a hand along the racks. In among the tat, she quickly saw, was the occasional mint – Dior, Worth – and she wondered if the owner really knew what he had. She picked out a white silk crêpe dress, with short sleeves and a wide collar, a tight waist and graceful folds that fell to the floor.

'Try it on,' the man behind the counter said. 'You'll look good in it, and you'll feel great, too.'

'How much is it?' Cherry said.

'Fifteen hundred.'

She laughed, but Joely was outraged: 'For an old frock!'

'It's a Worth,' the man said. 'A real collector's piece.'

Joely said, 'This is Camden High Street, not Bond Street. Besides, look, the darts are coming apart at the back.'

'It's beautiful,' said Cherry. 'Where's the changing room?'

The man said, 'Through the back.'

Five minutes later she came out looking like one million dollars. The white gave her fading tan a new lease of life. She turned around and the skirt swung in a leisurely circle. The man whistled.

'You need these,' said Joely, picking up a pair of white plastic sunglasses. 'Plus a big open Cadillac with Paul Newman at your side and the wind tugging at your headscarf.'

'I just need to be rich,' Cherry said.

'Hard cheese, darling, you just married a purveyor of wet fish.'

After several flamboyant twirls before a full-length mirror, Cherry reluctantly changed back again, then stayed a while, wondering what she might reasonably buy. Old Vogue patterns were selling from £15 to £50. It had been some years since she had made any clothes, and this might inspire her to retrieve her sewing machine from her mother's. In the end Cherry spent £12, knocked down from £20, on a pair of long-sleeved white gloves. John wouldn't mind: she might even wear them in bed to really show off her tan.

It was getting dark by the time they arrived back at the flat and John and Oliver had already called it a day, scrubbed the sooty black earth from under their nails and had the lapsang souchong brewing and crumpets laid out in the grill pan. Over tea, Joely reported on the high price of period frocks.

'They were selling them without even bothering to fix them up,' she said. 'It would only have taken a few stitches to put those darts back in the white dress, but he didn't care.'

John had been roaming the kitchen, finding knives, plates and jams and keeping his eye on the crumpets. 'I bet you looked great in that dress,' he said to Cherry. 'I wish I had been there.' He sounded genuinely disappointed to have missed the show. 'I'm going to start saving for it tomorrow. Didn't we have some quince and apple?'

'There's too much money about,' Oliver said. 'Everyone has gone crazy since the Big Bang. These guys in the City don't know what to do with their cash. Property comes first, but then what? They'll put their money into anything.'

'I wish somebody would put their money in me,' Cherry said, 'so I could start up a catering business on my own. I'm getting fed up with these last-minute fill-in jobs.'

'I'd hate to work for myself,' Joely said. 'It would take all the fun out of nicking the stationery.'

'Do you nick stationery?' Oliver asked.

'Joke, Oliver,' Joely said.

The following week Cherry started to put advertisements in the local paper offering her services as a caterer for small parties. Because of work and things to sort out in the flat, evening classes were an extra burden. They had missed the first one anyway, because of their honeymoon, and John gave up after only four lessons, though Cherry carried on a little longer. There was a couple of hours of homework each week and she usually did it the night before the next lesson, which is what she was doing one Tuesday in November when John phoned to say he had muddled up the days in his diary and as a result had to be at two places at once.

'Are you free to make a delivery to Chelsea?'

She sighed. Work had to come first. 'How am I going to get there?'

'Cab or tube. It's just one fish. I've got to take six crates of salmon up to Islington, so I'll need the van. Bernard'll still be here.'

The shop was in large, Victorian premises, tiled in blue and white, with a single large pane of glass for the shop window and the counter at the back beyond a small aquarium. John liked collecting marine memorabilia and around the walls were shells and seahorses, stuffed puffins and herring gulls, pots and nets. Bernard, bullet-haired with a silver ring in his left ear, handed her a parcel from the fridge. It weighed around three pounds.

'What is it?' she asked.

'Whitefish.'

'What sort of white fish?'

'That's its name, whitefish, *Coregonus wartmanni*, fresh water.'

She had never heard of it. 'Where's it going to?' She looked at a label stuck on the side of the plastic bag. 'David,' she said, squinting at it. 'Halsey Street, SW3. David who? God, John's hopeless.'

She found the street in an *A–Z*, took a tube to Sloane Square and walked around the back of Peter Jones. Halsey Street was a short, wide road of four-storey period houses, with black railings, first-floor balconies, basements and steps up to the front doors. Each one was half a million pounds' worth of prime London property, if it was a penny. She rang the bell. There was no reply. She tried again, then checked the label once more and rang a third time. She would have to find a phone in Sloane Square. There was no point in asking Directory Enquiries, because she didn't have the surname, but Bernard might still be at work, and he could check the address in the order book.

'Yes,' a woman's voice suddenly snapped in her ear on an intercom.

'John Dory's,' Cherry said. 'Whitefish.'

There was a pause, then: 'Bring it in.'

The catch buzzed and Cherry leaned against the door. It opened on to an unlit hall, closing behind her before she had a chance to get her bearings. She stood for a moment, squinting at the interior. Underfoot was a Persian runner. Boxes full of books and bric-à-brac lined the hallway and filled up the brass-rodded stairs. There were paintings and prints on the white walls. Light was coming from a door at the back of the stairs, but there was no sound.

Then: 'Down here.'

Stepping round the boxes, Cherry descended into the basement, where there were two rooms. She passed the first, which she took to be a kitchen, but was in darkness. It must have been a trick of the light: the occupied, second room was in fact the kitchen, and as she entered she felt herself step back to a time before she was born. Here was a culinary chiaroscuro with every shelf occupied, every hook hung from. There were dusty hams and salamis, dried peppers, herbs and bottles and jars of preserves. Hardly an inch of the shelves or the dresser and cupboards or even the wooden draining board was not covered, and to Cherry it smelled like a cross between an old-fashioned grocer's and a sous-chef's digs. There was little sign of tech-nological innovation: the gas stove was a simple four-ring affair; there was no freezer or microwave, yet the appreciation of food was abundantly evident: in the stone sink was a large omelette pan with a bit of egg still stuck to the side.

At a large pine table in the middle of the room, an elderly woman, breathing heavily, sat in a Windsor chair, padded by tapestry cushions and enveloped in a Japanese print silk dressing-gown, her dark grey hair swept smoothly back, gold reading glasses on her nose before deep-set eyes, her lips moist and loose. The only light in the room was from a Victorian lamp suspended from the ceiling just above her, illuminating the pages of books and notepads that covered half the table: some new, mostly old, some with the plastic covers of public libraries. Half a glass of white wine was set before her. Cherry imagined her to be hibernating, living out the winter and not putting a nose outdoors until the snowdrops were dead and buried. The two women exchanged unblinking stares.

'Whitefish,' the woman eventually said. Her accent was upper-class crystal from a lost generation, entirely unmodu-lated by late-twentieth-century trends.

'For somebody called David,' Cherry replied, 'but I didn't get the second name.'

The woman narrowed her eyes and looked at Cherry as if she were being insolent.

In the heat of the stare Cherry felt a sudden need to explain herself. 'My name is Cherry Ingram,' she said, standing on the dignity of her maiden name, which she still used for business.

'Let me see the fish,' the woman said, refusing to reciprocate the introduction.

Cherry went over to her and laid the bag on the table. In the process, she kicked an empty bottle at the woman's feet, which bumped against another and another until a whole crateful went down like skittles. She bent to pick them up.

'Leave them.' The old woman waved a hand wearily at the debris. 'Let the dead bury the dead. Show me this lord of the lake.'

Cherry unwrapped it carefully. It was about eighteen inches long, plumper than a trout, smaller than a salmon, and a peerless, silvery white. She proffered it to the woman, who prodded its light, scaly body with her expert, gnarled fingers. A large silver ring encompassed the second finger of her right hand. She then sniffed the fish deeply.

'What's its provenance?' she asked, sitting back.

'No idea,' Cherry said. 'John Dory just asked me to bring it over.'

She tutted dismissively. 'That can't be his real name.'

'His name is John, and he has a birthmark here,' she touched her own cheek.

'Ah, the stigmata of Saint Pierre. Very droll. I would like to meet him if I liked meeting people, which I no longer do. Nobody else has been able to find me this fish.'

She lifted its tail and let it drop to the table with a light smack, not once or twice but several times, and Cherry wondered what kind of test this was supposed to be.

'Soft bones,' the woman said. 'Oh, for soft bones.' It smacked a couple of times more, then she asked, 'How would you propose I cook it?'

'With fish, less is best,' Cherry said brightly. 'Probably just baked, like trout, in tin foil or greaseproof. You could brown a bit of garlic and onion, carrot and celery and herbs . . .'

'*A battuto.*'

'Exactly. But I haven't cooked one of these before.'

'Neither have I, but Norman was a huge fan.' She paused, leaving Cherry uncertain whether a story about a late husband was to follow, or if that was it. Perhaps he was the David: David Norman, Norman David. It rang no bells, though the woman had spoken his name as if Cherry should have known who he was. In a moment – satisfied, perhaps, that she had an appreciative, if ignorant, audience – the old woman continued: 'He urged me to go to the Hotel Hecht in Constance, and make love to the manager, and to tell him I had met a fellow countryman who had spoken in such glowing terms of the Bodensee Blaufelchen – which I have since learned is this whitefish *Coregonus* – that I was unable to sleep, travelling by day and by night via the Trans-Siberian Railway to taste them for myself under his hospitable roof.'

This entire story was not told without effort. It came in bursts of words, the woman's head constantly moving around, and the wineglass returning to her lips now and then. 'I have tried to buy one several times since. Every year more and more species, more varieties of produce are available. That's a bonus of modern life. It is also its bane. Do you know the provenance of this particular fish?'

Cherry tried again to answer the question. 'I suspect it *is* from Switzerland, maybe even Lake Constance,' she said, using knowledge gained from Swiss chefs to translate the Bodensee.

The woman was not impressed. 'But you don't know. I can't eat it if I don't know where it's from. It may come from Scotland. Mary, Queen of Scots introduced them to the lochs. Or it may come from some acid-rain butt in Sweden, or a mercury puddle on the Rhine. Can you telephone your Mr Dory and ask?'

'I can try.'

The woman pushed a phone across the table towards her, and Cherry called the shop, but the answering machine was on. She tried home, but there was no reply.

'Leave me his number so I can call him later. I can't cook it unless I know.'

'If I see him I'll tell him to call you,' Cherry said, writing their number on a piece of paper the woman tore from a notebook. 'But don't call him after nine-thirty, he'll be asleep.'

'Not after nine-thirty?' the woman repeated, surprised. Then she understood. 'I suppose he's up with the sprats.'

Cherry said he was, talking of which reminded her to look at the invoice pinned to the bag. 'Is this cash or account? I forgot to check.'

The woman sniffed and stared at her. She had a striking face, even though it sagged with a lifetime's good living. Her body was a dry twig but it held a dignity, a fundamental presence, which expected respect, much as someone important might, but she was not a familiar figure, not someone Cherry might have seen in the papers or on television.

'Cash,' the woman said.

Her leather bag was on her lap and she brought it up on to the table, opened it, took out a bottle opener and a packet of tissues and a small leather purse from which she counted twelve pounds, exactly, which was fortunate because Cherry had no change.

'On your way out,' she said, 'there's a box on the right of the door in the hall. Would you mind sliding it over here by my feet.'

Cherry went to the door where she found the box of estate-bottled Chablis. Good for her, she thought, as she dragged it across the parquet; she's going to go down like the Trans-Siberian Railway. She grinned at the woman and found herself holding out her hand. The woman's hand shook a little, and Cherry grasped it kindly. She would have liked to have got to know her better, but she knew she had come years too late.

An hour afterwards, back at the flat, she wondered if John's business was going to work. Twelve pounds for the fish didn't even cover her time delivering it. He was flopped on the sofa watching television in the front room, and as she came in he got up and kissed her, immediately apologising for having to send her on the errand. It had been a bad day, he said. She told him about the old woman and how anxious she had been about where the fish had come from, but he shook his head.

'I can never find out,' he said. 'There are so many people in between me and the fish who just don't care. This one came in through a wholesaler in Harwich, so it's the Continent rather than Scotland. I always ask, but the suppliers don't usually know. They just get on the blower to the next one down the line and all they're interested in is if the fish you want exists at all.'

'I said you'd phone her.'

'Okay. I'll tell her it's Lake Constance, that seems the likeliest bet. If she's as old as you say she is, a bit of pollution isn't going to do her any harm anyway. What's her number?'

'I thought you'd have it.'

'Why should I have it?'

'I don't know, I just thought she was a customer.'

'No, this is the first time I've dealt with her. It was ordered last week, by a man, an upper-crust bloke. The number will be in the book at work, but I don't have it.'

'I said if she called, she should call before nine-thirty.'

'Here?'

'Yes.'

He shrugged. 'Okay. If she calls, she calls.'

At 9.30 he went to bed, and Cherry stayed up a while, curled on the sofa finishing Harold Acton's book on Florence which she had taken on honeymoon and barely begun. Two hours later the phone rang, making her jump. She rushed to pick it up before it woke John. She always answered by just giving the number, as there were now two companies as well as two private lives operating under one roof. No one responded to her announcement of the number, but she knew there was someone on the line, and she had a good idea who it might be.

Eventually the old woman's voice came over clearly: 'Can I speak to Mr John Dory?'

'I'm afraid he's in bed.'

Another pause, then: 'That's you, isn't it? Cherry Ingram. Are you Mrs Dory?'

Cherry laughed. 'Yes, I suppose I am.'

'It's Mrs David,' she said, breathing heavily, another bottle of Chablis no doubt on its way to the ten-pin bowling alley, 'about the whitefish.'

The hair on Cherry's head filled with a thousand spiders and her blood turned to sorbet. She took a deep breath and said: 'Mrs David, we know the whitefish came from the Continent, through Harwich, but the wholesaler has no idea exactly where it's from.' She gripped the phone and squeezed her eyes tight shut. How could she deliberately lose a customer like this?

'Pity,' the old woman said after another pause. 'I was looking forward to fish tonight.' She hung up.

Slowly, Cherry put down the phone. She could not believe it. 'Fuck!' she shouted, pummelling the sofa cushions. 'Fuck, fuck, fuck, fuck, fuck! That was *Elizabeth* David. I thought she was *dead*!'

CHAPTER 15

Together,
Christmas 1989

Among John and Cherry's new and inescapable routines was the ritual of Christmas. If Sunday lunch was sacred at the Dorellis, Christmas Day was absolutely sacrosanct. There was no question of visiting Cherry's mother: she had to wait until Boxing Day. That was the schedule, begun on their first Christmas together and now fixed for ever, which meant that one vast luncheon would be followed the next day by another. On their third festive break together, Cherry was burdened with a further duty when Angelo decided to open his restaurant on New Year's Eve. John's father had extended the premises since giving him the fish shop, but business had not met expectations. Somehow it seemed only natural to try to help out.

The contrast between the two Christmas events could not have been greater. The uproar of the Dorelli household, the mess of paper and party hats, of chatter and laughter, games and practical jokes, the heat and the smoke, could in no way be compared to the quiet trio around the dining table in the back room of Grace Ingram's cottage in Ross-on-Wye. The climate was just not the same. Except in the lounge when a fire was lit, it was always cool in the cottage, and whereas the Dorellis' house meant getting down to shirtsleeves, here jerseys had to be worn at all times, sometimes even in bed.

Central heating, which was programmed to a minimum, had

arrived late in the Ingrams' cottage near Old Maid's Walk by the church at the top of the old town. This was the family home, where Grace and her five older siblings had been born, an ancient place of low ceilings and tiny windows, built for hunchback, dog-tired days of unremitting labour, thrifty larders and patched clothes, in a time of superstitions and old wives' tales. Tucked under the eaves, the bedrooms were not much bigger than cupboards and only Grace's room could accommodate a double bed, so when they stayed there, Cherry and John slept apart. Cherry was convinced the temperature in the house had dropped two degrees since her mother had lived on her own after her husband died five years earlier, and that morning, shortly after they had arrived, an old single-bar electric fire had been brought out of a cupboard to heat the dining room. A smell of burning dust was soon masked by the aromas of lunch.

'There's lots more breast, John,' Grace said, ladling the vegetable mix of leek, onion, celery and carrot which had been fried with the chopped neck of the goose. Roast potatoes and crisp watercress were spooned on top. At fifty-nine, she was small and birdlike, with similar Celtic dark looks to her daughter's. She liked John and she piled the food on his plate.

'The breast's great,' said John. 'And the bird isn't fatty at all, which is what you often think of with goose.'

'I still don't think this oven does them as well as the Aga,' said Grace. 'We used to keep geese when Cherry was little. Do you remember them, Cherry?'

'They were incredibly noisy, but I always felt safe with them around.' Cherry sensed they had had the same conversation over Christmas dinner the previous year.

'The problem is, they wander off,' said Grace. 'Most of them ended up down by the river, where the foxes got them.'

After the goose there was home-made Christmas pudding,

topped with holly and inflamed with brandy, during which Grace asked once again if they were sure they could not stay the night: it seemed such a long way to come just for lunch. John explained that though the next day was Monday, and a Bank Holiday, he needed to use the time to sort some things out in the shop before the full week that lay ahead. They would not leave until late though, to avoid the traffic. He produced a bottle of white port which he knew Grace liked.

'This'll help with the washing-up,' he said.

After they had washed and tidied up, they prepared to go out for a short walk before it grew dark. By the back door they put on their coats and pulled on their boots and waited for Grace, who had gone upstairs to change. John folded his arms about Cherry and held her tight.

'I'm sleepy,' she said dozily as she nuzzled into his shoulder.

'I'm horny as a hoot owl,' he growled, pressing his right hand firmly up inside the back of her woollen jacket and rubbing his cheeks in her hair. 'When was the last time we did it in the afternoon?'

'Florence, September the twelfth, 1987.'

They kissed each other languorously, sharing the rich tastes of the meal. As he moved his lips away, to her nose, to her ears, he said, 'I remember the holiday snaps. Desire and opportunity don't often happen together like that.'

'I think we could all do with some fresh air,' Grace said innocently, walking in on them, and they smiled and drew apart.

There was not much more than an hour of light left in the day and they walked briskly down through the old town to the river, across fields, through swing gates, and along John Kyrle's Walk. John, hand-in-hand with Cherry, kept up his banter of questions about what they passed on the way. He had a Londoner's curiosity about the countryside, amazed that anyone could tell two trees apart. It was as if, he once told Cherry, he lacked a spiritual side to his life, and he envied her familiarity with nature, its names and its rhythms. Grace pointed out a peregrine falcon soaring overhead, which had been breeding downriver at Symonds Yat, and he stopped to watch its flight. He remembered the falcon they had seen on their first picnic on the South Downs, and he reminded them about it. Grace said there were quite a few hawkers in the Welsh hills.

'What's the population of Ross?' John suddenly wanted to know.

'Ooh, I don't know now.' Grace was the only one in her family left in the town. 'You used to be able to count them, because you knew them all, and you'd never pass anyone without stopping for a chat or saying good day.'

John breathed deeply, invigorated by the country air, and when a young couple walked past them, he called out a greeting with such cheerfulness it alarmed them and they scurried past. Cherry laughed.

Not long after they returned home from the walk, Grace's spinster sister Em arrived, walking in through the back door without a knock, still treating the house as the family home. Part of the cast of the Christmas ritual, she had driven down from Hereford to join them for tea. A couple of years older than Grace, she had the family dark features and fine cheekbones but, unlike Grace's, her face had become pinched and sour: she seldom had a good word about anyone if a bad one could be found. There was another sister, Peggy, and her husband, Frank, who lived further north, in Ludlow, and a brother, Billy, who lived in Birmingham with his wife Jane. They had three children and several grandchildren.

John planted a hefty kiss on Em's cheek, enjoying her awkwardness and ignoring her attempts to avoid it: no one else kissed or touched. Tea and home-made Christmas cake were taken on a tray to the sitting room where an open wood fire had been burning most of the day. The sisters sat in the Parker Knoll chairs either side, in the same places their parents had probably sat, while Cherry drew the chintz curtains on the winter night and settled down with John on the couch. They talked about friends and relatives, and after a while Cherry got up and inspected the cards that covered the mantelpiece and bookshelves. There were one or two cards fewer each year; most of her dad's friends still kept in touch. She knew there would be no card from her half-brother Thomas, but she checked them all just the same.

Em asked if Cherry was still doing her Italian lessons, and she said an attempt in the autumn had again ended in failure, but she might have another go at them in the New Year, as they were hoping to go to Venice in the summer. At six o'clock Grace put on the television to see the news. It was still taken up with the end of the cold war and the opening of the Brandenburg Gate, but the main story was the execution of Nicolae and Elena Ceauşescu in Romania on Christmas Day.

'How can anyone be so hated?' Grace said, lighting a cigarette.

After the news John scanned the local paper, which he always liked to do, seeking the most curious stories to read out loud. But he was soon restless, and suggested they went to the pub.

'The pub?' Em made it clear she did not approve. 'There won't be anyone there.'

'We can't come to the country without going to a country pub,' said John.

'Even at Christmas?' said Em.

'Especially at Christmas,' replied Cherry, putting an arm through John's.

'I think that's a good idea,' Grace said.

'Will you come?' John asked.

'No, dear,' said Grace. 'I have things to do, but you two go off and enjoy yourselves.'

Cherry's support for the idea was a show of solidarity with John rather than a strong desire to visit the pub. She knew Em would be right: the place would not exactly be jumping, and she did not share John's enthusiasm for meeting the deadbeat locals who could think of nothing to do but down pints every night. But on the few times they had been there, John had enjoyed chatting to them, particularly such salts of the earth as the Free Miners from the Forest of Dean, men with thick accents, born in the Hundred of St Briavel and boasting about their gales and Gavellers, the Speech House and the Book of Dennis, and life in New Found Out, Strip And At It and other dark holes in the ground. John lapped them up but Cherry had heard these stories all her life and it still amazed her that men could be anything but ashamed of being engaged in such menial, filthy work.

The pub had low-beamed ceilings and a hushed air, above and beyond a one-armed bandit that played a repetitive, manic medley. There were only two other customers, bored, lank-haired lads fiddling with beer mats at a table. Cherry sat on a stool at the end of the bar and asked for a cider; John ordered a beer, choosing carefully from half a dozen local and guest specials. The landlord was from Birmingham, and there had probably been a dozen others since Cherry's teenage years, which was a good thing, as she had no wish to be reminded of the time she had spent propping up the bar.

'It's always such a contrast,' John said, keeping his voice low in this empty, echoing place. 'Christmas at your mothers, after the mêlée of my lot.'

'I'm sorry, I know it's boring.'

'Oh no, I like the peace, but I just think your mother might be bored. Anyway, I'd come just for the food. She's a better cook than my mum, though I wouldn't tell anyone else.'

'She likes us coming down, but she just doesn't always know how to show it. She's very independent. Even when Dad was alive, she'd go out and play bridge and he'd do his poaching, or he'd just sit in the kitchen, listening to the radio and drinking his cider while she sewed or watched television. They didn't bother each other. They just got on with their lives.'

Sometimes Cherry thought she missed her father more than her mother did. Edwin Ingram had been soft on Grace since they were at school, but he caught her only on the rebound. At the end of the war she had married someone else, a flyer called Jack, and they had had a baby, Thomas, after which Jack went away and did not come back.

'Does she ever hear from Thomas?' John asked.

Cherry shook her head. 'He used to send her a card every Christmas, but he doesn't even do that any more. I think it still hurts her.'

Thomas had been fourteen when Cherry was born, and she could just about remember an angry, sullen, stooping teenager. It seemed that he could never come to terms with the idea of a new father and sister, and he had left home when she was five, settling in South Africa. Cherry's grandmother had died shortly afterwards and she and her parents had moved back into the family home.

John shook his head. 'Thomas has never written to you?'

'I wouldn't expect him to,' she said.

Three middle-aged men entered the bar and one of them greeted Cherry. He was the father of an old schoolfriend and he offered them a drink which they declined. They swapped news for a few minutes while the publican drew three pints. Picking up the first of them, one of the men raised a toast to Ceauşescu, hoping that he would be eternally damned.

'You wouldn't even get a sin-eater for that one,' he said.

Cherry and John finished their drinks, said goodnight and stepped outside into the frosty, star-filled night.

'What's a sin-eater?' John asked, his arm wrapped warmly about her as they made their way over the lamplit, cobblestone path to the Ingram home.

'It was an old custom round here,' Cherry explained. 'When a person died you baked a loaf of bread and paid someone – usually an outcast, like a criminal or the town idiot, someone generally beyond the pale – to eat the bread, which passed on the sins of the dead person to the living one, so the dead person could go straight to heaven.'

'That's neat. How long ago did it go on?'

'Oh, I don't know. It probably hasn't happened in a couple of centuries.'

Grace and Em were just how they had left them, by the fire in the sitting room, watching television.

'You were quick,' Grace said.

'Aunt Em was right,' John said magnanimously. 'It was pretty quiet.'

Em looked pleased. They flopped on to the sofa.

'Do you want anything?' asked Grace. 'A glass of wine? Sherry?'

'I don't write about wine,' came a familiar voice from the television. 'I don't know enough about it.'

Cherry looked up, alert. 'That's Elizabeth David,' she said. On the screen, the cookery writer was sitting at a dining table with an interviewer, the wine writer Jancis Robinson. With a discomfort that showed she was neither used to, nor cared for, the camera, Mrs David was sniffing and tasting a full glass of red wine.

'It's a programme about her,' said Grace. 'It's nearly over now.'

'She's being very difficult,' said Em.

The camera cut to the kitchen where courgette flowers were being dunked in batter and fried. Cherry and John sat up on the edge of the sofa. The dishes were served at the table and Elizabeth David, between pauses and evasive stares, seemed impressed. She prodded them with her fork. There was a slowness, an anticipation, a palpable tension in the scene, which reminded Cherry so much of her own visit to Mrs David's Chelsea home.

'Who grows them?' she asked eventually.

'The owners' friend, Pasquale,' said Robinson who had done all her homework, and checked out the provenance of everything.

Mrs David was silent. She was not going to be drawn.

'True to form,' Robinson's voice came over the scene, 'she refused to play the interview game . . .'

Patient and bright-eyed behind her large, amber-framed glasses, Robinson tried every tack but was unable to prevent the interview grinding to an embarrassing halt. The tablecloth was the wrong colour. A light brown one had been used to suit the camera, but the Elizabeth David rule was 'white, white, white'. So that was the end of the interview with Elizabeth David. The restaurant owners, who seemed, by contrast, excessively pleasant and ordinary, were asked if they thought the event a success. They shrugged. How could they tell?

'How long has it been on?' Cherry asked.

'An hour,' Em said. 'They've been waiting at a restaurant in Abergavenny. Most of the programme has been spent wondering if she was going to turn up at all.'

Cherry smiled. She had to admire the woman's style. In the absence of a compliant subject, an actress came on to read some lines from one of Elizabeth David's cookery books, and the programme drew to a close with a quote, written out as a subtitle: '"Whoever has helped us to a greater understanding is entitled to our gratitude" – Norman Douglas.'

'Norman Douglas?' said Cherry, turning to John. 'Isn't he that relation your father came looking for?'

He shrugged. 'It's the same name.'

She said to Em, 'Was he in the programme?'

Em sniffed. 'They just said he had an influence on her, when she was young.'

'Did they show her kitchen?' John asked.

Em said, 'No, you didn't see her home. She and her three sisters all had birthdays over Christmas. Isn't that a coincidence? Hers was on Boxing Day. I suppose that's today. I don't know how old she is. Her mother sounded as if she had been a bit of a flibbertigibbet.'

'I didn't think she ever gave interviews, let alone television appearances,' said John.

'That was the first one she's ever given,' said Em. 'They said she hadn't even sat for a photograph for twenty years.'

'No wonder I didn't recognise her when I met her,' said Cherry.

Em sat forward. 'When did you meet her?' She sounded surprised.

'Didn't Mum tell you?' Cherry said, and once again she related the story of the visit, which still seemed fresh in her mind. She described the old woman in the kitchen, with no mention of the drink, which Em would have made too much of, and what happened with the phone call afterwards. Em listened attentively.

'The best client I never had,' said John when Cherry had finished the tale. 'I could have put a warrant above the shop door: "John Dory, by appointment to Elizabeth David". I'd have cleaned up.' He turned to Grace. 'Cherry told me you have a book signed by her.'

'Oh,' said Grace, 'that was so long ago. I don't think I would have recognised her now if they hadn't said who she was.'

Em said, 'What was so strange in the interview just now was that she said she spent that terrible winter of 1946 in Kensington. Why did she say that, when she was here, at the hotel?'

'Was that where you worked?' John asked Grace and she nodded.

'Why did she come here?' Cherry asked.

'The programme said she had come out of a bad marriage,' Em explained.

'She just wanted a quiet time,' said Grace. She was pulling distractedly at a thread in the arm of the chair. 'She was unsettled.'

'She looked a bit tiddly,' said John. 'What was she like when you knew her, Mrs I?'

'She liked her cider,' said Em, sniffing.

Grace said, 'She was lovely and ladylike, and she always dressed well in spite of the rationing. She had a red velvet coat. Of course, she had to eat what she could get, like the rest of us. Talking of which, I've put some goose in some greaseproof in a bag in the kitchen. I can't eat it all myself. You must take some Christmas cake, too.'

John said he would have it the following night, to extend the festivities. The grandfather clock in the hall struck ten and he got up, stretching loudly. It was time to make tracks. Cherry said she was annoyed to have missed the only programme worth watching over the whole Christmas break, and she hoped it would be repeated. Em said they shouldn't have gone to the pub and that it was time she was going home, too. But she hovered as they were getting into their coats and saying goodbye, and she stood with Grace on the back steps until they were out of sight.

The traffic was light and when they were on the main road Cherry reclined her seat and sat back, listening to a radio concert and the steady chug of their recently acquired diesel Citroën. She thought of her mother going off to work at the age of fourteen, and she wondered what Elizabeth David had looked like then, before her bones became brittle and her face became puckered and slack.

'Elizabeth David seems quite a character,' John said quietly, his mind on the same track. 'You were really lucky to see her in her kitchen. Nobody else seems to have done. She's never in the papers or on television. I had no idea what she looked like.'

'It's kind of old-fashioned,' Cherry said, 'being famous and not being a celebrity. Everyone knowing your name, but not knowing anything about you. She's just famous for what she does best. I admire her for that.'

'She obviously doesn't need the publicity,' John said. 'That big house in Chelsea must be worth a mint. I wonder why she denied ever being in Ross.'

'Perhaps she just didn't want to talk about it, if she'd had a bad marriage.'

She closed her eyes and thought of the old cookery writer. She would like to go back to that kitchen and talk to her again, over a glass or two from her bottomless cellar of Chablis. The car heater was warm against the frosty night and Schubert's *Trout*, playing on a tape, overcame the monotonous drone of the car engine. Still feeling full of Christmas lunch, she dozed for a while, and did not open her eyes again for more than an hour. When she did, she sat in silence until she saw a motorway sign indicating that London was fifty-two miles away. She yawned. Christmas was over. Real life was about to begin again.

'Oh God, Norman Douglas,' she said suddenly, and John, wide-eyed, gripped the wheel, glancing quickly at her.

'You made me jump. I thought you were asleep.'

'That must have been the Norman she was talking about when I saw her, the one who told her about the Bodensee whitefish.'

'Maybe.'

'Norman Douglas.' She yawned. 'It's odd the way he has cropped up. Have you ever read anything of his?'

John looked over to her. A hank of her hair had fallen over one eye and he reached out and brushed it back for her. She smiled and closed her eyes for a moment. Then she realised the music had stopped and she put the radio on.

'I tried to read a book called *South Wind*,' John said over the last bars of a concert. 'It was about some bishop on a Mediterranean island. I didn't get very far. It was rather old-fashioned. I gave up after that.'

'Have you still got it?'

'No, I chucked it out with the porn, when we got married.'

'What porn?'

'Oh, the usual, things like "Fishmongers' Wives", but I cancelled the subscription when I got a real one of my own.'

She gave him an admonishing slap on his thigh with the back of her hand, then she let it rest in his lap. The radio news came on, and they listened to the last events of the 1980s, and heard of the plans for a rock concert at the Brandenburg Gate in Berlin to see in the new decade. She thought of the year ahead, the same routines, more functions for catering companies, which she hoped wouldn't interfere too much with her Italian lessons, as they had the year before. She hoped they would be able to go back to Tuscany again.

When the news was over, she said, 'Have you made any New Year resolutions?'

He didn't answer while he negotiated an overtaking truck. When he was back in the central lane, he said, 'I would really like to have a child. I know we said we would wait till we got a larger place, but that isn't going to happen this year, not with the recession.'

Cherry had an image of Mrs David at the restaurant in Abergavenny, commanding so much respect, and at her kitchen table at home, doing just what she wanted to, being who she was, a woman fulfilled. 'I don't know,' she said. 'I'd like to do something with my life first.'

'What better thing can you do with your life than have kids?' John asked, and Cherry thought he sounded like his father. He sighed. 'It's not something we should think about. We should just do it, or it will never get done.'

'I will think about it,' she promised, and to reassure him, she rubbed her hand across his thigh. But she knew he was right: thinking about it would not make it happen.

New Year's Eve was hard. The Dorellis' restaurant was packed. The customers, made up principally of three large parties, were boisterous and demanding and it took some effort to get them out of the door by three o'clock in the morning, which was later than the licence allowed. At midnight, the staff had fore-gathered in the kitchen, and as the radio chimed in the new decade and a roar went up from the restaurant, they embraced. They weren't all there: Molly looked after the kitchen with Uncle Max while her husband, the *patron*, Angelo, ran the front-of-house with Isabel, now nearly thirty, who worked in the restaurant full-time. Cherry was waiting on table, too. Christopher, who was the most like John, had deserted his own family to help in the kitchen. The recession had recently put him out of work. His midnight kiss for Cherry had been generous.

'How are your feet?' Molly asked Cherry as she brought a tray of glasses into the kitchen.

'Not too bad,' said Cherry. How could she have any reason

to complain, she thought, when Molly and Angelo were both over sixty, and showing no signs of slowing down? 'Do you think you'll do this every year?'

'We have to work if we need money,' said Angelo, stacking a dishwasher. 'That is life.'

'You don't need money,' said Christopher, emptying a bottle of abandoned wine into a tumbler. 'You're a millionaire.'

'I am not a millionaire,' Angelo raised his voice angrily. No one batted an eyelid. 'What do you know?'

'You just like saying you're poor,' Christopher said amiably, drying up cutlery and letting it fall with a clatter into a large tray. 'Because then we'll feel sorry for you and come and help you in the restaurant for a pittance.'

Uncle Max chuckled. Christopher winked at Cherry, but she did not respond; she respected Angelo, and this was not the first time she had seen Christopher goading his father. John never did that.

Angelo stabbed a finger at his son. 'I'll leave no money for you.'

Christopher laughed. 'I thought you didn't have any anyway.'

Angelo marched out of the kitchen, throwing a cloth over his shoulder. Molly wiped her hands on a towel, and took a packet of cigarettes down from a shelf and handed them round. Isabel took off her shoes, and her mother said, 'The *zabaione* was popular. I thought there'd be some over for tomorrow. Tony and Sandy are coming up for lunch.'

'You don't know about being poor,' Angelo said as he marched back into the kitchen.

'Don't tell me, I know: you ate grass and barnacles in the war,' said Christopher.

'You have never seen anything like it.' Angelo appealed to Cherry. He was agitated, but his voice was slow and tired. 'Naples after the war. October 1943. Me and my friend

Massimo here were in the navy, in Taranto, when Italy surrend-
ered, and we walked home to Naples: three weeks in the hills,
living on nothing, and then finding nothing when we got there.
Less than nothing. People starving in the streets.'

'It looked like a refugee camp,' said Uncle Max, who was
spooning unused fresh tomato sauce into tubs. 'You couldn't
even find drinking water.'

'Both our families had died,' Angelo continued. 'My mother
and sister. I couldn't even find where they were buried. The
laundry business, where I had grown up, now it was full of
strangers. It was a disgrace, I can't tell you.'

'It was a brothel for the Americans,' Christopher said.

Angelo ignored him. 'So I went away, and I found Max
again.'

'And he found another orphan,' said Max. 'My family was
dead, too.'

'How dreadful,' said Cherry. 'So what did you do?'

'We were both aged twenty-one,' said Max. 'We walked all
the way back to the ship, and asked if we could join up again.
We worked with the English navy, and we decided we wanted
to come here.'

'Max had been the ship's cook,' Angelo explained, 'and
before I joined up I had been a fisherman, so we thought what
better place to start a fish and chip shop. Which is what we did
in our first business here.'

Cherry had heard part of this story before, but she always
listened attentively. This time she remembered Angelo's uncle
and she asked him if he had seen the television programme on
Elizabeth David on Boxing Day. He had not, nor had he heard
of Elizabeth David, though Molly said that she thought that she
might have had one of her books once. Angelo said he didn't
read cookery books. Christopher pointed out that his father did
not even read the newspapers.

'They are too depressing,' said Angelo. 'You don't learn anything from them. But I have learned two things in life . . .'

'You can't have enough money . . .' Christopher began for him.

'You can't have enough money, and you can't have enough children. That is what I have learned in life.'

An hour later Cherry was back home, tired and glad the evening was over. Christopher dropped her off at the front door, leaning over for a goodnight kiss and being presented with a frosty cheek. He drove off, and she let the car noise die at the end of the road before turning the key quietly in the latch. But the lights were on, John was up, making tea and reading a cookery book. He wore the white towelling dressing-gown she had given him for Christmas.

'What are you doing up?' she asked as she took off her coat. 'It's a holiday. The one day of the year you're meant to lie in.'

'I tried to stay in bed but my biological clock refuses to change. Besides, I wanted to make sure you got back safely.'

She went up to him and kissed him. When they disengaged he said, 'Anyway, you know I often can't sleep till I know you're home.' They kissed again. 'Happy New Year,' he said.

'Happy New Year.' She took his hand. 'Now come back to bed and we'll talk about New Year resolutions.'

CHAPTER 16

Looking Back, 1992

Cherry was making pastry in the kitchen one morning in May when she heard on the radio news that Elizabeth David was dead. She put down the dough, dusted her hands on her apron and wandered out into the garden where she stood for a moment by a bay tree in a tub, bathed in a calm morning light. The small urban garden was now tidy with pots and small beds of herbs which would provide an aromatic harvest, with horse-radish, rocket, salad burnet and mace. Clumps of thyme were well established, as was a rosemary bush where a heavy bee wandered about the blue flowers. Marigolds, dandelions and nasturtiums would provide colour. Everything was for the kitchen, even the violets' dark petals would be used to decorate desserts.

It had been four years since Cherry had met the cookery writer. Since then she had read several of her books and had come to appreciate why her mother's generation had found her such a breath of fresh air. Now, in this moment of recollection, it seemed as though Mrs David had influenced even this garden. Cherry thought that later she might buy a plant – parsley, perhaps – and find a corner for it, to mark the day.

Not long after she had returned to the kitchen and put the batch of bread rolls in the oven, John telephoned to ask if she had heard the news: he knew that she would be touched by it, and he asked if she had spoken to her mother. Cherry said she would do so later, at a cheap evening rate. Things had been looking up a little since she had started The Summer Pudding Catering Company a year earlier, and though it was hard work and it had meant abandoning her Italian evening classes, she enjoyed the independence. The business was still modest. It consisted of Cherry, a van, an overdraft and anyone she could encourage to lend a hand, which meant she was not quite free of John's relations. It would have been so much easier with permanent help, but there was not enough money for a full-time partner.

Joely was the next to call to share some thoughts about Elizabeth David and to reminisce about the picnic on the Downs. And when Cherry returned from an evening function she found a note from John, who had long been in bed, telling her to call Nick. So for the third time that day, she had a conversation about the picnic on the Downs, the falcon and the walk through the woods to Folkington, and the woman who was, of course, not Elizabeth David at all. Nick said he had now bought all her books.

Though it was late, Cherry knew her mother would still be up and she called her, too. Grace sounded genuinely moved by the news. Who else in Ross, Cherry asked, had been acquainted with Elizabeth David?

'I wouldn't know now,' Grace said. 'I haven't heard her name mentioned since she left.'

'I'm sorry I didn't ever see her again,' Cherry said. 'There are lots of things I would have liked to ask her. I'm sure I would have enjoyed getting to know her. I bought some parsley and planted it for her.'

'She liked parsley,' said Grace.

This pleased Cherry and she promised to try to go down to Ross soon. Almost as soon as she replaced the receiver, the phone rang and she grabbed it quickly in case it woke John. It was Nick again.

'Sorry to call at this hour,' he said in a whisper. 'I knew there was something else I wanted to tell you. I've got a friend who's interested in cookery and I said you might have some work, or at least you might bear her in mind if you're looking for some help.'

'As it happens,' Cherry said, 'I could use someone tomorrow night.'

Nick said his friend's name was Madeleine and gave a number, which Cherry called at once and she was glad to hear an enthusiastic and well-spoken young woman tell her that she was free the following evening. And so Madeleine, a doe-eyed blonde with a full figure, arrived in a sensible black dress at five o'clock the next afternoon. She was confident but not pushy, bright but not smart and she set about the tasks Cherry gave her with a methodical thoroughness. A few years younger than Cherry, she had recently returned to London, she said, after spending a year in Paris.

'How did you meet Nick?' Cherry asked, as they prepared the food on the kitchen table.

'Sainsbury's,' Madeleine said.

Cherry crossed her fingers behind her back to wish Madeleine luck. When they had finished preparing the food, wrapped it in tin foil, put it in cloth-covered dishes and piled it inside plastic boxes, they loaded the van and set off for the City.

'It was sad about Elizabeth David,' said Madeleine as they headed south. 'Nick told me you once met her. What was she like?'

Cherry told her what happened, and then said, 'I think we would have lost her custom either way. If I had lied and said the fish came from the Bodensee, she might have caught me out – the lake's probably dripping with industrial chemicals. I'm quite glad I told her the truth.' She laughed. 'And I told her how to cook it. I probably gave her one of her own recipes!'

Madeleine didn't laugh. She said Cherry had been privileged to meet Mrs David and had done the right thing. Cherry knew she was going to be pleased to have Madeleine around.

One Saturday morning a few weeks later, Joely arrived to take Cherry off to Camden market where they spent a few hours among the stalls. Joely had settled down now with Oliver, and she was working in a small west London hotel. She looked pallid but she was cheerful. Cherry used the excursion to look for a present for John's birthday which was a couple of weeks away. A stuffed fish in a glass case was irresistible and she paid a deposit, saying she would pick it up in the van during the week. The card that went with it would be inscribed 'The one that got away'.

On their way back to Cherry's, Joely remembered The New Look dress shop, and headed off towards it, only to discover that a second-hand bookshop had taken its place. They peered in through the window. It was gloomy and musty and piled high with volumes, and it was hard to imagine the entertaining shop that it had once been. On a shelf of books near the window the name of Norman Douglas caught Cherry's eye.

A bell tinkled when she opened the door but there was no sign of life. She went over to a shelf and took down *Old Calabria*, and wondered if it would be like *South Wind*, which John had found so heavy going. Perhaps because of Elizabeth David's recent death, or perhaps because of finding the stuffed fish – whatever it was, she now felt predisposed to try reading Norman Douglas. This edition of *Old Calabria* had been packaged as a contemporary classic, suggesting it would be accessible for the modern reader.

'What's that?' Joely asked.

'Just a travel book on Italy,' Cherry said, not wanting to start explaining the whole story. 'Something my Italian teacher recommended.'

'Can I help?' a clipped voice intervened.

The man had emerged from the back of the shop. He was around sixty, upright and bright-eyed with a craggy face and grey hair and Cherry recognised him at once.

'What happened to The New Look?' Joely asked.

'Recession, taxes, unpaid rent – the usual sum of human misery.' He looked at Cherry.

'Frank Kaplan,' she said in answer to his quizzical frown. 'I'm Cherry Ingram, a former pupil at your Italian evening classes. Are you still teaching?'

'Afraid so.'

'I couldn't keep up with the classes: work got in the way.'

'It's no excuse. You have to stick at it. Next term I'll probably be doing two a week. You might find the extra Monday class easier to get to. Is that a purchase?

'Yes, please. How much is it?' She handed him the book.

'Norman Douglas,' he said, turning to the title page where the price had been pencilled. 'No better writer on Italy.'

'I thought you said your teacher recommended it,' said Joely.

'Different teacher,' said Cherry quickly.

'Seven pounds fifty,' Kaplan said.

That evening, after Joely had left, Cherry settled to a quiet Saturday night in with John. He liked to cook, and while he busied about his pots and bowls, she sat at the kitchen table with a glass of Pinot Grigio and a small bowl of prawns. She put on her glasses, plucked the pink head off a prawn and sucked out its contents as she opened *Old Calabria* and started to read. Halfway through the introduction she stopped and looked up at John who was attending to a chip pan. A pile of washed mussels was waiting to be dumped in a garlic wine broth.

'It says Norman Douglas travelled to Calabria with a twelve-year-old boy called Eric he picked up in London,' she said.

'That sounds like him.'

'You knew he did things like that?'

'Yes, I found out a long time ago.'

'Why didn't you say?' She pulled off another prawn's tail and unwrapped the crinkly pink skin from its body, removing, as she did so, a purse of deep pink eggs on the end of her thumb, which she sucked.

'It was nothing to brag about,' John said. He began to empty the mussels into a big Le Creuset pan, which he slowly stirred with a large wooden spoon.

Cherry frowned. 'Does your father know his uncle was a paedophile?'

John continued stirring the mussels. 'When I found out about it, the first person I told was my brother, Christopher, but he already knew. He said he had tried to talk to Dad about it a couple of times, but he was always slapped down. When I brought the subject up with Dad, he wouldn't hear a word of it. He got very angry. He knows, but he's kind of proud to have a famous relative, proud to say he is related to an English writer, but not proud enough to take on board the whole, dirty old man.'

'I wonder what his mother thought.'

'Why don't you ask him tomorrow?'

Lunch at the Dorellis' the next day was the usual boisterous affair. As the latest bride, Cherry continued to take her place next to Angelo while young Isabel, unwed, continued to be consigned to the far end of the table. Conversationally, Cherry told Angelo she had just started reading *Old Calabria*. He said he had not read the book himself but he had heard it was good, and he offered her another helping of pavlova.

'You might be interested in it,' she said. 'Calabria is near Naples, isn't it?'

'More to the south. It's very wild, the *malavita*. When I was a boy there were still many bandits in the hills.'

'It sounds exciting. I'd like to go there.'

'No, you wouldn't like to go there. It's a very poor part of the country. Tuscany, Umbria are much better. You eat badly in Calabria and there is no culture, no history.'

It was clear he had no intention of reading the book. She waited until after lunch, when John was out in the garden with the children, and she was sharing a cigar with her father-in-law, before she expressed an interest in Angelo's parents and asked if she could see their picture. Angelo took down the silver frame from the top shelf in the bookcase and handed it to her.

'A beautiful couple,' he said.

'They certainly are.'

The young woman in the picture was vivacious and dark-eyed; the young man looked hearty and good company, not tuberculous at all. The Dorelli sisters may have inherited some of their grandmother's looks, and perhaps John's solid features owed something to his grandfather, but there was no great family resemblance that she could see. The picture was taken in an evening light and the couple were dressed up, at some outdoor fair. They looked too young to be parents, let alone the great-grandparents they were to become.

'I think the picture must have been taken just after they met, a few years before I was born. I know very little about my father. Just what my mother told me. Of course, I would like to know more.'

'What were their names?' Cherry asked.

'My mother was called Annetta. My father was Eric.'

'That's interesting,' she said carefully. 'Eric was the name of a young boy Norman Douglas took with him to Calabria when he wrote this book.' Cherry watched Angelo's face closely, but the pale grey eyes and the ingrained wrinkles of his honest face gave no clue that he might be trying to hide something.

'I don't know anything about that,' he said, taking the frame from her and placing it back out of reach. 'Eric is a common name.'

'Where did the picture come from?'

'My uncle Michele, my mother's brother. He was the only relative left alive that I could find in Naples. A strange man. The photograph was with a box of papers he had rescued from her belongings. You must remember how hungry everyone was. Everything she had would have been distributed. I was lucky the papers were not eaten, too. That's how I had the address of Uncle Norman: his letters to her were in the box with the photograph.'

'Were there any letters from your father?'

'No, my father had been dead for many years.'

'What happened to your uncle Michele?'

'I don't know. I did not keep in touch.'

'Do you still have the box?'

'No. It's a pity. It was a nice confectionery box, prettily decorated, from the Caffè d'Italia in the Via Roma. But Molly sold it with some other things to a shop in Camden soon after we met, when we didn't have much money.'

'And the letter?'

'They're in the attic somewhere with all the children's things. I don't know if I can find them now.'

'That's a shame,' Cherry said, knowing that he would not try to look for them, that they were lost forever.' And you have never wanted to go back to Naples?'

'Never.'

In the summer a small incident occurred which Cherry afterwards thought about quite a lot. She and Joely returned to Eastbourne, motoring down for a day in Joely's car. They had been invited by their old college to be external judges in a cookery demonstration given by a dozen chefs from Rimini in the Adriatic, who had come on a two-week course to study English cookery so that they could serve their English guests with proper English food. 'Fifty quid, a free lunch at the Grand and more Italian chefs than you can shake a stick at' was how Joely had sold the proposition to her. As it turned out, it was Joely who was more interested in the chefs, allowing herself to get lost with one of them between the college and the Grand Hotel lunch, leaving Cherry feeling anxious and awkward for more than an hour.

On their way home, Cherry said: 'What on earth do you think you were doing? Everyone knew what was going on.'

'You're such a prude,' Joely said.

'The flat tyre was such a pathetic excuse. It was like being back at school again.'

Joely laughed and said, 'Happiest days of my life.'

If John heard a whisper of Cherry doing something similar, she thought, he would die, and she asked, 'What about Oliver?'

'Oh, he's probably slavering over some lunch-time barmaid. They're all at it, even your John, I bet. You've got to do it to them first before they do it to you: it's the only way not to get hurt. Look at Nick. I loved that guy, but in the end I wasn't even second fiddle: I came in fifth or sixth.'

In the early autumn, Cherry happened to mention the extra Italian evening classes to Madeleine, and she immediately expressed interest. So they both enrolled for a year in Frank Kaplan's Monday session. Madeleine was becoming increasingly involved in Cherry's business, and Cherry was glad of her company socially, too. In addition, she felt sure they would encourage each other to keep up with the course.

In the class, there were one or two familiar faces whom Cherry recognised from her previous attempts, but most of the pupils were new. Kaplan strode in at the start of the lesson, and did not bother with introductions or formalities, talking to them in rapid Italian straight away. At first Cherry did not think he had recognised her, but just before the break he asked her to translate a sentence about going on holiday in Calabria with a young nephew. She did not get the answer quite right, and he threw it open to the rest of the class.

'How old is the nephew?' a Scot called Jamie Cooper Clarke wanted to know.

'When is a boy not a boy?' asked a middle-aged woman

called Muriel, who had been at all the previous classes.

'How old is the nephew?' Kaplan asked Cherry.

Cherry said, '*Dodici.*'

Muriel said she thought that in England boys were boys until they could get married – at eighteen. Jamie Cooper Clarke said that in Scotland it was sixteen, a talking point he tried to continue with Cherry and Madeleine as they queued for a cup of tea in the break. At the end of the lesson, as Cherry walked past Kaplan's desk, he looked up.

'Did you finish *Old Calabria*?' he asked.

'Yes, I did. Do you know what happened to Eric, the boy who went with him?'

Kaplan narrowed his eyes thoughtfully. 'A good question. He featured quite a lot in Douglas's life. His autobiography is dedicated to the boy. If I recall, he ended up in the colonial service in Africa.'

'Was Douglas really a paedophile?'

Kaplan let out an explosive laugh. 'Huh! I was going to say, "Is the Pope Catholic" but in the circumstances it wouldn't be too appropriate.' He looked directly at her, his blue eyes never more intense. 'Norman Douglas was a monster, the paedophile of the century – and there has been no shortage of competition. By all accounts he liked adventure with the dirtiest guttersnipes he could literally lay his hands on. He had absolutely no morals, he pursued a vice. It was simply sensation-seeking, showing off, and he was always getting into scrapes, in England and Austria and Italy and France.'

Cherry was shocked to uncover this common knowledge about a relation whom her father-in-law had talked of so reverentially for the past five years. But the evidence had been drifting this way for some time. It was not so surprising that John had been so reluctant to tell her about his illustrious forebear. Others would have been even more deeply affected by Douglas's habits.

Shaking her head as if to clear her thoughts she said, 'Oh my, what a sheltered life I have lead.'

CHAPTER 17

Thirty, Autumn 1993

Cherry took the leavened dough from the earthenware pancheon, dropped it on to the floured kitchen table with a thud and began knocking it back with gusto. As she pushed and squeezed and slapped the engorged mixture, she knew the chemistry was right: it welled between her fingers; the gas bubbles were redistributed; the gluten developed and the yeast was reinvigorated. She would beat the life out of it and she would beat life into it. All creation began with wheat winnowed from the chaff, with flour from the mill, with yeast from the wind, with a bun in the oven.

But still she did not want a baby. John wanted a baby, and John's father wanted a baby, but she wanted something more. A few hours ago her thirtieth birthday had drawn to an uneventful close. She did not want to get old. Her hands were starting to crack like her mother's, alcohol was at work on her jowls and she was coming up to what she thought might be a seven-year itch. They were getting no richer. Work was often little more than a chore.

It hadn't been much of a birthday. John had left by the time she awoke, and he was asleep by the time she had returned from a function she could not afford to turn down. At lunch-time a generous bunch of mixed flowers had been delivered with a note from John. He phoned soon afterwards and sounded disappointed she had not unwrapped the small pile of gifts he had left on the kitchen table. Cherry said she did not want to open them alone, and was waiting for Madeleine to come round. In the late afternoon her helper and partner arrived with a bottle of champagne. Cherry opened the parcels: the jersey she herself had chosen was fine, so were the chocolates, the white plastic fifties earrings and a Vivaldi CD. She had left John a thank-you note before she and Madeleine drove off to the evening function.

Now it was late, after midnight, the day gone. *The Four Seasons* was playing quietly from speakers in the kitchen and a light rain pattered on the uncurtained window panes. Autumn was setting in and the garden was dying back. These were her hours, when the streets slept and the world was lost to people's dreams. As she shaped the breakfast rolls and put them into the oven, she imagined the kitchen a hundred years ago, when a range would have filled the space beneath the chimney breast now occupied with shelves, and a copper would have bubbled with soups and stews, filling the room with steam and warmth and good smells. She poured another small brandy, which went so well with the birthday chocolates, and imagined a contented Edwardian mother, drinking tea by the fireside and dandling a baby on her knee. Perhaps there was also a daughter to dress, a son to be proud of, a husband who came home on time each evening, put on his slippers and had a fresh pot of tea. Why did these thoughts bring her comfort and contentment when she wanted no such life for herself? How could she feel nostalgia for something she had never known?

The hum of the shower pump broke into her reverie, announcing that John was getting up. It was a quarter past four, later than she had thought. With her mind still deep in the night, Cherry filled the kettle, and by the time John strode into the kitchen ten minutes later, the rolls were cooling on the grill and a pot of Assam tea was mashing. He sniffed deeply on the goodness that filled the air.

'Hmmm,' he said appreciatively, 'if you could put that smell in spray cans you could sell it to society women who could pretend they knew how to cook. Or to people trying to sell their houses: one squirt and the deal would be in the bag. Happy birthday for yesterday.' He kissed her on the cheek. 'Sorry I missed it.'

'You didn't miss a thing.'

He was depressingly cheerful at this hour of the day. His curly hair was wet as seaweed and his fragrances made Cherry feel in need of a shower and hair wash herself. Involuntarily, she scratched at her scalp.

'Never mind. We'll have a great meal on Saturday.'

'I've saved you some chocolates.'

'Oh, good. I'll have one tonight.' He poured a cup of the tea and broke open a steaming roll, which he layered with Breton *beurre doux* and three-fruit marmalade. 'These mornings are a bit like the international dateline,' he said. 'Tuesday night and Wednesday morning. Should be a film: "Yesterday's Woman Meets Tomorrow's Man."'

Cherry was scrubbing the pancheon in the sink. To her this was not a bright, fresh-cup-of-tea day, it was still the dregs of the dreamy night. A glass of brandy on the kitchen table was still waiting to be drunk and she felt more than half a day adrift.

'Starring Tuesday Weld and Wednesday Marsalis,' John went on, picking up two rolls and plunging them into his jacket pockets. 'Roll-mop rolls for lunch. Are you out tonight?'

'A buffet in Brent. I said I'd be there around five. I should be back before midnight. I'll try not to wake you.'

'Tomorrow?'

'I'm doing a Thursday Italian class.'

He said, 'We must go to bed together some time.'

He leaned over and kissed her on the cheek. She sighed. At

least she stayed up late, so they could meet over breakfast. Otherwise days might go by without them seeing each other at all. Was that why she often did not go to bed until he was up? She could no longer be sure. Lately, on these ever-darkening mornings, she had sometimes stayed up until *Farming Today* on the radio brought her news of life in the country. The night was making her pale and not helping with the ageing process at all.

When he had finished his breakfast, John rose from the table and said, 'Can I take two more? Bernard loves them.'

Without waiting for her assent he pushed another couple of warm rolls into his pockets. It was still dark outside, but already the shutters would be opening on the stalls at Billingsgate fish market on the Isle of Dogs and his mind would be on the slabs and crates of fresh catches that lay ahead. Cherry offered him another cheek as he passed on his way out.

'Ruby Tuesday meets Sheffield Wednesday,' he muttered to himself as he left.

The front door closed behind him, leaving dawn's breath on the mat, and as the sound of his Citroën died away, she felt the chill of the new day nip her ankles.

Two days later, on Friday, John came home with a new idea. He was going to order an aquarium of such vastness that it would fill the shop window. Cherry wondered if they could afford it, and John said they could not afford to pass up such a plan. There was money about again: the recession might be over and what he needed was a bit of publicity. Cherry was getting ready for an event, stacking prepared food from the larder on to the kitchen table.

She said, 'Don't forget to bring something home for tomorrow night.'

He said, 'How could I forget your birthday dinner?'

'Joely said she'd bring a pudding.'

He grimaced. Dinner parties were his particular show. He put on the kettle, fetched a bag of *porcini* and *bricioloni* dried wild mushrooms from a cupboard, tipped a handful into a cup and put on the kettle. It was a quarter to six, time for his supper. Cherry was in the outside larder when the doorbell rang and John went to answer it. As she returned to the kitchen, he was telling Madeleine about the aquarium.

'It will be enormous,' he said. 'You look cold. Do you want a tea?'

'I'm all right. We shouldn't be long.' Madeleine wore sling-back high heels and black tights, and beneath her black gaberdine that radiated the cold afternoon air was her work uniform of black pencil skirt and white blouse.

'I'm still not sure what to put in the aquarium,' John said. 'Lobsters are a bit crabby. I want something more exotic.

'Mermaids,' said Cherry.

Madeleine said, 'Now there's an idea.'

Cherry said, 'We'd better start loading up.'

'What is it tonight?' John asked.

'The usual,' Cherry replied. '*Boeuf bourguignon*.'

'City job, eh? Beef for the boys.' John had begun whisking three eggs in a tumbler. 'But "Fish For Real Fellas". I put that on the blackboard outside today. Want a hand?'

'No,' said Cherry.

'Fish For Real Fellas?' said Madeleine. 'Did it do any good?'

'A couple of gurnards looked like impulse buys.'

'I don't think I've had gurnard,' said Madeleine. 'Do you two want to come for supper tomorrow?'

'Joely and Oliver are coming over,' said Cherry.

'We're celebrating Cherry's thirtieth,' John said, adding a little naturally carbonated water to his sunny mix. 'Why don't you join us?'

'All right.' Madeleine sounded pleased to be asked. 'Nick's

got a new *hors d'oeuvre* he's been dying to try out on someone. He can bring it.'

John's grimace this time was designed for an audience, and Cherry laughed, knowing that he really was put out. It served him right for not checking with her before handing out invitations to her birthday dinner. Joely and Nick hadn't seen each other since they split up; perhaps it was time they were friends again.

They started to load the banquet into the beige van parked outside beneath the sickening yellow street light. When they had bought the vehicle, John had picked it out because, he said, it had the reassuring colour of brown soda bread. There were dents in the bodywork now, and a little rust combined with late autumn gloom to make The Summer Pudding Catering Company's liveried conveyance look as if it might contain kitchen scraps rather than gourmet meals. The back of the van, designed and largely built by John, was kitted out with shelves, coolboxes and storage units that would carry the bowls and dishes of food – meats and sauces, salads, puddings and fruits – as well as cutlery, crockery and condiments. It had been constructed to produce the minimum of spillage and rattle.

Just as the evening's courses were finally loaded, the telephone rang. The caller said he had seen The Summer Pudding advertisements and he wanted a wedding reception for fifty, around next Valentine's Day, with all courses containing aphrodisiac food. Cherry, late, said it would be no problem, took his number and promised to get back to him soon. It was not until the van was moving out into Camden Street that Cherry told Madeleine about the phone call. It was rather a silly idea, they agreed, but it might also be fun.

'I've got a baptism there next week,' said Madeleine as they passed the austere neoclassical Greek Orthodox Church. 'Nick's sister's kid.'

'You must be almost family by now.'

'I've moved in with him.'

'Really.' Cherry was surprised at the news. 'So Nick's finally settling down?'

'He wants a baby by next Christmas.'

'They all want babies,' Cherry said. 'Will you oblige?'

'In for a penny.' Madeleine laughed lightly. 'What about you and John? Are you two going to have children?'

'John would like to, and his family would make me a saint if I did. But I'm not in a rush. I've still got lots to do.'

'Like what?'

She sighed. 'I don't know.'

The birthday dinner was under control when Madeleine and Nick arrived the following evening with the first course, to join Joely and Oliver around the pine table in the Camden kitchen. John was ebullient and didn't even mind Nick providing the cold risotto made with fresh Chilean hop shoots and arboreal rice, drizzled with splashes of balsamic vinegar, and he joined in the general round of congratulation prompted by Joely and Oliver who, as pudding providers, had longest to wait for critical acclaim. They all got on well, in spite of past liaisons and apparent differences: Joely, crop-haired, skinny and streetwise, was a contrast to staid and steady Madeleine; Oliver, an increasingly large alien from the fast world of information technology, in which John was, like most people, vaguely interested, was quite unlike the worldly Nick, who managed to offend John by filling everyone's glass to the brim when they were anything less than half full.

'Steady on,' John said as the rough Sicilian red came around for the third time during what was, after all, only the first course. 'I won't know how much I've drunk.'

'My family is Macedonian,' said Nick with pride. 'Macedonians consider it impolite if there is any emptiness showing in a guest's glass, and they always fill it to the top. That is how you tell a Macedonian.'

Joely said, 'Elizabeth David said it's impolite, because it doesn't allow you to work out how many glasses you've drunk.'

'Is that right?' John asked, turning to Cherry as the fount of all Elizabeth David knowledge.

Cherry nodded. 'It was something Norman Douglas taught her.' She said it without thinking, without remembering that she was talking about an in-law several times removed.

'Who's he?' asked Nick.

'Oh, just some old literary bugger,' said John casually. He looked at Cherry. 'And a distant relation, as it happens.'

'Really?' said Nick. 'I didn't know there was any culture in the Dorelli DNA.'

'Don't worry about it,' said John. 'Only touches one generation in ten. Besides, I take after my mother.'

'I hope you cook like her.'

Like his father, John did not seem anxious to talk any further about his literary relation. While banter continued about the cooking, Cherry cleared away the plates and John prepared the main course: sea bream cooked beneath a pile of sea salt. He took it from the oven and, after showing the impressive and slightly improbable mound to the assembled company and explaining the benefits of cooking fish in heaps of salt, he put it on the side and began chipping away at the saline carcass to reveal the fish which he deftly sliced and served with baby carrots, *cavolfiori al stracinati* (cauliflower flowerets, par boiled, then mashed and browned in a pan of hot oil and garlic) and Cyprus new potatoes flavoured with fresh mint. It was all ready at the same time and he needed no help in serving it.

'I always thought that's what people with a drink problem did,' said Oliver as Joely topped up his glass. 'They have to count what they're drinking. People who are just enjoying themselves don't care. She did drink a lot, didn't she, Elizabeth David?'

'No more than some I know,' Cherry said defensively.

'Did you see that the contents of her house are up for auction?' Oliver said.

'The Chelsea house?' Cherry felt hurt, as if someone should have told her earlier, as if something had happened in the family and she had found out from a stranger.

'It was in the paper this morning,' said Oliver. 'Yes, I suppose it'll be all the stuff from the house you visited. Do you reckon there was anything worth snapping up?'

'I'd love to own an original Elizabeth David Le Creuset pan,' said Nick.

They should all go, said Joely, and she urged Cherry to find out where the auction was being held. Wine bottles were piling up. With a great clatter and further comments of appreciation, John cleared the plates away. Joely's contribution to the evening arrived: a chocolate cream mousse with paper-thin *cenci* biscuits, sprinkled with caster sugar and cut in the shape of hearts. After waiting so long in the wings, the relief of hearing general approval for her dish made her visibly relax, and she quickly became very drunk. Cherry, by this time, could not remember if she had had six glasses of wine or seven. Oliver attempted to say he would design an 'alcoholics' abacus' to count the number of drinks people had, but the two words became muddled up.

At around midnight Cherry brought out a marble slab on which were some simple cheeses – Dolcelatte, goat, an interesting Sussex Slipcoat – and a fresh loaf of wholewheat soda bread if anyone was still hungry. She also produced a chilled silver bowl of crushed pomegranate seeds, sprinkled with rosewater, lemon and sugar, and gave everyone a teaspoon. John complemented it with a couple of bottles of sweet white Beaume-de-Venise and Joely, tucking into everything, found her inability to connect her spoon with the pomegranate seeds excruciatingly funny.

'I don't know why you're laughing,' said Oliver. 'You've got to drive home.'

'Why can't you drive?'

'Because I'm drunk.'

Joely pealed with laughter again.

'We'll take you if you want,' said Nick. 'I haven't drunk much.'

'How can you tell?' Cherry asked.

Nick grinned, showing his fine white teeth, and he said, 'A Macedonian knows how to drink.'

'He was a shirt-lifter,' said John, looking suddenly alert. He had done well not to fall asleep at the table, which was his usual party trick. 'Alexander the Great. Liked to bunk up with the new recruits.'

'Of course he wasn't,' Nick replied indignantly. 'He was the greatest general in all history.'

John shook his head. 'Not what I read. He was a real bugger, that Alexander, rogered the ranks every day before breakfast.'

'Wogering the wanks?' Joely said poshly. 'Surely you mean wanking the wogers.' And she pealed with laughter again.

Cherry could not help laughing too, but Nick was upset. 'You don't know what you are talking about,' he said, as if he were addressing tiresome children. He looked at John. 'In Macedonia, culture does not skip a single generation.'

John grinned affably. 'Don't worry, darling, your secret's safe with us.'

But Nick did not find the jokes funny, and he suddenly seemed the only sober person at the table. It broke the evening up, and soon afterwards they rose, one by one, taking with them the bowls and pots they had brought with them, now scraped clean, and wishing Cherry happy birthday and wondering if they would see each other again before Christmas.

By the front door the cold air made them contrite and they all vowed to come to the launch of the aquarium, which John said would be in the New Year. Joely promised to dress as a mermaid, though everyone would have to put up with the sight of her breasts because her hair was so short. She kissed John on the lips with a smack and led the guests, giggling, into the night.

After they had gone, John asked Cherry if she was coming to bed. She said she would be along in a few minutes, after she had put a couple of things in to soak. As she pottered about, filling pans, scraping plates, covering up leftovers and putting them in the fridge, she wondered about John and his homophobic outbursts. Perhaps it was time the skeleton of a paedophile in the family closet was exorcised and laid to rest.

She did not mean to wash up, but after she had rinsed a few glasses and soaked a few dishes, she kept going. Just after three o'clock she climbed into bed, shaking John hard enough to stop his snoring, but not hard enough to wake him up.

CHAPTER 18

Venus in the Kitchen, Winter 1994

Work was piling up in the third week in February. Cherry had two mid-week functions, John was preparing for his aquarium opening on the Friday, and the aphrodisiac wedding party on Saturday was turning out to be the most ambitious project Cherry had undertaken. The event, which was to be held in the function room above a local pub, had begun in a relatively straightforward way, but as the date neared, the best man, who had booked the party, began warming to the theme: the menu changed several times, the demands steadily grew and the numbers crept up to more than eighty. Cherry liked people to be meticulous and know what they wanted, but the best man had also been anxious and excited, phoning her most days with new instructions, or to find out how it was going. A borrowed chest freezer was now sitting unceremoniously in her front room, which was also stacked with begged and borrowed pots and containers, and at dawn on Friday, while John went to pick up 300 oysters for her at Billingsgate, Cherry collected thirty brace of pheasant from Smithfield market. The birds were now sitting in a cold larder which had been converted from the outside lavatory.

Later that morning, as she was sorting out the ingredients in the kitchen, listening to Liszt on the radio, Madeleine arrived with a girl in heavy boots, denims and a big brown jumper who looked young enough to be still at school.

'This is Francine,' said Madeleine. 'She can help out tomorrow, too.'

'The more the merrier,' said Cherry leading them into the kitchen. 'I'll fetch aprons.'

Cherry then went through the ingredients – the dried apricots, prunes, cherries, mushrooms, cinnamon, saffron and cloves that formed the basis of the stuffing for the game birds – and talked through the crucial timing of the three courses.

'Is this supposed to turn people on?' asked Francine, curious but unconvinced.

'This and several crates of champagne,' said Cherry.

'John has got the oysters for the starter,' said Madeleine. 'I called him to see if he wanted a hand at the aquarium opening this afternoon. I said I'd get there half an hour beforehand.'

The phone rang.

'It's probably the best man with another change of plan,' Cherry said as she went into the hall. She was starting to feel harassed.

'Hello?' The voice was thin and cautious.

Cherry let out a small sigh. 'Hello, Mum.'

Grace wanted to know exactly when she and John would be arriving at the weekend. Cherry explained she had a function on Saturday night and would be driving down on Sunday afternoon, staying a night, and coming back on Monday, or perhaps Tuesday.

'What about John?'

'He has to be at work early on Monday. It's not worth him coming.'

It was precisely the same conversation they had had three days earlier. Although Grace was only sixty-three, she was forgetting things, and starting to sound old. Cherry asked her mother if she wanted to drive back with her and stay a few days, and perhaps come along to the Elizabeth David auction which was to be held some time the following week. But as usual these days, her mother, who had only ever visited John and Cherry once, not long after they moved in to their home, could not be persuaded to leave Ross.

It was only after she put down the phone that Cherry remembered she had meant to tell her mother about the Elizabeth David action. It had slipped to the back of her mind under the weight of planning the aphrodisiac wedding reception. Before she did anything else, she wanted to find out exactly when it was taking place. Phillips', the auctioneers, were in the phone book and when she called them she was surprised to find that viewing for the sale, due the following Tuesday in their Bayswater showroom, had already begun. If she went now, she could get a catalogue to show her mother at the weekend. There was no time to be lost. She phoned Joely, who said she would have loved to come, but hotel work prevented her from getting away.

When Cherry returned to the kitchen and told Madeleine that there was a chance of going to the preview, her partner had no hesitation in urging her to go at once, saying that she and Francine would be quite happy to finish off the work for the reception. Cherry, excited, kissed her on the cheek and told her she did not know what she would do without her.

Fifteen minutes later, in coat and headscarf, Cherry was rattling round the Circle Line to Bayswater, looking forward with mixed feelings to scrutinising the contents of Elizabeth David's Halsey Street home. Viewing was in the first-floor sale room of the auction house, which took up nearly a block off Moscow Road. Signs led her up the stairs and into a long room, draped with blue curtains and lit by tall casement windows. Several dozen people were shuffling around and a young assistant handed her a clip of photocopied sheets. Cherry put on her glasses and peered at them.

'The catalogues have sold out,' the young woman said. 'But more are being printed. We didn't estimate such a demand.'

Cherry was immediately drawn towards the centrepiece of the exhibition, a grouping of kitchen furniture near the rostrum. Here was the answer to the confusion she had had about the rooms in the basement: there had been not one kitchen but two: one for summer, one for winter. In this four-bedroomed Chelsea house, resisting fitted units and central heating, Elizabeth David had spent the last forty years of her life. Here were just some of the items she had accumulated; a famous clutter of books and implements which reflected her inspirations and passions. There was her five-plank pine table, the very one Cherry had seen her sitting at, and a nineteenth-century farmhouse dresser. Other small tables and cabinets were set around it, and the whole was arranged to look like a working kitchen, with jars and pots, graters and whisks, plates and bowls. The only thing lacking was, rather essentially, something to eat. But Cherry was enchanted, recalling the intimacy of the occasion when she had visited this extraordinary woman. She put her hand on the table; picked up a wooden spoon; ran her fingers around the edge of a bowl. It was almost as if she had been invited personally into the kitchen again, this time to share its secrets, to know its hospitality, to be offered lunch.

In all there were 177 lots: forty-seven of ceramics, seven of glassware, thirteen of utensils and cutlery, thirty-six of miscellaneous items, three of textiles, eleven of paintings and prints, eight of books, five of ephemera, twenty-six of metalware, mostly kitchen equipment, and twenty-one of furniture, including the kitchen table. Each item bore a specially printed tag with the lot number written on it in a blue felt-tip pen. There was no questioning the items' provenance. Long tables down each side of the room were so carefully arranged that the discerning David readers could identify the implements grouped as they had appeared in line drawings in her books, and the occasional remark from a prospective buyer showed who was in the know. Cherry moved with awe among them, touching now and then the items Mrs David had touched, hoping to feel the magic of her heroine's life filter through her: a silver nutmeg grater from Tiffany's, a personalised Tabasco holder, a lignum vitae rolling pin, an *hachoir*, Mouli and mandoline. There was the Le Creuset casserole Mrs David had introduced to Britain, grubby with use, and the potato diable, reassuringly blackened and deliberately never washed. A real favourite must have been the old picnic bag, worn down by countless pleasurable pastoral outings, with a Thermos flask, wooden trencher, fifties glass coffee cups and corkscrew. There were also prosaic and sensible aluminium cooking pots and Tupperware containers: it did not for one moment occur to Cherry that it was unusual for one of the major London auction houses to be selling second-hand Tupperware. Every so often she would stop and breathe deeply, inhaling the legacy of the most famous private kitchen in the world.

Yet she also had the feeling that, however impressive the collection was, it was not complete. In particular there was no sign of the cast-iron omelette pan she had seen in Mrs David's sink, and there were none of the famous headscarves, though there were bundles of collected postcards, calling cards, menus, cuttings and sketches, and a trunk of muslins and damasks.

With a tinge of regret, it dawned on Cherry that the great cook's most precious items could not have been here, but would have been passed on to close friends and relatives. She scoured the stapled, photocopied catalogue pages. The fulsome Foreword, written by Stephen Gray whom Cherry took to be a relative, explained that her books had gone to the Warburg Institute in London, and to the Guildhall Library in the City. But there were some left, put out on small bookcases, as they might have been in her much more cluttered home. Others were guarded in glass display cabinets behind the kitchen tableau. Cherry looked along their shelves. All seven of Elizabeth David's cookbooks were there in various lots, none in the original hardback.

A 1955 paperback edition of her first book, *A Book of Mediterranean Food*, was on the shelf. Grace's hardback edition would have fetched quite a price. At Cherry's request, an assistant unlocked the glass cabinet door, slid it open and handed her the book. Under his gaze she began turning the pages, looking for anything to show that this was a special copy. Her eyes fell on the last paragraph on the page of Acknowledgements: 'Above all I have a debt of gratitude to the late Mr Norman Douglas, whose great knowledge and enchanting talk taught me so much about the Mediterranean.'

Next, she asked for the paperback *Italian Food*, published in 1954. Elizabeth David's livid red pen had excised whole paragraphs and added amendments for the next edition. An incisive slash removed all mention of the Elizabeth David shop in Sloane Square which she had helped to found but with whom she had fallen out. Cherry could sense in that vermilion scar the author's frostiest indignation.

It was only after she had returned the paperback to the shelf that she saw the small green clothbound book with a title in faded, barely legible gold print. The assistant unlocked the case once more, pushed back the glass panel, reached inside and handed her Elizabeth David's copy of *Old Calabria*. It was not an original edition; on the spine was printed New Adelphi Library in the same faded gold as the title. Cherry opened the book at the first page, which was blank save for an inscription in a neat hand in black ink: '21 May 1940. N'. She stared at it for a few moments before flicking through the next 400 pages, anxious for more messages from the past. There were none. She reached the back cover, and inside it another inscription was carelessly scribbled in pencil: 'Always do as you please and send everybody to Hell, and take the consequences. Damned good Rule in Life. N'.

Cherry's heart quickened and nervously, involuntarily, she laughed. In her hands she had evidence of the connection between two of the most influential arbiters of taste who together spanned the twentieth century. It also seemed to have a special place in her own life, as a souvenir of the extraordinary woman she had met, and as a legacy from Douglas for the man she had married. The fact that she was now touching the book, more than half a century after the inscription had been penned, seemed confirmation that their lives were somehow predestined and intertwined.

Reluctantly, Cherry returned the book to the assistant, who put it back on the shelf and relocked the case. There was no sign of other works by Douglas, no other clues to illuminate the relationship between the two. But *Old Calabria* was an eloquent memento of the pair and Cherry wondered seriously about coming to the auction the following Thursday and putting in a bid. The catalogue gave no price guide for the lot that contained the book, though another lot, which included half a dozen paperback copies of her cookbooks, had a reserve price of £80–£120, which, though high, was not completely out of reach. John would not be too concerned how much she spent, but she had a more realistic grasp of their financial situation, and she was slightly uneasy about spending so much.

The thought of her husband caused her to glance at her watch and she was shocked to see how long she had spent in the showroom. The aquarium opening in Camden would soon be starting and there was still a lot to do for Saturday's event. With one last look around, she left the auctioneers and took the tube home again. It was after four o'clock and the rush-hour crowds left no seats free. There was barely room to unfold the evening tabloid: NATO forces were standing by to pound the Serbs around Sarajevo; Hillary Clinton's younger brother was threatening to stand for the Senate; Ellington, the last coal mine in north-east England, had closed with the loss of 1,160 jobs; and Torville and Dean were set to carry the torch into the Winter Olympics in Norway. As far as Cherry was concerned, none of the day's news stories had anything approaching the significance of Elizabeth David's auction. As she turned to the Foreign News, a brief item caught her eye: NUREYEV ISLAND SALE. It read: 'Li Galli, a three-island archipelago off the Amalfi coast which belonged to Rudolf Nureyev, is expected to go on sale later this year for 4.8 billion lire (£2 million). The dancer, who died last year at the age of 54 of an AIDS-related disease, bought the property, known as the Siren Islands, in 1989.' Nothing is owned, Cherry thought, neither islands nor omelette pans. They are only borrowed for a while from the common wealth.

The flat was quiet and empty when she returned. The helpers had gone, but there was a note on the kitchen table. *All done – see you up there*, it said in Madeleine's copperplate, finishing-school handwriting. But there was still a lot to do: too much to contemplate now. Cherry put on the kettle for a cup of Earl Grey tea and changed into a starched white blouse, petticoats and a duck-egg blue fifties skirt with matching stiletto shoes, which would probably make her overdressed in a fish shop, but John liked to see her dressed up and this was his night. Her hair quickly washed and blow-dried into life, make-up lightly touched up, she pulled on a headscarf and coat and took a cab to the fishmonger's shop.

The taxi stopped just short of the large crowd which spilled over the pavement outside the shop – made up, it was clear, not just of guests, but of passers-by who were straining to see what was going on. A flashlight popped a couple of times and laughter came out in waves. On the edge of the crowd were

Joely and Oliver. Cherry paid the cab driver and went over to meet them.

'How is it?' she asked.

'The event of the year.' Joely was hopping from one foot to another.

'Bought any good omelette pans?' Oliver enquired, grinning.

'Was it interesting?' Joely wanted to know.

'It was extraordinary. Moving. Spooky. Inspirational. Bizarre.'

'I'm sorry I couldn't come. But I'll definitely come to the auction next week.'

'You haven't got your mermaid costume on.'

'Yes I have, the top half – underneath.' Joely waved her arms wide and looked down at her waif-sized body encompassed in a forties land-girl outfit. 'I put on a siren suit but nobody's got the joke and it's too hard to explain. It was a complete waste of time.' She laughed. 'But the seal's going down well.'

'The seal?'

'Didn't you know about the seal?'

'The surprises never cease.'

'Lucky you.'

Before Cherry could ask if she should expect any other surprises, there came a honking bark from the shop, a loud splash and a cheer. A huge commotion and shrieks were followed by a parting of the crowd as the glistening, whiskery black seal slapped out of the shop across the pavement towards the road, waving its head and sniffing the crowd, which it regarded with great round button eyes. Joely instinctively ran forward to stop it waddling under a bus. John, wet, happy and in a broad blue-and-white-striped apron, tried to grab the animal from behind but it remained impervious to all injunctions until the shrill whistle of a man Cherry took to be the animal's minder caught its attention. It turned its supercilious, snooty nose, barked and cheerfully accepted the red ball the minder threw, tossing it around as it headed back into the fray.

'Hi!' John waved a raw herring at Cherry. 'Come and have some wine. I've saved you some fish.'

'Who's your friend?'

'Sally the seal. Cute, isn't she?'

'You'll have the animal rights lobby after you, never mind the Health Inspector.'

'Nonsense, she's in her element, like a kid in a sweet factory.'

He tossed the herring in the air, and with a deep 'aarp', Sally chucked away the ball, caught the fish and smacked it down in a single swallow, to general applause. The whole shop window was now taken up by the new aquarium, beside which was a plank to facilitate Sally's entry and exit. The water was slopping wildly.

John put his arm around Cherry and led her through the crowd into the shop, squeezing in through the door. Angelo was there, with half the Dorelli family and Madeleine was beside the aquarium, listening to a bald, middle-aged man, but otherwise she knew only a handful of the guests who were made up of wholesalers, restaurateurs, customers and fellow shop-keepers. Nick and Francine said hello as John and Cherry pushed passed, apologising.

'The hostess with the mostest, looking stunning as usual, Cherry,' said Nick cheerfully.

Cherry smiled thinly. 'It's not my party.'

'It's quite a turnout,' said Nick.

'Anything for free drinks,' said John, slapping him on the shoulder. 'And a bit of a show. People like a bit of a show.'

'Chablis, Cherry?' Bernard, also in a blue-striped apron, was behind the counter splashing out the wine. With the glass, he offered her a toothpick with a roll-mop herring on it: 'Fish kebab?' There was also a tray of various smoked fish and shell-fish, and there were several small piles of battered squid and whitebait in which Cherry thought she recognised Madeleine's touch.

'How was the auction preview?' John asked, giving her a moment of intense interest between his shifting glances among the guests. 'See any bargains?'

'There was a copy of *Old Calabria* with an inscription from Norman Douglas . . .'

An enormously distracting splash and a roar from the drenched crowd announced the fact that Sally had clambered the plank and dropped back in.

'I'll tell you about it later,' said Cherry, upstaged. 'You got the oysters?'

'In the freezer. I'm glad you came. I thought you might have too much to do for tomorrow.'

Cherry thought it an odd thing for him to say. 'Of course I'd come.'

Sally was now gliding gracefully around in the blue water. Bernard picked another herring off the slab and hurled it over the heads of the crowd into the top of the tank. The animal caught sight of the silver scales, rolled over as it turned and made a dash for the surface, caught the fish in one mouthful, flipped its tail and dived again, creating a small wall of water that sped to the side of the tank and crashed over the edge. The whole floor of the shop had become a giant puddle and half the crowd was wet, including Madeleine who, soaked and unprotesting, was making her way towards them. Her blonde hair hung in hanks, her blue eyes sparkled in her wet face, and her white blouse clung damply to her flesh, stretching across her soft bra and showing every detail of her full breasts. Cherry flushed a little as she thought how wonderfully sexy she looked.

The crush was not easing; the doorway at times was completely blocked, and the party looked as if it were settling in for a while. A familiar voice was suddenly at her ear.

'Isn't this fantastic?' It was Angelo. 'He is so clever, that boy. I love aquariums. I used to go to the aquarium in Naples all the time when I was a boy. They had seals there, too. But they ate them, in the war. They fed General Clarke on seal from the aquarium when he arrived with the American forces. There was nothing else to give him. When I went back I found all the glass was broken, all the fish eaten, not a drop of water left to drink.'

'That must have been quite a feast,' Cherry said.

'What?' said Angelo.

He could not hear above the chatter that echoed against the tiled walls, and before she could repeat herself, he was being steered towards other guests by a cheerfully smiling Molly, who wore the same raspberry pink suit she had worn for John and Cherry's wedding. Cut off from the few people she knew, Cherry found that each way she turned she was cornered: a mollusc supplier wanted to take her to Galicia to sample the mussels of La Toja ('I think I've been there,' she said. 'Or was it Tossa?'); a shopkeeper repeatedly said how wonderful John Dory was for the street ('It's where he belongs,' she said); an elderly woman said she was married to a fishmonger for forty years and could still smell him when she woke up every day, years after he was dead. Cherry did not stay late. After a couple of hours she slipped out without disturbing John who was deep in conversation with Francine.

She took a cab home, changed into jeans and stayed up a while, listening to the radio, slicing pistachio nuts, and wishing that her life might make her spiritually richer and far more interesting than it was as a mere caterer married to a fishmonger. 'You his wife?', 'You with 'im?', 'Are you Mrs Dory?' What would it have been like to be Elizabeth David? Clever, elegant, rich, famous beyond her own lifetime, so good at what she did best, spreading pleasure and as fulfilled as anyone stepping down from her own luncheon table. She had been her own woman, with intelligent books to her credit, honoured by universities, institutions, a nation. Certainly, Cherry enjoyed food and cookery, but she wanted to be more than just a good cook.

She began experimenting with the Loving Cup for the aphrodisiac wedding feast, toasting bread, dousing sugar lumps in orange-flower essence, spooning in caster sugar, nutmeg, cinnamon, ginger, and adding sploshes of sherry, soda and ale. She had drunk a jug of it by the time she fell into an empty bed at two o'clock.

John was still absent when she woke with the slightly familiar feeling of a cast-iron water tank pressing down on her brow. It was five past seven, and she arose cautiously, hand on forehead, to prepare the enormous tasks of the day, taking delivery of an early consignment of carnations and roses and making her first sortie to the venue by nine. The pub was a large nineteenth-century establishment and the upstairs function room was high-ceilinged and generous. At one end a door led on to the stairs that brought people up from the pub entrance shared with the lounge bar, at the other was a raised dais, at either side of which was a door leading to a corridor and a warren of store rooms, closets, lavatories, pantries and the kitchen. Because the kitchen was not much larger than a galley, several rooms were used for the overspill of the food, drink, crockery, coolboxes, microwaves, five boxes of champagne and fifteen of wine.

Madeleine and Francine arrived shortly after nine. Madeleine said she had enjoyed the aquarium party, in spite of the drenching. Francine said she had left after being cornered by a mollusc salesman who wanted to take her to Spain. John had last been seen sitting in the wet in a corner, pouring his heart out to Sally the seal.

The morning was spent in unrelenting preparation, driving

backwards and forwards to Cherry's house to bring all the necessary food and equipment. The best man telephoned during one of the visits, and Cherry heard a thump in the bedroom, a sign she took to mean that John had found his way home. Three other girls had arrived for work at the pub at eleven o'clock and, as instructed, they set out two lines of trestle tables stretching the length of the room, plus a table for six on the raised dais, where the bride and groom would dine. Jugs of Loving Cup were placed at intervals on the tables with small vases of single roses, cotton napkins and a specially printed menu decorated with rather unpleasant-looking cherubs.

At two forty-five a chamber quartet – two violinists, a cellist and a pianist – arrived, and Cherry slipped to the Ladies to change into her working long black skirt. The guests made a boisterous entry at three. The best man, an immaculate figure with a neat moustache, grey morning suit and salmon-pink tie, put his head round the kitchen door to ask if everything was okay. Cherry said they were just fine, and they agreed to serve the lunch in fifteen minutes, after telegrams had been read and speeches made. It was up to Francine and the three other girls to do the serving, ensuring, among other things, that everyone had full glasses of Loving Cup. Madeleine and Cherry stayed in the kitchen preparing the dishes and supervising the event. Oysters, prepared in champagne and fish glaze and served with parsley and herbs on toast, were the first course to go in. To cast an eye over the proceedings and make sure everything was all right, Cherry took in one of the trays and was greeted with an unexpected ripple of applause. Everyone was seated, but she sensed something was not quite right. It was only when they got back to the kitchen that Francine put her finger on it.

'They're all blokes,' she said.

'Even the bride?' asked Madeleine.

'Yes, she looks lovely, though.'

They turned to Cherry, who shrugged; it was news to her too. Madeleine wiped her hands on her apron, picked up a tray of oysters and went to have a look.

'We're outnumbered sixteen to one and still haven't got a hope,' she said on her return.

'What a waste of our talent,' one of the girls commented, picking up another tray.

'I wonder if the bride went to the stag night,' Francine said, following her out.

But there was little time for chat. The speed of events, of plates coming and going, rose to a sweltering pace: the kitchen, poorly ventilated, was an oven in itself and for a while Cherry believed that the main course, the pheasant, was a terrible mistake. In spite of all the haste and effort she could muster, it had taken much longer than she had imagined, and synchronising the accompanying vegetables was not going to be easy. She kept telling the girls to go back into the function room to make sure the wineglasses were, in the Macedonian tradition, continually topped up. In a belated moment of inspiration, she piled the small stuffed joints on stainless-steel serving platters, doused them in cognac, gave the girls oven gloves and set the spirit alight as they left the kitchen: the cheer from the function room showed that once more style had triumphed over content.

The break between the main meal and the pudding was less crucial. The girls reported that everyone seemed remarkably happy: japes were beginning, laughter was raised; signs of affection were being shown and the corridors around the kitchen seemed busy with activity. A sense of appreciation nevertheless prevailed and when the *coup de grâce* was presented, a marmalade of carnations made of freshly crushed blue dianthus and accompanied by green pistachio cream, the response was genuine, if discordant. Almost unwittingly,

Cherry caught the adulation in full flight. It was only at this juncture in a meal that she felt she could safely leave the kitchen again, and she took a tray of the carnation *compôte* into the room just as the applause was beginning.

As she stepped through the door, the groom, seated at the table on the dais, stood up and announced: 'Gentlemen, I give you the cook!'

The cry at once went up around the room: 'The cook! The cook!' Glasses were raised and there were cheers and applause, as spoons started to clack rhythmically on the tables: 'More cook! More cook!' though some deliberately mispronounced the word. The tray was taken from her and unseen hands led her up on to the dais and lifted her on to the bridal table where her court shoes narrowly missed a serving boat of pistachio cream. She was embarrassed, of course, and reddened deeply, but she also felt a thrill at the sight of the sea of appreciative faces, and the general applause. They were a mixed crowd, some in jeans, some in shorts, some in morning suits, old and young, some fat and some fatally thin.

The bride and groom were smiling up at her. In his make-up, plucked eyebrows and organza gown, the bride could easily have passed for a woman. She certainly seemed to have made the groom – who looked younger, in his early twenties, perhaps – a happy man. When Cherry attempted to get down they both made moves to keep her back up. So she picked up the side of her black skirt in dainty thumb and forefinger, raised it a couple of inches and gave a little curtsy, which was met with a roar of approval. This was more like it, she thought, as the bride and groom each took a hand and helped her down on to a chair. Life should be full of moments such as this.

The glow of adulation warmed her through the rest of the late afternoon as she supervised the washing and clearing up. By seven o'clock, the party was in full swing and the caterers' work was largely done. The chamber orchestra had left and a disco was throbbing. Francine reported that some food had been thrown about, some shirts were coming off and at least one couple was in a deep embrace. It was time to go. Coming to the end of the chores, Cherry went to the Ladies to change back into her jeans, but both lavatories were being used by the guests, who felt no need to be segregated. In one cubicle three men were naked, giggling, entwined.

'Don't mind us,' one of them said cheerfully.

To her surprise, Cherry didn't mind them at all and, rather than being embarrassed, she laughed at his impish grin. They seemed like little boys, and she envied them their free spirit. These were the heirs of Norman Douglas, taking up his Rule in Life, doing as they damn well pleased, and sending everybody to Hell. How could she possibly care if they saw her change out of her black dress? When she returned to the kitchen the trips to the van began. It took nearly an hour to clear everything away and Cherry was taking a last look around when a familiar figure appeared in the doorway.

'Venus in the Kitchen.' Frank Kaplan's eyes twinkled and his tight mouth was pulled in a lopsided grin. He wore a midnight-blue suit and tie with a white carnation in the buttonhole and he held a cigarette as if it should have been in a holder. 'Or, "Love's Cookery Book" by Pilaff Bey, otherwise known as Norman Douglas. I realised as soon as I saw the Marmalade of Carnation. The bride is the son of my niece, by the way. Sweet boy. Always wanted a white wedding. His mother still doesn't know. Now you have to come to dinner with me, on Tuesday week. Meet me outside the bookshop.'

'Tuesday?' Cherry echoed, dumbfounded.

'I'll tell you my Norman Douglas stories. I met him on Capri, you know, in '51. He started me out on my career.' He put a business card from the bookshop down on the work surface, ignoring her look of surprise. 'I'll call you to confirm.' He turned to go just as Madeleine was coming into the kitchen with one of the girls. 'Wonderful lunch,' he said to her. 'And such adulation. Anyone would think she was Elizabeth David.'

CHAPTER 19

The Auction,
22 February, 1994

It was a starless evening and much later than anticipated when The Summer Pudding Catering Company van drove into Ross-on-Wye on the last Sunday in February. There had been a lot of clearing up to do after the aphrodisiac party, and the morning had slipped away to such an extent that at one point Cherry wondered about telephoning her mother to cancel the two-day visit altogether.

The journey took more than three hours, mostly off the motor-way and in the dark. Beside her in the van was her overnight bag with a couple of sections from the Sunday papers folded up inside. She had been surprised at their interest in Elizabeth David: 'The Keats of the Kitchen' one headline ran; another compared her cracked, blackened and deliberately unwashed potato *diable* to the Turin shroud. It was now estimated that the whole lot might fetch as much as £20,000, and Cherry began to worry that the publicity might push the book lot containing *Old Calabria* up past the hundred-pound mark and thus out of her reach.

The streets were lifeless, except for a knot of bored teenagers by the seventeenth-century arcaded market hall. At the top of the hill, not far from the church, she came to a stop, took out her bag, locked the van and walked down a cobbled lane to the house. Before she had reached the front gate, she could see there were no lights on and no curtains had been drawn. Her immediate thoughts were that her mother must have forgotten she was coming and was out visiting one of the neighbours. She clicked open the gate, went around the garden path to the back door, set down her bags, and took the key from under a geranium pot. But the back door was open.

As she switched on the light, she was immediately confronted with a blanket of dark smoke and a smell of burning. She sped over to the stove, turned off the oven and opened its door, standing back to avoid the black cloud and blast of heat that came out like a vengeful genie, making her eyes water and causing her to run, coughing, out of the back door. She opened the kitchen windows and as the smoke started to clear, made her way back to the oven to retrieve the burnt offering. It was, or had been, a cake.

She turned on the light in the hall, heard the tick-tock of the long-case clock and inhaled the more familiar, damp country smell that central heating had failed to eradicate. The smoke alarm John had fixed over the kitchen door was silent and she knew its battery would be flat. When she turned on the centre light in the sitting room it revealed her mother in her old Parker Knoll chair, her head slumped forward, her right arm hanging over, and a cigarette below, in the hearth – burnt out, mercifully – on the tiles. Her heart pounding, Cherry looked at the figure, waiting to witness any signs of life. It seemed an age before a slow inhalation almost imperceptibly inflated the small figure and Cherry reached out and shook a skinny shoulder. 'Mum? Mum!'

Her mother came quickly awake, her small, bright, dark eyes blinking, and she said with the unexpected huskiness of sleep in her voice, 'Hello, darling.' Then, sniffing the air, she added, 'Oh, shit, is that your cake?'

'*Mum!*' Cherry was shocked.

'Sorry, dear. Excuse my French.'

She started to get up, but Cherry told her to sit down. 'Everything is all right,' she almost shouted, 'but you're lucky to be alive.' The fright had made her angry. 'I suppose the battery's gone in the smoke alarm?'

'I took it out. It kept going off, it was such a nuisance.'

'That was the signal that it was going flat. We'll have to get another one tomorrow.'

'I baked a Dundee for your tea. Is John here?'

'He'll come next time.'

'Oh yes, so you said. Such a shame. I know he loves Dundee.'

'I'll put the kettle on,' Cherry said. 'No, don't get up. You stay there.'

The kitchen was cooler now, but there was not much point in closing the door and windows until the smoke had gone. Cherry was cooling down, too, and she gave a shiver as she held her hands in front of the kettle warming on the blue flames. Voices from the television set, just switched on, drifted out of the front room, above which her mother raised her own voice to ask about the journey. There was half a small unsliced wholemeal loaf in the bread bin and while Cherry kept up the small talk, she hunted through the cupboards to see if there was anything else to replace the tea-time Dundee. They contained the familiar potential cascades of rusting cake tins and graters, jelly moulds and Kilner jars, pipes and pastry cutters shaped as hearts, diamonds, circles and stars. The rag-and-bone man wouldn't give the time of day for them, never mind a London auction house. In spring Cherry would return, as she did every year, to clear out the cupboards, to chuck away the outdated cream of tartar, arrowroot, cornflour and gelatin, and bin any flour or oats crawling with weevils. Her mother had never got used to the idea that she had no one to cook for any longer.

It was getting late: tea would be combined with supper. Cherry settled for fresh bread, a chunk of crumbling white

Caerphilly, a couple of tomatoes, some home-made pickles and an apple, getting some for her mother, too. She would have liked a glass of wine rather than tea, but there was none in the house. Taking the tray into the sitting room, she set it on a small table between the two Parker Knoll chairs. The moment she did so, her mother decided it was time to go to the lavatory.

'I won't be a minute.'

Cherry drew the chintz curtains, rearranged the lighting, turned down the volume on the television and looked at a couple of recent postcards from friends on the brick mantelpiece. They were propped against a framed photograph of her father, Edwin. He was a slight figure, a second husband living in the shadow of the first, just as Cherry had sometimes felt that she lived in the shadow of her step-brother. She picked up the unfocused colour photograph of Edwin sitting on a fence in an apple orchard not far from the house. He was small and dark like Grace, a childhood sweetheart who had caught her on the rebound. Second best. He had been a kind man, if not very forceful or bright, and there had been something reassuring about him sitting in the kitchen at night listening to old favourites on the radio and sipping cider. In the daytime he went fishing, and some nights he went poaching. They didn't need the rabbits, but he had done it since he was a boy and he liked to keep his hand in. With indecent swiftness his ferrets had followed him to the grave. These days Grace did not mention him much.

When Grace returned, Cherry asked her if she often fell asleep during the day. Grace denied that she did. It was probably just age, she said, that had made her nod off that night.

'When did you last see the doctor?' Cherry asked.

'I don't need to see the doctor. I'm slowing up, that's all. What else can I expect at my time of life?'

'You shouldn't expect to be incinerated in your own house. I think you should go and see a doctor, or else I'll worry about you and I don't like worrying about you; you're too far away. I just want you to see a doctor, that's all.'

'All right. But they never do any good.'

There was no point in continuing this conversation, and over supper Cherry told her mother what she had seen at the Elizabeth David preview. Grace listened with interest and Cherry showed her the newspaper articles and the photocopied catalogue, which Grace, putting on her reading glasses, studied carefully. Cherry said she had been lucky to get it, they were in such short supply.

'Your hardback edition of *Mediterranean Food* might be worth a few pounds,' Cherry said. 'There weren't any hardback books of hers there at all.'

'I wouldn't like to sell it,' Grace said.

When Cherry went up to her old room later, she thought about her mother, the youngest of six, returning here after her husband had run off. The bed tucked into the eaves had been Grace's bed – as a girl growing up, and as a young wife, alone, with her first baby. Cherry opened the small leaded window that looked out on to the little back garden and breathed in the aroma of riverbanks and windblown trees. Then she slipped between the cold sheets and slept like a log, as she always did on her first night home.

The following morning she did not wake until past nine o'clock. Her mother was already up, and after breakfast and a tour of the garden, they went shopping in town. Cherry was surprised at how slow her mother's walking had become. They passed by a shop her mother said used to sell bric-à-brac.

'Mrs David often went in there to buy little knick-knacks,' she said. 'Perhaps some of them will be in the sale.'

At the top of the town Cherry tried to persuade her mother to go for a coffee in the Royal Hotel, but Grace said she would be just as happy with a bit of carrot cake in the vegetarian café. Her mother didn't like things to be too grand, which frustrated Cherry who wanted the best for her. Grace's life had not been indulgent.

'Was Elizabeth David lonely when she was here?' Cherry asked over coffee and cakes.

'I don't know,' Grace said. 'Perhaps she was, buying plates and jugs and candle holders when she didn't have a home.'

'How well did you know her?'

'A maid doesn't really get to know the guests. But I got used to her. I took her hot-water bottles and breakfast in bed – dried eggs and wartime flour. She didn't like the carrot jam. And though she drank it, she said she hated tea.'

'Did she really loathe the food?'

'She didn't complain about all of it. Not in words. But she could give you a look. Well, none of us was keen on the food. It was a terrible winter and no one was happy, except that the war was over, of course. But the food was awful: it was so hard to get. And the weather was dreadful. There was a baby died of cold in its cot on one of the farms. It wasn't just the cold and the snow, there was such flooding. Cattle and sheep were swept down the Wye: great bloated carcasses. Whole orchards became lakes and the trees turned to rafts, and all the allotments were washed away. After all we'd been through, it seemed so unfair. Mrs David wasn't the only one missed a good table.'

'Did she have any boyfriends?'

'Someone came with her, but he didn't stay long.'

'Was that Mr David?'

'I wouldn't know.'

'There was nobody else?'

'Boys from here wouldn't go near a woman like that – such a striking woman, so well mannered, so polite. You don't hear voices like hers any more, not even on the BBC. She kept herself to herself. She used to sit at a corner table, usually with her head in a book, or writing, she did lots of writing. But she did like her cider.' Her mother lowered her voice, as if ghosts were listening. 'She'd go round the pubs, and once or twice we had to help her into bed, though she wouldn't remember the next morning, and you wouldn't want to remind her.'

In the afternoon, the smoke alarm fixed, Cherry took a walk down by the River Wye. Trees were black skeletons picked over by slow, flapping crows, and the lifeless grass of the meadows was scattered with turnips to sustain pregnant sheep. It was bleak and wintry and exhilarating. When she returned, it was time to pack and drive back to town. She really would have liked to have stayed a little longer. Before leaving, she hunted out an old clockwork timer from the back of a kitchen drawer and stood it on the dresser in the kitchen, urging her mother to use it from now on whenever she was cooking, as it might wake her if she had nodded off. Her mother said, 'What a good idea.' Cherry knew it would never be used.

'I'll call you tomorrow night,' Cherry said, 'and let you know how the auction went.'

'Yes, I'd like to hear all about it. Give my love to your John, and tell him he has to come and see me soon.'

Going back to London always seemed to take longer than going down, and the journey was interminable. It was nearly eleven o'clock when she walked in through the front door. The lights were on in the lounge and she hadn't taken her coat off when John appeared in his dressing-gown. His hair was a little ruffled.

She said, 'I thought you would be asleep.'

He said, 'I was reading. Do you want tea?'

'Yes,' she said, and he asked after her mother. She hung up her coat while he put on the kettle, and she told him about the near-disaster of the burnt cake.

'My God!' His voice shot up an octave and his heavy brows

were deeply furrowed. 'She could have died. What are we going to do with her? We'll have to get Social Services to look in on her. I'll call them tomorrow.'

'There's nothing we can do. The neighbours pop in and they have our number.'

'We must do something. I didn't realise she was getting so forgetful.'

'The last time I went to see her I found the kettle in the fridge.'

'You never told me.'

Cherry shrugged. 'And in Ross this morning the cobbler came out of his shop to tell her he'd had a pair of her shoes for six months. She said she thought she had lost them.'

'Lost her shoes? Children lose shoes, like kittens lose mittens, but grown-ups don't do things like that. Why didn't you tell me?'

'They were just little things.'

'They're not little things. They're life-threatening.'

He handed her a mug of tea. He was agitated and the mark on his cheek appeared to be larger and darker than usual. Cherry looked away, her eyes roaming the table. Open and face down was a book about marine mammals. He was becoming angry and she didn't know why.

'It happens,' she said, finding herself now siding with her mother. 'She's just getting old.'

'Why don't you tell me these things? Why do you always keep things to yourself? You don't tell me anything.'

'What do you mean?' She didn't know what he was getting at and she looked at him curiously. 'Like what?'

'I don't know.' He went to the freezer and took out the bowl of an ice-cream maker and holding a teaspoon as if it were an assassin's dagger, he began stabbing at its solid, cinnamon-flavored contents. 'Sometimes I think I'm the last person to know what's going on in your life. I mean, if I hadn't still been awake tonight and I hadn't seen you until tomorrow afternoon, would you have told me about your mother then?'

'I expect so.'

'You expect so!'

Cherry pulled out a chair and sat down, wondering why he was making such a fuss. It seemed harder and harder to talk these days. 'We just don't see each other very much, it's true, but it's always been like that.'

John finally dug out a large lump of ice cream which he shovelled awkwardly into his mouth. As he sucked on it, between sharp intakes of breath he said, 'It's not just that we hardly ever see each other, but when I am here, I don't . . . I don't quite know what I'm doing here. I feel intrusive in your life.'

'Do I make you feel like that?'

'I do try to talk to you when we get together. I attempt to get some dialogue going, find out who we are, what you're up to.'

'What I'm up to?'

'I like to know what you're doing, of course. I don't want to interfere . . .'

She was not going to let him get away with this. 'Yes, you do.'

'I don't.'

'You do. You want to know about all the functions I go to . . .'

'I'm interested.'

'You want to tell me who to get in touch with, what to call my business, who to have for supper, how to cook fish . . .'

'I want to know what you're doing. I can't always imagine you when I am not with you – the customers who chat you up when you're all dressed up in your black and looking so elegant.'

'I get chatted up by drunks. It's not that much fun.'

'And by shirt-lifters.'

A penny was beginning to drop. Cherry hadn't told him

about the aphrodisiac celebration, that it had turned out to be entirely gay. It wasn't because she didn't want to – she just hadn't got around to it. Madeleine, however, might have passed on the news.

'God,' she said, 'why are you so homophobic? Is it because you're frightened Norman Douglas might be lurking in your genes?'

'In my jeans?' His voice began to rise. 'There's fuck-all lurking in my jeans. I'm just a sad, miserable bastard, who hates the idea of people enjoying themselves, especially by indulging in lots of jolly sexual activity, because I'm not bloody getting any myself!'

Cherry rose, mustering all her dignity. 'If this was wine,' she said, raising her tea mug, 'I would pour it over your head.'

'Yes! Yes! Pour things over me! Wet my body. Give me some attention!' He flung back his arms and bent backwards over the kitchen table. 'Dance on the table for me like you did for the poofs.'

Cherry emptied her tea down the sink and said, 'Good night, John.'

Her smooth exit was impaired by a sudden and alarming thump coming from the bathroom. It was followed by the unmistakable sound of movement and Cherry stopped in her tracks.

'Are we alone?' she asked.

'No.' John's fieriness evaporated in an instant and he suddenly sounded extremely sheepish.

'What do you mean, "No"? Who's in there?'

'Just don't go in the bathroom,' he muttered.

'Who is it?' Cherry's mind was racing. Madeleine was high on the list, and she remembered her looking so wet and accessible in the fish shop, making her way towards them.

John said, 'I just promised to look after Sally overnight.'

For a moment Cherry couldn't think who Sally was. Then, with disbelief, she remembered. 'The seal? You're joking. That's disgusting. Where am I going to wash?'

'Kitchen sink?'

She was shocked. She stared at him steadily and wondered if she could detect instability. This was completely unacceptable behaviour. It was insane.

'It just came up,' he said without looking at her. 'I couldn't do anything about it. I went round to see Malcolm, his trainer, this afternoon, with some fish. That was the deal for Sally's guest appearance – a month's supply of fish. And he was in the middle of an appendicitis attack. I got him to hospital and I think he's all right but he had the animal in a special van, ready to take him down to a gig in Dorset.'

'A gig? Where's the RSPCA? Are they all asleep? I'm going to phone them myself.'

'When I got back I realised the key he'd given me wasn't for the house, but for the van, and I couldn't leave the seal locked up in it all night; he might have been nicked by joy riders. So I brought him back here. Somebody phoned a couple of hours ago, a friend of Malcolm's. He said he'd be round to get her later tonight or early tomorrow morning.'

It took a moment for this information to sink in, then Cherry said, 'And you have the bloody nerve to tell me that *I* don't tell *you* anything. If I'm going to sleep in this house at all tonight I'll sleep on the sofa. And if that animal isn't out of here by tomorrow, I am moving right out for good. It's either her or me, is that clear?'

She picked up her bag and strode from the room, slamming the door behind her. Nothing would keep her in the same room as her husband a moment longer, not even the removal of her make-up and the cleaning of her teeth, two of the most important rituals in her life. She took a couple of coats off their hooks in the hall, slammed the front-room door behind her and turned the television on to drown out any sounds from the bathroom. Fully clothed, she lay down on the couch, pulled the coats over her and tried to sleep.

An hour later she was woken by whispers, and the barking seal crashing about the hall. Then the front door shut and a few minutes later a vehicle drew away, its sound receding like a bad dream evaporating into the dawn. The animal had gone, but Cherry stayed awake for some time, thinking about life, about her mother, about John, and wondering if it wasn't time for a major change. She tried to imagine life on her own, and she tried to imagine life with a baby, but she found neither idea easy to conceive.

Deep slumber finally arrived and she knew nothing again until the phone rang at half-past nine. Joely was calling to arrange to meet for the Elizabeth David auction, which began at noon. A vague attempt to clean up the bathroom had been made but it was still rather wet and it smelt of herrings. Cherry, nauseated, washed in the kitchen sink, then changed into crisp striped blouse and mushroom-coloured wool skirt, put on big, circular, white plastic earrings and tied back her hair with a Jaeger scarf the way Elizabeth David looked in a drawing Cherry had seen in one of her books. It seemed appropriate. She made sure she had her chequebook and credit card.

Joely was waiting at the entrance to Bayswater station, her thin frame hung with an old fake Dalmatian-skin coat. She tucked her arm in Cherry's and led her through the cosmopolitan throng of Queensgate towards the auction house.

'Great do on Friday,' Joely said. 'Ooh, look at those Belgian pastries. Where did John get the seal from? She was such a star!'

'He got it from somebody called Malcolm who has just had an appendectomy, as a result of which the animal spent last night in our bathroom.'

Joely's high-pitched laugh attracted glances.

'It wasn't funny,' Cherry protested. 'The bathroom stinks of herrings.' Joely still refused to see the serious side, and when Cherry said, 'I can't believe I actually said to him, "It's either her or me",' Joely's hoots were too infectious. Arm in arm, laughing like drains, they turned into the cul-de-sac off Moscow Road.

The sale was scheduled to begin in a quarter of an hour, and they joined the orderly crush on the auction house stairs which was moving slowly forward. There was a kind of spirituality in the air: this was a culinary Compostela, and shuffling devotees were waiting to touch the relics of the saint. Officials at the top of the stairs were looking concerned, craning their necks to peer into the auction room and signalling to colleagues out of sight. They had run out of catalogues again. When Cherry and Joely reached them they held out their hands to prevent the women going into the packed room. After a couple of minutes, they were directed down the corridor, where they entered the back of the sale room. Every seat in the place was taken, and people were standing down the sides and at the front, where there was such a press around the rostrum that there had been no space for Cherry and Joely and all those behind them to get in. Many of the women were about the same age as Cherry's mother, perhaps a little younger: women who would have been inspired as young housewives when Elizabeth David's books became popular. They did not look like radicals, but these were the women who had boldly cast beetroot out of the salad bowl and put herbs in their omelette pans, who were excited by travel and would prefer to buy odd-shaped food from a market stall than any perfect specimens a supermarket had to offer.

Not helping the proceedings was a television team at the front of the room, their lamps aimed at an interviewee. 'Prue Leith,' Joely said helpfully. 'I read that she's after the table.'

They looked around them to see who else they could spot. Several television foodies were there, quite a few men, as well as the solid bank of middle-class, middle-aged women. There was a delay as the people were shuffled into orderly place. Cherry showed Joely her catalogue and told her what she had seen in the preview display, confiding her desire to purchase the lot that contained *Old Calabria*, though still not explaining the Norman Douglas connection. Joely was excited and she wondered if there was anything she might like herself.

'Isn't there an omelette pan?' she asked.

'You couldn't afford the omelette pan,' Cherry said, rather shocked at Joely's ambition.

'The omelette pan has been divided among the four nephews,' a woman beside them supplied helpfully. 'They are scattered all around the world and they've agreed to have it on a rotating annual basis. Don't you think that's wonderful?'

Joely looked at her, wide-eyed. 'Stunning,' she said, 'but it's all right, actually, I didn't really want it. I've got one already. Who are the nephews? Are they famous foodies? Is there a David dynasty.'

'I don't know,' the woman admitted. 'She was such a shy woman herself.'

'Greta Garbo of the gourmets,' Joely said.

'Exactly,' the woman agreed, failing to notice the touch of irony. 'But with much better taste.'

A gavel brought the proceedings to a start. The auctioneer, who had put the sale together, was sharp and businesslike. His voice was clear and resonant and he managed to inspire a feeling of awe about the property, in spite of the blunt commercial transactions that were about to begin. It seemed like a celebration, a picnic with games, a country-house fête which had let the locals in.

There was a great hush as the gavel came down for the first

lot, a part-glazed earthenware crock and three brown glazed storage jars. Bidding was tentative. Five, ten, eleven, twelve, fifteen pounds . . . twenty, twenty-five, thirty, fifty. Bang! Fish-shaped platters, sheep-shaped moulds. Bit by bit, the cupboards were emptied. Acorn thimble holders, open-weave baskets. Any number of the items might have been bought for a few farthings at the junk shop in Ross. There were gasps and murmurs, shouts of delight and groans of despair, and though there were some obvious dealers, buying was on the whole democratic and most people seemed to have a shot at what they wanted.

Three cheese graters and a nutmeg grater went for £220, an earthenware pot with wooden spoons went for £400. 'Bring your old wooden spoons to Phillips',' the auctioneer said. Five mediocre still-life watercolours of flower vases went for £900, five times the estimated price. The chances of getting the copy of *Old Calabria* were growing thin. After more than an hour, after Ceramics, Miscellaneous Items, Textiles, and Paintings and Prints came the books. Cherry's heart was in her mouth. Before bidding had begun she had thought the lot in which the Norman Douglas book was included might fetch £100 or £150, and she had imagined she was erring on the pessimistic side. Now she thought it more likely to be £200, a sum she now persuaded herself that she could afford: it was scary to think she had already doubled her original ceiling without any change in her financial affairs.

When the lot was announced, the first bid was for £50, then £100, almost before she had time to think.

'Two hundred,' Joely called out gamely.

'Sshh, Joely! What are you doing?'

'Two fifty,' said the auctioneer in response to an unseen bid.

'Three hundred,' said Joely.

There was a pause. Cherry had images of leaving her watch

and wedding ring at the cashiers, talking her way out of an ugly situation, phoning John, phoning Oliver, waiting for someone to bail them out. It wasn't me. It was my friend. 'Three twenty-five . . . five hundred.'

Suddenly the bids were away and running, slipping out of reach with the speed of a soap bar flying through bathtime fingers, until almost as suddenly they came to a stop. Nine hundred pounds. Bang! Cherry felt a kind of elation. Never in a thousand years could she have spent such a sum on a book, though she had come as close as she ever would – or Joely had for her. But she was glad it didn't go cheaply; the lot was truly valued. It had been worth it. In the end, she thought, by way of reconciling herself to the loss, she didn't really want the book that much. As Norman Douglas, whose fortunes had ebbed and flowed like the tide, would probably have said, it was just Much Ado About Nothing.

'That was hopeless,' Joely whispered. 'We didn't stand a chance.'

They stayed on to the finish, through the Ephemera and Metalware to the Furniture finale. The cookery writer Prue Leith gave a shriek of excitement as she sealed the bid for the kitchen table at £1,100, and her good fortune was greeted with a round of applause. Cameras popped, necks craned. The sideboard took the top price of £1,800.

When it was over some began reluctantly to shuffle slowly out. Others gathered in knots around the lucky buyers, to congratulate and commiserate, to recall the highlights and the opportunities that had come and gone. Press photographers set Prue Leith up at her table with the £400 pot of spoons and the flashlights blinked away. Everyone felt they had played their part. Cherry was elated to have been at this valedictory performance, even if she had to share the moment with so many others. Joely wanted a closer look at everything and everyone, especially any famous foodies, and they resisted the easy exit at the back of the room, instead inching their way towards the front.

Cherry's scarf bobbed among the crowd, her head held high above the upturned blouse collar, her darting, dark eyes sharp and bright and a little wary. An elderly man in a cravat squeezed by. He stopped and turned. In a loud, croaking whisper he said: 'Liza?' Others turned their heads, and he said it again, raising his voice in incredulity and attracting more interest. 'Liza? Is that you?' Cherry looked at him and he smiled, his eyes dewy with affection, and said, 'I'm so sorry. For a minute there I thought you were Liza.'

CHAPTER 20

Late Harvest,
Spring 1994

Cherry met Frank Kaplan outside the bookshop the following Tuesday evening and they travelled by bus to a pasta house in Clerkenwell. It was more of a café than a restaurant but, Kaplan assured her, it served the kind of macaroni of which Norman Douglas would have approved. The *patron*, an Italian cockney of Angelo's generation, greeted Kaplan as an old friend, and took their coats. The restaurant was only half full and they chose a table in a corner where they could talk. With little discussion, they agreed to the *patron's* suggestions of *macaroni vongole* in a parsley sauce with fresh Venus mussels, followed by some zucchini and meatballs. To drink, said Kaplan, they would start with a litre of *rosso* and take it from there.

'So,' Cherry said, 'tell me about Norman Douglas. How did you meet him?'

'I was sixteen.' Kaplan broke some bread and tucked his napkin into his white shirt collar in preparation for an antipasto of artichoke hearts and salami which, unbidden, had just arrived. 'We went on a family holiday to Capri. We were there mainly because my father was a great fan of Gracie Fields.'

'Who was she?' She tasted a corner of a slice of salami, savouring it as she chewed.

'How soon are popular idols forgotten! Gracie Fields was a professional northerner, the Lancashire Lass from Rochdale, with a thumping great sing-along voice and a ghastly matey tone, who set up home on the island. When she performed in Britain she often urged her audiences to visit her, and many of them took her up on her word. Everyone associated her with "the isle of C'pree".'

'What made her go there?'

'*South Wind*. She was captivated by it, like millions of others, and not long after it came out, she wanted to visit Douglas's fictional "Nepenthe". In the early thirties she bought a house in Marina Piccola, and she died there in the late seventies.'

'And how did you meet Douglas?'

'He was sitting outside a restaurant in the Marina Grande, holding forth at a table full of friends including Gracie Fields. You could tell at once he was the centre of attention. I was with my older brother and neither of us knew who he was but my father pointed out this white-haired old chap.' Kaplan mimicked a stern patriarch: '"See that man over there with Our Gracie. He's a bounder. Don't let me ever catch either of you going anywhere near him, or I will thrash you to within an inch of your worthless lives." Of course, this completely intrigued us. When we got home I tried to find out everything about him I could. I enjoyed hunting down his books: it started my drift into the second-hand book business. In the end I read everything he ever wrote and everything that was ever written about him. And I learned all about the island, too, from Suetonius to Gracie Fields. Have you been to Capri?'

'No, I'd love to go,' Cherry said. 'But I thought you said you met Douglas? The least I expected were some tales of disgrace and excess.'

'I exaggerated,' Kaplan said, putting his hand lightly on hers. 'I was desperate for your company at dinner.'

Surprised, she withdrew her hand. 'Do you often lie?' She wasn't cross, but she pinned him with an unwavering stare.

'Mankind has a natural love of the lie itself,' he said meeting her gaze. 'In this case it was merely a means to what I had hoped might be an end. Besides, people who go seeking the truth all the time are invariably dull.' His shunned hand picked up his glass. 'You really must go to Capri. It's wonderful, however much tourists have Hollywood-ised it.'

Cherry looked down at her food. She did not want to go behind John's back, but her curiosity had been roused for too long. 'My father-in-law comes from Naples,' she said finally, looking up. 'His father was an English musician called Eric Douglas, a nephew of Norman Douglas.'

'Really?' Kaplan frowned. 'He had hundreds of nephews and nieces, but I didn't know any of them were actually related to him.'

'After the war, John's father came to England to look for Norman Douglas.'

'He'd probably have been back in Capri by then. What happened to Eric Douglas?'

'Apparently he died of TB just after John's father was born.'

'And when you asked me about the Eric in *Old Calabria* a while ago, you wondered if it might be the same person.'

'Yes.'

Kaplan shrugged, but he seemed to be giving the matter some thought. 'Just coincidence, I suppose. There are obviously things even I didn't know about our dear Uncle Norman. However, there is not much I don't know about Capri.'

For the rest of the meal, Kaplan entertained Cherry with stories of outrages committed on the island, explaining the mysteries of Tiberius's *spintriae*, choreographers of rude trios of boys and girls, which put Cherry in mind of the gays in the lavatory at the aphrodisiac wedding. The German industrialist and homosexual Fritz Krupp, on the other hand, said Kaplan, commanded servants to let off fireworks each time he ejaculated, and Kaplan wondered what effects such a practice might have on the night sky today. Towards the end of the meal, after they had squeezed the last drop from the carafe, the *patron* brought some Marsala, a plate of cheese and a *macédoine* of fresh fruit. Cherry told him how she had met Elizabeth David, and how Mrs David had talked of Norman and the Bodensee whitefish. Kaplan agreed that she probably did mean Norman Douglas.

'They had a lot in common,' he said. 'And of course their books were just what was needed, the right thing at the right time. He cheered everyone up after the first war and she did the same after the second. Neither of them was prolific – a handful of books each and then they petered out, both in their different ways washed up. Somehow unfulfilled.'

Cherry thought of the woman she had met in Chelsea. 'I don't know,' she said. 'They achieved more than most.'

It was after midnight by the time they left the restaurant, only realising when they got up to leave that they were the last ones there. Helping her on with her coat, the *patron* told Cherry he hoped to see her again. On Roseberry Avenue Kaplan hailed a cab and as they settled into the back seat, he took Cherry's hand and asked, 'Will you sleep with me?'

She said, 'No.' But the suggestion that a young woman might sleep with an old man suddenly did not seem preposterous.

'Are you monogamous or should I take this as a personal rejection?'

'Monotonously monogamous, all my married life.' She smiled ruefully.

'Well, you shouldn't be so stingy. You're far too delightful to be wasted on just one man, however much of an angel he might be.'

When they parted he squeezed her hand and said, 'Let me know if you decide to stray.'

She pecked him on the cheek, as she might have done her father. And she said she would see him at the Italian class the following week.

*

A few days later Kaplan telephoned to say that Elizabeth David's last book, *Harvest of the Cold Months: the Social History of Ice and Ices*, had just been published, and he had put a copy by for Cherry. Mrs David might have been writing it, they speculated, when Cherry delivered the whitefish to the house in Chelsea. On Sunday, Cherry wanted to stay quietly at home, hoping she might read the book. So as not to offend the Dorellis, she told John she was not feeling well.

It was unlike Cherry to be ill: nobody could recall her missing a Sunday lunch. Molly was concerned for her health and Angelo suggested that she might be pregnant. There had been no pregnancies in the family for a couple of years and Cherry had long since become a little tired of Angelo's constant talk about children. Lucy and Brian's children were in their late teens; Pauline and Christopher's oldest was now eight; their youngest, Pippa, two. At lunch John sat next to Pippa and helped to cut up her food, playing games to help her to eat it all. Sitting next to Angelo at the head of the table was a balding, portly man called Patrick who was nearer Angelo's age than thirty-five-year-old Isabel Dorelli's whom he had recently begun courting. Towards the end of the meal, after the children had got down from the table to start their boisterous games in the garden, Angelo offered this last potential in-law a cigar and began talking about his Italian roots.

'Those are my parents,' he said, pointing proudly to the picture on the bookcase. 'They're about the same age in that photo as their oldest great-grandchildren are now. I don't remember my father. He died of tuberculosis. He met my mother when he was visiting the San Carlo opera house. He was a violinist. The rest of my family died in the war . . .'

John rose from the table and followed Christopher out into the garden. The trees were in bud, and the grass was muddy from a winter of children's play. James, Christopher's eldest, propelled a football towards them. Absently, and with his hands deep in his pockets, John kicked it back. He wore an olive-green jersey and he shook his shoulders against the damp and cold day. Christopher lit a cigarette.

'Violinist at the San Carlo,' John said quietly. 'Funny how none of us is musical. Even though they say it skips a generation.'

'Maybe he said he was on the fiddle,' said Christopher, 'and it didn't translate.'

'Who do you think he really was?' John asked.

'No idea,' Christopher said. 'Just a guy on holiday.'

'What about her? Annetta?'

Christopher shook his head. 'Who knows.'

John said, 'Maybe she was one of Uncle Norman's "nieces".'

In the middle of the following week Cherry met Joely for coffee in the sky-blue Amalfi café in Old Compton Street, Soho. The word delicatessen, Cherry thought as she arrived, might have been introduced into the English language via the Italian family grocers in this short, intimate street. Hung with hams, spiced with olives and smelling of fresh pasta, shops such as I Camisi were recommended by Elizabeth David to her readers who wanted to reinvent a taste of the Mediterranean after the war. I Camisi was still there, and a few other traditional premises hung on – a bulging newsagent's, an old vintner's, a catering outfitter's, the Algerian Coffee House, Pâtisserie Valerie and the Amalfi café – but the street had become a homosexual playground with bulging brasseries, body-piercing studios, drag dress shops and men-only bars.

It was an unexpectedly sunny, halcyon day and, sitting on a blue chair at a round metal table, Cherry had cast off her headscarf. Eating almond cakes and drinking cappuccinos, she and Joely watched the crop-haired, multi-pierced parade go by. A young man roared past on a sparkling chrome Harley-Davidson dressed in a crash helmet and white underpants.

'They've hijacked the moral low ground,' Joely said.

Cherry said, 'They always seem to have fun.'

'AIDS isn't much of a laugh.'

'It doesn't seem to worry them. They seem to get off on danger. Do and die.'

'I just passed a girlie show where they're only charging a quid a peep. I charged more than that at primary school twenty year ago for a look at my knickers. This is more than a recession: heterosexuality is bankrupt. We're witnessing the end of romance.'

'John's got a down on gays,' Cherry said. She meant it to sound supportive, as if he were a robust champion of hetero-sexuality and old-fashioned romance.

Joely replied flatly, 'Yes, I noticed that when we came round for supper. What's he got against them?'

'I don't think he has, really. He just gets jumpy about . . . things.' She suddenly thought she did not want to have this conversation.

'How is it for you?' Joely asked, looking at her with her quizzical green eyes.

Cherry shrugged. She felt a sense of betrayal talking about John. 'No fireworks. What about you and Oliver?'

'Oh, we're all right. I just close my eyes and think of England – that's the cricket team as well as the football and rugby teams.' She said it as if she had said it a dozen time before, then she said, 'He's a nice guy, but I think he's insecure.'

'Oliver?'

'No, your John. About his love life, about you.'

Cherry felt uncomfortable for having read the message wrong, for inviting Joely's inquisition. 'There isn't much to be insecure about.'

'He doesn't turn you on any more.'

'No.'

'And he knows it.'

Cherry put down her cup. 'It's not my fault . . .' she began. But all of a sudden there was a boulder in her throat and her words tumbled over it, dispersing up the back of her nose and gripping her chest in upsetting spasms. She grabbed a paper napkin to wipe her eyes and nose. Joely put an arm around her, but she would not be comforted.

Joely said, 'Nobody's saying it's your fault.'

'Please, please, I can't talk about it at the moment.'

But they both knew that if their friendship meant anything, Cherry was going to have to explain herself some day soon. They paid up as soon as they could and left. On the train home Cherry felt heavy-hearted and when she reached her front door her feet were leaden and did not want to enter her own flat, where she would be surrounded by her relationship, her daily grind, waiting for John to come home. On the mat there was a note from Madeleine to say that, for reasons too complicated to mention, she had left The Summer Pudding Catering Company van parked in a meter bay just up the road.

Cherry needed no other prompting. She picked up her own van keys and turned on her heels. At first she did not know where she was driving. The sun was still bright, bringing with it an urge to go south. Heading back through the centre of town, she took to the A24, this time remembering not Joely but John: they had been up and down the road so many times. Everything had changed so much. It was hard enough trying to understand it herself, let alone trying to explain it to someone else, even someone as close as Joely. Everyone liked John. That wasn't the point. Liking somebody was as easy as pie. The fact was that she didn't know what to do with him any more. He was just there in her life, like a relation. She recalled a Norman Douglas menu:

'Not for every day – but then no dish is.' And she heard her own voice: 'I have been monotonously monogamous all my married life' – the phrase rang through her mind like a dirge, a lament, an epitaph. She felt that something was in transition, that something important was dying, and it made her desperately sorry for herself.

Within a couple of hours she was standing 500 feet above the sea on the chalk-white cliffs of Beachy Head. The wind was buffeting the few shrubs that clung to the headland and ruffling the feathers of jackdaws and gulls. Down to the left was Eastbourne where this phase of her life had begun. Out to sea, ships broke the horizon: Channel traffic, North Sea and Atlantic bound. Far, far below the red-and-white lighthouse looked no bigger than a pin, and as the wind whipped at her unrestrained hair she pushed both her hands through it, pulling it back to give her an unrestricted look at the grey swirling sea.

'Oh, John Dory, John Dory, John Dory,' she wailed into the wind. 'Where has it all gone?' She did not know if it was he or she who was lost and she also called out her own name. All those years slipped away. Time wasted. Love gone. She let the tears flow.

'You all right?' An earnest young man was at her side. He wore spectacles, a Parka and trainers and was about Cherry's age.

'What?'

'I'm from the Samaritans. We man a post here – to stop people jumping. I don't believe you are going to jump.'

Cherry sighed and laughed and finished crying all at the same time. 'No,' she said, stepping back from the brink. 'I'm not going to jump.'

She wandered back towards the van, pausing at a memorial commemorating the purchase of all the land around Beachy Head from Eastbourne to Folkington by Rupert Gwynne, MP for Eastbourne from 1910 until his death in 1924, when his daughter, Elizabeth, would have been ten. She climbed back in the van and drove slowly through the Seven Sisters Country Park, then followed the meandering Cuckmere to the Downs and the figure of the Long Man at Wilmington who looked chilly and deathly white.

At Folkington she parked at the edge of the woods and went into the church. In spite of the bright sun outside, it smelt like a damp barn. She wandered around, rereading the wall plaques she had looked at with John the day they had met. Now, she knew, it was not the name of David she was looking for, but the Gwynnes, residents of Folkington Manor. Rupert Sackville Gwynne's mother's family had come from Fifeshire, and his wife was the Honourable Stella Ridley, daughter of the first Viscount Ridley of Yorkshire. This was the root stock of Elizabeth David: stubborn Yorkshire, upright Scot, with the county set of the South Downs grafted on.

Outside, in the small, underpopulated cemetery, there was a new grave, a grassy hump in the shape of a body, lying next to the headstone of the honourable Stella Ridley. Cherry felt a prickle at the back of her neck. She had not thought about where Elizabeth David now lay. Slowly, reverently, she walked towards the unweathered black tombstone: it was elegantly carved for Elizabeth's youngest sister, Felicité Violet Gwynne, who had lived with her and been closer to her than anyone else. She had died in 1986, the year before Cherry met the cookery writer. There was no sign of Elizabeth's grave. She had not returned to the family fold: she was still out there, Cherry thought, not yet at rest.

As she drove back to town, she searched for some optimism. 'At least I'm alive, at least I've got a home, at least I'm in work.' She put her foot down to try to beat the rush hour, which she nearly did, arriving back at five o'clock. John was not back yet and there was a message on the telephone answering machine. Its unhurried, almost Welsh, tones pulled her up sharp.

'Cherry? This is Em. I'm in the hospital in Hereford. Your mother's been taken in.'

She had left the ward number and Cherry called her straight back. 'What's happened?' she asked her aunt when she was finally put through.

'It looks like a stroke but they're not saying anything. They're doing tests.' Like the rest of the family, Grace's sister was not given to overstatement: all of them could not help but tell things how they were.

'Will she be all right?'

'I think you should come down.'

'I'll come right away.'

Cherry was seized by a fear that by the time she reached Hereford, it would be too late. John was just leaving work when she called to tell him what had happened, and that she was going to drive down there now in the van. He pointed out that she did not know how long she was going to be away, and Madeleine might need the van for the business. He insisted on coming straight home to give her the Citroën.

'But you'll need it,' she said.

'No problem. If you're still at your mother's at the weekend I'll come down by train.'

Cherry felt her life was coming unhinged. She packed a bag and included *Harvest of the Cold Months*. It might be a long stay.

In the bleak, neon hospital ward, where nurses clumped in sensible shoes and curtains rasped around beds like harbingers of death, Grace looked small and helpless and out of place. Her hair was thin and unkempt, her skin was dull white and dry, and her body was quite unable to fill out the voluminous folds of a flannel nightgown. Propped like a doll on several plump pillows, she was not quite awake, not quite asleep. A glucose drip was plumbed into a vein in her right arm and the notice at the end of her bed said: NIL BY MOUTH.

Cherry kissed her mother on the cheek, causing her to stir with a colourless smile. 'Hello, dear,' she said. 'I've cooked your supper.' Her mouth fell away on the right side and her words spilled carelessly out, like a drunk's. Her eyes flickered and closed. 'Stilton soup.'

'They've drugged her up,' said Em who was at the bedside. 'They say she has to stay in overnight so they can keep an eye on her. They'll have the results of the tests in the morning.'

It was nearly eleven o'clock. 'When did they bring her here?'

'Just after lunch. Mrs Kyle found her and called an ambulance. I've been with her since then. Some of the neighbours have been up. Not the Jamesons though, nor Sylvia Williams.'

'I'll stay with her now,' Cherry said.

After Em left, Cherry asked a nurse about her mother's stroke, but the nurse replied that they wouldn't know anything until they had the results of the tests. There was nothing they could do at the moment except keep an eye on her, taking her pulse and temperature every half an hour. Grace's condition remained unchanged and Cherry was not encouraged to stay the night. At one o'clock, with Grace apparently asleep, she drove back to Ross-on-Wye. In thirty years she had never stayed in her mother's house alone.

At seven the next morning she was woken by a phone call from the hospital with the message that her mother had indeed suffered a stroke, but her condition was complicated by anaemia and pneumonia, and an ambulance was now leaving to transport her to the cottage hospital in Ross. They asked if Grace had been a Social Services case. The combination of ailments sounded alarming, but at least they all now had a name. John telephoned to find out the news. He was overwhelmingly sympathetic, and she was surprised at how pleased she felt to hear from him. He said he had spoken to Madeleine, who by the way sent her love, and she had said that she could manage the Summer Pudding functions for the next week or so.

Cherry soon settled into the cottage hospital, a large red-brick building in walking distance of her mother's home. She took books and papers, knowing it could be a long haul. Grace had her own room with a view over the town, and Cherry sat by the window in a Lloyd loom chair. On the first day, her mother awoke around lunch-time and seemed fairly *compos mentis*, but her eyes were unsteady and often roamed. She had no recollection as to how she had come to be there and Cherry had to explain what had happened to her.

'I am a nuisance,' Grace said, breathing heavily and slurring the words that were rasping and weak. 'Bringing you and your John all the way down here. Will he be here soon?'

Cherry explained he would be down at the weekend, and asked if she was comfortable.

'Just my old bones, dear. What are you reading?'

'Elizabeth David. It's her last book, which they have just published, about ice-creams.'

'Lovely Mrs David. So refined.' Grace's loose lips and wild stare now made Cherry unsure how conscious she was of what she was saying. 'Came to us because she was in trouble. She'd walked out on him. Good for her. Bastard. Bastard. Fucking bastard.' Her head waved and lolled on the pillow, and Cherry took a tissue to wipe her salivating mouth. 'And she was . . . she was in trouble. Such trouble, oh, such trouble. She was so unhappy, but she didn't know how to cry. Strong woman. Hair on her teeth. Drank like a forester. Lovely woman. She said nothing, but you knew she cared. In such trouble. God, it was cold. Babies died. Everything died, frozen, washed away, cattle, sheep. So many babies. No coal, no fuel, no fucking food anywhere. We were...' She breathed in deeply. 'I was pregnant. What else would you do but lie with any bastard to keep warm? Everything died. Everything you touched. Everything you wanted. We wanted life.' She started to sing in a thin, reedy voice: 'I lay with a man who lied to a man that I'd lain with the Prince of Wales.' She sighed deeply, then: 'No one went dancing. There was so little whistling. So very little uncalled-for whistling. She never belonged. Why did she come here? Should have gone home. They would have understood. We told her they would have understood, but she wouldn't go. The war was over. They had to understand. They would have understood. Can they cook me an omelette? Nothing fancy. Just an egg and some water and some butter in the pan.'

Cherry didn't answer. She thought it part of the narrative, but Grace asked for an omelette again so she went to see if she could find somebody to cook one up. When she returned, Grace was asleep.

Late that evening, with Grace still sleeping, Cherry returned to her mother's home for a bath, to report to the neighbours and to make a few phone calls. There was little food in the house, so she walked into the High Street and bought herself a takeaway pizza and two bottles of St Emilion. 'To be miserly towards your friends is not pretty; to be miserly towards yourself is contemptible.' Douglas's maxims were becoming a part of her life. Before she sat down to eat she took from the kitchen bookshelves that hardback edition of *Mediterranean Food*, which had probably been sitting in the same place for forty years. She turned to the first page and saw the familiar neat writing, in green ink:

To Grace, With best wishes and undying thanks, Mrs David.
She wondered exactly when and where this simple message

had been written. It had never held any significance before. Now it seemed laden with meaning. She turned the book over, looking for clues.

Inside the back flap was a black-and-white photograph of the author, taken in Cairo when she was nearly thirty, about the same age as Cherry. The shadowy lighting made it look as if she were in the corner of a souk. She wore a white blouse and had a locket round her neck. Her hair flew off a little to the left and her attractive, sharp features were emphasised by the fine lips which did not quite smile but turned down a little at one end, adding a note of arrogance, a challenge that had not been taken up.

That night Cherry dreamed of the post-war winter in Ross: the snow and the floods, and the cold hearths and empty plates, of dancing that had stopped and babies that had died. When she woke it was to the bright songs of blackbirds and immediately she recognised a familiar mustiness in her head. She wondered how long the knocking on the front door had been going on as she slowly got out of bed and put on her dressing-gown over her blue cotton nightdress. The postman had been around as long as Cherry could remember. He had a letter for her and he wanted to know how her mother was.

'You'll give her my best,' he said. 'A lot of us here like to remember her.'

She phoned the hospital and heard that her mother was still sleeping, so she did not rush getting up, having a bath and breakfast. Over a mug of tea she opened the letter, which was from John. Inside was a postcard with a picture of Tower Bridge and just a line wishing her good luck. Also enclosed was an unopened letter addressed to her and she recognised her teacher's writing.

Kaplan's letter said that he had been wrong. Douglas did have real nephews: John Sholto, his older brother's son, had become the seventeenth Laird of Tilquhillie; and his younger sister Mary, who died of tuberculosis aged thirty-two in 1903, had two children with her husband who was called Fairbairn. None of them fitted with Cherry's description of Eric Douglas, and Kaplan had now become intrigued to find out what had happened to Eric Wolton, the boy who had accompanied Douglas to Calabria. Hoping for a lead, he had written to everyone called Wolton listed in the London telephone directory. Meantime he was enclosing a photocopy of a photograph of Eric Wolton taken from a biography. Cherry flipped over the letter and stared at the picture. This smiling man, in his mid-thirties, pipe clamped between teeth, could well have been the same person who some fifteen years earlier had been pictured with John's grandmother in the photo that now stood on the Dorelli sideboard. It was an extraordinary revelation, but it was not the answer: it was just the start of another round of questions.

She was disturbed from her thoughts by the telephone. It was John. He wanted to know how her mother was and if there was anything he could do. Cherry was in no rush to tell him, let alone his father, that he might be descended not from Norman Douglas, but from his catamite.

Just after nine o'clock, Cherry arrived at the hospital. Grace's condition was unchanged, and the staff said she had spent a quiet night. Her breathing was still difficult and they were wondering whether to reintroduce the glucose drip. Half an hour later she awoke, and during the course of the morning there were visits from a couple of neighbours and friends from the Forest of Dean.

Every now and then Cherry would go over to her mother, to wipe her face or adjust the covers. She seemed to have become so ill so fast. Her breathing was bad and she was coughing a lot. Sleep came and went. She had still not had any solid foods and at lunch-time a young doctor came in. He added little to

Cherry's knowledge about her mother's condition but he said she was 'comfortable'. He woke Grace and asked her how she felt.

She said, 'A bit poorly.'

'I see you're not eating,' he said. 'We'll have to put your drip back in.'

After he had gone, Cherry sat beside her mother and held her hand. 'The postman sends his love,' she said.

'Frank? So many men.' Her eyes closed again. 'So many babies.' Ten minutes later she muttered in her sleep, 'I'm so sorry about the babies. Forgive me.'

'Forgive you what?' Cherry was concerned. There had been a stillborn sister when Cherry was four. Though she was not meant to, she had seen it on her mother's bed, white, withered and nameless like a dead lamb. 'What is there to forgive?' she asked.

Grace suddenly raised her head and looked at Cherry with absolute intensity. The afternoon sun was shining on the white plastered wall behind her daughter, putting her face half in shadow, and her hair flew out to one side. Her mother's voice suddenly found remarkable strength and it was harsh and unforgiving.

'Your breakfast, Mrs David. Yes, yes, I'm sorry, it's the same as usual. That's all there is, a turd on toast, and you should be grateful for that, you stuck-up cow.' Still staring at Cherry she raised her voice to screaming pitch, spittle flying. 'You fucking toffee-nosed, stuck-up fucking bitch!'

The commotion brought a nurse rushing in. Cherry was rigid with shock. In a moment her mother was herself again, oblivious of what she had just said and done, complaining how hot it was and asking if it was Sunday, and was she going to go home soon, and how the pains had started moving down her legs. Then she fell asleep.

Two friends dropped by during the afternoon. Grace did not wake while the first was there, and though she opened her eyes for the second, she did not recognise him. Em came around seven o'clock and sat and talked to Cherry for a while.

'She has been rather delirious,' Cherry said. 'She talked about having lots of babies.'

'No doubt she did,' said Em. 'She wasn't called the town bicycle for nothing.'

Cherry clenched her fists tight in anger, stood up and walked out of the hospital and did not allow herself an explosion of vitriol until she was back in her mother's home. Dear God, sometimes she remembered why she had left home as soon as she had been able. She made herself supper, and cooled her heels for a couple of hours until she knew Em must have left, then she returned to the hospital. Grace awoke around ten o'clock. She seemed calm, and when Cherry held her frail hand she gripped it quite firmly.

'Promise me just one thing,' she said in a hoarse whisper.

'What?' Cherry asked.

'About the funeral arrangements.'

'You're not going to die.'

'You must promise me.' She sounded desperate.

Cherry hesitated, but there was nothing else she could say, except, 'All right.'

'I want a sin-eater.'

'A sin-eater?'

'You promised,' she entreated.

'I know, but . . .'

'I must be forgiven. They are all waiting for me. I can't see them unless I have a sin-eater. You cannot let me down.' Tears sprang from the corners of her pale, almost sightless eyes.

'Who is waiting for you?'

'Just promise me.'

Cherry held back her own tears as she leaned over and kissed the wet cheeks. 'I promise,' she said.

Soon her mother was asleep again, breathing slowly, rhythmically, but Cherry knew she should not leave her side. Just after three o'clock, Grace gave a kind of hiccup and made a rattling, choking noise, and Cherry unwillingly recalled a phrase in the introduction to *Mediterranean Food*: 'Anyone who has lived for long in Greece will be familiar with the sound of air gruesomely whistling through sheep's lungs frying in oil.' Grace stopped breathing.

Cherry sat with her for a full five minutes before she alerted the night staff. She didn't stay to see her mother laid out. She put on her coat, tucked her books and papers in a bag, and made her way home. Crying came fitfully. She wouldn't sleep. She stood in the kitchen and thought there was nobody else awake in the world. Then she tied her mother's apron around her and took out some flour, and she began to make the dough for an unleavened cottage loaf for the sin-eater's feast.

Cherry squeezed and slapped and shaped the dough, breathing life, her own life, into it. This would be the finest cottage loaf the house had seen, and when the coffin was brought to the house the following day, the golden, crusty loaf would be placed on the lid. There it would stay until the night before the funeral, when it would be devoured to the last stale crumb. It would be eaten by its maker. Cherry would be Grace's sin-eater. She would shrive her own mother of the trespasses of a lifetime, whatever they had been. And as she ate the dry loaf, she would also hope for forgiveness of her own sins: the sins of her past and the sins that she sincerely hoped were to come.

CHAPTER 21

Alone, Summer 1994

Grace was buried beside her husband in the churchyard of St Mary-the-Virgin on a bleak day in March, when a keening wind howled and the rain came down like a dog. From the plateau of the burial ground the red sandstone cliff fell into a misty abyss, hiding any sign of the horseshoe bend in the River Wye and the Old Meadow below. Awash at the graveside were the blood relations: two aunts, one uncle, some cousins and a few distant kin – some who had not met since the funeral of Grace's husband ten years earlier, some even longer ago than that. More than three dozen friends and neighbours swelled the black-clad gathering and though Grace had not been a churchgoer, the vicar had expressed the community's sense of loss for 'our sister, Eleanor Grace Ingram, daughter of Nancy and Thomas Pearson, also of this parish . . .'

Cherry was red-eyed from her night of feasting on the sin-eater's dry loaf. She had not returned to London, and John had been up and down several times, arriving early in the morning of the funeral when not a crumb was left on the lid of the coffin that now lay drowning in a puddle of red earth. Cherry tossed a handful of soil on the pine box, relieved to think that her mother's soul had been redeemed. Then she stood back, sheltering beneath a big coloured umbrella beside the solid, reassuring figure of her husband. Rain dripped down the neck of her ankle-length gaberdine as she looked around at the gathering: here were her mother's friends, the crowd that summed up her life, all with their own secrets which would, like Grace's, follow them to the grave.

After the service most of them came back to the house for tea. The majority were middle-aged, but there was a cousin and a couple of childhood friends from Cherry's schooldays who still lived in Ross. Joely had come down, without Oliver, to add support. Madeleine had phoned the day before to offer apologies: her pregnancy was making her ill. During the wakeful, sin-eating night, Cherry had thought of Madeleine's imminent child carrying on the human race.

It was a traditional tea, a thick Ceylon brew, with wafer-thin cucumber sandwiches sprinkled with malt vinegar and a little sea salt. Since it was nearly Easter, Cherry had also baked simnel cake. She assumed the role of hostess, and John, occasionally blowing his nose or wiping an index finger across an eye, had no difficulty in finding the right things to say, introducing himself enthusiastically to anyone who did not happen to know him, wanting to know how they knew Grace and how far they had come.

In the absence of a will, there was an assumption that the house now belonged to Cherry. She had tried to get in touch with her step-brother, Thomas, the morning after her mother died. Directory Enquiries gave her his number in South Africa but when she called there was an answering machine, so she left a message for him to call back. Then she wrote to him telling him his mother had died. That had been six days ago, and he had not phoned. Thomas was just one thing she had to clear up. Her Uncle Billy from Birmingham and his wife Jane were standing by the lounge door, and she made her way over to them.

'Your simnel cake's nearly as good as your mother's,' he said.

'I want to know the family secret of how you all keep so slim,' said Aunt Jane. 'Did Grace leave all her recipes?'

'I don't think she left anything we can't see here,' Cherry said, answering the question she imagined they wanted to ask. 'I've been through all her papers and there seems to be nothing put by. She lived on a state pension, nothing more. The house was all paid for before she was born.'

'It will go to you, though,' said Uncle Billy.

'There will be death duties.'

'I dare say. But you'll have the house.' He sounded as if it was decided, that it was written in stone.

'I wrote to Thomas, but he hasn't had time to reply.'

'You're the only child.'

'Everyone should take something, some keepsake. Is there anything you want?'

'A keepsake?' He looked puzzled, as if it were something he had not thought about, then he said, 'Well, I held back when your father died, but I wouldn't mind taking a look in the garden shed.' And with little further encouragement he slunk off into the kitchen to let himself out of the back door into the rain.

'I've always liked that picture of roses in the hall,' his wife said, as if struggling for small talk.

'It's yours,' said Cherry, and while Jane went to examine her booty, she circulated among the family, friends and neighbours, inviting them to look out for souvenirs. One by one they went on a tour of the house, searching for something to remember Grace by. Em did not have to be asked twice. She said she would like the three-piece suite and the long-case clock in the hall, both of which had belonged to their mother. Her sister Peggy, from Ludlow, left her husband Kenneth on the sofa, saying, 'I'll take a look upstairs. It might help clear some space.'

Cherry smiled and called after her, 'There's her ring and her watch if you want them.'

John had initially been taken aback by Cherry's fit of

generosity, but when he saw how happy it made her, he quickly accepted her way of spreading Grace's memory among her relatives and friends. An hour later, the guests began to leave with their mementos, some tucked in their pockets, some in boxes, others producing roof racks and struggling in the dark and rain to strap furniture on top of their cars. John helped shift a small table out to a waiting hatchback, but on his return he balked at aiding and abetting a couple struggling to dig up a rose tree near the front door. Back in the house, he headed for the cellar under the hall stairs where he opened a few bottles from one of the boxes of wine he had brought down from town. Joely was the first to hear the corks pop, and she was waiting with a small tray of motley glasses at the top of the cellar stairs.

'Seen any souvenirs you fancy?' John said as he started pouring.

'I'm coming back later with a pantechnicon. What's Cherry going to do with the house?'

'She's determined to sell it. We could probably take out a second mortgage to pay the death duties, and it would be tight, but if it were me I'd give it a go. I love it here. It's all part of her family inheritance and I can't understand her not wanting to keep it, but she seems determined. I'll miss it, and I'll miss her mum, too. She was great.'

'I only met her a few times, and she seemed a good soul.' Joely took a glass from the tray for him, and one for herself. 'Here's to Grace.' They raised their glasses and took a sip.

'They weren't a demonstrative family,' said John, 'not like my lot. They never seemed close. But Cherry didn't have much family and I'm sure she'll miss Grace a lot.'

'She's taking it very well.'

'I don't think it has really sunk in.'

Cherry came out of the front room into the hall looking calm and composed. Her dark eyes were still a little puffed, but they shone and, as John had more than once told her, she always looked great in black.

'Oh, good,' she said, spotting the tray. 'You two have been introduced to the wine. Why don't you introduce me?'

'*Vin*, meet a fan,' Joely said, handing her a glass. 'Did you mean them to take everything?'

Cherry sunk half the glass in one go. 'Everything I didn't want,' she said. They were both gazing at her, and she raised her eyebrows and her glass, and she smiled. 'Chin chin.'

The rest of the contents of the glass disappeared and she held it out for more. All she had wanted of her mother's possessions was that signed first edition of *Mediterranean Food*, which, thanks to John, was now safely tucked alongside her other Elizabeth David books on the kitchen shelf in Camden Town. She had been prepared to give a lot for that signed copy of *Old Calabria*, but this book was priceless. It would not leave her side from now on. From her mother's kitchen came the clatter of cupboards being cleared. She took a sip from the second glass of wine, and a sense of freedom beat louder in her heart. As each item left the house, another layer of clutter was peeled away, increasing the feeling that the past could never catch up with her.

The burning of boats had begun.

Cherry was an orphan now, with no parents, no children, no guilt or responsibilities except to someone she did not love. Over the coming weeks, grief over her mother's death continued to lie in ambush, catching her when she least expected it and hurling her into pits of sadness in which she hid, indulging these moments alone. She was on a roller-coaster, and her giddy new pastime was part of the white-knuckle ride.

Cherry began sinning on April the first. A young blade with a flop of blond locks had caught her eye at a function in the City and they screwed hard and fast on the roof of the building in the glow of an atrium dome. '*Sfoga o schiatta*,' Douglas had said: do it or die a slow death.

Her dreams were disturbed by a confusion of sex and death. Skeletons rattled in the cupboards, bodies were naturally naked and in limbo, and silver cords led to enchanting, fancy-free fucks. She saw her mother's vagina as a moist late-summer fruit, a bletted medlar, that squeezed her into the world with barely a second thought. On another night she saw it dry as the chalk Downs, uncared for, unlovely, untouched.

One night she awoke hearing a boy groaning and moaning and complaining that he had never felt so ill in his life. She got out of bed and put her feet in her slippers, then stole out into the hall where she put the light on. The voice had gone, but she was drawn to the spare room and she opened the door. There was no one there.

Over a plate of spaghetti after classes one Monday evening Kaplan told her that all the Woltons listed in the London phone book had replied to his letters and they had been helpful, but no one knew Eric Wolton, or Norman Douglas. He was now following some leads to East Anglia, to Darlington and the north.

At the beginning of May Cherry visited Ross, arriving just after lunch. There was the lawyer to see to sort out some finances, and check that the sale of the contents of the house had gone through. Local charities had scooped what was left of the clothes. The garden was overgrown and though blood-red tulips and apple blossom did their best, it did not look excited by the prospect of summer.

Inside, the curtains plundered, half the carpet carried away, the house was cold and bleak. A sweet smell of embalming fluids followed Cherry around, refusing to leave her alone. She had brought a sleeping bag and a Lilo, but in only a few minutes of walking through the echoing rooms she had decided to book in at a hotel. Whatever it cost, it would be better than staying here. As she was leaving, she noticed a few letters piled on a window-ledge, which the estate agents, who had a key to show prospective buyers around, had failed to send on. They were circulars mostly, but one was handwritten and brightened with South African stamps. She immediately tore it open. It was written with black ink in an unfamiliar, untidy hand.

Dear Cherry,

Thank you for letting me know about Grace's death. I am sorry to have taken a few weeks to reply, but I have been travelling. Please believe me when I say that, though I have little idea who you are these days, my thoughts are with you during what must be a very upsetting time.

As you are undoubtedly aware, there was a gulf between me and Grace. You may or may not know that I left her when I found out I was not her real son, and her continual refusal subsequently to tell me who my mother and father were made me angry. I even spent money on a private investigator in London to try to discover the truth. Perhaps I was wrong, but I was hurt.

I ask you now, if you do come across anything among her papers that might tell me anything about my mother or father, ANYTHING AT ALL, please let me know. It is very important to me, and to my two children (Yvette, 16, Scott, 14). I think they have a right to know, too.

Cherry leaned against the window-ledge, and read the letter through again. All this time she had thought that her brother had deserted her and her mother because her own father had entered Grace's life, and though Cherry seldom thought about Thomas, he had always been there, one among many shadows that shaped her background. Now he was gone, fallen out of the family tree, and it was as if there had been another death in the family. Intrigue took his place, and she wanted to find out more. Grace had kept her papers in a single leather suitcase in the attic, and Cherry had taken it to London where John had shown an interest. They had both gone through them all, but there were no surprises. Grace wasn't a squirrel, nor was she romantic or nostalgic: much of the evidence of her life had been discarded as she went along.

The phone in the house had long been cut off, so Cherry went to the High Street to call Aunt Em in Hereford. She told her about Thomas's letter and demanded to know the truth.

'I know nothing about it,' Em said and the more she was pressed, the more intransigent she became, making Cherry recall a phrase her mother had once let slip: 'That woman lies like a rug.' Eventually she gave up and called her Aunt Peggy in Ludlow.

'I'll need to talk to Kenneth first,' she said at once. 'He's gone shopping in town.'

'You do know something.'

'I do and I don't.'

'I'll come over now.'

An hour later Cherry was in her aunt's neat bungalow on the outskirts of Ludlow, further north on the Welsh border, a cup of tea in her hand and a yapping Jack Russell staring suspiciously at her headscarf. Peggy, older than Grace, was the musical member of the family, and an upright piano stood near the French windows. When they used to gather there, they had to sing. Like all the Pearsons, she was trim, but she was fair and her hair was curled and short. She wore spangled glasses, and when they were seated alongside each other on a bright patterned sofa, she offered Cherry a chocolate from a box. As Cherry took one, she noticed that her aunt was wearing Grace's watch and she wondered if she had put it on especially, to show her appreciation. In that slightly sing-song accent that bordered on Welsh, which all the family had grown up with, Peggy started to tell the tale.

'Em just called me. She didn't want you to know, but I don't see why not.' She tucked a rogue drip of chocolate back into her painted red mouth with a crooked little finger, as if it were a sophisticated thing to do. She was going to enjoy telling this tale about her little sister: she had waited a long time to tell it. 'When your mother first got pregnant she was just sixteen. It seems young now, but it wasn't so uncommon then: she'd been in service two years. Some said it was an accident, some said she'd done it deliberately to catch him, but Grace was always a lively girl and she often got into trouble. However it happened, there's no doubting Pretty Jack, as we called him, was quite a catch. He'd turned lots of heads, and none was as surprised as Grace when he agreed to get married. He was twenty-two, old enough to get me and Em and a dozen other women in Ross interested. But it was Grace that bagged him, and he bagged her. Then . . . oh, it was a tragedy. The baby died at birth, and Grace was very frightened that without a child she would lose Jack, too. He was away: he hadn't been demobbed. Within twenty-four hours the midwife had found her another baby boy. So your mother lied to Jack. She wrote and told him they'd had a bonny boy, bouncy and fit. He found out later, that's why he left. And when young Thomas found out, he left, too.'

'How did they find out?'

'We don't know, Grace never said. I suspect there was gossip, but I couldn't really say. Both times it nearly broke her heart. Whatever else, she had certainly looked after that boy.'

'So who were Thomas's real mother and father?'

'None of us knew.'

'The midwife must have known.'

'Agatha Prentice? You wouldn't remember her, she was a

terrible martinet and wild horses wouldn't have dragged anything out of her. If they had, half the women in the county would have pulled up their chairs for a listen. Your mother always insisted Agatha had never told her where the boy came from. Perhaps she didn't know, but she must have been curious. What was so strange was that Thomas had such an uncanny family likeness: dark eyes, strong cheekbones. Do you remember him much?'

'No. Except he seemed tall and he kind of . . . sulked a lot.'

'He was angry, and it sounds as if he still is.'

'There must be registers of adoptions.'

'Not in a case like this. Things were different. In those days, just after the war, when everything was hard, midwives ruled the roost. They had to act as judges and social workers, doctors and baby traders. That's not to say anything they did was wrong, even if they did sometimes forget to slap the first breaths into any poor misshaped mite. There were thousands of orphans after the war and we'd just been through that terrible winter. Men weren't coming home and the divorce rate went through the roof. Judges gave up their holidays that year to get all the cases settled.'

'It wasn't Em's baby?' Cherry wondered aloud.

Peggy gave a tittering laugh. 'Good Lord, no. What an imagination you do have.'

'I just thought . . . Have you heard of a cookery writer called Elizabeth David?'

'Of course. Your mother was a great admirer of hers. She stayed at the hotel where your mother worked. What about her?'

'Oh, I don't know . . . What happened to Jack?'

Peggy shrugged. 'There were rumours. Some said he was in London, some said he'd gone to live in Tangier. We wondered if there might be something among your mother's papers.'

'Not a scrap. No letters, no photographs, nothing relating to Thomas or Jack at all. Everything had been tidied up.'

'We're not a sentimental lot, us Pearsons.'

'Was Jack gay?'

Peggy sighed. 'Some said so, I don't know. Kenneth always says, "Tangier if you're queer". He was in the Royal Welch. Another cup?'

There were a thousand other questions Cherry wanted to ask, but Peggy was not the one with the answers. The one with the answers had nothing to say: she was dead and buried and her secrets had gone with her.

Spring warmed to summer and Cherry kept busy. House apart, there was the business to look after and she could not always count on an increasingly pregnant Madeleine, who seemed to mellow as motherhood approached, becoming more voluptuous by the day. Nick already acted the proud father and several times he dragged John to the pub for an early wetting of the baby's head. John was as pleased as Nick about the baby and he went willingly. Sometimes Madeleine went, too. A couple of times just John and Madeleine went.

Cherry sensed John's longing for a child, and one Sunday at breakfast, soon after Grace died, he said: 'I just see it as part of a responsibility for the human race. Your mother has gone. We should pass on our lives.'

'Not just yet,' Cherry said.

Her newfound adultery had not improved her domestic sex life, as she had thought it might. John was different from the others: he was the man she took her make-up off with, the man whose habits lay like the evidence of unruly children all over the flat. The thought of having sex at home in bed reminded her of coffins and winding sheets, of duty and death. Anyway, she saw him less and less. Work was busy, especially now that she could not always rely on Madeleine, and it was enhanced by her growing reputation as the supplier of aphrodisiac wedding parties, mostly heterosexual now, and none received quite like the first.

Evening classes continued and before the end of the summer term she dined with Kaplan again. He brought along a musty book, from which he had photocopied the picture of Eric Wolton, and Cherry confirmed that it was probably the same Eric in the photograph on Angelo's shelf.

'I've had no luck tracking him down here,' Kaplan said. 'But a footnote at the back of the book says that after the First World War Eric Wolton joined the Tanganvikan Police.'

'He became a policeman?' Cherry raised her eyebrows.

Not a bad job for a London lad with no prospects. Douglas probably helped him find it through his Foreign Office connections. I might try to put an advertisement in one of the East African newspapers.'

Cherry wished him luck but her enthusiasm for finding out what happened to Eric was waning, along with her interest in his family. At the end of the meal, when pear sorbets were finished, Kaplan looked at Cherry and said, 'You've got a twinkle in your eye. Have you strayed without telling me?'

She smiled and put her hand on his. 'Did you really think you would be the first to know?'

'Love labour's lost,' he said ruefully.

'Much ado about nothing,' she replied.

She had grown fond of Kaplan, which was one reason why she could not sleep with him. She didn't want him on the roller-coaster. She preferred him as a dispassionate critic and friend.

He sighed and said, 'When am I going to meet your young man?'

'John? He said he would come to Muriel's party at the end of term.'

'Does he stray?' Kaplan asked, as if one stray was as good as another.

Cherry laughed. 'Maybe,' she said. 'I don't know.'

*

One sunny day in early June Cherry met Joely in the old fruit market in Covent Garden, within sight of the Elizabeth David kitchenware shop. Joely wore leopardskin-patterned trousers and a patchwork jacket, and her tired, flour-white face was accentuated by a boyish haircut bright with henna. Cherry was pleased to see her and uncharacteristically kissed her on both cheeks. Her smile immediately summoned the waiter and they ordered two coffees.

'Why are you so perky?' Joely asked. 'What are you on?'

'Cappuccino and doughnuts. You're looking okay yourself. I like the jacket.'

'Yeah? I bought it to cheer myself up. I've had enough of kitchens and cooking. Some days I think I couldn't eat another crumb. To be honest, I fancy going on holiday somewhere without any kitchens or restaurants. Maybe somewhere with just a fruit garden to wander round twice a day. But Oliver can't get any time off. He's working his little socks off because he's worried he might be out of a job soon – new technology's putting lots of people out of work. Just as I'm thinking maybe I should have a kid before it's too late. It's a bummer. But maybe we'll just do it anyway. What about you?'

'I'm in work, not having any children and I'm okay.'

'Are you going away this summer?'

'I'm still sorting out the house in Ross. Fingers crossed though, there's a buyer who seems serious, and the sale might be through in a few weeks.'

'So you're going to be rich and live happily ever after?'

'Hardly, after the tax man's through, but I might take a break. There are things I'd like to do.'

'You don't fancy the two of us going off on holiday together, just for a change?'

Cherry could think of few things more tacky than two

women like them on holiday: on their own, on the make, comparing notes, starting rumours, standing out a mile. 'Nothing personal,' she said, 'but not just now.'

'Just a thought.' Joely shrugged and looked as if she hadn't meant the suggestion to be taken too seriously. 'How is it with you and John?'

'Just fine.' Cherry smiled and tugged at the knot on the headscarf at the back of her neck.

'Really?'

'Yup.'

'Sally the seal not causing any more problems?'

Cherry smiled. 'No.'

Joely let the silence of an angel pass overhead, then she said: 'Well, that's good. Those almond cakes suddenly look rather decadent. Forget the fruit garden, I'm going to book a singles holiday in a Belgian pâtisserie.'

It wasn't quite an end-of-term party at Muriel's. This was a midsummer party, she said, which she held every year in her three-storey Victorian pile in Muswell Hill, and as nobody else had any ideas for an end-of-year celebration, the class agreed to pitch in with Muriel's crowd. In fact, as the day approached, it became clear that they might have something in common with the other guests, as invitations had gone out to the Monday Basic Computer Skills class and the Wednesday Photography evening class. Muriel turned out to be something of an evening-class groupie. Madeleine couldn't come: she was due to have the baby any second. John said he had been looking forward to the evening, though he could not promise to stay too late. Cherry hoped there would be dancing. She put on a scarlet dress with a petticoat that made it all but impossible to get into the car, a Jaeger headscarf, scarlet plastic earrings, white plastic beads at her throat, seamed stockings and scarlet high heels. John was in his best herring-bone tweed suit, old-fogey brogues and flippant kipper tie, on which there was a picture of a mermaid, which he refused to change.

Muriel was in her late fifties and, by the look of it, had lived in this house a long time: perhaps there had been a husband once, or perhaps there was money in her family, because she did mostly voluntary work for local arts groups. There were two lodgers in the house, one in his twenties, one in his fifties, who were on front-door duty and generally helping out. It was still light when Cherry and John arrived at nine o'clock and everyone was out in the spacious back garden.

'*Buona sera*,' Muriel greeted them. 'Oh, I love your dress, Cherry. What colour do you call that?'

'*Rosso scarlatto*.'

'Oh, your accent is so perfect, I don't know how you do it.' She turned to John: 'She's the cleverest one in the class.'

'I believe it,' John said.

'Do you speak any languages?' Muriel asked.

'No, I sell fish. Do you like fish?'

'Oh, I do. I have some carp at the end of the garden and one hasn't been looking well. Come and see, perhaps you can do something about it.'

Most of the class was there, and as Muriel led John off across the grass, which Cherry avoided, knowing her heels would pin her to the ground, her classmate Jamie Cooper Clarke came over.

'You look hip,' he said. 'We'll have to take that dress for a spin.'

At eleven o'clock, past his bedtime, John announced he had to go home. There was still light in the sky: the night was warm and the party was starting to come alive. Cherry prepared to leave with him, but he was insistent that she should continue to enjoy the evening with her friends. She was sorry Kaplan had not turned up but she stayed on a while after John had left, and soon the music in the back room enticed her into the house where she and Jamie took to the floor. She kicked off her red shoes, unknotted her headscarf, and spun her scarlet skirt around. Then she danced with the lodgers and anyone else who asked. There was no tiring her and she enjoyed the fresh, sweet perspiration that ran over her lips and coursed down her back. This was not an evening to turn anyone down.

At midnight Frank Kaplan appeared at the door with a half drunk bottle of whisky. He was in a grey suit, without a tie, his collar undone, as if he had just come from a function. He was greeted with general good will, moving around among the guests, among his pupils, speaking only in Italian when it suited him, when it caused frustration or created a challenge, speaking German occasionally, sometimes French. Cherry met his dangerous blue eyes with her own predatory stare. She continued to dance, to whirl her skirts, to toss her hair, to keep her feet on the ground as infrequently as possible. Kaplan did not dance. He drank and talked and laughed and waited.

In a while, she came to him with his shoes in her hand, out of breath, dripping, glowing, hot. She handed Jamie her glass to fill and she imagined for a moment that Kaplan's interest might drift towards the young Scot, but his focus was entirely on her.

'I'm sorry I don't dance," Kaplan said.

She said, 'It's our imperfections that make us.'

He said, 'I sent you a letter today.'

She said 'What was in it?'

He said, 'Another letter, from a stranger.'

She said, 'Ah, the comfort of strangers. Shall we get some air?'

They stepped out into the garden and she abandoned her shoes, walking besides him down a path to the shadow of an overgrown pear tree, sharing the whisky bottle, putting an arm through his, a cool dew rising through her stockinged feet. The night was warm and dark and deep and edged with a sheer thrill, a hair-raising recognition that everything could happen, that anything was allowed. In the beginning there were fireworks and in the end there was damp squibs and dullness. In between it was up to everyone to find pyrotechnics to light up their skys.

'*Sfoga o schiatta,*' Kaplan whispered as he unzipped her dress. 'Let's not die a slow death.'

At four o'clock in the morning Camden Town was warming to the glow of the first light of day and, as the hum of the shower faded in the garden flat, Cherry, still in her party dress, and not long returned, took a batch of fresh rolls from the oven. Five minutes later John came into the kitchen to find her at the table, pouring tea. Everything was tidy. There was no washing-up and no books or papers lying about.

'Have a good time?' he asked in his growling morning voice.

'Great,' she said.

'Are these rolls fresh or are they something you made earlier?'

'I made the dough this afternoon.'

'Yesterday afternoon,' he corrected as he sat down opposite her.

She said, 'John, I am leaving you today.'

He said nothing for a moment, breaking open a roll and layering it with unsalted butter. Then: 'Where are you going?'

'I'm going away for a while. On my own. The money has come through from the house. I will keep it all. You keep the flat.'

He had one foot crooked over the other beneath the table and it moved rapidly, nervously, up and down. But he remained outwardly calm: the news was not a complete surprise.

'What about the business?' he asked.

'Madeleine can look after it, you told me that yourself.'

'She wasn't pregnant then.'

'The business was only ever as good as its last meal. It isn't worth anything. A few hundred pounds for the van, perhaps.'

He sighed deeply and rubbed his hands over his face, and for a moment she was worried he was going to make a scene. But he said, 'I am, as the cod said to the fishwife, absolutely gutted. I know you didn't like me for it, but I couldn't help being jealous sometimes. I loved you so much. And the more you love, the more jealous you are.'

'We're just two different people,' she said.

He said, 'So often I feel I just don't have a clue who you are.'

'Me neither,' she said.

He sniffed deeply. 'When are you leaving?'

'This morning.'

'Where exactly are you going?'

'Away, just away.'

He shook his head. His voice kept catching. 'What upsets me most is all I can think of is: How am I going to get through Sunday lunch with the family?' He laughed.

She said nothing.

She would not miss Sunday lunch in Barnet. The family that once seemed so warm and friendly now seemed cloying, brutish and dull. The house that had been so comfortable and welcoming, with chairs that needed fixing and china that did not match, now appeared tasteless and shabby.

John could read her thoughts well enough. There was nothing that he had that she wanted. He got up.

'Kiss me goodbye,' he said, 'and I'll get off to work.'

She stood up, and for the first time in a long while they put their arms around each other and held each other tight.

After a few minutes he said, 'Remember the good things, too.'

She nodded, not trusting herself to speak.

He whispered hoarsely, 'I'm sorry about some of the jokes.'

She laughed in a hiccup of tears. When she drew away again, she didn't look at him, but turned her head towards the stove, not moving until she heard the front door close. Two seconds later the key was back in the lock and he returned to the kitchen table where he picked up two more rolls. 'Forgot Bernard,' he said, sniffing and wiping the back of his hand across his nose. Then the front door closed again, the Citroën started up and he drove away.

Cherry did not go to bed. She changed out of her party clothes, and neither knew nor cared what John would do with everything she left behind. She packed a single case, and included her mother's copy of *Mediterranean Food*. She had a last look round, checking her passport and the air ticket to Naples. Tomorrow lunch-time she would be in a shady restaurant in Capri. That would be her starting point for a whole new life, whatever that might be.

As she waited for the cab by the front door, the morning post dropped on to the doormat. She immediately picked up and opened an envelope addressed to her in Kaplan's handwriting. It contained a letter from somebody else, in Tanzania. She took out her glasses and frowned as she tried to make out the unsteady hand. The diesel engine of a taxi cab slowed outside as she finished reading. She took off her glasses, tore the letter into small pieces, stepped outside with her suitcase, put the scraps of letter in the dustbin, and closed the front door for the last time.

CHAPTER 22

The Last Lunch, Capri, 1951

Eric Wolton sat on the right hand of Norman Douglas at an umbrageous table outside a restaurant on the Marina Grande on the isle of Capri. Above them a striped awning flapped lazily at the behest of the sultry south wind, and before them the white tablecloth was dazzling with anticipation. The breeze caught the tips of the small waves in the Bay of Naples and flicked spray into the air; the sky was drowsy, opaque with a lazy sun. By the quayside, a ferry was docking, ready to disgorge the latest crop of tourists, some here for the day, some for a fortnight, some to see Gracie Fields and some to find their pleasures on the Via Krupp. Several would fall in love with the island for the first time. Naples, the island's careless chaperon, watched through half-closed eyes; Vesuvius was sleeping; and the Sorrento peninsula stood silent guard over the secrets of the Siren Islands. Eric, in a white linen suit and club tie, and sucking on a pipe, felt proprietorial about this view, about the folds of the hills, about the fishing boats like Ciro's, about the seductive breeze and the ravishing quality of the light. To him, this was home.

There were a dozen guests at the table, talking, animated, bonded in their affection for Douglas. He was eighty-three, on his last legs, his features crinkled and reddened, though his face was still hard-nosed, square-jawed and firm. Walking was difficult, and age had donated him a stomach that made his seated body the shape of half a sack of potatoes, but he was not stooped or cowed. His hair was quite white, with an amber streak, his eyebrows also yellowed by nicotine. His stick, made from wood which grew only in the island of Zamorgla, was hooked over the back of his chair, capped with a fisherman's cotton sun hat. A snuffbox was by his wineglass, and between small plates of Felino salami and Castellammare olives was a box of half-smoked cigars which he would later try out, a puff at a time. Viewing the world from behind gold-rimmed glasses, his eyes were alert, and his spirit was high: already he had sent back a plate of saffron rice because it did not match the deep yellow of the died handkerchief he produced. And he refused the Lacrimi Cristi, insisting on wine from the flask.

'Eric, go with the *patron* and make sure the wine is properly weighed. He's making far too much money – he's going on holiday to America this year. I can't get up. Peppito has fallen asleep on my knee.'

Douglas caressed the dark head of hair in his lap, which belonged to the boy who had been sitting on his left. Without thinking twice, Eric stood up and went inside. He knew Uncle Norman's rule: treat them as thieves and they will respect you. It wasn't the English way, it was the Italian way, and generally he was right. Ettore, a *scugnizzo* from Naples who had been at the table, followed him into the cool of the restaurant interior to watch. He must have been the same age Eric was when he arrived in Naples all those years ago: he might have been Michele's twin. Eric asked the boy if he wanted anything to eat or drink. He wanted an ice-cream, he said, and Eric ordered one, along with a swift beer for himself. As they watched the wine being respectfully weighed, he asked Ettore if he knew the Gran Caffè d'Italia on the Via Toledo, which used to make a marvellous *spremuta di amarena*. He did not.

When they stepped outside again, Helen shot him a glance, as if he had just picked the boy up. She had hardly spoken at the table, and any ideas that she would not be too humiliated were starting to fade. Her hair was white now, her figure plump and countrified. Eric thought she had grown much older than he and he sometimes realised that he treated her as if she were his mother. He paid for his sex now, in Dar. Their life together was as arid as Africa. He hoped she would not cry too much when they returned to the hotel. At least she was sitting next to Kenneth Macpherson, the amiable and intelligent Scot who owned Villa Tuoro and who had been looking after Douglas.

Eric took his seat at the table, which was beginning to fill up with bowls and dishes. First to arrive was grilled and barbecued fish.

'Name your *poisson*,' Douglas said.

'Brain food for Boris,' said Gracie Fields, forking some sardines and whole baby octopus on to the plate of the man at her side, a local repairman with whom she was currently in love. He sat stony-faced in an immaculate dark silk suit. Her white hair was in waves, her teeth pearly, and she wore a bright flower-print blouse and pale pink slacks. Faith Mackenzie, in a large straw hat, had lobster, Macpherson settled for *braciola*, a roll of pork filled with *provolone*, *prosciutto*, raisins and eggs. Nancy Cunard, wearing an elaborate hair net and jangling bracelets, had lamb *alla pizzaiola*; Harold Acton, in a Panama, was happy with *ossobuco*; Graham Greene, returning from a distant reverie, tucked his napkin into his shirt collar and ate *coniglio all'ischitana*, rabbit from Ischia which had been raised in the dark to produce almost transparent flesh. Helen had langoustine, Eric had a Margherita pizza all to himself.

A variety of other wafer-thin *pizze* were sliced and put out for general consumption. There were salads of tuna and beans, of crumbled bread, onions, tomato, anchovies and basil, and dumplings made from mozzarella, egg, potatoes and *prosciutto*. There were strips of red peppers with anchovies and capers all gleaming with oil, and slices of *buttáriga*, the compressed dried eggs of grey mullet, and a dish of *zucchini* flowers fried in batter.

Bowls of stuffed olives were replenished, salami plates emptied, salads of onion and tomato were covered with torn-up basil leaves and drizzled with oil. Douglas ate boiled eggs, leaving the yolks, and sent back the mozzarella because it wasn't absolutely dripping, saying if it were to be eaten it would have to be fried. He had his own supply of Parmesan in his pocket.

Faith Mackenzie, gracious and with impeccable manners, said, 'Lobster always reminds me of Edith Sitwell summoning her maid.' She mimicked the eccentric writer's imperious tones: '"I think the red lunch today, Mary."'

'What was the red lunch?' Harold Acton asked.

'Lobster, strawberries and Burgundy!'

'Hah,' said Norman, 'and guess where she got that from.'

'Osbert and Sachie Sitwell introduced me to you in Florence,' said Nancy Cunard, who was sitting opposite Douglas next to an empty chair. 'You were fifty-four and I was twenty-seven: twice my age, I remember thinking, and you told me never to be rude unless I really meant to be.'

'"I like to taste my friends, not eat them." That's what he told to me,' said Gracie Fields, roaring with laughter. Her Lancashire accent had not deserted her. '"Taste them, not eat them!" I said, "Whatever do you mean? You're not licking anything of mine!"' And she crackled with laughter again.

'When I wanted to ensnare a certain young actor,' said Faith Mackenzie, 'I asked Norman what aphrodisiac I should use, and he said, "First take a well-trussed crane . . ."'

'Whenever he sees me in the garden these days,' said Macpherson, 'he asks me about my "bottomical Kewriosities".'

'I first met Uncle Norman in Florence,' said Harold Acton, looking dapper beneath his Panama, 'in Betti's, that restaurant David Lawrence used as a background for *Aaron's Rod*. We were with Reggie Turner and I thought it was going to be just some common midday meal, when lo . . . in you came, and you proceeded to take over the role of Amphitryon and conjure a rollicking Illyrian feast. I always thought Hogarth should have painted you, and how at ease Hume or Gibbon would have been in your company . . .'

'Have you tried the salami?' Nancy Cunard said, sliding the plate towards him. 'It's terribly good.'

Not all the guests at Norman's table added their memories to this paean. Graham Greene sat in silence at one end, watching, taking notes. Nor did Eric make a contribution: his role in Douglas's life was not up for scrutiny; his memories were private, not for everyone to share, and anyway he felt out of his depth in this glittering circle. He was just happy to be in southern Italy once more, even if he would never see Annetta again. The laundry was no longer there, Uncle Norman had reported, and there was no sign of her or her aunt. She had had two children, a boy and girl, but he had not been able to find out what had happened to them. Annetta's brother, Michele, who had tried to give Eric such a beating on their first meeting, was in an asylum and recognised no one.

In spite of the heat, in spite of the impossible dreams, Eric suddenly shivered at the thought of all the love he had lost and he stared past the group at the sea. The island's aromas, borne by the wind, sped over the table, collecting the essence of the oil, the garlic and wine. This was the smell of the best time in his life, when nothing went wrong, when each day was so good to wake to. He wondered if it still affected new visitors in this way. He looked towards the ferry that had just docked. On the quay, coming towards them, was a striking young woman in a fresh, gracefully swirling white skirt, in espadrilles, with her hair in a scarlet scarf and a shopping bag on her arm. She stopped to buy fruit from a stall and Eric thought she was foreign, perhaps French.

'Are you allowed back to Florence, Norman?' Nancy asked.

'I'm not travelling any more, Chawlie,' he said. 'I'll soon be part of the soil: probably the most good I'll ever do this island. When I returned to Italy in '46, the visa people in the embassy in London said they did not give permits for English people to live in Italy. I told them that was all right, because I wasn't coming here to live, I was coming here to die!'

'And they made you an honorary citizen of Capri,' Faith Mackenzie said. 'That's so nice.'

Ettore got up from the table and went over to Eric, taking out a tin cigarette case and giving it to him. Goodness knew where he had got it from. Eric was embarrassed but Douglas urged him to accept it.

'He's a generous boy,' Douglas said, 'and he likes you. Be flattered to accept the gift.'

Eric thanked him, and opened the case. There was an inscription in German inside the lid and he was sure it was nothing to do with anyone present. Perhaps it had been dipped from a visitor's pocket while fireworks were going off.

'Well, I don't know what we're all doing here,' said Harold Acton. 'The last time I saw Uncle Norman he said he never wanted to be in the company of anyone older than fourteen. We were all far too hidebound and set in our ways . . .'

'Children can teach us so much,' said Douglas, looking down at Peppito. 'We forget that. We think we have to teach them. Pure arrogance.'

Eric wondered what on earth he himself had taught the old man that he did not already know. And what Peppito, lying there, was teaching him now. Someone brushed behind him. The woman in the white dress from the ferry had arrived at the table and was standing at Douglas's side. A large bracelet hung on her wrist and the collar of her shirt blouse was turned up. She was a striking woman, in her thirties, dark-eyed and strong-boned, not naturally pretty, like Annetta, but lovely, sophisticated, in control, with an exciting, untouchable air. The waiters, busy as they were, had not let her pass unnoticed. But she had eyes only for Douglas and she bent to kiss the old man on both cheeks.

'Hello, Norman, darling,' she said.

'Ah, there you are, Lizzy,' Douglas said, as if he had last seen her a few hours ago. 'I am so glad you are late. It would have ruined my memories of you had you been on time. You look perfect: rationing has obviously done you the world of good. Not too far a walk from the ferry, I hope. What have you got there?'

'Figs and plums.' She opened the bags to show him and he pulled out a fig.

'*Fica*, Eric?' Douglas handed him one with a wink and tried one himself, breaking open the fruit and sucking at a corner.

Eric took a bite and offered it to Helen, but she declined. 'Very good,' he said, refusing to respond with any sexual innuendo.

'Where did you get them from?' Douglas asked.

'The stall down there, by the steps.'

'Next time, my dear, try Graziella two stalls further on, though leave it two days till they're at their best. Now, let me introduce you. This is Mr Eric Wolton and his wife, Helen. Eric Wolton, Mrs Elizabeth David. They are from Tanganyika in Bampopo land. Eric is my oldest and dearest friend. I rescued him from a life of certain crime more than forty years ago, and since then he has brought me nothing but credit.'

'I've heard so much about you, Mr Wolton,' she said, her voice rich and slow. Eric took her outstretched hand, gripping it lightly. Her raw umber eyes held his. She looked as if she had been up to mischief and did not care a jot. She also looked genuinely pleased to meet him. Flattered, Eric grinned widely and felt they had the whole world in common. Perhaps it was just Uncle Norman.

'I've been hearing about you, too, from Uncle Norman.' He

still pronounced uncle as 'un-caw'. 'I'm looking forward to reading your book.'

'I'll give you a copy. Are you staying long?'

He stepped back to include Helen. 'A few days, then we're going to Germany.'

She reached over and shook Helen by the hand. Helen said she was pleased to meet her, but she said it in German, by mistake.

'*Sehr angenehm*,' Mrs David said.

'And you?' Eric swiftly interrupted. 'Will you be here long?'

'I hope to write another book, about Italian cooking, and I have a great wish to visit the south.'

'You'll love it,' Eric said. 'Uncle Norman and I had a grand time there, except for the malaria and the bugs.'

'I don't think I'll be writing about the bugs.'

'Like you, Eric,' said Douglas, 'Mrs David has come to have a last look at me before I die.'

'That's what you said in Antibes,' she reminded him.

'Liza Gwynne!' Nancy Cunard suddenly said, disengaging herself from a conversation with Faith Mackenzie. 'Antibes, of course! When we were trying to get the old bugger to leave. Norman said that a fine new cookery writer was joining us for lunch, but I didn't realise it was you.'

Elizabeth David walked round the table to greet Nancy Cunard, kissing her on both cheeks before taking her place in the empty seat next to her. The two had much to catch up on since the last time they all met. War had ruined the farm at Réanville, Nancy Cunard said, along with her press. Elizabeth said she had had 'a few little adventures', and she was glad to be back in the Mediterranean again.

'We were all desperately worried about Norman,' said Nancy, shaking her head. 'Weren't we, dear? You're such an ox sometimes. But I knew when you finally reached Portugal, because someone in New York called to say it had been reported in the *New York Times*. That must have been in late January 1941. The headline was simply: NORMAN DOUGLAS IS SAFE.'

'Good heavens!' Harold Acton interjected. 'I wish they'd say the same thing about me.'

'It's libellous, Norman,' Gracie Fields said with a hearty chuckle. 'Didn't you sue?'

They all laughed. Eric grinned. Helen went pale. On the quayside two boys had stopped to stare at the lunching group, and their father pointed them out. This must have been the most famous table in Capri that day and they were not the first passers-by to remark upon it. Throughout the meal others stopped in greeting, both friends and strangers, most of whom were Gracie Fields fans. There was some traffic still on the quay. A lorry was driving slowly along it, followed by a black Citroën, perhaps the last vehicles off the ferry. On the lorry's side was written *Acquario di Napoli, Stazione Zoologica Nazionale*.

Eric touched Douglas's arm. 'Look,' he said. 'It's from Lo Bianco's aquarium in Naples.' Though his Italian was perfect, when speaking in English he still called the city 'Ny-paws'. He remembered his thirteenth birthday, his first day in Italy, in the south, when he went to feed the octopuses with Lo Bianco and the stingrays gave him a shock. Douglas pulled his glasses down his nose and peered across at it.

'So it is,' he said. 'Wonderful man, Lo Bianco.'

Macpherson said, 'It's good to see the aquarium is functioning again.'

'What happened to it?' Eric asked, over Helen's head.

'Ransacked,' Macpherson said. 'By the Neapolitans, and who can blame them? They were starving to death at the end of the war.'

'Man's usual inhumanity to man,' Douglas said. 'It'll be the same again in a hundred years.'

Macpherson said, 'General Clark was presented with a steak of a manatee, of the order Sirenia, boiled and served in garlic sauce. A perfect gift from Siren Land.'

'What did that taste like?' Eric asked.

'The meat is dark red,' said Douglas. 'Quite solid and rather gamey.'

'I don't think I would have liked eating it,' Eric said, and he looked across the table, catching Mrs David's eye. 'Do you have a recipe for mermaids?' he asked.

She smiled. 'Not yet.'

Nancy Cunard filled her old friend's glass to the brim from the glass flask on the table and looked around for a waiter to order some more.

'What are you eating, Liza?' Douglas asked. 'What will stir your memories in these lands of sun and sea and olive trees?'

She took a sip of her wine and looked around the table. Her sharp nose sniffed deeply, and her tongue played over her lips. A young waiter, who had arrived to fill the empty flask, hovered at her side. Faith Mackenzie recommended the lobster, Harold Acton said the *ossobuco* would restore a mental pabulum. Gracie Fields declared the octopus the most Mediterranean of foods and Macpherson said the stuffed olives were terribly good. Finally, Mrs David took a fresh green plum from her bag and handed it to the sleek-haired young waiter.'

'*Mi lavate la prugna, per favore*,' she said.

The waiter hesitated, unsure he understood these foreigners and their requests. Then he shrugged and said, '*Prego.*' As he took the fruit into the restaurant to wash, she watched him with a steady gaze.

'There you are, Lizzy,' Douglas said, looking, too, at the waiter as he sped away. 'What do you want better than that?'

She met his twinkling eyes with her own dazzling stare. 'We share many tastes, dear Norman, but your appetite has always been just a little bit larger than mine.'

He picked up his glass and raised it to her. She picked up hers and waved it back, and they did not take their eyes off each other as they drank. Lulls in the conversation were rare. One came now, while everyone savoured their food, aware that a toast had been proposed for which they were not invited to drink. But Nancy Cunard could not bear the silence for long.

'Where's Mr David?' she wanted to know.

Elizabeth David took another sip before replying. 'Oh, on a horse somewhere. I should have listened to Norman.'

'But you did as you pleased,' Douglas said, 'and you took the consequences. That's how it should be.'

Nancy smiled. 'Dear Norman, there are so many things we all have to remember you for. What would you like us to remember you by?'

Faith Mackenzie said, 'Do you remember when Constantine FitzGibbon wanted to write your autobiography? And you said, "Say what you like as long as you tell the truth, but I don't know how you're going to get around Eric."'

There was a silence. Helen let out a small squeak, and Faith Mackenzie, suddenly realising the implications of what she had said, put her hand over her mouth to try to put the words back. She looked mortified. Everyone glanced at Eric, crushed between the grand old man and the humiliated Helen, between enormous pride and unbearable shame. Douglas turned to him and squeezed his thigh, then picked up his glass again.

'If, as a memorial, I leave behind me nothing but Eric,' he said, addressing his protégé with rare sentimentality, 'it will suffice to prove to posterity that I have not lived in vain.'

'Here's to Eric,' said Macpherson, tactfully jumping in, 'who has played an immeasurable part in making Norman the immortal man he is.'

The company raised their glasses in toast to Eric. But Eric did not bask in this glory. Modestly, and with some discomfort, he looked away, beyond the table to the quayside. The aquarium lorry had come to a halt and a man had climbed down from the driver's cab. He walked to the back of the vehicle, opened the back doors and jumped inside. A ramp was lowered and a seal barked happily as it emerged into the daylight and slid down on to the quay. The Citroën, meanwhile, had pulled up alongside and the driver had stepped out. He had dark wavy hair and was large and big-featured, like Lo Bianco, though he was light-skinned, which helped to highlight a birthmark the shape of a kidney bean on his left cheek.

'Oh, do look,' said Gracie Fields. 'There's a seal right on the quay.'

Everyone at the table turned to watch except for Harold Acton, who noticed that Ettore had just begun peeling a peach. 'Did I ever tell you how I got to Peking?' he asked, removing his Panama hat.

An attractive young woman, with fair hair and a full figure, climbed out of the passenger seat of the Citroën with a baby suckling at her breast. Like its father, it had a small birthmark on its cheek. The man kissed the woman fully on the lips, stroked the baby's head, and put his arm around them both. Together they watched the seal's progress. Even from where he sat, Eric could see that the baby was small and crinkly, freshly born, a delicious bun warm from the oven. It was a simple idyll: a man, a woman, a child, a happy family relationship and one, Eric realised, that no one who was sitting around this table had ever experienced. Nor was it a state any of them ever wanted to enjoy. He was suddenly overwhelmingly happy for this unknown new life, for this child of the post-war decade. It would grow up in a world that was free from harm. The war was over. There was food again. And Norman Douglas would soon be dead.

The seal looked at the water. Then its nose rose snootily in the air, sniffing the soft breeze. It pushed its flippers down on the quay and launched itself into the Marina Grande with a delicate splash. For a moment there was a silence as it was lost from view. Then, a hundred yards out, it surfaced and everyone cheered as it rolled and dived beyond the harbour wall, free at last, heading towards the distant islands of Siren Land. The south wind rattled the awnings, creaked at the cypresses, drew the perfumes from the hills and the songs from the sirens: '*Hoio hoiotoho-swar, eia-weia opopoil; Ai! Ai! Papaiax attatai papai pai; io, moi, moi, omoi otototototoi; wallawa-hupla, ja, ja, atcha!*'

CHAPTER 23

The Reply

Dar-es-Salaam
Tanzania
East Africa
12th June 1994

Dear Mr Kaplan

Thank you for your ad. which appeared in our paper called
SUNDAY NEWS of 28th May 1994, a copy of which I enclose.

Excuse me for the bad writing, but I was attacked by a stroke on
18.6.85 and although I was treated in the hospital, I still have lost
my handwriting and I shiver as I write.

I knew Mr Wolton very well.

In October 1957 I was transferred to Moshi (one of the Districts
of Tanganyika). I was a police inspector. There I found Mr Wolton.
He had retired from the Police and was working as a Public
Prosecutor. I shared the same building with him (while working)
until at 0900 hrs when he went to court, every morning. I was 31
years old (the law provides that one has to retire on reaching the age
of 55).

But while I was working with him I used to hear the stories
that he was a Police Superintendent, which was a usual custom for
a Police Officer to be employed as a Public Prosecutor on
retirement.

In the first half of 1958, one morning, Mr Wolton went to the

firearm shop to buy a revolver. Suddenly he fell down and died.
This is the little I know of Mr Wolton's life.
Yours sincerely
  David S. Nkulita